William Wyatt Gill

Historical Sketches of Savage Life in Polynesia

with illustrative clan songs

William Wyatt Gill

Historical Sketches of Savage Life in Polynesia
with illustrative clan songs

ISBN/EAN: 9783337314811

Printed in Europe, USA, Canada, Australia, Japan

Cover: Foto ©Andreas Hilbeck / pixelio.de

More available books at **www.hansebooks.com**

HISTORICAL SKETCHES

OF

SAVAGE LIFE IN POLYNESIA;

WITH

ILLUSTRATIVE CLAN SONGS.

BY THE

REV. WILLIAM WYATT GILL, B.A.,

AUTHOR OF "MYTHS AND SONGS FROM THE SOUTH PACIFIC."

WELLINGTON:
GEORGE DIDSBURY, GOVERNMENT PRINTER.
—
1880.

INTRODUCTORY REMARKS.

THE flattering reception accorded to a former[1] volume has induced me to collect and publish a series of Historical Sketches with Illustrative Songs, which may not be without interest to students of ethnology and others. Some of them have already appeared in a serial publication. During a long residence on Mangaia, shut out to a great extent from the civilized world, I enjoyed great facilities for the study of the natives themselves and their traditions. I soon found that they had two sets of traditions — one referring to their gods, and to the supposed experiences of men after death; another relating veritable history. The natives themselves carefully distinguish the two. Thus, historical songs are called " pe'e ;" the others, " kapa," &c. In the native mind the series now presented to the English public is a natural sequence to "Myths and Songs ;" the mythical, or, as they would say, the spiritual, necessarily taking precedence of the historical or human.

In such researches we cannot be too careful to distinguish history from myth. But when we find hostile clans, in their epics, giving substantially the same account of the historical past, the most sceptical must yield to the force of evidence. I say substantially, as in some of the earlier stories there is a great air of exaggeration—*e.g.*, " The Story of Mokè," " The Twin Kites," and " The Expelled God." But the reader will observe that in all three stories the national feeling was invoked against other islanders. In the great mass of song and story there exists the wholesome corrective of clan rivalries to prevent such

---

[1] " Myths and Songs from the South Pacific," with a preface by Professor Max Müller.

self-laudatory exaggerations. I have endeavoured to relate the stories as the natives give them, without improvement or elimination.

When first we settled down amongst these islanders and attempted to acquire their language, I was often puzzled by references to past events, scraps of song, myths, and proverbs—the force of which depended upon an accurate acquaintance with the circumstances which originally led to their utterance. Two courses lay open to me—either to ignore their ancient religion and their undoubted history, or to study both for their own sake, and especially with a view to understand native thought and feeling. I chose the latter course.

The ignorance of these islanders of the art of writing fully accounts for the absence of many really ancient compositions. It was not that they were deficient in natural ability, or in desire to perpetuate the knowledge of the remote past. What race unacquainted with the use of metals ever invented an alphabet or made any considerable stride in civilization? Each clan, as it rose to importance, was assiduous in composing and preserving its own songs and history, but was willing enough to cast into the shade those of its fallen rivals. A few of the prayers in " Myths and Songs " are believed to be of great antiquity, being independent of clan jealousies ; constituting, in fact, the liturgy of each succeeding generation. I have been the more anxious to put these things on permanent record, as the correct knowledge of the past is rapidly fading away, and will probably soon become extinct.

WILLIAM WYATT GILL.

Rarotonga, Hervey Group, South Pacific,
16th December, 1878.

CONTENTS.

CONTENTS.

HISTORICAL SKETCHES

OF

SAVAGE LIFE IN POLYNESIA.

CHAPTER I.

SUMMARY REVENGE.

" ANA-NUI," or the Big Cave, is celebrated in the annals of the " Aitu," or god tribe, as the scene of the first great misfortune which overtook them in the latter days of Rangi.

Their ancestors came from Iti (Tahiti), and settled down on the eastern part of the island where they first landed. On one occasion a grand feast was to come off in honor of the gods. As this tribe were noted fishermen, they were all busy. After spending the day in the sea, the entire tribe, with their wives and children, slept on the sandy floor of the Big Cave. This cavern, as the name implies, is very spacious, but has this drawback : the centre is open to the dews and rains of heaven. The entrance is very narrow, admitting only one person at a time. Near this entrance are great boulders, which render access and egress alike difficult.

A large turtle having been caught, custom required that it should at once be presented to the king, who lived near Rongo's *marae*, or sacred grove, on the western part of Mangaia. This king was Tama-tapu, whose father Tui came from Rarotonga, where the name is still one of dignity and power. By courtesy Tui shared regal honors with Rangi, sitting with him on " the sacred sandstone " (*kea inamoa*), and being appointed by him to guard by his prayers the sea-side from evil-minded spirits coming from the sun-setting, whilst Rangi kept a sharp look-out against bad spirits from the east.   Tui was dead, and his regal duties descended to his son Tama-tapu, who set the first example of wanton bloodshedding in war.

When about a mile from "Orongo" the two turtle-carriers perceived a strong fragrant smell.   The fact was, Tama-tapu, dressed up to the height of heathen extravagance, and highly scented, had that morning gone into the interior.   Hearing foot-steps approaching, he hid himself in the bush at a spot known as Okara.   Said one of the Aitu, "It must be the fragrance of that villain's clothes," little thinking that Tama-tapu was listening to the disparaging remark.   On they walked to the residence of the seashore king, and, depositing the turtle, immediately returned.

Tama-tapu was stung to the quick.   Slowly returning to his home he gave vent to his feelings, weeping long and loud, and then planned his revenge.   Conch-shell in hand, he started off to the south-west part of the island, where his mother's clan (she was a native of Mangaia) resided.   This clan was called "Te-tui-kura"—"The red-marked;" they worshipped "Tekuraaki," a god introduced by Tui from Rarotonga.

He quickly assembled his royal clan by blowing his conch-shell. They were indignant at the story of the humiliation he had under-gone.   A hurried feast was at once prepared for Tama-tapu ; each person partaking of it was thereby pledged to avenge his quarrel. It was arranged that they should divide themselves into two parties, one to prepare candle-nut torches, and the other to cut green calabashes to serve, when hollowed out, as dark lanterns. The rendezvous was the marae of Motoro, in the interior, at dusk.

At the appointed time every warrior belonging to "the red-marked" tribe was at the appointed place of meeting.   Their first employment was to clothe the incensed Tama-tapu; each indi-vidual came forward with a piece of the finest cloth, which was wrapped round his person.   It is said that in all as many as two hundred pieces were thus collected about him, so that he was almost buried under the pile.

Torrents of rain now fell,—a good omen in their estimation. But the irate king never moved, as his presence at the marae, as well as his incantations, were deemed necessary to the success of

the expedition.   The expedition now started, under the guidance
of the warrior chief Matataukiu.   Each warrior carried in his left
hand a green calabash, scooped out in such a way as to admit a
candle-nut torch ; but these torches were on no account to be lit
until they should get near the scene of slaughter.   For the present,
a single torch was to guide the warriors on their way.

They first halted at Tevaenga, a distance of two and a half
miles, to slay Turuia, the original priest of Taue-Ngakiau, god of
the devoted tribe.   The old man was clubbed in his sleep, and on
the following day laid on the altar of Rongo.   Passing on another
two miles to the district of Karanga, they slew two more chiefs of
the tribe they were intent on annihilating.   Elated with these
successes, they hurried on to the " Big Cave," where the devoted
tribe slept on during the tempest of rain without sentinels or the
least presentiment of danger.

On nearing the cave, some of the assailants made their way
over the rocks to guard the opening at the roof of the cavern, lest
any should mount the rugged path and so escape ; but the main
body went along the sandy beach to the proper entrance to the
cave.   When tolerably near they lighted their torches with difficulty, and carefully covered them with the green calabashes,
taking precaution that the light should fall only on the ground,
like the dark lanterns of police at home.

Silently, yet rapidly, they approached their victims.   Their
leader, Matataukiu, on arriving at the narrow entrance, gave the
signal to his followers by throwing away his calabash, thus gaining
the advantage of a bright light to enable him the more effectually
to execute his bloody purpose.   The overhanging rocks sheltered
their candle-nut torches from rain.

" The red-marked ".tribe now rushed pell-mell upon these poor
defenceless Aitus, who in many instances were despatched in their
sleep.   Like sheep penned up in a fold, they were slaughtered at
the will of these cruel men, without regard to age or sex.   One
powerful man, Pâpâkea, the chief warrior of the devoted tribe,
darted through the ranks of the attacking party and made for the
ocean, intending to swim out a short distance, and then, under
cover of darkness, to come ashore again at another part of the

---

* The long sound, as represented by (-), must be understood wherever the
circumflex accent is used.

island.   Although closely pursued, he would certainly have
escaped but for a deep hollow in the reef, into which he unfortunately fell.   As Pâpâkea rose to the surface his skull was cleft by
his foe.   The place where he fell still bears his name.   Of the
large number cooped up inside that cave, only one—a man named
Teruatonga—escaped, by climbing up to the opening in the roof.
The pathway by which he climbed is not very difficult.   At the
top he saw an ironwood sword ready to descend upon his head.
But as the light of the torch fell upon the trembling Aitu, who
had given himself up as lost, the chief of that detachment of "the
red-marked" tribe saw the face of an old friend who permitted
him to escape.

It is said that the blood of the massacred tribe tinged the
waters of the reef, and even extended to the ocean.

In Mangaian story the slaughter of the god (Tane) tribe, at
the Big Cave, ranks as the first bloody surprise of which subsequent history furnishes endless instances.   The engagement which
followed at Tangikura is the second battle ever fought on this
island.   The most careful consideration of the entire stream of
their history convinces me that this never-forgiven and cruel
attack took place about 450 years ago.   It is curious that all
the prominent names in this story—Matataukiu, Rautakanini,
Pâpâkea—are still kept up in their respective families.

THE WRONGS OF THE AITU TRIBE; COMPOSED BY KOROA,
CIRCA 1817.

A "crying" (*tangi*) song pertaining to the "death-talk" of Arokapiti.

TUMU.	INTRODUCTION.
Solo.	*Solo.*
Tiô ra, kotia te ue i Tangikura,	Sing we the dark lanterns made at Tangi-
Ei pueke ia Ana-nui,	To light up the Big Cave, [kura
Ko te Aitu te atua ê!	Where the god tribe was wrapt in repose.
Chorus.	*Chorus.*
E ngaec mai e Teruatonga ê !	Alas! Teruatonga alone did escape !
PAPA.	FOUNDATION.
Solo.	*Solo.*
Pamiro te one ra, e Tevaki ô !	At Pamiro[1] was the hiding-place of Tevaki.

---

[1] "Pamiro" is the name of a spot where, in the days of Mautara, Tevaki took
refuge after the slaughter of his first family.   Twice in the history of this tribe *the
entire race was exterminated all but one member;* Teruatonga was the favoured
individual in the first instance at the Big Cave, and Tevaki in the comparatively
modern age of Mautara.

Chorus.

Pamiro te one i poro ai
Ei akapou ia tatou
I te anau oki a Teraki ra i Tekutikuti.

Solo.

I Tekutikuti Takiri, e ua kapitia Tuarau
E te tueru, tei Ruaoata i te vairanga.

· Chorus.

Ua motu au ki Aratangaroa ê !

UNUUNU TAI.

Solo.

Te umu aitu, na verarera o Iti ra ê !

Chorus.

Te umu aitu, na verarera o Iti.
Tei Ana-nui na tauna,
Na pararua a Matataukiu,
Tae a kauvai te pera i Avaavaroa.
Tei Okara ma tara koumu,
Kua akarongo te ariki Tama-tapu,
Auâ e kai i te ua i te ika
    I te onu a Rongo :
Kua vaia i te aunga puâriri paoa
    No taua tae ra.
Te vai ra i Pâpâkea, e ake karea i taru-
    arere.

UNUUNU RUA.

Solo.

Veroia Matakere i te ngau roa ra ô !

Chorus.

Veroia Matakere i te ngau roa,
I turanga râui i Teueue i raro io Moana,
Tei Kurupcupeu te ariki paa
O Teraki nei, O Tenau ariki,
O Temoeau te ivi i akamoeia i
Ia Tirango i te are korero.
    Na Ivi paa tei akaô ?
    Te manga i kai ai.
Te vai ra i Pâpâkea, e ake karea i taru-
    arere.

UNUUNU TORU.

Solo.

Pokia Ana-nui e!

Chorus.

At Pamiro he adjured his sons
    To die a brave death—
A death befitting the children of Teraki.

Solo.

The eldest, Takiri, was speared ; the next,
    Tuarau,
Was hunted to death, and lies deep in the
    cave Raupa.

Chorus.

The sire was with difficulty saved.

FIRST OFFSHOOT.

Solo.

The flaming ovens[1] devoured the god
    tribe.

Chorus.

The flaming ovens devoured those from Iti.
At the Big Cave perished a multitude,
Deceived by Matataukiu's dark torches :
Torrents of blood flowed into the ocean.
By the roadside at Okara.
The royal Tama-tapu heard the whisper,
" Why should *he* taste the daintiest of
    fishes,—
The turtle sacred to Rongo ?
Ah ! I perceive the rich perfume
From the dress of that fool ! "
Pâpâkea stumbled on the reef ; the brave
    was utterly undone.
Sing we, &c.

SECOND OFFSHOOT.

Solo.

Matakere was speared in the open plain.

Chorus.

Matakere was speared in the open plain,
Amongst the rocks not far from the sea,
Condemned to wander from place to place
Was the childless old man Teraki.
Was not his mother, " the Soft-sleeper,"
Descended from the great Tirango,[2]
    Daughter of Ivi the priest ?
    Hence the wisdom of the son.
Pâpâkea stumbled on the reef ; the brave
    was utterly undone.
Sing we, &c.

THIRD OFFSHOOT.

Solo.

They were caught in the Big Cave.

---

[1] A subsequent atrocious murder of this devoted Aitu tribe, twice enacted against them.

[2] Tirango was the famous warrior of the Tongan clan who exterminated the Tekama tribe ; but was eventually slain in battle. The spot where he fell is well known.

Chorus.

Pokia Ana-nui e te matakeinanga,
O Rautakanini ra, e ngati i Te-tui-kura
　　E ariki Tama-tapu.
Kua kapi te rangi ia Iva,
Takaia e Rongo ia ê te enua.
O te kautuarau, e ko te ua e pa,
　　Kua ki te roto i Mangaia.
Kavea i uta i te tukono i te mana o te
　ariki.
Te vai rai Pâpâker, e ake karea i taru-
　arere!

Chorus.

They were caught in the Big Cave by
　their foes,
By Rautakanini and "the red-marked"
　tribe,
　　Sent by king Tama-tapu.
The heavens became as black as Hades :
By the fiat of Rongo the island was
　flooded.
The fine cloth was all soaked in the storm.
　　The valleys of Mangaia were covered,
Only hills could be seen : O thou wonder-
　working king !
Pâpâkea stumbled on the reef; the brave
　was utterly undone.
　　Sing we, &c.

CHAPTER II.

Ivitu, nephew to Rangi, collected a number of friends, and at Tangikura, the head-quarters of "the red-marked" tribe, gave battle to Matataukiu and Tama-tapu, in the vain hope of avenging the treacherous slaughter of the Aitu or god-tribe. Ivitu's party of 140 was defeated; the leader and most of his warriors perished.

In the heat of the conflict two of the vanquished escaped unhurt to the rocks of Tevaenga, on the north of the island, which, unlike the wild home of Rori, in after days, in the east, are everywhere covered with the densest tropical vegetation. Lofty forest trees of various kinds overshadow smaller plants, and beautiful creepers everywhere hide the naked rock from view. At mid-day it is twilight, and the painful silence of the primeval forest is pleasantly relieved by the occasional twittering of drowsy birds. On one occasion the writer, having lost his way, wandered about for hours amongst these rocks and trees, and only gained the exterior by walking opposite to the setting sun. In the patches of soil between the stones a considerable variety of wild food grows. Amongst these is the *márarau*, or sweet yam, which tastes like the sweet potato; also the noble indigenous true yam (*ui parai*), in addition to the ordinary pandanus, *nono*,[1] and other edible but inferior fruits.

This magnificent hiding-place, nowhere less than two miles wide, extends for several miles; but there are only two places where fresh water can be obtained. One of these is so exposed as to be of little use to a poor fugitive. The well-protected perennial fountain was close to the hiding-place of Uriitepitokura and his father Temoaakaui. Any one may trace the course of the stream under the vast pile of rocks from the neighbouring valley; but the secret pathway by which the fugitives descended from their

---

[1] *Morinda citrifolia.*

eyrie to fill their calabashes is unknown, having been built up so lately as 1846. The sense of security induced by Christianity causes such knowledge to die out, save in tradition.

The home of these hermits, which bears the name of the son, is a tolerably wide cleft between the rocks, close by the secret road to the deep fountain. The overhanging rock forms a convenient roof, whilst the dried leaves of the *Barringtonia*[1] and other trees made a soft bed for father and son. From the extreme end they could, by moonlight, feast their eyes with a view of the fertile valley of Tevaenga, with ranges of pleasant hills in the distance. The cave is at a considerable height from the ground; the rocks being perpendicular, they were safe from surprise on that side.

They had one faithful friend,—an aunt of Uriitepitokura. She alone was in the secret of their hiding-place, and at dusk would occasionally bring a basket of cooked food, which was hoisted up by means of a long rope made of hibiscus bark. It is a wonderful thing that for the period of *four years* she should have continued to feed these fugitives without betraying her secret.

These occasional supplies were, of course, supplemented by what they could collect in the forest. During those four weary years of exile they did not once venture into the interior.

Amongst the rocks of that part of the island there was at that time abundance of beautiful birds: two or three varieties of the pigeon; several sorts of sea-roving birds, who incubate in the stones and hollow trees of that part of the island; besides the true wood-pecker and the linnet. The bird most easily caught by Uriitepito-kura and Temoaakaui was the *titi* (so called from its cry). In the month of December it leaves its burrowings in the red mountain soil, and comes to the rocks near the sea to fatten its young on small fish. By day it hides in holes, and sleeps. The hunter has only to call at the entrance to the dark cave, in a plaintive tone, *E titi e*, when the foolish bird, imagining it to be the voice of its mate, comes out of its secure hiding-place, and, dazzled by the un-welcome light, allows itself to be caught by the hand. In size and colour it closely resembles the dove, but the breast is of a light yellow.

---

[1] The flowers of the *Barringtonia speciosa* are very beautiful. Its broad, glossy leaf is used for dressing wounds; the fruit, when grated, furnishes a powerful fish poison; the timber makes the best canoes.

Unlike Rori, they ate[1] all they could catch, carefully collecting the best feathers in the driest part of their cave. They were in great want of warm clothing, but dared not beat out the bark of the banyan tree growing on the neighbouring rocks, for fear of being discovered by their foes in the interior. A noble substitute was at length devised,—they would manufacture dresses of birds' feathers! Of feathers they had abundance; but how to work them into a dress? In the rocks of Tevaenga grow the best and longest *orongá (Urtica argentea)* for the manufacture of fish-nets. This plant usually grows out of the very stones under the shadow of lofty trees. They stripped off a quantity of this bark, and, carefully scraping it, exposed it to the sun by day and dew by night until fit for use. The custom of the natives is to twist this bark into twine with the palm of the hand upon the bare thigh. With this string the hermits of Tevaenga ingeniously wove together the beautiful white, green, blue, and yellow feathers of the birds they had eaten. This cloth was doubled, in form like a sheet, with a slit to admit the head of the wearer. Such a dress would be called a *tiputa* of feathers. Thus clothed, father and son could defy the cold of winter, and the frequent heavy showers of the tropics.

Two grand head-dresses were subsequently made of feathers. The shape was conical, and bore the name of *pare piki*. This was the nearest approximation to our "crown" existing in their language. Captain Cook refers to these head-dresses of gay feathers interwoven with fine *cinet*. The finishing touch was the insertion of a number of the long red tail-feathers of the tropic bird. Such a prize was considered to be well worth fighting for.

Rori worked in wood and stone; these fugitives excelled in the manufacture of fine and valuable fish-nets. The palm was given to the *nariki*, which is invariably six yards long and four wide. The meshes are so small that only the very tip of the finger can be admitted. Such valuable heirlooms are only used on grand occasions. The making of one such net might well occupy father and son for a whole year.

It is said that two *nariki* nets were completed by Uriitepitokura

---

[1] Rori regarded these same birds as minor divinities. To one family the *land crab* was sacred, to another not. To one the *centipede*, to another not. To one the pretty blackbird was an embodiment of his god, to another the same bird was food.

2

and his father, with the express purpose of purchasing the protection of some powerful chief. No serf dared possess such valuable property. Their commendable diligence was shown by the preparation of *five* other fine nets, of inferior value and only two yards long, called *kukuti*. They then set to work upon a coarse long net (six yards in length) known as a *tata*, and used daily in times of peace to catch larger fish. The making of all these nets, a fortune still in the eyes of a Mangaian, might well occupy two men for a period of four years.

The drum of peace had sounded, so that the fear of being clubbed to death at their first appearance in the interior was removed. But of what avail would this be without the friendship of some chief to supply them with food and a plot of land? Their surviving relatives were slaves of the conquerors, and could only pity them by stealth.

But Temoaakani was not destined to enjoy the reward of his incessant toil; for in the last year of their residence in the *makatea* (rocks) he sickened and died of privation and anxiety, for their supplies came no more. Ere he died he revealed to his son a plan he had devised to insure his safety. About a mile from their solitary home on the margin of the forest was the principal pathway to the beach, by which those in the interior obtained their occasional supplies of sea-water and fish. Midway lay a pile of rocks close to the narrow and rugged path where Uriitepitokura should conceal himself and watch patiently those passing, until a suitable young person should attract his notice. Two small eye-like apertures[1] in the stone would enable him to see without being himself observed. To the girl that pleased his fancy he should offer marriage, and the possession of all their accumulated treasures.

In the interior lived Akamârama, considered to be a great beauty. Her parents were very proud of her, and compelled the fair one to *noo are pana*, i.e., to live entirely inside a house specially erected for the purpose, in order to blanch her complexion and fatten her against the day when a certain grand dance should come off. The object contemplated by the parents was an eligible marriage with some young chief.

---

[1] A year or two ago a native of this district, accustomed with his friends to use this pathway to the beach by night for the purpose of fishing, was so irritated by the apt resemblance of the rock to human eyes that he one day borrowed a sledge-hammer and utterly demolished this natural curiosity.

The great requisites of a Polynesian beauty are to be fat, and as fair as their dusky skins will permit. To insure this, favourite children, whether boys or girls, were regularly fattened and imprisoned till nightfall, when a little gentle exercise was permitted. If refractory, the guardian would even whip the culprit for not eating more. Songs were made in honor of the fair one on occasion of her *début*.

Now Akamârama had grown tired of this fattening process. One day she was left in the care of an easy-going old uncle. The wilful girl thought this a favourable opportunity to obtain a little liberty, though perchance at the expense of her complexion. Seizing the empty calabashes, she contrived to elude her guardian's notice, and darted through the forest by the accustomed pathway to the sea.

Here was Uriitepitokura's opportunity; for, finding her alone, he emerged from his curious hiding-place and followed the fair fat girl. Imagining that she was pursued by her uncle, she looked back, and to her astonishment saw a tall strange youth dressed in a magnificent *tiputa* of feathers of many colours, surmounted by a magnificent head-dress. She had never before seen anything half so fine, and was lost in admiration, whilst the young hermit in a few words told his sad history and entreated her protection. He had priceless treasures; they should all be the property of Akamârama and her father, if she would marry him.

She returned to her home and received the scolding she deserved for thus endangering her complexion; but Akamârama flatly refused to go on with the fattening process. Daily altercations now took place with her parents, who were amazed at the sudden change that had come over their daughter. To various suggestions of marriage from her parents she invariably turned a deaf ear. In despair they begged her to say whom she would marry (for a proposal of marriage may emanate with propriety from a *woman of rank* to an equal or to an inferior). She now revealed her attachment to an exile in the rocks on the outskirts of their own forest; not forgetting to dilate on his wonderful dress of variegated feathers, and the hint of still more precious treasures of fish-nets. The astonished parents gave their entire but not unselfish consent.

To-morrow, guided by their pretty daughter, they would fetch the hermit and arrange the marriage with him. A secret visit from

Akamârama told all that had so auspiciously occurred, and removed all his fears.   At the time appointed, Uriitepitokura boldly showed himself to the friends of the future wife, dressed up with special care in all the finery bequeathed to him.   The fugitive was nothing loth to leave his old dwelling in the cleft of the rocks for a comfortable dwelling in the interior.   But first he conducted his new friends to his eyrie to fetch the nets, and the other dress of feathers, not forgetting the wonderful conical hat.

To remove these treasures required the assistance of several strong men.   At the home of Akamârama numbers had collected to see a man who had seemingly dropped down from the clouds. Uriitepitokura now formally made a presentation of the nets, &c., to the father and uncle of his bride, as an equivalent for protection and food in the future.   The gift was graciously accepted, and a small return present made to him as an inferior, in token of ratification of the agreement.   One or two of the nets were that same day given to the paramount chief to secure his good-will and powerful aid in protecting the slave.

Akamârama was led by her parents to the side of the bridegroom, who wished to put on her the beautiful dress that had been prepared for the happy occasion.   But she would not consent; she, however, gladly put on the *pare piki* or glorious head-dress so coveted in ancient times.   They sat together on a piece of the finest whitest native cloth, to receive the presents of admiring friends to husband and wife separately.   They then both partook of food in symbol of their future union, all present rejoicing in the good things provided for the occasion.   Such only was the marriage ceremony of those days.   Finally, tradition asserts that Uriitepitokura and Akamârama had no reason to repent their union in after-days, although denied the greatly coveted gift of offspring.

Such is the old story connected with the well-known " Cave of Uri-i-te-pito-kura," called in short " *To-uri*."

CHAPTER III.

On the southern part of Mangaia is a small lake named Tiriara, which receives all the streams from the valleys on that side of the island. It discharges its superfluous waters into the sea through a narrow passage under the vast belt of rocks which, like a massive wall, surround the fertile portion of the island. The distance from this lake to the ocean in a straight line is about a mile. Amongst the gloomy rocks and chasms which occupy this intervening district there loves to wander, according to ancient story, a female named Tumuteanaoa, or Echo. Though rarely seen, one cannot doubt her presence, for, say what you may, Echo delights to repeat your words with singular distinctness. This rock nymph has a numerous offspring, which have the visible form of *rats*. In later times they gave birth to the common rat which now everywhere infests the island. Tumuteanaoa is likewise the mother of fresh-water eels, shrimps, and a small delicious fish called the *kokopu*, which abounds in this little lake.

The renowned Mokè was the son of Tavare the profound sleeper, so named because she was in the habit of sleeping from the month of Pipiri (July) until the bread-fruit was ripe and crabs were plentiful (February). During all these months her limbs were rigid; but at length the fervid rays of the sun relaxed her muscles and put an end to her sleep. Her illegitimate son first saw the light at a spot called Ukuroi, in one of the most sequestered and picturesque valleys on that side of Mangaia. He was excessively small and feeble at birth, so that he was left on the greensward near the fountain-head to perish. A sudden freshet swept him from his native valley to the lake, and bore him right under the rocks, where in semi-darkness, and unknown to all beside, Echo fed this waif on frothy bubbles collected from the little eddies on the surface of the lake. Mokè grew apace under this careful nurture. At length he was permitted to drift on with the waters of the lake through the unexplored fissures and caves until he reached the sea. A slight hollow in the rocks near the reef is still known as "the Cave of Tavare." Here the profound sleeper happened to be resting one day after fishing, when she joyfully recognized her now noble boy fearlessly drifting out into the main ocean. She rushed to detain Mokè, and, after swimming a considerable distance, succeeded in bringing him ashore to her temporary abode. In this cave by the shore she fed him bountifully with fish, and other substantial food, until he grew up to be a man of gigantic proportions, actually attaining the height of sixty feet!

He now made his way into the interior of the island, and astonished his countrymen, hitherto unaware of his existence, with many proofs of his enormous strength and bravery. On the western shore, on the sandstone rock, often washed by the sea, are two hollows in the shape of a man's foot, designated "the footprints of Mokè." They are half a mile apart. The *left* footprint is two feet eight inches in length; width of heel nine inches, the broadest part being sixteen inches. The *right* footprint is somewhat smaller.

One memorable day a fleet of double canoes arrived from Rarotonga, with no less than 200 warriors on board, led on by the brave Kateateoru. The place where they landed is in a straight line from Rarotonga, and is named Avarua, because these formidable visitors started from a part of Rarotonga so named. The Rarotongan warriors lived peacefully enough at first, but eventually enraged Mokè by the murder of Tepuvai, the third king of Mangaia. The giant resolved upon obtaining revenge, but for the present concealed his purpose. Under the guise of friendship Mokè induced the strangers to visit the south of the island, where he lived. They did so; and led by their favourite the giant they made their way to the neighbourhood of the lake, of course helping themselves to all the food they could find. Not the slightest opposition was offered to their rather unceremonious proceedings. On a hill overlooking the lake was the dwelling of Mokè; and farther on lay the district of Tamarua, where he resolved to fight the invaders. On the morning of the fatal day he selected two beautiful *ariri* shells (*Turbo petholatus*), one for

himself, and one for his adversary Kateatcoru. Secret in-
structions were given for his forces to hide themselves in a certain
spot at Tamarua. The narrow pathways between the deep *taro*
swamps were obliterated. This done, Mokè returned to look at his
shells: to his joy, the one representing his foes was turned upside
down. He interpreted this as a sure omen of their destruction.
He forthwith went after the Rarotongans, who had no idea that
he was playing them false. Apparently they had little to fear,
seeing that the giant was quite alone, and carried only a stout
walking-stick. He led them in a very friendly way to Tamarua,
so that the visitors might enjoy the good things of that district.
In a short time they scattered themselves all over the broad and
fertile valley, climbing cocoanut trees along the edge of the *taro*
swamps. While thus employed the whole male population of the
island rushed out from their ambush, and speared their visitors
without mercy. In attempting to escape from the morass,
numbers sank up to the middle, or deeper still, and were picked
off by their foes. Under such circumstances the utmost bravery
could effect but little. Mokè killed all who attempted to return
by floundering through the swamps, hoping to gain *terra firma.*
The stout walking-stick of the giant proved to be a truly formidable weapon. Some assert that it was in fact " Timapere," " the
whisker-away," whose blows were ever fatal. Be that as it may,
twenty Mangaians fell that day ; whilst, of the 200 Rarotongan
warriors who landed on these shores, only one escaped with his
life. Kateatcoru was expressly spared, in order that he might
convey to his native land the fame of Mokè.

A great double canoe sailed back to Rarotonga with a fair
wind, with Kateatcoru as the only voyager. Great was the grief
and indignation of his countrymen upon learning the tragical fate
of the warriors. Immediate preparations were made for a second
descent upon Mangaia.

Nor was Mokè idle. Certain that so brave a race as the
Rarotongans would speedily return, in order to be revenged for
the slaughter of their friends, he built a fortification consisting of
rough stones, 162 feet in length, on the hill opposite to the
ancient landing-place. Every bush near the edge of the cliff was
cut down, so that the expected invaders might see that Mokè was
not unprepared for the contest. The giant next lopped off the

tops of the dense growth of ironwood trees which at that time covered the sandy beach. Their bare limbs, reduced to the height of ordinary men, were carefully wound round and round with native cloth, so as to give the appearance of human heads. On the short lateral branches long native dresses were suspended ; spears were carefully poised as if in human hands ; so that at a little distance there seemed to be on the beach, close to the landing-place, a strong army drawn up in battle array. Not a leaf was permitted to grow up to prevent the full effect of this harmless demonstration. The reason for it seems to have been that in ancient times the population of this island was far inferior to that of Rarotonga ; so that in a fair fight they would have been utterly unable to repel the invaders.

At length the Rarotongan fleet of war canoes hove in sight. Kateateoru acted as pilot ; but the famous Teuaopokere, full thirty feet in height, was their leader and chief warrior. Upon approaching the place of debarkation, they were greatly daunted by the sight of the fortification, and especially at the seemingly formidable army drawn up to oppose their landing. Behind the sham warriors there was a small band of veritable combatants. But Mokè could nowhere be seen. Teuaopokere at first felt excessively mortified at the non-appearance of the giant he had come so far (120 miles) to destroy in single combat.

All this time Mokè concealed his enormous person by standing in the ocean near the landing-place, where the water is many fathoms deep. His long locks floated in the breakers ; a large pearl oyster-shell concealed his face. At last the pilot caught sight of the head of the hidden warrior, and bade him show himself to Teuaopokere. Mokè shouted, " Let the great Raro-tongan chief first show himself !" which he willingly did, standing well armed on the deck of his great canoe, full thirty feet high ! Mokè now slowly emerged from his briny hiding-place, and stepped on a projecting point of the reef, holding an enormous stone in his right hand. To the eyes of the terrified invaders his gigantic form seemed to pierce the skies, being twice the height of Teuaopokere. Without a moment's delay the invading fleet turned their canoes, and sailed straight back to Rarotonga. To hasten their flight, the giant Mokè hastily broke off three points of rock, and hurled them after the retreating fleet. They fell short of the mark on the reef with the noise of thunder, causing the entire island to tremble.

These legendary stones are pointed out on the reef, each standing about a mile apart, and weighing about twenty tons apiece! As one might suppose, Mangaia was never again troubled with warlike visitors from the sister island. Mokè is said to have charged Amu, the fourth king, to despatch all strangers on landing.

On the eastern part of the island, close by the scene of the slaughter of the Rarotongans, is a strong but rough wall, also built by the giant. In front, towards the interior, is a beautiful piece of rising ground, very gently undulating, and terminating in a grassy knoll. It is fabled that the giant lies buried, face downwards, here, close to the scene of his signal victory, the undulations of the soil exactly corresponding with the natural curve of his back.

Such is the wild story of Mokè. That a brave and gigantic man of that name once lived and repelled a formidable band of Rarotongan warriors is borne out by the traditions of the sister island. In fact, they assert that his notable device to augment the slender ranks of his army was afterwards imitated at Rarotonga. One of Iro's party of exiles, named Auau, married into the Makea clan, and told them how Mokè had once frightened away a superior invading force. The story of Iro is related in a subsequent chapter. In the reigning family at Rarotonga the memorial name "Takau,"[1] *i.e.*, twenty, is still kept up, with reference to the number slain by *their* warriors. In a similar way the feats of the Mangaians were commemorated by the name "Te-upoku-rau," *i.e.*, "the two hundred heads." Each generation of admiring Mangaians doubtless added some new marvel to this famous warrior of remote times.

Opposite to one of his fortifications is a wall. The intervening space of seven feet four inches is said to be an accurate measurement of the breadth of the shoulders of the giant!

Mokè was the *third* warrior chief of Mangaia; he flourished about three hundred and eighty or four hundred years ago.

---

[1] The present Queen of Rarotonga is Makea *Takau*. Makea is merely a hereditary title (like Pharaoh, Candace, &c.); the true name is Takau.

CHAPTER IV.

In 1865 I visited for the first time the pretty island of Mauke, about one hundred miles to the north of Mangaia. A chief and a deacon who accompanied me were well feasted and most kindly treated by the Mauke people. An aged man, who said that he was a native of Atiu, inquired of the visitors whether they had ever heard of Akatereariki. The deacon replied that he had heard of his visit to Mangaia in the olden time; adding, the land which once belonged to his famous Mangaian wife was now his. The deacon forthwith chanted an ancient song in praise of Akatereariki, to the astonishment and delight of all present. As the song proceeded the old Atiuan wept freely, saying that, though now naturalized at Mangaia, it was originally derived from Atiu, and referred to *his* ancestors. Upon our return to Mangaia I wrote down the song from the lips of the deacon.

The song refers to *kite-flying*. In times of peace this was the great delight of aged men. Kites were usually five feet in length, covered with native cloth, on which were the devices appropriate to their tribe,—a sort of heraldry. The tail[1] was twenty fathoms in length, ornamented with a bunch of feathers and abundance of *sere ti* leaves. Parties were got up of not less than ten kite-flyers; the point of honor being that the kite should fly high, and be lost to view in the clouds. Songs made for the occasion were chanted meantime. It was no uncommon event for them to sleep on the mountain, after well securing the kites to the trees. Of course the upshot of all this would be a grand feast, in which the victor got the biggest share. So serious was this employment that each

---

[1] The *long* tails had six bunches of *leaves*, to correspond with the number of the Pleiades. *Short*-tailed kites had but four, in imitation of the constellation "Pirie-reua."

kite bore its own name, and tears of joy were shed by these grey-bearded children as they witnessed the successful flight. When desirous at length of putting an end to their sport, if the wind were too strong to allow the string to be pulled in, it was customary to fill a little basket with mountain fern or grass, and whirl it along the string. The strong trade winds would speedily convey this "messenger" to the kite, which now slowly descends to the earth.

Children's kites were, and still are, extemporized out of the leaves of the gigantic chestnut tree. Sometimes one sees a boy (no longer grandfathers) flying a properly-made kite.

Akê, a chief of Atiu, was famous for his kite-flying; no kite in all the island could compare with his. On one occasion, when a strong north wind was blowing, he let go his "twin kites," which bore the name of "The sorrowful ones." A huge basket of stout string was exhausted; the kites were the admiration of crowds of spectators, when unfortunately the string broke, and the kites were lost. Akê, knowing that the wind was favourable for Auau (Mangaia), remarked to his son Akatereariki that in all likelihood his favourite "twin kites" would reach that island. The son of Akê at once prepared his *titira*, or double canoe, to sail to Auau in search of the lost kites. With a good supply of cocoanuts for food and water, and attended by a number of Akê's vassals, he set off on his voyage. In a couple of nights Akatere-ariki made Auau, and landed opposite to the *marae* of Rongo on the western part of the island. He inquired whether any one had seen "the twin kites of Akê." The Mangaians said that a pair of foreign kites had recently come ashore on the east of the island, exciting great interest as coming from another land. Akatereariki went to look at them, and found that they were indeed his father's famous kites.

The *real* object of his visit to Mangaia was to get a hand-some wife, under guise of kite-seeking. The prettiest woman on the island at that time was *Matakore*, only daughter of Tiaio, supreme temporal *and* spiritual sovereign, whose principal resi-dence was in the sacred district of Keia. Akatereariki was deeply smitten by her charms, but could obtain no response. Nor was he the only suitor for the hand of the lovely girl. The famous Tairieterangi had sailed in his big canoe from Rarotonga to fetch

her as his wife, but she would not deign him a smile. It was
known that he had gone back with his friends in order to seek
enchantments and love charms to enable him to win the obdurate
Matakore.

Tiaio did not permit strangers to enter his dwelling. But one
evening when the doors were secured, and the candle-nut torches
of the supreme chief cheerfully burning inside, the crafty admirer
of Matakore hid himself under the eaves of the thatch, and softly
recited or chanted the subjoined song. The astonished girl was
greatly delighted, and coaxed her father to open the door and
allow the musical stranger to come in. Tiaio that night feasted
Akatereariki, who at length avowed his love to Matakore, and
entreated the consent of her parents.

Akatereariki's suit was successful; the beautiful girl became
his wife. After some time Akatereariki intimated to Tiaio his
wish to return to Atiu with his wife. The supreme chief consented,
but his brother, Pukenga, was violently opposed to their going.
But go they did, and that by way of Rarotonga. When about
halfway to Rarotonga they fell in with a great decked double
canoe, bound to Mangaia. It was Tairiiterangi and his warrior
friends, about to solicit for a second time the hand of the fair
Matakore.

The canoes were laid alongside of each other. As soon as
Tairiiterangi saw the lovely girl quietly sitting behind her husband,
he became mad with anger. A fight ensued. The Rarotongans
slew Akatereariki and most of his companions,—even Matakore
perished. The bodies of the slain were thrown to the sharks,
excepting the unfortunate bride. Ere long the great canoe of
Tairiiterangi sailed into the harbour of Ngatangiia; the body of
Matakore was carefully anointed with oil, and kept on one of the
maraes.

Those spared by the victorious Tairiiterangi succeeded in getting
back to their homes in Mangaia, and told the sad tale of the death
of Matakore and her husband, and others. Burning for revenge,
her uncle Pukenga, a man of great strength, with a number of his
followers, set sail for Rarotonga. Landing at Ngatangiia, he
marched straight up to the marae where the body lay exposed,
and bewailed the unhappy end of his pretty niece, without any
active opposition on the part of the Rarotongans. The corpse was

now enveloped in a 'paua, or sort of mourning used only for the best-beloved.

Pukenga publicly challenged Tairiiterangi to compete with him in a race. The challenge of the Mangaian chief was accepted, and a long plot of ground was cleared for the purpose. Numbers assembled to witness the race. Four times they ran the entire distance, when Tairiiterangi was completely exhausted, and lay panting on the ground. Pukenga continued to run alone without any apparent sign of weariness. After having for the eighth time traversed the whole distance with seeming ease to the amazement of all, he suddenly seized his club, and with one blow dashed out the brains of Tairiiterangi.

Pukenga and his party succeeded in making good their retreat to their canoe, and even carried off the body of his beloved niece. They eventually reached Mangaia in safety. But from that day it became customary to murder all visitors touching the reef. The fierce hostility towards strangers which was manifested in 1823, when the Rev. J. Williams first endeavoured to land Christian teachers, is attributed to the battles in the time of Mokè, two generations prior to the death of Matakore, and to the contests with Tairiiterangi.

When referring to any one of unusual strength, it is to this day usually said, " *Pukenga oai e ngi ai raua ?* " (" Who can compare with Pukenga ? ")

Tiaio reigned about 340 years ago ; he was the *fifth* sovereign of Mangaia.

The father of Matakore is the Tiaio who was clubbed to death for wearing in his ears the flower of the scarlet *Hibiscus* in front of the *marae* of Motoro, and *was afterwards deified*, and associated with Motoro in worship. Tiaio was believed to be enshrined in the eel, and especially in the shark.

THE SONG OF THE TWIN KITES.

Adapted by Pai, circa 1770.

Tumu.	Introduction.
Kua rere te pa manu naau, e Akê,	Thy kites, O Akê, have sped their flight
No nunga i Atiu,	Far away from Atiu.
Ei akaariki i to tere ê !	Thine is a peaceful errand.
Te ui tôkere i tangi reka ê !	How softly sounds that drum !

PAPA.

Tangi reka mai, e reira e,
 O te pau i karavau
 Na Akatereariki.
 Nani e rutu ê?
 Na te mana o Manii kuke mai ei?

FOUNDATION.

Ah! soft indeed its notes;
 The drum which ever sounds
 Is Akatereariki's.
 Who shall beat it?
 Who has the skill of Manii[1] to attempt it?

UNUUNU TAI.

I rere, i rere ki te matangi ê!
I te matangi o te pa manu a Rongo,
 O te pa manu a Rongo ai,
 Ko te manu i rakei,
 Ko te kiakiato rai,
 Ei moenga i ka oro ei.
O te taupiri tau ki te manu ê!
Te ui tôkere i tangi reka ê!

FIRST OFFSHOOT.

They sped, they sped on the wind.
The winds favoured the kites[2] of Rongo;
Those beautiful kites of Rongo;—
 Kites gaily decked out,
 Strengthened on the back,
 And covered with devices;—they fly!
Wonderful tails have those kites.
How softly sounds that drum!

UNUUNU RUA.

Turua te manu o tai enua ê!
 O tai enua' i!
Kua piri te arorangi o tai enua;
 Kua piri te arorangi.
Taku manu, taku manu,
Miria e te matangi, parea e te matangi.
 Kua motu paa i Ruaunga.
 "Mata-ruerue" nga tama ê!
O te taupiri tau ki te manu ê!
Te ui tôkere i tangi reka ê!
 Ai e ruaoo ê! E rangai ê!

SECOND OFFSHOOT.

A second time thy kites reached other lands;
 Ah, distant lands!
A strange horizon has encompassed them.
 Clouds hide them from view.
Alas! my kites, my kites, ill-treated
And hurried far away by the winds,
May fall perchance on Mangaia![3]
Ye "sorrowful children"[4] of mine!
Wonderful tails have those kites.
How softly sounds that drum!
 Ai e ruaoo ê! E rangai ê!

---

[1] "Manii," an Atiuan chief slain in Mangaia because he would not part with his beautiful breast ornament. The spot where he fell is a place of pilgrimage even now to his countrymen; it is called Matatia.

[2] Rongo presided over peace and war, the dead, and *kite-flying*.

[3] I have substituted the name of the island for that of the particular spot where it is pretended that the kites fell, after coming a hundred miles.

[4] The name of these "*twin*" kites; they are regarded as the "*children*" of Akê. The tragic fate of Matakore is doubtless a fact. It is universally believed to be such by the natives. The song, in its original form, must be *over* 340 years old.

CHAPTER V.

THE Tekama clan anciently dwelt at Karanga, on the north-east of Mangaia. They originally came from Vaiiria, an inland district of Tahiti. The first resting-place of these fugitives was Atiu; but, being expelled that island, they sailed for Mangaia, where they were well received. Marrying women of the island, they ultimately became formidable in point of numbers. At last they devised a notable expedient for obtaining possession of the entire island.

Close to the frowning rocks, some hundreds of feet high, was a large taro path called Puamâtâ. It should be weeded, and the weeding should be done by moonlight—a favourite time with the natives on account of the delicious coolness after a sultry day. The leading men of the different districts were invited to assist. None refused the invitation, as it was announced that a great feast was in preparation, and no Native neglects to attend to eating and drinking.

The preparation for the feast went on day by day; but it afterwards transpired that the fish was secretly devoured by the Tekama tribe, pieces of green wood instead being cut into the shape of fish, well wrapped up in leaves, and ostentatiously baked in the oven. So, too, of Native puddings, usually made of banana, taro, and cocoanut. Hundreds of new cocoanut-leaf baskets were plaited, to enable the guests the more conveniently to carry away their respective divisions of food. Such a feast had not yet been seen.

On the appointed beautiful moonlight night the visitors from the different districts slowly assembled for the proposed weeding. But the real purpose of the Tekama was a very different one, each individual being secretly armed with a light club or a small war-axe easily hidden in the dress. When the first party of six or eight made their appearance the men of the Tekama clan feigned to be diligently weeding. Under the pretence of a cordial greeting they went through the *reru tâki*, or frightful Mangaian war-dance, in which the performers leap wildly into the air, slay imaginary foes,

and wind up with a wild, prolonged yell. In doing this they contrived to surround their guests, and then, without the slightest
warning, dealt them death-blows on the head. The screams of the
victims were lost in the prolonged final yell of the war-dance.

In this novel fashion, under the mask of warm friendship,
several arrivals were entirely disposed of. It is believed that a
great number were killed that night. The slain were either hastily
covered with the long grass of the taro patch, or summarily
trodden down in the mire.

Unluckily for the murderers, as one party arrived within a
hundred yards of the tragic scene, a bit of rising ground concealing them from the sight of the Tekama, they distinctly heard a
death-shriek after the cessation. of the war-dance. They immediately turned back and fled to their homes, everywhere spreading
the news of the treachery of the Tekama.

Next day the surviving male population of the island under
Tirango assembled to avenge the death of their friends. They did
not find the Tekama unprepared for battle. The spot chosen by
them is excellent for the purpose of defence. On either side of
their entrenchments were miry taro patches. At the back is the
narrow path for flight to the desolate rocks, where they would be
safe for a while if defeated. But despite these natural advantages
the Tekama were routed in this fight, known as the battle of
Rangiue. In their flight to the rocks they threw aside all their
valuable ironwood weapons. The first anxiety of their chief, upon
collecting his now broken clan for a second engagement some time
afterwards, was to provide a new supply of spears and clubs.
Unable to obtain ironwood of the requisite size and length, they
cut down *máriri* trees, spears made from which are as sharp-
pointed as the best ironwood, but exceedingly brittle. This great
undertaking accomplished, they gave battle again at Putoa, but
lost great numbers on account of the ill quality of their weapons.

Once more the scattered remnants of the fallen tribe made a
desperate stand. This time it was at Maungarua; the attacking
party divided themselves into two companies, so that, whilst the
fragment of the Tekama was engaged in front, the others taking
an apparently impracticable path attacked the bewildered foe in
the rear. Thus there was no chance whatever of escape. Almost
every male of the tribe was slain, the women being, according to

custom, reserved for the victors. Thus the famous weeding, with which the name Tekama is indelibly associated in the Mangaian mind, became the cause of the speedy and utter destruction of the clan.

The bodies of those treacherously slain by the Tekama were allowed to rot in the mud of the taro patch. The one great taro patch now forms two, and is kept well planted, as though it had never been a graveyard. But the natives of that district superstitiously believe that at the full moon, when the unsuspecting guests were slain and sunk there, the water assumes a blood-red appearance! At my visit I noticed a quantity of curious grass with a deep red tint. My aged guide remarked that this grass grows rankly only where human blood has been shed! Since that day I have seen abundance of the same sort of grass in various parts of the island where no such crime as *te tauna i Puamâtâ* ("the slaughter at Puamâtâ") was ever committed.

The date fixed for these events by the most intelligent natives is the period immediately preceding the first *umu Aitu* for the extirpation of the worshippers of Tanè, which would be about three hundred years ago.

It is said that one or two young children survived the destruction of the tribe, and amalgamated with their mother's clan, the Tongans.

The following extract from the war-dirge in honor of Tuopapa (*circa* 1790) refers to this moonlight weeding, and to the two ovens for the destruction of the Aitu :—

Pokia, e Tanè-kai-ai, te tâuna i Pua-mâtâ,	Alas for Tanè-devoured-of-fire; and those at Puamâtâ,
Pokia, pokia, pokia e ! Era tokovaru !	Caught, slain, and buried in the mud,
Kua pau ua te tâuna o Tekama	eight at a time !
I te umu Aitu.	Hence the overthrow of the Tekama.
Takina, e Tongaiti, te vairakau,	Weep for the fiery ovens !
A ngaa te kano i te kava.	Lead on, brave Tongan,[1] thy warriors.
A mate ! a mate ! !	Break through the centre of the enemy.
Rumakina e ! Era tokoiva !	Death to you ! death to you ! !
Kua pau ua te tauna o Tiroa	Hurl them in, nine at a time !
I te umu Aitu.	The entire tribe of Tiroa[2] has perished
	In those fearful ovens.

---

[1] Tiranga, the leader of the attack in the battle on the following day. For his bravery he was afterwards declared temporal "lord of Mangaia."

[2] Priest of Tanè Ngakiau, offered in sacrifice to Rongo about the time when the tribe to which he ministered was thrown "nine at a time" to the flames.

It was evidently believed in 1790 that the destruction of the Tekama and the fiery ovens were events not far apart.

4

CHAPTER VI.

On a gentle slope at Putoa, on the east of Mangaia, just where the mountain fern—that unerring token of barrenness—gives place to coarse long grass, and almost under the shadow of the high rocks, is a circular hollow, now only thirty-four feet across and comparatively shallow. It has evidently been the work of man in some former age. Tradition says this hollow was once of great extent and depth, but successive displacements of clay and stones from the neighbouring hills during the heavy floods of summer have well-nigh filled it up. In 1854 a rainstorm of terrific violence brought down a vast quantity of *débris* upon the lower and fertile grounds in that entire district, almost depriving many families of the means of subsistence.

At first sight an individual accustomed to South Sea Island life would pronounce this to be a monstrous oven for baking the *ti* root (*Dracæna terminalis*). But on closer investigation this would seem incredible, as no *ti* ovens were ever half so large as this must originally have been. The real purpose for which this vast hole was dug is a topic of unfailing interest to every Mangaian.

The "Aitu" or god tribe was, as we have seen, almost extinguished at the " Big Cave," for speaking ill of the king Tamatapu. In the battle which followed, most of their connections and friends perished. And yet in a few generations after the " Aitu " tribe reappears in history. Possibly a few escaped the hand of Mata-taukiu, by not sleeping at the " Big Cave." But the received explanation is that six canoes full of the worshippers of the same god drifted here from Iti (Tahiti). Thus this tribe again grew really formidable for numbers, and spread themselves all over Putoa and the contiguous district of Ivirua.

The god of this tribe was *Tanè;* but there were many Tanès

or lesser divinities included under that name. Nevertheless all worshippers of Tanè were regarded as forming one great tribe.

These driftaways from Iti, whose names are preserved, brought no wives with them, but intermarried with the older families on the island. So strong did they feel themselves to be that Panteanua resolved to set up a grand *marae* shaded by a noble grove of trees at Ivirua. The site of the grand *marae* was well chosen, being on rising ground overlooking the fertile valley. The *marae* itself—the best-built on the island—was 100 feet long and 25 feet broad. It is now in ruins, and planted with paper mulberry (*Morus papyrifera*) for the manufacture of native cloth. Great stones are buried deep in the soil, three feet, however, being exposed to view on all sides. In all other *maraes* the centre is filled with earth, a thick layer of snow-white pebbles covering the whole. But the "god tribe" resolved that this should excel all other *maraes*; they therefore *determined to fill "Maputâ"* (as it is called) *with human heads cut off for the purpose!* and this they did!

Revenge for the many cruelties practised upon their tribe was doubtless the motive for this bloody consecration. Night attacks were made upon the older settlers for the purpose of securing a number of heads.

Cocoanuts are tied together by fours, for the convenience of carrying. A man usually carries two or three such bundles on one end of an old spear, and an equal number on the other. The "Aitu" tribe substituted human heads reeking with blood, tying them together by the hair. Entire families were slain when assembled at their evening meal. Hence the proverb, "Hasten our meal, or the Aitu will be upon us, bringing terror, chilliness, and death." Hence the custom[1] of eating the evening meal *before* the setting of the sun, to avoid a surprise.

The *marae* was at last filled up; a covering of earth was laid on the human heads; sea-pebbles (still traceable) ornamented the surface; and the whole was dedicated to Tanè-ngaki-au (Tanè-striving-for-power).

The Aitu had triumphed; but the relatives of the murdered did *not* forget what had occurred. Several years elapsed ere they

---

[1] They now eat by lamp-light.

dared wreak their vengeance upon the wrong-doers. The mode of revenge adopted was novel and fearful.

In the dry season (from July to December) taro is scarce. In the olden times these islanders subsisted on old cocoanuts and wild yams during these months. But nuts alone are too rich, so that it became customary to dig up roots of *ti*. These roots were cooked in great ovens dug for the purpose, and afterwards kept in store for the winter months to eat with hard cocoanuts. *Ti* is remarkably sweet and agreeable to the European palate.

The chief of the primitive tribe of Ngariki at that time (*circa* A.D. 1620) was *Ungakute*, who announced an extraordinary oven of *ti*. It was dug in the midst of the little homesteads of the Aitu clan, on the boundary line dividing Tamarua from Ivirua, the original settlement made by their ancestors. The *ti* tree was usually planted in avenues near their dwellings, so as to be ready for cooking whenever the chief might give the welcome order to their people.

Ungakute's oven was professedly for *all Mangaia*, in place of the twenty or thirty ovens usually prepared. The proper parties to dig and get ready ovens of this sort were the Aitu clan, as the original Tanè was "Tanè-papa-kai"="Tanè-giver-of-food," and under his wing all subsequent Tanès took refuge. On a given day great logs of firewood and firestones were collected. Next morning an enormous hole or oven was dug. All being ready, on the third day a great crowd of men, women, and children came bearing great uncooked *ti* roots. The firewood was at a given signal carefully piled up so as completely to fill the hollow; and on the top enormous stones of black basalt were laid, so as to cover the whole. The wood was now lighted in different places, and speedily the whole was in a fierce blaze. When the wood (more than half of which was green) was burnt out, the firestones, now red-hot, sank to the centre of the deep hollow. Now was the moment of danger, when the bravest and most adept selected long *green* branches of the chestnut with a hook at the end in order to pull these heated stones into proper order, so as to form, in fact, a red-hot pavement, on which the *ti* roots might be thoroughly and equally baked. This dangerous feat accomplished, laminæ stripped off banana stalks with abundance of the juiciest leaves were thickly strewed over these glowing stones. Green limbs of trees were

then laid over the oven, to enable men carefully to pack the roots
without burning their feet. As the oven was filled with *ti*, these
sticks were gradually withdrawn.

In packing these roots the least valuable part is placed downwards, the slender juicy tops upwards. Each person ties something on his own half-dozen or more big roots, so that there may
be no confusion when the oven is opened. The roots require to
be packed closely, to prevent heat from escaping upwards. When
the oven is at last completely filled up with *ti*, the biggest roots
being in the centre, the whole is covered over with a vast quantity
of leaves. Finally the oven is covered in with earth to the depth
of *three* feet. A large oven requires two whole days and nights
for the contents to get thoroughly done. Upon opening the oven,
each person is careful to take only his own bundle of *ti* roots.
This is, strictly speaking, a steaming oven—the very best mode of
cooking this sort of food. The process, however, is very laborious;
hence *ti* ovens were made only by order of the chiefs.

The foregoing is a description of an ordinary *ti* oven. But
Ungakute intended that his should be of a very different character. The greater portion of the Aitu clan attended, and, *as in
duty bound*, lent their aid in digging the oven, it being a time of
peace. The only possible ground of suspicion was the gigantic
proportions of this oven, the smoke of which, according to the
tribal songs, "blackened the entire heavens." As soon as the
tremendous fire lessened, the Aitu and others approached the edge
of the oven with long green hooked sticks, apparently ready at
the giving of the word to arrange the firestones in order.

Ungakute shouted in stentorian tones, " Ka uru te umu ! "=
" *Rake the oven !* " At this each member of the devoted tribe
found himself suddenly seized by his neighbour, and hurled down
into the deep oven, lurid with red-hot charcoal and stones ! Two
of them in falling succeeded in dragging down each his man. *But
none of those who fell ever got up again;* for those who had
planned this fearful tragedy had taken care to have at hand the
heavy ironwood spades used the day previously in digging the
oven, and kept *professedly* for the purpose of closing it over with
earth, in *reality* in order to force back into the burning mass
below those who might struggle to get up the sides. Even the
half-grown lads belonging to the Aitu tribe were hurled into the

oven and perished miserably with their parents. The bodies of this unhappy tribe were left to be totally consumed in the fire of this memorable oven, which was of course at once abandoned.

The wives and mothers of the dead fled in horror to the rocks, and remained there until some few months afterwards, when the drum of peace was beaten. Several Aitu who were not present at the dreadful oven survived this wholesale destruction of their tribe. The sovereignty of the island reverted to the original clan of Ngariki, Ungakute being formally declared "temporal lord of Mangaia." The remnants of the "god" tribe became slaves to those who had cooked their nearest relatives.

Most incredible does it seem that in a subsequent age, when the remnants of the Aitu clan had again increased in numbers, this trick should have been successfully repeated. *Yet such was the case* (A.D. *circa* 1660). No new offence had been given; but the *marae*, filled up with the heads of their ancestors, had not yet been forgiven. Nothing but the utter extinction of this Aitu tribe would satisfy the malice of the clan who boasted to have sprung out of the shades.

The leading chief amongst this dominant tribe, the worshippers of Motoro, was *Kaveutu*, who emulated the fame of Ungakute. This time the oven was dug at the foot of a hill near the rocks on the *north* of the island. This wild and desolate neighbourhood is called Angaitu. As the crest of the hills is further removed, this second oven is much larger than that at Putoa, being more recent, and from its position less liable to be filled up with stones and clay. At the present time it is forty-eight feet across, quite round, and much deeper than the older one. Like that at Putoa, it is said to have been originally much larger and deeper. This second oven was also dug at a boundary line, dividing Tevaenga from Karanga. Again the services of the ill-fated tribe were called into requisition to dig another monstrous oven to their own destruction. In all respects the second catastrophe was similar to the first, except that in the latter instance none of the dominant tribe perished with their victims. Moreover Kaveutu and his friend so arranged their plans that nearly all the ramifications of the doomed tribe worshipping Tane perished in the flames, women and children included.

As Koroa sang in modern times (1817)—

Te umu Aitu, na veravera o Iti ra ê!   The flaming ovens devoured the Aitu ;
Te umu Aitu, na veravera o Iti.   The flaming ovens devoured those from Iti.

The known survivors were the priest Tepunga, Tevaki, and Teko, wife of the famous Mautara. Kaveutu was proud of having become in his turn despotic temporal sovereign, and especially proud of having wreaked full vengeance on the defenceless remnants of the Aitu.

To this day these gaping holes in the clayey soil are known as " nga umu Aitu "="ovens for the Aitu tribe." Truly the heathen are " hateful and hating each other."

At the " death-talk " of Arokapiti (1817), Koroa recited a song (his own), of which I give a verse :—

Mani nga toa o te Aitu ;
O te Aitu, ei kaunio ia Maputû
  I te kapua anga mai,
  O nga kapu o Tetuma ê !
E aaki mai nga ponga ê ! ·
  Kua tae oki i te tuuri karaii[1]
    E te tatakanini.
Kua piri ake, e Tevaki e, ei Putuputu-
  kiau
Eiaa ra o te ata kura i iti ê!

Hail to (the memory of) the warriors of
  the Aitu tribe,
Who filled up the marae of Maputu
Against the day of its dedication !
What rows of human heads !—
A crime ne'er to be forgiven,
Were in after-days exterminated.
None were saved but Tevaki,
Who worshipped the red light in the east.

_____

[1] "Tuuri karaii "=turning up stones under which little crabs (serfs) hide—*i.e.*, extermination.

CHAPTER VII.

THE EXPELLED GOD.

CIRCA A.D. 1660.

IN the interval between the vast ovens by which the Aitu tribe was consumed, the priest Ue landed at Karanga on the north-east part of the island. He came to Mangaia in a double canoe, professedly in search of his god *Tanè*. His original home was on the eastern side of Taiarapu, the peninsula forming the southern part of Tahiti, where Tanè was once worshipped, but was ignominiously expelled on account of his "man-devouring" propensities—*i.e.*, great numbers of persons wasted away in consequence of his anger. Tanè was known by the appellation of *"the yellow-toothed god,"*—*yellow with eating mankind !*

The sacred sennit, or finely-plaited cocoanut fibre, was the supposed shrine of this ferocious deity. A strong feeling of opposition having arisen to the worship of Tanè at Tahiti, the priest carefully hid the unpopular god in an empty cocoanut shell, securely plugged the tiny aperture, and threw it into the sea, adjuring Tanè to seek a new home in some distant land.

After a few weeks the sorrowing priest resolved to abandon his ancestral lands and go in search of the expelled god. Launching his canoe and spreading the mat sail, Ue started off on his eventful voyage with a steady trade breeze. He touched at several islands on his way, without hearing anything of Tanè hidden in an empty calabash. At last reaching Auau (Mangaia), he resolved to rest himself awhile after a voyage of some four hundred miles.

Ue's first care was to set up a *marae* to Tanè at a spot about a mile from where he first set foot on the soil. Noticing, however, that the planet "Anui, Tanè's eye," *i.e.*, the morning star, rose a little on one side of the *marae*, Ue was dissatisfied. He sought carefully for a new site, eventually fixing upon the slope of a hill, now covered with cocoanut trees, known as "Maungaroa," due east. Here the anxious priest built a new *marae* to his expelled divinity, and was delighted to find that "Tanè's eye" rose directly over it, just as had been the case at his old *marae* at Taiarapu.

Ue now started off to the place where he had originally landed, with a large scoop-net to get *fish* for the dedication of his new *marae*. After the most diligent fishing he obtained only a minnow. Advancing, however, towards the due east part of the reef in a straight line with Maungaroa in the interior, when despairing of his errand, he noticed something floating towards him on the sea. It proved to be merely a cocoanut-shell well stopped. On opening it he heard a chirp; it was his long-lost god Tanè, who henceforth was known as Tauè-kio, or Tanè-the-chirper.

The delighted priest at once carried off the cocoanut-shell and the still imprisoned god to his subsequently famous *marae*, and carefully deposited his new-found treasure there. Tanè, an outcast from Tahiti, and long a waif on the illimitable ocean, had found a new and congenial home!

But the troubles of Ue were not over. When all was completed he found that the older driftaways from Iti (Tahiti), who worshipped Tanè-ngaki-au (Tanè-striving-for-power), looked upon this new Tanè and his temple with no favour. *Their* great *marae* at Maputû had been solemnly dedicated with human heads reeking with blood—the new *marae* with a minnow, and a cocoanut-shell containing only a bit of sennit! As for the alleged "chirping," who but Ue and his insignificant clique had ever heard it?

Ue desired to settle down in the neighbourhood of his god; but the land thereabouts had long ago been all parcelled out amongst the older settlers. Eventually the worshippers of Tanè-striving-for-power drove the unfortunate priest to seek refuge on the margin of the sea, at a most sterile and desolate spot near the hiding-place of Rori in later times. Almost dying of hunger in this most barren place, where scarcely a leaf can be seen, Ue made up his mind to leave this inhospitable island for ever.

A single friend, Mataroi, celebrated for his skill in manufacturing stone adzes sacred to Tanè, volunteered to share the fortunes of Ue. These two kindred spirits crossed the island, seeking the point due west where Ue set up his third and last *marae* in honor of his god. A more useful memorial was the enclosing of a spring with large smooth stones, still known as "the fountain of Ue." Within the past few years the stones have been removed for building purposes. Ue and his friend set sail and left the island for ever.

5

Such is the story of Ue and his *marae* at Maungaroa. The persecutors of Ue all perished (save two) in the second fearful oven at Angaitu. Tevaki, one of the survivors, worshipped at Maungaroa, a spot most sacred in the eyes of all his numerous descendants, until idolatry was finally subverted by God's blessing upon the labours of Davida and Tiere.

THE EXPELLED GOD.
INTERLUDE TO THE FETE OF PARIMA.
By Tuka.—Circa 1816.

FIRST BAND.

Ia Ua te vari i te marae ;	Ue set up the first altar ;
Te vari i Putoa, na itiki o Tanè è !	His home was at Putoa,
Uia, uia Tanè e, ei ata è !	Where the morning star stood o'er him.

SECOND BAND.

Tiroa te pia i Itianga ;	Tiroa was offered in sacrifice ;
Kua kapitia Matariki,	Matariki, alas! shared his fate ;
O na pia o Tanè è !	Both were priests of Tanè,
E rua katoa i âriki nei.	Offered to their relentless gods.

FIRST BAND.

Pangeara Tepunga i Ngaua.	E'en Tepunga was laid on the altar.
Te kapu i te upoku,—	The sacrifice was headless !
Kua rika te kiri o Mautara,	Mautara himself was horror-stricken
O na raverave na Ngariki nei.	At the atrocities of the tribe Ngariki.

SECOND BAND.

Kua ora Tevaki ia Raumea,	Tevaki alone was saved by Raumea ;
Ei tamaru na Mautara,	Under the shadow of the great Mautara
E ora'i Kaukare nei.	His only son Kaukare was secure.

FIRST BAND.

Kua ora Iva-nui-tarava etu,	The band of Orion now shines brilliantly,
E Mere, kua kake oa te pa etu nei.	Sirius too, and all the stars of heaven.

SECOND BAND.

Kaa kake te uri a Vairanga	The posterity of Vairanga[1] yet survive ;
O ngati Kâki, tei takina i te râ nei.	The descendants of Kâki now prosper.

FIRST BAND.

Taki na i te ra iâ iti,	Prosperity now smiles upon Mataroi,
Te râ ia Roi, ei tukirua	Despite the two great attempts
Ite pou tai o Tanè è, reià !	To destroy the tribe of Tanè.

SECOND BAND.

Reia e te utu, paoa e Aumea,	Once the stars[2] fought, valiantly did Au-
Na Mere te vai e vâ 'i mai,—	mea (Aldebaran)
	And Sirius fight the Pleiades,

---

[1] Vairanga, Kâki, Mataroi, are the names of three chiefs of the original drift canoes from Tahiti. Ue came later.

[2] Star-worship was indelibly associated with this tribe. Aldebaran and Sirius are *red* stars, *as if* shadowing forth the lurid ovens which in a former age consumed their worshippers.

Te vai ia atea : *na umu Ailu*
*Na Kaveutu te amo ia Ngati Tanè
nei.*

And were victorious. *Thus were the
Ailu*
Consumed in the fiery ovens of Kaveutu.[1]

CHORUS.

Taki na ake Ngariki ê!
E maunga i te râ nei.

Mighty is the tribe of Ngariki!
A mountain touching the sun![2]

Towards midnight the music and dancing ceased. The performers arranged themselves into two bodies, reciting alternately stanza by stanza until the last, when both parties met and recited the final verse with tremendous emphasis. The drum was again beaten, and the *kapa,* or semi-drama, proceeded. This chanting or plaintive recitation was the true Polynesian mode of singing. Singing, as we understand the term, is in the native mind indelibly associated with Christianity.

---

[1] Both ovens are, for poetical purposes, attributed to the author of the second. Kaveutu was of the same tribe as Ungakute, and *possibly* a descendant of his.

[2] A delicate compliment to Pangemiro, the warrior chief of Mangaia at the time, as being a member of that tribe.

CHAPTER VIII.

LATTERLY inquiries have been made at the neighbouring islands to ascertain the fate of Ue after leaving Mangaia. He reached Aitutaki, where his descendants, the "Ngati Ue," = "the clan of Ue," still flourish. In extravagance the story of his subsequent adventures, as told by his descendants, exceeds all others. It is as follows :—

· A fleet of warriors from Samoa once invaded Aitutaki, destroying the entire island. These fierce Upolu men reserved the king, *Temaeva*, for eating long after the fighting men of Aitutaki had been devoured. As escape was deemed impossible, the unhappy king was allowed a little liberty. One evening he saw Tuoarangi —a man who was supposed to be dead—steal out of his concealment in the bush, and launch a small canoe in order to escape to Rarotonga. Temaeva entreated the fugitive, should he arrive in safety, to proceed at once to Arorangi, and inquire of his daughter Maraerua (who had married the king there) whether she had a brave son willing to avenge the wrongs of his grandfather. "For," · added the captive Temaeva, "I shall be eaten up *to-morrow*; already the firewood and wrapping-leaves are gathered for my oven, and the taro to be eaten with my poor body has been taken up."

In those times the nights were unusually prolonged, unlike the brief nights of a degenerate age. Tuoarangi safely reached Rarotonga, and, proceeding to the home of Maraerua, told his mournful tale. At once her grown-up son, Maronna, resolved to go to the help of his unfortunate grandfather. Taking off his magnificent head-dress, he therewith purchased a large double canoe, which he named " Rautiparakiauau " = " The fading *ti* leaves of Auau," *i.e.*, " *Ripe for destruction*." A number of brave Rarotongan warriors accompanied Marouna. Ere starting on his voyage he slew two or three men with his own hand, to evince his bravery and as an omen of success.

That same night Marouna reached Mangaia! On proceeding to the interior his further progress was opposed by Ue at the fountain called by his name. These men being of equal strength and cunning, neither could get an advantage over the other. They therefore saluted by pressing noses, and became the best of friends. Marouna now invited Ue and Mataroi to accompany him to Aitutaki to avenge the wrongs of his grandfather, King Temaeva. This being agreed to, they all started off in that famous craft, "Ripe for destruction," and in that night of wondrous duration reached Atiu, where the redoubtable Kaurâ and Tara joined the expedition. Long ere break of day they reached Aitutaki, the final goal of their midnight wanderings. The Samoan sentinel at the entrance to the lagoon was at once despatched; a second sentinel guarding the sandy beach likewise fell. Further on, a vast block of sandstone is pointed out, where two more were destroyed; so that the slumbering warriors in the interior received no intimation of impending danger. The canoe was dragged up amongst some neighbouring taro patches, and there hidden in the mud, defiling the stream, which to this day is, in consequence, called "*Vaieu*," or "*Muddy brook*."

Temaeva was still alive, and expecting to be cooked in the morning. After greeting his brave grandson for the first time, he gave them some ripe bananas to eat. Marouna and his followers now proceeded to the houses where the successful invaders from Upolu were sleeping. Each head was gently lifted up: if heavy, being clearly the head of a warrior, it was immediately clubbed; but, if the head proved to be light, the owner was permitted to sleep on till daylight, as it was evidently the head of a coward. In this way the leading enemies of Temaeva were quietly disposed of. At daylight the astonished and affrighted survivors made a feeble defence, and were to a man put to death.

In the division of lands which followed, the enfranchised king bestowed great possessions upon Ue and Kaurâ. At the present time their respective clans form a considerable portion of the population of that beautiful little island; but, unhappily, in after days these clans fought fiercely against each other, the tribe of Ue gaining the victory. In the fifth generation from Ue, Christianity was introduced to Aitutaki.

That a descent was made upon Aitutaki by a hostile fleet from Upolu is doubtless true : that Temaeva, in the last extremity, gained help from Rarotonga, Mangaia, and Atiu, is very probable. But the Polynesian love of the marvellous is excessive ; hence a complete voyage of the group, which might well occupy a fortnight, is made in a single night of unheard-of duration.

The Mangaian story makes Ue and Mataroi start off alone in search of a new home. The Aitutakian account represents Ue and Marouna as becoming friends after a smart trial of strength.

In 1864 the late Rev. C. Barff told me that the tutelar god of Huahine was Tanè, whose worship once prevailed over Tahiti, and that people and god came originally from Manuâ, the eastern portion of the Samoan group. The proof of this, he remarked, was found in ancient traditions and songs pointing to Manuâ. These dovetailed with the statements of the old men of that island, or cluster of islets, when, in company with the lamented Williams, he introduced Christianity to Samoa in 1830.

The original Tanè of Mangaia was " Tanè-giver-of-food," deified by his son, Papaanuku. Then came " Tanè-striving-for-power," whose worshippers were all condemned to furnish sacrifices to Rongo, tutelar god of Mangaia. Next in order came " Tanè-the-chirper," often called " Tanè-of-the-shadow " (Tanè-i-te-ata), in allusion to the star of day appearing directly over the head of Ue at Maungaroa.

There is a close analogy between these Tanès of Polynesia and the Baals of Phœnicia. *Tanè*, like *habbaal*, means *husband* ; both undergo numberless modifications ; Tanè and Baal are invariably associated with the worship of heavenly bodies. Tanè is the fifth son of Vâtea and Papa, *and is enshrined in the sun* ($= Râ$). Sometimes the morning star is lauded as *"the eye of Tanè ;"* at other times Jupiter, by mistake for Venus, attained this distinction. Of course the older colonists adhered firmly to *their* myth concerning the sun as "the *right* eye of Vâtea " ($=$ noon), parent of gods and men ; his *left* eye being the moon.

Tanè is invariably regarded as a male divinity, and had innumerable modifications (*habbalim*), a few of which I subjoin :—

1. Tanè, *i.e.*, Tanè-papu-kai.	*Tanè*-piler-up (*i.e.*, giver) of food.
2. Tanè-ngaki-au.	Tanè-striving-for-power.
3. Tanè-kio, or Tanè-i-te-ata.	Tanè-the-chirper, or Tanè-of-the-shadow; also known as Tanè-of-the-yellow-teeth.
4. Tanè-i-te-utu.	Tanè-of-the-Barringtonia-tree.
5. Tanè-i-te-kea.	Tanè-consecrator-of-kings.[1]
6. Tanè-tukia-rangi.	Tanè-the-heaven-striker.
7. Tanè-kai-aro.	Tanè-the-man-eater.
8. Tanè-i-te-roa.	Tanè-the-tall.
9. Tanè-marò-uka.	Tanè-shearer-of-thatch (for dwellings).
10. Tanè-mata-ariki.	Tanè-of-the-royal-face.
11. Tanè-arua-moana.[2]	Tanè-guardian-of-the-ocean.
12. Tanè-ere-tue.	Tanè-the-storm-wave.
13. Tanè-vaerua.	Tanè-the-spirit.
14. Tanè-i-te-io.	Tanè-inspirer-of-bravery.
&c., &c., &c.	

The first four only possessed ironwood representations admitted to the king's god-house.

The natives of Atiu lived in dread of Tanè-mei-tai, *i.e.*, Tanè-out-of-the-ocean.

The Mitiaro people believed that their island was beautified by Tanè-tarava, or Tanè-the-all-sufficient.

The tribe of Tanè, discarding the myth of Ina, regarded *thunder* as "*the voice of Tanè.*"

UE FINDING HIS GOD TANE; COMPOSED BY TUKA, CIRCA A.D. 1817.
For the "Death-talk of Arokapiti."[3]

TUMU.	INTRODUCTION.
Te etu tangi a Terangai,	'Twas the loved star of Terangai[4]
E vâ'i mai i Maungaroa,	That stood o'er Maungaroa,—
Na Ue e akatere!	The guide of Ue.
Ua karo i te ata e kake è!	How he gazed on its rising!

PAPA.	FOUNDATION.
Terau oki to tama râ rire	Terau,[5] too, was thy son,
I ravea'i e Tanè nei,	Adopted by the tribe of Tanè,
Ei koatu i Maungaroa na Ue,	To pray at Maungaroa on behalf of Ue
No vara nei te pia.	(*i.e.*, the tribe of Tanè),—
Ei vari au ki Maungaroa ra è!	He the priest of (the tribe of) Vara.[6]
	My boast is of Maungaroa!

[1] Literally Tanè-of-the-sacred-sandstone.

[2] To whom libations were offered of chewed *Piper mythisticum*, that he might send abundance of sprats, &c.

[3] Arokapiti was a famous modern chief of the tribe of Tanè. His god was Tanè-kio; hence the burden of the preceding song is the arrival and settlement of his god at Mangaia.

[4] Terangai was the original founder of the existing tribe of Tanè. He came from Iti, *i.e.*, Tahiti.

[5] Terau was the son of Vara, priest of Motoro. His own god was Tanè. As priest of Motoro he swayed the island. Hence the introduction of his name into this song.

[6] Vara is here evidently put for the priestly tribe, of which he was the founder.

UNUUNU TAI.

Te etu tangi è a Terangai ê!　・
A Terangai, tei Tupuaki enua,
Ua ketu aere mai!
Ua ketu aere mai.
Mei ia Ue mai te atua
Eiia koe tau ai ê?　Ei Avaavaiê.
Ua akatere e Tanè ê!
Ua karo i te ata e kake akê!

FIRST OFFSHOOT.

The loved star of Terangai—
Of Terangai whose home was at Tupuaki,
He earnestly sought;—
Ah! how earnestly did he seek
A new home for his god.
At what place did it land? At Avaavaie.
Behold the guide of (the tribe of) Tanè!
How he gazes on its rising!

UNUUNU RUA.

Akatere atu ê i te kavainga ê!
I te kavainga tei mua i te marae,
I te titara tapu ra,
I te titara tapu ra'i!
Taii te pipi i to marae,
O te ara patu i Maungaroa
Tei takina e Ue ê.
Ua akatere e Tanè ê!
Ua karo i te ata e kake akê!

SECOND OFFSHOOT.

Be thou the guide, thou harbinger of day!
Yes, thou harbinger of day, guide to the
　　marae.
To the sacred shrine itself,—
E'en to the sacred shrine itself!
Let wild vines cover thy marae,
So well-built on Maungaroa,
The result of the toil of Ue.
Behold the guide of (the tribe of) Tanè!
How he gazes on its rising!

UNUUNU TORU.

Tiria mai ê, no kai maki ê,
No kai maki i te tama takitai ê!
I te tama akaaroa! I te tama akaaroa'i,
Ua kaukau i te tai ê!
E atua nio renga ra ia Iti.
Eiia koe tau ai? Ei Avaavaiê.
Ua akatere e Tanè ê!
Ua karo i te ata e kake akê!

THIRD OFFSHOOT.

Expelled for occasioning sickness,
For occasioning sickness amongst child-
　ren—
E'en amongst the best-beloved,
Thou didst float o'er the ocean,
A yellow-toothed god from Iti (i.e., Tahiti).
At what place did it land? At Avaavaiê.
Behold the guide of (the tribe of) Tanè!
How he gazes on its rising!

UNUUNU A.

Eketia i raro ê, i Karangaiti ê!
I Karangaiti, i te tautai ngere ê!
Aore e mataika.　Aore paa e taia,
　　Aore paa e taia'i.
Ngaro atu ai, e Ue e, i te taruku
Tei Poiritama rai; tei Avaavaiê.
Ua akatere e Tanè ê!
Ua karo i te ata e kake akê!

FOURTH OFFSHOOT.

He[1] went on the reef at Karangaiti;
Yes, at Karangaiti he fished in rain,
He failed to obtain an offering, utterly
　failed;
　　He obtained nothing.
Ue put down his net
At Poiritama, and (successfully) at Ava-
　avaie.
Behold the guide of (the tribe of) Tanè!
How he gazes on its rising!

AKAREINGA.

Ai e ruaoo! E rangai ê!

FINALE.

Ai e ruaoo! E rangai ê!

---

[1] "He," i.e., Ue.

CHAPTER IX.

ONE day the accustomed present of food from the chiefs was brought to Mautara, as priest of Motoro, garnished by the cooked head of Tepunga. Now Tepunga was priest of Tanè, the god worshipped by Mautara himself. Of course this was a studied insult to the wily priest of Ngariki, who for the present dissembled his anger. Mautara did not taste the head of Tepunga: not, however, as objecting to such diet, but because it would draw down upon him the anger of his own divinity. The corpse had first been offered to Great Rongo; and then, contrary to all precedent, the offering had been despoiled of its head.

Mautara thirsted for revenge. At a meeting of chiefs at the grand *marae* of their god Motoro, Mautara fell into an ecstasy produced by swallowing an unusual quantity of *Piper mythisticum*. With eyes ready to start out of their sockets and in great agitation, he said in unearthly tones, " I, Motoro, require of So-and-so, my faithful worshippers and distinguished chiefs, a most costly offering. On a given day the first-born of each must be slain and eaten in my honor by the tribe of Ngariki, descended from Great Rongo !"

From this fearful command no appeal lay. Mautara professed to be horror-stricken, but he had merely been the mouthpiece of their god. *On the day appointed these children, the flower of the ruling clan, were killed, cooked, and eaten by the assembled tribe* in supposed obedience to the will of Motoro ! Tepunga was amply avenged. Mautara in after years confessed that it was all a trick of his own, to wreak his vengeance upon those who had so barbarously insulted him.

Tevaki, uncle of the crafty Mautara, now became priest of Tanè, the last of his race. It was he who put the priest of Motoro up to the cruel trick of demanding the first-born of the ruling tribe. Four preceding priests of Tanè had all been laid in sacrifice on the bloody altar of Rongo. Tevaki and his four grown-up sons must be slain. The sons fell fighting, the eldest, Tuarau, at Tama-

G

rua, where for some days he was concealed in a dense growth of
brushwood. The spot where he was clubbed is now the site of the
schoolhouse of that village.

The now childless Tevaki hid himself in the rocks of Tevaenga.
Daily search was made for him by his foes. One rainy night he
descended from his lofty and almost inaccessible hiding-place into
the interior in the hope of meeting his nephew Mautara, whose
priestly duties detained him a few days at that part of the island.
A venerable chestnut-tree is pointed out as the place where he took
shelter during the storm, until he believed that his foes were all
wrapped in sleep. At length he started a second time for the hut
of Mautara, which was surrounded by the members of the hostile
tribe. The trembling old man succeeded in reaching the house
unobserved. After a weeping welcome the hungry fugitive ate a
good meal, and consulted with Mautara as to the best means of
securing his safety. That his foes would relent was out of the
question, his offence being that he was the last of the hated tribe
of Tanè, and priest of that rival god.

It was resolved that Tevaki should start at once for Putoa, and
hide in the rocks and thickets of that neighbourhood. The rain
still fell in torrents. With leaves of gigantic taro *(Arum costatum)*
for umbrellas, the elder sons of Mautara (Teuanuku and Raumea)
led the childless old man to a cave in the district indicated. A
quantity of cooked taro left with him sufficed for the present.
Fortunately, the two young men got back before dawn, so that
their nocturnal travels were unsuspected.

Mautara soon afterwards returned to his own hereditary lands
on the southern part of the island. The house of the priest was
set up at the head of the valley, where six minor valleys open to
view in lovely perspective. Tevaki's residence at Putoa becoming
suspected, under cover of a dark night the same young men conducted the hunted hated priest of Tanè to the well-built reed
dwelling of Mautara.

Upon his arrival, Tevaki was hidden inside the " pa tikoru," or
that part of the dwelling curtained off with a piece of sacred cloth.
On no pretence whatever could this sanctuary be invaded. His
presence there was for a long time kept a profound secret. Meanwhile, the rocks of Putoa which he had just left were thoroughly
searched by the foes of Tevaki. Eventually the truth leaked out,

and constant watch was kept near the dwelling of Mautara for the old man, should he unwittingly put himself in the power of his foes by leaving the charmed dwelling of the priest. Even Tokoau, the factotum of Mautara, proposed again and again that Tevaki should be eaten; for Tokoau was passionately fond of human flesh. A minute's walk outside the house would have cost Tevaki his life. Such was the wonderful ascendency which Mautara maintained, that his old uncle lived a *whole year* inside the curtained partition. Namu was concealed with difficulty for *one month* by his father-in-law, and at last had to run for his life when the sanctuary was invaded.[1]

At the expiration of the year (*circa* A.D. 1720), the battle of Arera was fought, putting an end to the supremacy of the original tribe which had so persistently sought the life of Tevaki. The utter rout of Ruanae at Puknatoi, some two years later, removed all fear, as Teuanuku was declared warrior chief of Mangaia.

Tevaki became now a man of consequence, and lived to a very advanced age. He become the father of a boy who grew to manhood under the fostering care of his cousins, and eventually became the founder of the present numerous tribe called " Ngati Tanè "="the descendants of the god Tanè," who claim almost half the island as their own. Thus the last survivor of the Aitu became the author of a new and altogether prosperous clan.

The tribe of Tanè has the honor of first embracing the word of God in 1824. Their honest pride is that they early gave up their idols and embraced Christianity. Parima and Rakoia were distinguished chiefs of this clan, who did all they could to aid the cause of truth and righteousness in their day. Numerous deacons and evangelists have been furnished by this family.

In 1854, Kaveriri, one of their number, " counted not his life dear unto him, so that he might finish his course with joy, and the ministry he had received of the Lord Jesus." He was one of five who were slain and eaten by the·savage natives of the island of Fate, one of the New Hebrides.

The rival "gods," Motoro and Tanè, now repose quietly in the museum of the London Missionary Society.

---

[1] This "curtained sanctuary" of Mautara has become proverbial. Native preachers love to urge poor sinners, hunted by Satan, to take *sure refuge* inside "te pa tikoru o Jesu "="the curtained sanctuary of Christ."

CHAPTER X.

BATHING one day in the pretty lake associated with the name of the giant Mokè, I was desirous to track the course by which its deep waters pass on to the ocean under the rocks. A dense growth of *hibiscus* overhangs, and in some places touches, the waters. Not being an expert swimmer, with the assistance of a native I lashed together with *hibiscus* bark two cocoanut troughs which happened to be at hand. Unitedly they bore my weight; a dry cocoanut branch served as a paddle. On this extempore canoe I paddled under the spacious opening. The lofty roof grew lower as I advanced, and a feeling of awe crept over me as I solitarily paddled on to the farthest part of the " Cave of Tangiia."[1]

Finding my farther progress stopped, I turned and gazed upon the novel scene—the dark waters underneath, the dome-like walls of the cave blackened with age around, while overhead a vast mass of hardened coral sustained a most luxurious tropical vegetation. Through the spacious entrance the best view of the pretty lake was obtained, reflecting on its still bosom the rocks and trees which surround it. Beyond lay the fertile taro patches, the rich soil of which, carried by freshets into the lake, made it so black. Noble cocoanut groves adorned the base of the range of hills in the distance. The upper part of these hills was covered with slender ironwood trees, mistaken by Captain Cook for willows.

At the farthest part of the " Cave of Tangiia " is the gorge through which the swollen waters of the lake sullenly rush into the ocean. In the dry season, when the lake is shallow, it is easy to crawl through this opening into a spacious but gloomy cavern, ever associated in the minds of these islanders with the name of Panako, who here found a safe asylum from his foes.

The lofty open cave into which I had paddled was formerly

---

[1] Nearly 200 feet long.

regarded as the abode of the god *Tangiia,* whose name means
" a murmuring " of waters. Tangiia was supposed to be enshrined in the hideous ironwood idol now in the London Missionary Society's museum. He was regarded as the fourth son of
Vâtea (noon) and Papa (foundation) ; being one of those who
accompanied Rangi from Avaiki, or the nether world, to this upper
world of light. This mythical personage must be distinguished
from the great historical warrior chief of the same name from
Tahiti, who was one of the first settlers at Rarotonga, and whose
son Motoro, drowned by his brother at sea, was afterwards worshipped at Mangaia.

On a pleasant fertile slope near the lake stood the sacred grove
or *marae* of Tangiia, long since demolished, and now well planted
with arrowroot.

The worshippers of this god were once numerous and powerful,
but, being devoted to furnish sacrifices to Rongo, became in time
almost extinct, a very few only surviving to this day.

Forty years ago, the Christian pioneer Davida had been labour-
ing on this island some few years with marked success. Those
who had been baptized united in building a Christian village on
the margin of the sea. The Sabbath was very strictly observed by
these early converts. But the heathen living in the interior openly
showed their contempt for that sacred day by pursuing their usual
occupations. On a bright Sunday morning, Tapaivi went to the
lake after *kokopu,* a fish especially plentiful in the inner cave,
where Panako once took refuge. The waters being low, Tapaivi
and his assistant crept in without difficulty. Their fishing greatly
prospered ; but somehow they failed to notice that the waters had
suddenly risen, and they were in fact imprisoned. A storm from
the south had occasioned a sudden rising of the ocean, thus preventing the egress of the waters of the lake, which now rapidly
filled the Cave of Panako.

Very uneasily did these poor fellows wait in utter darkness for
the subsidence of the waters. Hour after hour passed, but the
waters continued to rise. Dismissing all thought about fish, and
anxious only to get out of their gloomy prison, they repeatedly
dived for the narrow opening. Each time they rose they struck
their heads against the solid rock instead of clearing the entrance.
Exhausted by their efforts they impatiently waited for help. In

the afternoon of that Sabbath, their friends, wondering at their
long absence, went to the lake, and, finding that its waters had
risen to an unusual height, at once divined the truth.

A long pole was quickly cut down. Approaching as nearly as
they could on a raft, they inserted it in the opening. Two men
held firmly the outer end, whilst the third crept under the water,
holding on by the pole, and finally, emerging into the inner cave, he
found the Sabbath-breakers very uncomfortable in mind and body.
Explaining the process, all three quickly dived for the inner end
of the long pole, and with its aid succeeded in finding the true
opening, and soon rejoiced to see the light of day. Tapaivi and his
friend shortly after joined the Christian party, being, as he assured
me, effectually cured of Sabbath-breaking.

But this cave derives its name and permanent interest from the
circumstance that the royal Panako having fought a most disastrous
battle under the shadow of the vast overhanging rocks close to the
lake, he and the other survivors took shelter in this almost inaccessible cave, the waters of the lake being low. His force was now
reduced to forty warriors, with twenty lads fit to carry stones and
their fathers' spears. Most of the women remained with their
relatives in the interior, to await the will of the victors—to be
slain, or reduced to slavery, or to be married to the murderers of
their husbands and children.

Panako and his tribe had plenty of room inside their cave. As
it was the dry season, sufficient light came in through the aperture
to relieve the gloom. One or two warriors kept strict watch at the
entrance throughout the day, whilst the rest slept. At nightfall
all hands issued forth by twos and threes to forage. Occasionally
some of these were caught and slain, but generally speaking the
poor fellows contrived to get back with their scanty spoil. To put
an end to their nightly depredations a row of long stakes was driven
into the muddy bottom of the lake, and at the top firmly tied
together. Death at no distant date now stared them in the face,
as the vigilance of their foes cut off all further supplies of food.

Of brackish water they had a plentiful supply. They caught
abundance of shrimps, eels, &c., which they cooked inside the cave.
To eat with the fish they had only *maramara*, or sweet-scented
black loam from the bottom of "the cave of Tangiia." This fragrant earth was thickly plastered on the walls of their gloomy abode,

to be cooked and eaten at leisure when dry. Sick people with capricious appetites still send to the lake for *maramara*, which contains a quantity of vegetable matter from the valleys. I have several times tasted it, but, notwithstanding the praises of the natives, could not swallow it. Month after month passed away in this dreadful prison-house; they must soon perish, as their foes kept away the women in the interior, who would have brought supplies. The usual result of their own foraging parties was merely the obtaining of a supply of firewood to cook their fish and *maramara*.

Panako knew that about a mile from the lake, at Tamarua, lived a warrior named Onè, whose ancestors had ever been on good terms with his own. Could not Onè help them, being on the winning side? He determined to leave the cave and have an interview with him. That night, after considerable labour, two or three stakes were pulled out of the mud, leaving a free passage for a man, while above water nothing unusual could be seen. Being an excellent swimmer, at dawn Panako bravely dived through the opening in the palisading, and, rising to the surface, caught a sere leaf of the *hibiscus* (nearly round, and fully ten inches in diameter) that happened to be floating near. Holding the stem between his teeth, Panako gently swam on his back, his body hidden in the black waters of the lake. Amid the myriads of yellow leaves silently drifting on the lake in the winter season, this attracted no attention.

Fortunately for Panako a heavy rain compelled his foes to keep inside their huts during his exit across. Arrived at the farthest point of the lake, a distance of a quarter of a mile, he emerged from the water amidst some tall bushes, and put on a woman's petticoat he had brought with him firmly rolled up. He then plaited a few taro leaves for a head-dress, covering his neck and bosom with thick wreaths of the same, in the approved fashion of the women of those days.

Thus arrayed in female attire, Panako slowly ascended the hill, collecting dry sticks as if for firewood, carried, woman-fashion, under the arm. The crafty Panako was seen by several of the warriors, who sat at the entrance of their huts watching the rain; but his disguise and imitation of female gait were so perfect that the figure slowly moving through the trees on the slope of the hill was considered to be a woman belonging to the conquering tribes. Who else could dare to move about by daylight in front of a hostile camp?

Once screened from observation by tall reeds and trees, Panako, avoiding the usual narrow track, pressed on, tremblingly but rapidly, to the dwelling of his friend. Onè was astonished at the temerity of Panako, whom he had never expected to see alive again. Onè was disposed to succour the royal fugitive, if there were any chance at all of success. A plan of operations was agreed upon, and the night fixed when Onè should bring all his Tongan tribe to attack those who so vigilantly guarded the cave night by night.

To ratify this treaty a ripe bunch of bananas was given to Panako; but, instead of eating it, he broke it up into little clusters, and, disposing them as best he could in the folds of his petticoat, he took up his bundle of sticks, and departed by the way he came, unknown to any but Onè.

The rain still poured down. The royal fugitive got back to the margin of the lake; doffing now his head-gear and wreaths, besides the large bundle of sticks, he provided himself, as in the first instance, with a fallen leaf of the *hibiscus,* and noiselessly swam on his back towards the cave. Once beyond reach of pursuit, he dived through the opening in the palisades, and soon was amongst his miserable friends. He bade them not to despair, for Onè would come to their rescue. The ripe bananas, a priceless boon to the starving fugitives, were carefully portioned out. That all might have a taste it was needful to divide each banana into three portions.

A consultation was now held how best to secure the favour of Rongo, the divine arbiter of the destinies of war. The best blood must be spilt to secure victory. The man next in rank to Panako was Tiroa, priest of Tanè, who offered to die. On the morrow the self-devoted victim took a sad farewell of his friends, and openly left the cave, heroically entering the encampment of his foes. Of course they at once speared him, and, it is said, laid his body on the altar of Rongo, without divining why he courted death at their hands, as the visit of Panako to Onè had not transpired.

Next day Onè assembled the Tongan tribe, and made his appearance amongst the cave-watchers, who gave him a good reception. At twilight he proposed that he and his tribe should keep guard all night to cut off all stragglers from the cave. This would permit his friends to obtain a good night's rest after their incessant watching. This was at once agreed to.

Now it was the usual practice in times of war for armed night guards to play quoits in order to keep themselves awake. Onè looked about for a suitable place for his deadly purpose, and found one not far from the cavern where Panako had taken refuge. On my visiting this spot it was evident that only one person at a time could enter, whilst the interior will accommodate scores. At the opening were stationed a number of Onè's warriors, in order to cut off stragglers from the camp of the victors who might be attracted by the supposed quoit-playing. Every now and then the war-dance was performed, *as if Onè had succeeded in killing some of the poor wretches from the cave* prowling about for food, whilst, in reality, he had turned his spear against his former associates.

That fearful night, the fugitives, inspired with new courage, came out of their gloomy stronghold and united with Onè in the work of slaughter. Their faces were blackened, and strips of white *tapa* wound round the forehead, to distinguish their own united force from their foes. Again and again the war-dance was performed as they succeeded in cutting off numbers of the enemies of Panako, who had come to see what made their companions so merry. The bodies of the slain were at once dragged out of sight, so that new-comers had no suspicion of the fate of their friends, and were in their turn put to death.

In this way Panako was amply revenged upon the ancient tribe of Ngariki, the remnant of which, for the first time in their history, took refuge on the rocks. A neighbouring taro patch, "Kume-kume," is still pointed out as the spot where the dead bodies of their foes were trampled down out of sight in deep mire.

Wondrous change for the miserable cave-dwellers! Panako and his clan were now at liberty to move freely over the island, breathing the fresh air, and eating what little food remained. Panako was declared supreme chief of Mangaia. How long he enjoyed that dignity is uncertain, but half a dozen years would be a long time for heathen to live in peace. The chiefs whose rule lasted longer are but few, and their names well known. As long as Onè lived, the united tribes continued in harmony. But after his death his place as chief was occupied by the warlike Ngauta,

7

"eight times lord of Mangaia," who was unwilling that Panako should enjoy the supreme dignity, because everybody knew that but for the cunning and bravery of the Tongans Panako and his associates must have perished of starvation. These quarrels were fomented by Tekaraka, at whose instigation a battle was fought at Arakoa, on the west side of the island. In this engagement Panako and many others of his clan were slain by Ngauta, who now assumed the government of the island.

The famous league between Onè and Panako is known as "the sere-leaf compact,'' in allusion to its brevity. The royal conch-shell used by Panako in his journeyings round the island is in my possession.[1] The "Tekaraka" who occasioned the destruction of Panako is the man of that name mentioned in New Zealand annals. Others assert that *this* Tekaraka was named after the companion of Tauai, who, expelled from Mangaia, found a home in the distant island called "The Fish of Mâui."

The breaking up of "the sere-leaf alliance" and the fall of Panako in the battle of Arakoa are referred to in the—

WAR DIRGE FOR TUOPAPA.

By Teinaakia, A.D. 1700.

FIRST SPEAKER.

Ka ano au e momotu i taù ivi ei ô noku ; Noou tera autua, e taù taeakc o, noku tera.	I am resolved to put an end to our alliance ; Take this, friend, as a parting gift from me.

SECOND SPEAKER.

Ae, eaa to ara i vâ' i ai koe ia taua ?	But why thus rudely put an end to our friendship ?

FIRST SPEAKER.

Oro mai, ei tara ua na taua, Na te arekorero, a titiri atu taua.	It is the wish of the wise men of our tribe ; Perhaps 'twere better to disregard their words.

SECOND SPEAKER.

Ei kona ra, e Onè, ka aere au ka êra Ia Ngariki ia tau i runga i tai motu.	Farewell, Onè ; I go to deceive and drive The ancient tribe of Ngariki off' the island.

FIRST SPEAKER.

Akaruke atu, a kitea koe.	Take care, or you will be found out.

[1] Now deposited in the British Museum.

(*Another Scene.*)

SECOND SPEAKER.

Ie ui atu te ura o Tekaraka e,
I ana mai ïa i te aa ô.
I ana mai ua au i aaki i te tamaki ;
Te kotikoti a tuua ia maira korua e Onò
   roa.

If any ask why Tekaraka comes here,
And what object he has in view,
'Tis to warn you of impending danger ;
Eel-like you will be chopped in pieces by
   Onò's tribe.

FIRST SPEAKER.

E Tutavake e, tena oa te veu ; teia toku
   taeake.

Ye gods, a fight is at hand! How precious a friend !

SECOND SPEAKER.

Koni toou taeake i aakina'i koe ?

Who is this friend that kindly put you
   on your guard ?

FIRST SPEAKER.

O Tekaraka te toâ.

Tekaraka told me.

SECOND SPEAKER.

Ae, ua kite ia i te maro ?

Did he actually see the war-girdle put
   on ?

FIRST SPEAKER.

Ae, te taeko!

He pretends that he did.

SECOND SPEAKER.

Ae, e amo oa tena inau ia tu korua ia ta,
Aitoa korua ia ta !

'Tis false ; he wishes us to strike the first
   blow,
So that the blame may rest upon us.

A SINGLE VOICE.

E Tengaungau ôi, e tu ra, umea to maro ;
   Inapo nei ua koe !

Brave chieftain! rise, adjust thy war-
   girdle ;
This night may be thy last.

THE ENTIRE CLAN.[1]

Tera te ivi o Tongaiti ei ngaere ia Tutavake :
Tukua mai te ariki o Rongo ei kave i te
   puruki !
         Iekôkô !

Here come the Tongans inspired by
   Tutavake :
Sovereign appointed by Rongo, lead the
   attack.
         (War-dance performed.)

Era a pia te kaû o Tutavake,
  Ei taeva i te raugi tao.
Ka eva Ngariki i te Mereikau,
  Ra riro oki te taeko,
  Ka ta i te ivi roa ô !
Noo akera Panako ia puruki
I te taparere i Arakoa,
I te tauenga râ i te aini.
Karo tika ra, e Rongo, i te raipoko !

The deadly spears are now uncovered,
And every preparation made for battle.
Ngariki has foolishly taken the initiative.
The deceiver attained his purpose ;
The long-dominant tribe is doomed.
The royal Panako fought his last battle
On the hill-slope of Arakoa,
When the sun was low in the heavens.
Ah! Rongo, he was deceived to his death.

The above is the commencement of this celebrated war-dirge,
the extracts given elsewhere being the continuation, with occa-

---

[1] Standing in two rows, facing each other.

sional pauses as new events in the history of the clan to which the deceased belonged are taken up. The chant is caught up from the lips of the solo, who repeats a single line relating to some new disaster or success.

The destruction of Panako's foes by the aid of Onè and his clan are descanted on in *Tuka's* war-dirge for his relative Tuopapa, A.D. 1790.

TIAURU (WHOSE FATHER WAS BURIED IN THE TARO PATCH).

E karo mai koe inku.	Pray have some respect for me.
E tara ra, e Ngauta, i tai naau tara.	Oh, Ngauta, make some peaceful settle-ment.

NGAUTA, LORD OF MANGAIA.

Eaa taku tara ka tara'i ?	What can I say to please thee ?
Kua tara atu uao—	Say what I may, still thou wilt plot
Tera taau, o taü rae ra !	To cleave this poor skull of mine.
E ariki mana koe !	(Derisively)—If thou be a mighty king
Ie oro, ukea mai tei Kumekume !	Be revenged for those buried in yon taro-
E taea ra on ?	patch.
	Darest thou attempt *that* ?

TIAURU (FOAMING WITH RAGE).

Eaa to reira !	To *me*, that were but child's play !
Tena au. Tena au.	Here am *I*. Here am *I*.
Aore e pa, aore e arui i to rae kere?	Who dare stop me ? Who shall save thy
E manga koe na te araü !	black skull ?
	This club shall scatter thy brains.

Despite these boasts of Tiauru, he and most of his clan were miserably slain by Ngauta, and trampled down in a neighbouring eel-swamp, in emulation of the prowess of his uncle Onè, associated with Panako not many years previously.

CHAPTER XI.

In the days of the invincible Ngauta, some twenty men were fishing with a long drag-net on the northern side of the island. Late in the afternoon was, as it is still, the most favourable time for catching *kanae*—a species of mullet frequenting that part of Mangaia. At dusk a division of the finny spoil was made, each fisherman receiving one large mullet as his portion, without counting inferior fish.

Now these fishermen were all of the subject tribe; but one of their number had a young friend, named Taipiro, belonging to the then dominant Tongan clan, who helped to drive the fish into the net by beating the sea with cocoanut fronds. Taipiro had seen about a dozen summers. When the division was being made his friend said more than once, "Let not this boy be forgotten." But, whether from accident or design, whilst all the others received an equal share, Taipiro had nothing. His friend, grieved at this, cut his own fish in two and gave the boy the best half.

They now proceeded towards the interior by a very rugged but well-shaded path, now but little used. As it was quite dark by the time the party emerged into the valley, they concluded to sleep in a cave close by, a common practice with the islanders. The proper entrance to "the cave of Taipiro," as it has ever since been called, is very narrow, so that one has to sidle in. Near this entrance Taipiro sat down, saying to his friend, "Here let us sleep apart from the rest."

Some of them now busied themselves in getting a light by rubbing together two bits of dry wood. In a short time, they made a blazing fire out of the dry sticks which covered the ground; and in accordance with native etiquette each broiled his own share of fish on the red-hot embers, and then supped with a keen appetite on the remainder of taro they had carried with them.

In a short time the fishermen, wearied with their day's work, fell asleep on the dry leaves which thickly strewed the floor of their ill-covered cave. The fire was dying out, when Taipiro cautiously crept through the narrow entrance and crossed the hills to Tamarua, where Ngauta and his principal warriors then lived. Aided by the light of the newly-risen moon, the hurried journey could well be accomplished in an hour.

Close to the dwelling of the "lord of Mangaia" lived Vaerua-rau, the king of those days. Ngauta and Vaeruarau were both roused from sleep to hear Taipiro's tale of the dishonor put upon the dominant clan in the person of one of its youngest members. Vaeruarau at once went to a little *marae* named Ariana, where the royal war conch-shell lay, and sounded it long and loud. The warriors of that neighbourhood started out of their sleep at this summons, adjusted their war dresses in the moonlight, and assembled forthwith at the dwelling of Ngauta. Led by Ngauta and Vaeruarau they first made for the level central hill, which is about half-way to the cave. On this supposed " crown" of Mangaia, Vaeruarau adjusted on each the girdle sacred to Rongo, invoking the aid of their raven-haired god of war. A little past midnight they set out to Tevaenga, where helplessly stretched out on the earthen floor of the cave their unconscious victims dreamed not of danger.

It was near dawn by the time Ngauta and his party arrived at the cave. The three entrances to it were closely guarded, so that escape was utterly impossible. When the meshes of the fatal net were thus drawn closely around the unconscious victims, Taipiro stealthily advanced to the principal entrance, where his friend lay sound asleep. Cautiously rousing him, the boy begged the fisherman to follow him outside the cave. The man, still half asleep, mechanically obeyed, little thinking that this was to save his life.

As soon as they were fairly out of danger a terrible war-shout was raised by Ngauta, effectually rousing the devoted sleepers. The cruel warriors rushed upon the horrified and defenceless fishermen. Upon a large flat-topped stone commanding the narrow entrance stood a fierce warrior felling the few who, dashing past their foes inside, vainly hoped for life. Of the entire party not one escaped save the friend of Taipiro!

Such is the darkness of the heathen mind that these poor fellows were believed to have been justly slain.

To this day, if a number of natives are dividing out fish, somebody will playfully say, " Remember Taipiro, lest we be served as those were who grudged him an equal share."

The conch-shell used by Vaeruarau on this occasion has been carefully preserved in the family of the worthy old king of Mangaia. No one but the reigning sovereign might use it. The king made me a present of it.

An amusing story was told me by the king relative to his ancestor Vaeruarau. In the incessant fighting of Ngauta's younger days the kingly family was almost exterminated, only a royal female and her infant son surviving. The drum of peace had been beaten, and the infant Vaeruarau carried to O-Rongo, the *marae* of the god of war, as the future king and high priest. A grand feasting in honor of the gods at the cessation of war and the installation of a king was to come off.

Every preparation for the feast was completed; all the great men of the time were waiting; but who should perform the necessary " karakia," or " prayers"? Buanga, the mother of the infant king, *could not*, being disqualified by her sex, though well versed in these " prayers." The baby-king Vaeruarau was too young to learn. Not a creature else on the island was eligible to perform such sacred functions. What was to be done? A happy thought struck the mother. Though her child, high priest of the gods, was too young to perform the accustomed prayers, he was not too young to *cry !* She therefore gave the young king a smart blow on the back, causing him to cry lustily. This was enough; the royal voice had sounded in the hearing of the gods, although not quite in the right way! It was to be accepted in the place of the " prayers" or " grace ; " and of course the feast was immediately proceeded with to the satisfaction of all parties.

Vaeruarau was eventually murdered at Ngauta's suggestion in after-days. He fell at Ariana, his little *marae*, and was greatly lamented. Divine honors were paid to him after his decease. Rori carved an ironwood representation of the murdered king. This image was duly installed amongst the principal gods of

Mangaia! For some time the worship of Vaeruarau prospered; but this god being at length accused of the crime of "man-eating," *i.e.*, of occasioning sickness and death amongst his worshippers, he was ignominiously expelled from the house of the gods. The "god" was secretly hidden in the rocks near the pleasant home of Rori at Ivirua. Secret visits of respect were paid to this disgraced divinity down to 1824, when idolatry was finally subverted.

Is not a counterpart of all this found in so-called Christian countries, in the canonization of saints, in the offerings, and in the inferior worship paid to them?

An allusion to Taipiro's exploit occurs in

THE WAR-DIRGE FOR TUOPAPA.

By his nephew Teinaakia, *circa* A.D. 1790.

Naai teia tutia ?	Who occasioned this slaughter ?
Na Taipiro i aere te po, i aere te ao,	Taipiro, who travelled night and day
I rauka'i tona ariki,	To gain a great name
I pau ei te tauna i ana-nui.	By destroying the sleepers in the great cave.
Era ei ia Rongo Mangaia !	Ah ! Rongo, thou art sovereign of Mangaia.
Kokii o te toa a puta i te rangi.	
A kako, e Ngauta, a motu o Teipe :	Seize the war-spears, lift them high.
A motu o Paia, era tumungamanga !	Ngauta loves war, and has given over Teipe.
Arutoa mai koe, tane atu au.	O Paia, these warriors must die !
	If one army be brave, so too is the other.
A kai Tutavake i te aunga toto,	Tutavake[1] delights in human blood,
E kapua tangata i tera peiaa ;—	And long rows of human heads,
Peiaa Tongaiti i kai ai.	Secured by the bravery of the Tongans.
Na tera eretonga e mau Mangaia na Tekea.	Mangaia ever belongs to the bravest.
E kapa rakau to Rongo ;	Rongo's dance is a dance of spears.
Ei au ngangare ;	Peace is but transient.
Aore e tainga miro i teia.	In this case no provocation[2] was given.
E ta Turanga e ta Teipe.	Attack Turanga[3] and Teipe.
Porutu i te rangi tao :	Spears rain from the skies.
Euoa te rangi tao :	Reverse now these spears.
Ua kaki i te rangi tao :	Nay ; we thirst to fight,
Ua ka te ngakau !	Our hearts are burning with rage.

---

[1] "Tutavake" is the demon from the shades who slew Tukaitaua, the first who shed human blood in this world of ours.

[2] *I.e.*, no blood was first shed by the fishermen.

[3] "Turanga" and "Teipe" are put for their respective worshippers.

CHAPTER XII.

FEMALE TREACHERY.

CIRCA A.D. 1674.

DURING the latter part of the iron sway of Ngauta, the great Tongan and Teipe clans, long united and supreme, quarrelled. The ground of the quarrel was the belief (for it was never proved) that the head of the Teipe tribe maliciously injured the beautiful yam vines growing in front of Ngauta's dwelling, and furthermore fouled the stream of which the great chief daily drank.

A challenge was sent to Arepec to prepare for battle. Although the challenge was manfully accepted, the chief of Teipe felt that his days were numbered. A wild spot on the crest of a hill overlooking his pleasant home in better days was chosen for the final feast. But the engagement itself came off in a narrow rocky gorge, known as the "Ikuari," overhung with a noble species of gigantic laurel and other trees. The reason for selecting this most extraordinary battle-field was that it was the favourite path to the sea used by his daughter Taaumârama, the real author of their troubles. The rock on which Ngauta for some time stood alone, keeping his foes at bay until his friends could come to his rescue, is still pointed out. Teipe was utterly routed, the fugitives flying in various directions for shelter in the rocks.

One band of eleven, all nearly related to each other, rushed towards the shore to a long cave with a narrow opening close to the sea. This entrance was completely hidden by trees and wild creepers, so that a stranger might pass and repass a thousand times without detecting its existence. It is now known as "Tungâpi."

Here these unfortunate warriors hid themselves for a long time. The ruling party made several bootless searches for them, but, discovering no traces whatever, believed them to be all dead. During these weary months the sweet-tasted but minute kernel of the pandanus drupe was their main support. Their plan was

8

to bring the ripe fruit to the mouth of the cave and spend the
livelong day in pounding the hard shells and carefully picking
out the nutritious morsels so hard to get at. Now and then
they got a taste of the ill-smelling and unsavoury *Morinda citrifolia*, and especially of a species of sweet yam. Fish was obtained, too, with great caution and constant fear of detection.
These hungry fugitives abstained from eating land crabs, which
abound in all solitary places, hiding under stones. Nor did they
attempt to catch the pigeons, at that time plentiful. The reason
for this was that they imagined themselves to be under the
special protection of these rock-gods. The only water they
drank was painfully collected from the crannies of the rocks.

One evening Inangaro, the head man amongst them, when
wandering in quest of berries to satisfy the cravings of
hunger, observed a basket of cooked taro temporarily left there
by a woman engaged with her friends in catching fish on the
reef, according to native custom. Unhappily for Inangaro, he
resolved to get possession of the taro. Should he steal it? The
owner would be sure to report her loss to Nganta, a search would
be instituted, detection and death would possibly result. Should
he murder the owner of the basket? Of course she had companions who would discover the crime, and vengeance would
certainly follow. Inangaro resolved to *make love* to the fair
owner for the sake of her food.

He accordingly hid himself until Inaango, the owner of the
basket, made her appearance alone. He begged the astonished
woman to give him a single taro. She good-naturedly emptied
out for him the contents of her basket, which was afterwards
equally divided to his friends inside the cave.

Inangaro, a young and handsome fellow, pretended to be
smitten with the charms of Inaango, and entreated her not to
reveal the secret of his existence to her companions. The dusky
beauty promised secrecy, and failed not to bring her lover supplies of food from time to time. After a time her visits became
a matter of course, and Inangaro very unwisely showed her the
interior of the cave where the fugitives, her pensioners, were
cowering over a fire roasting *nono* apples.

On one occasion, when Ngaae was roaming alone over the
rocks and along gloomy ravines collecting pandanus fruit, he
heard a female voice chanting a song. He drew nearer and

nearer through the bush to listen, without being himself perceived, and found that it was Kurauri (better known in later days as Puiariki) engaged in stripping bark off the branches and long rope-like roots of the banyan-tree. This almost imperishable tree grows everywhere amongst the most inaccessible rocks. To collect its bark has been from time immemorial woman's dangerous employment. It is used for making coarse native cloth.

Kurauri too was provided with a small basket of taro greatly coveted by Ngaae. Upon showing himself she proved to be as good-natured as Inaango. They were old acquaintances, but Kurauri had imagined that the fugitives had all perished of hunger. She returned to the interior with plenty of bark, but contrived on one pretence or another to meet her lover constantly without exciting the suspicions of her friends. The best she could get was taken to Ngaae and his companions, the food being divided out with the strictest impartiality.

Now Inangaro, the elder brother of Ngaae, did not really care a rush for Inaango, but her food could not be dispensed with. Kurauri, their new lady-friend, was the real object of attraction to him. Here was an awkward predicament—Kurauri was really loved by two brothers. The younger one generously gave up to the elder, who was a poet, and in their frequent wanderings through the rocks composed for Kurauri the accompanying song, in sorrowful commemoration of the want and suffering the exiles had so long endured.

Their condition was now vastly improved, so that they scarcely ever ventured to a distance from the sequestered cave, lest they should be overtaken and slain. The two women continually visited the interior, but luckily never met.

On one occasion, however, after enjoying a scanty meal furnished by Kurauri, it was prophetically remarked, "We shall perish whenever one of our kind protectresses becomes aware that we have a second. We cannot escape, because we have shown them our asylum."

Now it happened shortly after this that these patronesses of the fugitives went fishing with a number of other women. Kurauri was very successful, and early in the evening extinguished her torch and ran to her friends in the cave with what she had obtained. To avoid detection she did not stay a minute, but, relighting her torch, resumed her fishing with her companions, who had not observed her brief absence.

The hungry fugitives at once cooked the fish in the interior of their retreat, and enjoyed their unusually good supper. The meal was scarcely over, when Inaango made her appearance with her basket of fish. The infatuated chief of the party, Inangaro, said to her, " We have but just finished what Kurauri brought us." At this Ngaae interposed, " Speak gently, brother, for we owe our lives to her."

Bitter jealousy at once sprang up in the mind of this woman, who now for the first time became aware that they had a second lady-protector. She had imagined that she reigned supreme in the affections of the noble-looking Inangaro.

On looking round, Inaango was found suddenly to have decamped. The poor fugitives now realized their critical position: she had doubtless gone to seek revenge. And who had ever received pity at the hands of the terrible Nganta? No time was to be lost. Great stones were at once rolled to the narrow entrance of the cave, in the hope of effectually concealing it. Two of their number, Vivi and Tito, started off by themselves to another part of the island, ever hiding by day in the densest thickets near the sea, travelling, although with great difficulty, by night. Some years later, Vivi and Tito were slain by the fierce Tamangoru in the interior.

The other nine betook themselves to a noble Barringtonia-tree, hoping to be effectually hidden by its broad and glossy leaves. As soon as Ngauta heard from his cousin that a cave full of fugitives existed near the sea, he immediately summoned his warriors, and with lighted torches proceeded to the shore in search of the unhappy creatures. It was expressly stipulated that Ngaae should be spared on account of the rebuke administered by him to his brother. The armed party wearied themselves in their search for the cave, the entrance to which had so cleverly been closed. As the morning star appeared, one of their number laid down his head on the gnarled root of a huge tree to rest himself, when he noticed a whistling of wind as if through some hole. The man rose and sought for the supposed cave, but could discover nothing. Again he lay down to rest, and again a rush of air arrested his attention. Listening attentively, he became convinced that a cave of no ordinary size was near. He therefore summoned the whole party to relight their torches and join him in the search. And now they quickly detected the true opening to the cavern, which is very spacious inside, with an aperture for egress at the farther end. The large stones were removed, abundant evidence of the recent occupation was to be seen, but the fugitives themselves had mysteriously disappeared.

The search was recommenced with new zeal outside. It was early dawn, and yet no clue had been discovered. At last, wearied with the fruitless labour, they all gathered together under a Barringtonia-tree of enormous proportions to rest awhile. Some of the tired warriors were soon wrapped in profound slumber. But one of their number lay on his back watching the increasing light of morning. It seemed to him that there was something unusually dark in the uppermost branches of the tree ; it must be the men they were in search of, hiding in the magnificent foliage.

In a second the whole party were on their feet, brandishing their long spears. First of all the trembling Ngaae was ordered to come down, which he did. Seven poor exiles were speared to death on the branches. One of them bravely leaped down expecting instant death, but somehow managed to get off unobserved. But human footsteps covered with blood attracted the notice of some of the attacking party. For a long way they were tracked with ease, but finally were lost in the sea. The warlike clan of Ngauta returned to the interior well satisfied with their morning's work.

The last of the retreating clan lingered on the edge of the cliff over which the pathway passes, to watch the sea, when in his direct line of vision he saw a head cautiously peeping out of a great block of coral standing on the reef. The head quickly disappeared, having caught sight of the armed warrior standing against the blue sky. Guessing this to be the escaped victim, the pitiless foe at once retraced his steps to the shore, and, climbing up the coral rock, clubbed the poor creature whose crouching form closely fitted the hollow where he lay. Such was the unhappy fate of Teuarâvai.

Ngaae was duly delivered up to Inaango, the author of all this mischief. He was content to marry her, although he well knew that, if at any time he should have the misfortune to displease her, his life would be the forfeit.

Inangaro was selected for an offering to "Great Rongo." It was to obtain this suitable sacrifice that Ngauta so willingly set off in search of the fugitives. The nose and ears of this handsome man were cut off and divided out by Ranuo, the king of those days, to all the landowners and chiefs on occasion of beating the drum of peace.

Ere the corpse was mutilated, the very day it was solemnly exposed to the gaze of men and gods (according to the faith of former times), Kurauri made her appearance, carrying in her hand two pieces of dark mourning native cloth to cover the nude body on the altar. She was sternly ordered back, but refused to obey, well knowing that she, being a member of the winning tribe, would not be slain. After carefully wrapping up her dead lover, she clasped his neck in her arms, and gave vent to her grief in the song which Inangaro had composed for her in happier days. The warriors and chiefs around listened with undisguised admiration, and the song, such as it is, took its place amongst the literary treasures of the tribe.

The news of this unwonted scene spread, and Inaango, the bitter rival of Kurauri, rushed towards the sacrifice, intending to drag away her hated relative. This unseemly fray was not permitted, so that she was compelled to listen to the song in question, with the pathetic additions of her rival. She, however, gave vent to her utter disgust and contempt of the whole proceeding by repeatedly growling, " Aitoa ! aitoa ! " (Serve him right ! serve him right !)

Amongst those present was a young man named Iro, who, with his near relatives, was some years later driven off the island to perish at sea, but reached the south-eastern coast of Rarotonga. A year or two afterwards a season of severe scarcity occurred at that island, when the refugee Iro and the rest of his clan climbed a lofty mountain named Teroune, in the hope of obtaining a supply of wild yams. He there recollected the song of Inangaro, and through its words gave expression to his grief for the land of his birth, to the great delight of his newly-acquired Rarotongan friends. The descendants of the little Mangaian colony at Titikaveka, Rarotonga, to this day resort to the mountain referred to as an unfailing resource in time of scarcity, never omitting to recite the following song:—

THE SONG OF INANGARO.
Circa 1670.

TUMU.

To aoa i makuku,
Kua vai reka te tane.
Kua iri tau kakara ê !

PAPA.

Naai rai e ngaki
I te onge roa i taukauri e tu ê ?

UNUUNU TAI.

Mai tu e, e ruao, mei Kurauri,
Mei Kurauri te ngara ê,
Ka roiroi i te ngira ia Inangaro tu ê !

UNUUNU RUA.

I ngaki, i ngaki ki Kopaka ê,
Ko te uru kura ê, ko te uru kura.
Ko ara momotu rai e tu ê !

UNUUNU TORU.

Naai ra e ngaki
Ko te kumukumu ?
Kura io aaki ko Ngaae e tu ê !

UNUUNU A.

I ngaki, i ngaki, ki Oenga ê,
Te enua tapu o Ngariki,
Enua kimi oki au ê !
Ko ara momotu au e tu ê !

INTRODUCTION.

Under you ancient banyan tree
Was I first seen by my lover,
Covered with sweet-scented flowers.

FOUNDATION.

Who now shall gather food
For these starving, wretched exiles ?

FIRST OFFSHOOT.

Long has Kurauri waited ;
Wearied out was Kurauri,
Hoping again to meet Inangaro.

SECOND OFFSHOOT.

He was wearily gathering wild berries,
Such as grow on the rugged red cliffs ;—
Sweet-tasted pandanus kernels his only
food !

THIRD OFFSHOOT.

Who now shall gather food
By torchlight fishing,
When Kurauri gave the spoil to Ngaae ?

FOURTH OFFSHOOT.

Sometimes thou didst venture
Into the sacred land of the kings,—
I following thee with my basket ;—
Sweet-tasted pandanus kernels thy only
food !

When Christianity inaugurated the present friendly inter-course between the islands of the group, the Mangaians were not a little surprised that this ancient song had long been familiar to the natives of all the neighbouring islands. So that this irregular fragment has become a literary curiosity amongst the islanders themselves. Its rough form and unusual expressions are evidence of considerable age, as it was only at a later day that the highest development of native poetry took place under the rule of the priestly clan of Mautara.

The spear wielded by Ngauta on this and many other occa-sions was thirty feet in length, and is said to be sacredly pre-served in a dry cave. No consideration would induce one of the few collateral descendants of this distinguished warrior to reveal the precise whereabouts of this cavern, which is believed to be filled with memorials of the departed glory of their once-powerful clan. A lizard of enormous proportions and dreadful eyes, and a centipede of unheard-of size, are superstitiously believed to be the guardians of these hidden treasures. Woe betide the daring youth who should seek to enrich himself at the expense of the dead !

The final overthrow of Teipe at the battle of the "Ikuari" is alluded to in

THE WAR-DIRGE FOR TUOPAPA.

By Teinaakia, *circa* 1790.

Vâia Rongo puâ akaneke atu Ngauta ia Paia,
  Ua tae Rongo vârâia.
Era na tauokura e naki i te parai o Tutavake.
  No Rongo tera autua :
  No Tonga-iti tera auaro.
Ka aere Tepei i Te-ikuari.
Ka aere Tekuru i te opunga o te râ.
Tera oa na kai-tamua a Tutavake
Oi atu korua, e au taeake, ia atea.
  Oi tika ; oi atu.
Taumaa i te uru i te tokotoko ei vaerua tou,
Ei momotu i te mokotua o Tongaiti.
  Piritoa! piritoa!! piritoa!!!
  Taina ra !
Ka aranga oki Teipe i te ivi raia ô !
  E varu ata i te patinkâ
I koa 'i, i kiritia 'i nga rakau e varu.
  Te aoa mai na tai,
  Na tangi ravakau.
Taumaa Tevaki i te paratao ô !
  Kâreia !
  Aue te vairakau ê !
Ei kona râ Tirango e pa 'i.
  Aue te pa moa ê !
  Era te matuati.
Ka peke iia, e Paia, teia kopu,—
  Teia vakamui tane ?
Ka ati iia ? ka oro iia ?
Eea tu atu ?   Eea tau atu ?
I nunga i tai motu putaonga 'tu
I Marotangiia, i Tearataukanii,
I Te ara tuaririki, te ua o te rangi ê !
Era, ka ariu !   Tueruia atu Rongo
Ia tu a papa tavaki i te kopunga râ
I te avatea ; oe mate io, oe ora atu !
Ka ao Tutavake i ora ake !

The tribes of Ngauta and Arepee are at enmity ;
  Rongo has decreed their fall.
Here are plenty of spears for the impending fight.
  Let Rongo take the lead :
  Let the Tongans do his bidding.
Tepei will fight at the " Ikuari ; "
The battle-field is towards the setting of the sun.
Ah ! the first-ripe fruits of death have been plucked.
Alter the battle-field to some open spot.
  Move on !   Move on !
On the rough rocks brave men are fighting
And breaking the very backbone of the Tongans.
  Crash !   crash !!   crash !!! go the spears.
  Slay them !
Teipe is doomed now Ngauta attacks them,
  On a series of platforms,
Eight in number, secured with stakes and ropes.
  They were taken in the rear
  By their crafty foes.
Skulls are splitting on every side.
  (War dance performed.)
Ah the clashing of spears !
Descendants of Tirango, destroy your foes !
  They are but ensnared birds.
  They fly for their lives.
Whither indeed shall the vanquished fly,—
  This vast host ?
Where can shelter be found, or life be safe ?
Can another stand be made ?   Is all hope gone ?
The fugitives are scattered hither and thither
In the rocks and caves of Marotangiia,
Crowding " the narrow path " in a heavy ruin.
Some are hunted by Rongo[1] from rock to rock ;
Like wearied tropic birds they drop dead in the valleys.
Many perish, but few survive.
What a day of woe the day after the battle !

---

[1] " Rongo," god of war, is put in place of those who do his bidding.

CHAPTER XIII.

THE SERF AND HIS MASTER.

In the palmy days of the clan Ngariki, Autea and his family lived at Ivirua, on the lands and under the immediate protection of a chief named Mouna.[1] Autea was supposed to be on excellent terms with his master, who was of a most genial disposition. Underneath this apparent friendship there lay concealed in the mind of the serf the bitter recollection of the defeat and slaughter of his own clan Tanè. The following well-known incident revealed the truth :

One morning Autea went fishing off a huge rent in the reef, known as Vaingatara, occasioned by the discharge of the freshwater streams of that part of the island into the ocean. The place is famed for the abundance of *nanue*, a fine fish common throughout the Eastern Pacific.

At midday Mouna started off alone in his slender *puka* canoe to share the sport. Happening to lose his hook, he asked Autea to lend him one. Autea replied that he had only one of the sort required, and that was the hook he was angling with. Anxious not to return home empty-handed, Mouna set to work upon the shell of an *ariri* (*Turbo petholatus*) which he had picked up on the reef. A piece of red quartz, sharp as flint, was his only implement. (In those days a man always carried about with him in his girdle a piece of this quartz, as we carry a pocket-knife.) Knowing that there was not a breath of wind to ruffle the glassy sea, Mouna chipped away at the shell until the hook was completed. In a few seconds more it was fastened to the line, and baited. Looking up, he was alarmed to find that he had drifted out to sea ; indeed, he almost despaired of regaining the distant shore of his island home. Earnestly invoking the aid of his god Teipe, he paddled back with might and main. Happily the current turned in his favour, and he again arrived

---

[1] To be carefully distinguished from an earlier Mouna who slew the king Tiaio. See p. 29 of " Myths and Songs."

on the fishing-ground in time to secure a basket of fish ere sunset.

The serf witnessed the drifting out to sea. He returned to the interior inwardly chuckling at the apparent certainty that one of the leading warriors of the dominant and hated tribe of Teipe would never again set foot on land. Judge then his surprise, as darkness came on, at hearing the well-known voice of the master calling his wife to cook the fish.

Next morning Mouna desired his son to run about the adjoining premises of Autea *as if in play,* so as to discover where his fishhooks and lines were drying in the sun, and to be sure to bring them stealthily to him. In a few minutes the boy returned with a number of hooks of different sizes tied together. Amongst them were several intended for *nanue.* His surmise had proved correct: the serf cherished the grudge of his clan against his master. A message was at once sent by the boy to Autea, for him to depart. When it was delivered, the serf, knowing its justice and irrevocableness, wept bitterly with his wife and children. Gathering up a few portable articles, without a word of farewell or even a sight of his master, Autea made a sorrowful journey across the hills to Tevaenga, where he had two brothers living as serfs to a very exacting and disagreeable chief.

The fugitives found shelter, though a very poor one, at Tevaenga. When the brothers heard the story of ejectment from the lips of Autea, they severely blamed him. They composed a commemorative song, which they were permitted to chant at the ensuing *fête* of their lord. Of this song only the subjoined fragment is now remembered. The irregularity of the original attests its comparative antiquity :—

Nai tanu au i te kakara tupu.	I was as a fragrant flower growing near the house.
Kia atea koe ô, o kino te karo ê!	'Twas thine own folly drove thee far away.
Nai kino pan te karo e reire ê!	
Autea e! nai miri koia 'i te akamouponga ê!	Alas, the greatness of this folly!
Mai te are taeake ô, mai te are taeake ê!	Oh Autea, thy sin led to this cruel revenge!
Tatou e tokotoru katoa ô!	In early life we lived—we lived together. Once more misfortune unites us all three.

Scarcely a day passes on Mangaia but a serf is advised to "remember Autea." The fate of Autea was tragic. The three brothers went fishing with a net on the outer edge of the reef at

Atuakoro, when an immense wave swept all three into the ocean. The bodies were never recovered.

It was by no means necessary, or even usual, to give a *vivâ voce* notice to a serf to quit. It was enough for the master to sit down on the ground near the threshold of the serf's hut and procure fire by the use of firesticks (*ikâ aî*). At other times the lord of the soil would plant his short spear (anciently used as a staff) into the serf's taro-swamp, to signify that his gift had had been resumed. For the lord of the soil to be often seen in the serf's plantation was a sure sign that he meant to eject. The ordinary method was, and indeed still is, for the master to weed the sloping sides of the serf's taro-patch. The *formal* method of ejectment is to "put down the *râui*," which is simply a green cocoanut frond, platted in three places on either side of the midrib, as a rough representation of the human form. This platted frond is firmly secured by pegs driven into the earth. The symbolism is, the real proprietor of the soil taking possession of it with his hands and legs! If, as frequently happens, the *râui* is disputed and chopped in pieces, the lord of the soil in a tempest of rage declares his *spine* (*i.e.*, the midrib of the frond) has been chopped in two! In the olden times death was the only adequate compensation for such an insult.

CHAPTER XIV.

MAUTARA THE CANNIBAL.

CIRCA A.D. 1666–74.

AMONGST the fugitives who escaped after one of the early battles of Ngauta was a powerful fellow named Mautara, who sought shelter amid the secluded glens and vine-clad rocks of Ivirua. For several years he lived on without the knowledge of the victorious and hostile families of the interior. He subsisted upon wild fruits, which are plentiful in that neighbourhood; in the winter season he dug up a species of yam, which grows luxuriantly wherever the sun can penetrate the dense foliage. His home was an extensive, circular, deep cavern, which still bears his name. The approach to the "cave of Mautara" is by a natural narrow pathway over loose stones. It is a region of perpetual humidity. One might wander for days over these moss-grown, fern-hidden rocks, without suspecting the proximity of this secure hiding-place. Most of the caverns of this island are at a considerable elevation; occasionally, as in this instance, it is needful to *descend* again by a difficult path, shaded by trees, in which the pretty *ngoio* (a species of dove) builds her nest and rears her speckled brood in safety. A feeble light struggles into this strange abode through two gloomy apertures.

Mautara was a cannibal. He chose this cave on account of its close proximity to a pathway to the sea known as "Anarea." Then, as now, young folks were accustomed to go that way to the beach, in order to fish, or to fill their calabashes with salt water. Solitary stragglers were sure to disappear without a clue to their fate. These victims were conveyed to the great cave to be cooked at sunset. As the whole of the prolonged sway of Ngauta was unsettled, continual fighting being the order of the day, it was impossible for the relatives to ascertain what had become of these missing ones.

Dusk of evening and morning twilight were the only periods when Mautara deemed it safe to go in quest of prey. He slept through the day in his lair to avoid detection. His usual place for digging up wild yams was in the neighbourhood of the present Iviruan mission premises.

Like Ngako of later days, he sometimes preyed upon stragglers of his own and other tribes in adversity. Occasionally he would come upon some one asleep in the rocks ; a blow from his club would despatch the victim. At other times a slip-noose of strongly-platted sennit would enable him noiselessly to strangle the poor wretch.

He had become so accustomed to this mode of life that, having one morning secured a victim at the narrow pathway to the sea where only one can pass at a time between the perpendicular rocks, he unwisely ventured to steal some taro for a feast.

It happened, however, that at the edge of the magnificent pile of rocks at his back was a small *marae*, where, at that early hour, Kauate and his son Reketia were paying their respects to their tribal divinity. Their royal clan had been worsted in a later battle of Ngauta's at Tamarua, known as " the fight at Punanga." The bodies of Tiauru and the rest of the slain were sunk in a neighbouring eel-swamp. The standing-place of the victorious Ngauta is marked by two large stones.

Kauate and his son at once recognized Mautara, and resolved to intercept him. The favourite weapon of the cannibal was the " aro," which he had planted upright in the soft banks of the taro-patch. The grand point, of course, was to secure the weapon before Mautara should be aware of their approach. Swiftly and stealthily they descended to the valley, and then crept round a great rock which lay between them and the taro-patch, in which the cannibal was busy, utterly unconscious of danger. In another moment father and son darted out from behind the rock and rushed along the narrow pathway to secure the club. Mautara, now aware of his critical position, made a desperate effort to grasp the trusty club which had so often befriended him ; and would doubtless have succeeded but for the deep mud of the taro-patch, in which he piteously floundered. When tolerably near the coveted weapon, Kauate snatched it out of the soil, and, whirling it round, dealt his foe a terrible blow on the head. A second blow finished Mautara, whose body was hastily dragged out of the mud to the neighbouring *hibiscus* bush.

Hitherto Kauate and Reketia had not tasted human flesh, but they resolved now to begin upon so promising a subject. So corpulent was Mautara that they contented themselves with cutting off the thighs to cook, leaving the unwieldy carcase to rot. The place where this unholy feast was cooked is a grotto, "Turuatua," formed by a curiously-overhanging rock, where natives love now to recline during the heat of the midday sun.

The taro-patch where the savage met with his deserts is commemoratively called "Pakâ"—" Fallen," and is in the possession of Katuke, the native pastor of the village.

Though Kauate and Reketia were exiles, they were not friendless. They informed those who by stealth supplied their wants of the tragical end of the cannibal, who had been the pest of the neighbourhood. A careful search was instituted to ascertain the headquarters of Mautara. The red clay marks on the pointed rocks revealed the secret. In one of the dreariest recesses of that gloomy cave was found his sleeping-place of dry grass and fern, with abundant evidence of his nefarious occupation in past times.

Kauate and Reketia on more than one occasion made their way to Putoa, to consult with the afterwards famous warrior, Ngangati, and the celebrated "mouthpiece of the god Motoro," how to restore the supremacy of the ancient tribe to which they belonged. The true name of the celebrated priest was "Rongo-i-mua"="Rongo-the-Leader;" but, when about the time of these midnight conferences he took to eating human flesh, the priest of Motoro was nicknamed "Mautara," after the cannibal slain by Kauate. Strangely enough, this nickname was far from being disagreeable to the priest, and ever after stuck to him; so that at this moment the name in question recalls to a native of Mangaia the memory not of the miserable solitary cannibal of Ivirua, but of the great man who founded a tribe which for a century swayed the destinies of Mangaia.

The priest, in a drunken ecstasy, assured the fugitives that only in one way could the worshippers of Motoro be restored to power and prosperity, and that was by the sacrifice of Kauate himself. With a strange heroism Kauate agreed to die on behalf of his tribe ! Not, however, as a altar-offering to Rongo—that were impossible; but *Kauate should seek a violent death at the hand of his foes.*

Kauate was the tallest man of his time. He one day wrenched off by main force a bunch of green bananas belonging to one of the hereditary foes of his clan, and buried it in the earth near the public road to ripen. A moment's glance convinced the indignant owner that no ordinary man could perform such a feat. It must have been done by tall Kauate. A careful search was made to discover where it was buried. It was soon found. As on the fifth night the bananas would be ripe, the tribe of Ngauta were on the alert and well armed. It was said that Kauate, aware of all this, begged his son to live ; but Reketia refused to leave his father. On their way to disinter the bananas they both fell at the hands of their foes.

The subsequent well-planned and successful surprise of Ngangati, in which " every slave slew his own master," and the invincible Ngauta was slain by his nephew, as well as all the glories of his prolonged rule, were all attributed to the costly offering of the conquered chief Kauate. This circumstance, regarded as the turning-point in their history, was commemorated in song.

FETE SONG OF RUAKURA.

By Tangarerua, *circa* A.D. 1700.

Reketia urunga i Mataira
  Kauate te are o Ngariki.
Kua motu koe ia Motoro, ka ta ê!
  O Ngariki oki te puanga.

Reketia was slain by his foes,
  With Kauate chief of the royal clan.
'Twas the fiat of Motoro that ye should die,
  To resuscitate the fortunes of Ngariki.

Pua i Tevaenga, o te Tikute,
  O Ngati Marua :
Te ivi matakeinanga ia Ngariki ê !

Born in Tevaenga, son of Tikute,
  Originally from the land of shadows,
Thou wast the proud head of our tribe.

Noo i Ivirua, kopu tangata o Motoro,
  Amu te tuarangi ê !

Ye lived at Ivirua, worshippers of the god Motoro,
  Like the famed Amu (long ago).

Ei tauka ia Ngariki ;
O Vaeruarangi au ê !

Descendant of Vaeruarangi,
Why didst thou not live to rule Ngariki ?

CHAPTER XV

THE CANNIBAL TANGAKA.

CIRCA A.D. 1680.

AFTER one of the battles of Ngangati, a warrior named Tangaka, belonging to the long since extinct tribe of Kanae, took refuge in the rocks of Veitatei. He contrived to subsist by stealing food from the interior on moonless nights, and by digging for wild roots. Contrary to the custom of exiles, instead of worshipping he *ate* the frugivorous bat, which, paralyzed by cold, is easily struck down with a stick at daybreak.

It was a period of incessant warfare. Luckily for Tangaka, the battles of Ngangati were fought at no great distance from his hiding-place. From all these battle-fields he reaped a rich harvest of spoil. Those who had relatives amongst the slain, as soon as the fighting was over, sought out and removed them. The rest were left to rot where they had fallen, for dogs were then unknown. At nightfall, Tangaka, with a sharp bamboo-knife, cut off the legs and arms of the dead, as being the most delicious bits, and, tying them together, carried them off to his cave. The cannibal grew quite dainty amid such abundance.

His grim abode, still called the Cave of Tangaka, was not more than half a mile distant, so that he could easily make two or three trips in a night. It was known that some one had dismembered the slain for the purpose of eating, but no one cared to inquire what had become of the bodies of their foes.

The Cave of Tangaka is very difficult of access. The surrounding scenery is pleasing. The cave itself is a hole, a little over forty feet in depth, about midway in a perpendicular rock of more than a hundred feet, overhung with trees and bushes. This lair is well concealed by an enormous splinter of the solid rock. After climbing up a natural pathway of loose stones, covered with beautiful creepers, the guide said, "This is the way to the Cave of Tangaka." In a few moments he climbed up the almost perpendicular rock by dexterously inserting his tocs in small crevices, and clinging with his hands to projecting ledges. I declined to follow, as it would be impossible for any one with shoes to do so with safety.

Upon a second visit we discovered a second entrance to this cave. A short *détour* through the bush brought us to the foot of a huge stone. A pandanus-tree growing above it completely hid from view this side-entrance. Carefully avoiding the serrated edges of the thick-growing pandanus leaves, we entered the narrowest part of the rent. At first it seemed impossible to get in, but following a native lad I contrived to squeeze in sideways. In the middle of this narrow, gloomy passage are several rope-like roots of the banyan-tree, which have found their way down from the distant top, and lodge in the scanty soil at the bottom.

After a time the narrow passage widened considerably, and we found ourselves right under the cave once inhabited by the cannibal. It was comparatively easy now to climb on a ledge of rocks, and thence to pass by means of a plank into what had once been the home of Tangaka. The dividing chasm is nine feet wide. From this point I made a rough sketch of the natural rent in the rock; but no pencil can give an adequate idea of the wildness and solitude of the spot. Ferns of exquisite delicacy grow out of the rock. Far above was a tiny patch of blue sky, bounded by the giant branches of ancient ironwood trees. This secret entrance was used by Tangaka when broad daylight rendered it inexpedient to use the direct one which I first visited. He was wont to bring his prey to the direct entrance at night. To a native it is nothing to climb the almost perpendicular rock, and then to haul up the heaviest burden by means of stout sennit cords. He was too crafty to cook his disgusting food in the cave, where the smoke and fire might attract the notice of his foes. A natural round hollow at the bottom of the deep chasm, in its widest part, was his oven; and a better one for his purpose could not be imagined.

About a mile distant from this stronghold was another resort of this cannibal. One of the main routes from the interior to the beach, named Raurau, passes over a small cavity of the rock. A person inside can distinctly see any one climbing the rugged pathway, but cannot himself be seen. Here Tangaka used to lie in wait for his victims. The cave was one day occupied by

9

Tiaio,[1] who was fed by his sister Koua. As Koua had married into the victorious tribe she could easily do this.

As soon as Tangaka discovered his victim, he went in, pretending friendship for the fugitive from a later battle-field. As Tiaio was ignorant of Tangaka's cannibal propensities, he was off his guard, and in a moment the fatal slip-noose was passed over his head. After a brief struggle Tangaka succeeded in carrying off the dead body of Tiaio to his usual haunt. Early next morning Koua came as usual to bring food to her brother, but he could not be found. On carefully examining the earthen floor of the little cave, she discovered traces of the death-struggle and drops of blood. At this distance of time the family name of Tiaio is still kept up in remembrance of their unfortunate ancestor.

As soon as this supply of food was exhausted, Tangaka returned to this little cave to watch for a new victim. The names of several of his unhappy victims are still remembered. A favourite occupation of his was to watch for travellers along the pleasant hill-range opposite to his eyrie. It was easy for him to intercept any solitary woman or child on descending to the lower lands covered with bush.

A party of young girls started early one morning from Keia to collect chestnuts which had fallen in the night. The clump of trees they visited was within a short distance of the hiding-place of the cannibal. With great glee he watched the party descend towards the chestnut trees, and soon passed out by his secret path to hide in the tall reeds for a victim.

The girls soon filled their baskets and returned home. But one of their number, less expert than her friends, lingered behind, securing her basket with *hibiscus* bark. A sharp turn in the narrow pathway hid her companions from view. At this moment Tangaka emerged from his hiding-place, and, creeping stealthily behind the poor girl, threw the fatal cord around her neck and strangled her. He speedily dragged the body and the basket behind some stones, until nightfall should enable him to bear both to his lair.

The companions of the murdered girl waited long for her on the hill-top ; finding that no response was given to their loud

---

[1] So named after the god Tiaio.

calls, fear naturally took possession of their minds, and they hastened back to relate the mysterious disappearance of the poor girl. Raupo, the father of the missing young woman, went that same day with his friends to seek for her, but in vain.

The paramount chief, Ngangati, with the priest Mautara, then a youth, called a meeting of all the principal men to endeavour to find out what had become of Raupo's daughter. Manini stated what was known only to himself, that Tangaka was yet living, and that doubtless he had eaten the poor girl. In fact, Manini was related to the cannibal, and occasionally supplied him with food, but now gave him up to destruction, because he had eaten the daughter of his friend. Manini headed the avenging party, and led them by a rough and circuitous way to the farther end of the chasm opposite to that by which we laboriously entered. Then, noiselessly clambering over the masses of fallen stone, they hid themselves under the shelving rocks close to the entrance of the cave. The spears provided for the occasion were about twelve feet in length; these were firmly planted in the rocky soil.

Meanwhile Raupo, unarmed to avoid suspicion, went up the direct pathway, and looked across the chasm, and saw the ferocious Tangaka, his own near kinsman, fast asleep, it being midday. He could not get across, and probably did not wish to, as the narrow plank had been withdrawn by the wily cannibal. Raupo called him by name, and Tangaka started up with a grunt of displeasure at the unexpected intrusion. So long had the cannibal lived in the rocks that he did not know that the girl he had murdered was his own cousin; still less did he suspect that it was to avenge her death that Raupo had tracked him to his very den.

Raupo blandly assured his relative Tangaka that he had come to fetch him to live with him in the interior. Tangaka smiled, but asked in what part of the island their future home should be. Raupo said, "I will give you a fine taro plantation in Veitatei. You shall eat the firm small taro for which it is famous."

Tangaka shook his head at this proposal. Did he think it inconveniently near to the scene of his many crimes?

Raupo next proposed that they should both go to Tevaenga, and there "eat the yellow soft taro for which that district is noted." It was quite true that Raupo's lands were in that part of the island. Tangaka caught at this, and expressed his entire willingness to give up his solitary life in the rocks and thickets. Raupo said, " We will go at once. The drum of peace has beaten ; you have nothing to fear." The cannibal now got the plank and laid it across the chasm. The moment Tangaka stepped upon it, Raupo kicked the plank with his foot, thus precipitating the monster down headlong to a depth of thirty-six feet. His brains were not dashed out on the rock, for Manini and the rest were on the watch, and, as he fell, firmly held the spears they had planted upright in the soil, and thus transfixed the cannibal. Many were the spear wounds in his body. After extinguishing the last remains of life, the battered corpse was righteously left to moulder in the very hollow where he had been accustomed to cook his victims. One could not help sitting a few minutes on the edge of this oven, ruminating on the striking contrast between the past reign of cruelty and " the gentle reign of Jesus."

Raupo soon discovered several packages in leaves hidden away in a recess of the cave—the remains of his poor daughter. It is said that the head enabled the sorrow-stricken parent to identify the remains. The cord, knife (of bamboo), and club were all there. There is, therefore, no little propriety in the the constantly-recurring allusions in native preaching and praying to " Satan going about, *like Tangaka*, seeking whom he may devour."

CHAPTER XVI.

ONE day having occasion to visit the opposite side of the island, and the morning being cool, I crossed over the hills on foot, accompanied by an intelligent young man as a guide. We were half-way on our road when my companion proposed that we should diverge slightly from the narrow track in order " to see where Vivi rolled himself down." I gladly assented. A few minutes' walk along a narrow hill-ridge through the crisp fern which we crunched under our feet, brought us to a conical eminence, up which we climbed. On either side was a deep valley with precipitous sides. It might be just possible for a barefooted native to get down alive by holding on to the tufts of fern and branches of trees which here and there shoot out of the clayey soil. A false step, or the snapping of a bough, would precipitate him to the bottom—a depth of some six hundred feet. "Down there," said my guide, "rolled poor Vivi." We rested a few minutes in the shade of some graceful ironwood trees (*Casuarina equisetifolia*), the wiry leaves of which closely resemble the stems of fine grass. In the distance was the blue ocean, scarcely distinguishable from the azure sky. Nearer rose that impregnable rocky defence against the violence of old ocean which encircles the island, and is itself covered with dense forest. Between it and where we sat it was pleasant to trace out the hills and valleys of Veitatei. The plaintive murmur of the wind through the numerous clumps of ironwood-trees seemed like the distant music of the waves.

The following is the story of Vivi then related to me.

The tribe of Teipe, once very numerous, was devoted to the furnishing of sacrifices to Rongo from an early period. During the former part of Ngauta's supremacy they enjoyed exemption from this terrible fate. But when that great warrior turned his hand against them their doom was sealed. Repeated defeats in battle reduced the clan of Teipe to a mere fragment; as, how-

ever, their sisters and daughters were in many instances married
into the winning tribes, a few of the males were sheltered and
fed.   But even they lived as it were by sufferance, and might be
killed at pleasure.   At the period referred to Tuanui was paramount chief of Mangaia ; Mautara, who at that time lived at the
mouth of the valley at our feet, was inferior only to Tuanui in
importance.   Hearing that his distant relatives, Vivi and Tito,
were yet living in the forest near the sea, he sent a trusty messenger inviting them to come by night into the interior and
secrete themselves in this lonely valley, where he could easily
supply them with food.   Very joyfully, but in the end unfortunately, they left the few surviving members of their tribe to
shift as they could upon wild roots and fruits, whilst they looked
forward to happier days under the protecting care of the priest
of Motoro.   Vivi and Tito hid themselves in the dense thickets
which at that time covered the bottom of the valley, which is
very narrow.   Rarely did any one pass this way, as it lies out of
the ordinary track, and the sides are for the most part inaccessible.   Here, if anywhere, they seemed secure under the secret
patronage of Mautara, whose son Kakakina brought them food
out of the abundance which was supplied to the supposed
" mouthpiece of the god " by the chiefs.

The principal warriors took up their abode near this famous
priest, partly in order to learn the commands of their god, and
partly in order to assist Mautara in disposing of his food.
Amongst this number was the bold and unscrupulous Tamangoru,
who, having noticed that the food brought day by day from all
parts of the island disappeared with a rapidity not warranted by
the small family of the priest, set a watch to discover what
became of it.   At last he found that Mautara was guilty of
succouring these forlorn creatures, Vivi and Tito.   Without
giving a hint to his priest, on the following morning Tamangoru
collected a number of his friends to hunt the fugitives.   As
soon as the poor fellows discovered their danger they ran up to
the head of the valley, in the hope of gaining the crest of the
hill where we were sitting, and of so being able easily to balk
their pursuers by hiding in another valley.   Vivi, being swifter of
foot, gained the top of the hill, whilst his younger brother, Tito,
was yet only at the base.   The ascent must have been an
arduous task, but fear works wonders.

Now Tamangoru had foreseen this movement, and from the first setting out had left the body of his followers in order to run up the parallel valley, and so intercept his victims. Hence it happened that Vivi and Tamangoru met face to face on the spot where we were resting. But poor Vivi was unarmed, and, indeed, had he been armed, he would have been no match for his fierce antagonist, who was regarded as the best warrior of his day. Standing in Vivi's path with his uplifted club, Tamangoru uttered the words which have since passed into a proverb, " Run where thou wilt, thou shalt not escape." The unhappy fugitive, seeing that there was no hope, at once threw himself down the hill which he had just climbed. He rolled heavily to the very bottom, repeatedly striking against projecting stones, sharp roots, and branches of trees.

Tamangoru, disappointed at the sudden disappearance of Vivi, dashed down into the valley by a circuitous but safe pathway at a little distance. Once at the bottom of the gorge, he ran at full speed, lest any of his friends should deprive him of the honor of slaying his victim. With his own hand he clubbed the battered, insensible, but still breathing form of· one who had never injured him.

Tamangoru now searched everywhere for Tito, who was hiding in some thick brushwood. Tamangoru is said to have split his skull with a single stroke of his wooden sword.

Meanwhile Kakakina, in utter ignorance of what was going on, was carrying a large bunch of bananas for the unfortunate fugitives. Thus to befriend two members of the devoted tribe was a mortal sin in the estimation of Tamangoru. The boy was murdered and his body hidden in the fern, but was subsequently discovered by his brave elder brothers and buried. Over that grave were uttered threats of vengeance against the ancient ruling tribe to which the wanton murderer belonged. In the battle-field of Mâueue, which took place about two years afterwards, all engaged in these murders· were slain, with the exception of Tamangoru, who was reserved by a retributive Providence for a more ignominious end.

A single family, consisting of three brothers, alone survives out of the once numerous tribe of Teipe. A long line of ancestors were all slain, and for the most laid on the altar of " Great Rongo," the relentless god of war. These survivors are members of the Church. Nothing but Christianity could have saved their lives. Females were offered in sacrifice as well as males, although less often. One of the three survivors has lived many years in our family. Occasionally his countrymen chaff him about his having narrowly escaped the fate of his ancestors; but although said in joke—and nothing can prevent these islanders from joking on all kinds of subjects—I have invariably seen him turn ghastly pale as the fearful vision rose up before his mind.

A "CRYING" SONG FOR VIVI AND TITO; BY KOROA.

Pertaining to the "Death-talk" of Puvai.—*Circa* A.D. 1795.

Solo.
Tiô ra Vivi oki nga tokorua
A Tepeipei.

Solo.
Sing we of Vivi and his brother—
Devoted Teipe.

Chorus.
Un kimikimi Ngariki ê!
Na ivi taito ia Tito te vi para ô!

Chorus.
Ngariki was bent on their destruction.
Shortlived was the shelter afforded to Tito!

PAPA.
Solo.
Tei utâ Tito ê i!

FOUNDATION.
Solo.
Ah, Tito was hiding in yon valley.

Chorus.
Tei utâ Tito i te vao mangarua,
Po rua oki au e pokia io.

Chorus.
Yes, Tito was hidden in a secluded valley.
'Twas but the second day when he was caught.

Solo.
Pokia io i te kaiví i te karava,
Un amanga te rima o te tamaki.

Solo.
Caught on the very crest of the hill,
The hands of his foes were upon him.

Chorus.
I uta i Teauiti i te vao ô!

Chorus.
In the vale of Teauiti (he perished)!

UNUUNU TAI.
Solo.
Vivi ô tueruia ra ô!

FIRST OFFSHOOT.
Solo.
Poor Vivi was hunted to death.

Chorus.
Vivi e tueruia, ua atava nga tapuae
O te Tuma nengaia Tepei î.
Tei miri Tito i Tetanga a teuanuku,
To are rau mê kopiopiotâ.
Eiaa te ao i toe ai ô!

Chorus.
Alas! Vivi was hunted to death, by
The relentless foes of his tribe.
Tito vainly hoped to escape,—
Hiding in a fern-leaved hut.
(Said Tamangoru:) Not one of the vanquished shall live.

Solo.
Tio ra, &c.

Solo.
Sing we, &c.

UNUUNU RUA.
Solo.
Tipia i nunga e taka i raro!

SECOND OFFSHOOT.
Solo.
The victim rolled down from the hill-top.

Chorus.	*Chorus.*
Tipia i nunga e taka i raro :	Ah ! he rolled down from the crest of
E taka i raro i te nii taparere	the hill :
I te ainia i te tataingo o Vaiariki.	From that dizzy height he rolled and lay,
Oai te puta in uta ?	A scarcely-breathing mass at the bottom.
Mautara koi i te kiko o Tane.	Who invited him to the interior ?
Eiaa te ao i toe ai ê !	Mautara, the saviour of Tanè.
	(Said Tamangoru :) Not one of the van-
	quished shall live.

Solo.	*Solo.*
Tio ra, &c.	Sing we, &c.

A LAMENT FOR VIVO AND TITO. A "TIAU," OR PARTIAL WEEPING. BY KOROA.

Circa A.D. 1795.

Tumu.	Introduction.
Pukiekie e kore rai Tokoano ai.	Helpless, entirely helpless, were the sons
E oro ei Vivi ê !	of Tokoano.
Mei uta i te vao !	Hence the flight of Vivi
Tai puku kakengata, e korua ê !	From the deep valley
	To the steep hill where both perished !

Papa.	Foundation.
Kimiia koe i Tepikoiti i te makiten,	Ye were sought out of the deepest recesses,
Te are ao na Mautara,	To become vassals of Mautara.
Te kino nei a uta e taeakekore	*Even there* the jealous foe tracked
I Tito i te tamaki, e Ano ê !	And slew the well-beloved Tito !

Unuunu Tai.	First Offshoot.
Pukiekie kore, e korô, tei Avaavata-	Utterly friendless, they first hid near the
kina,—	ocean,—
Tei Avaavatakina.	Near the ocean.
Ko te ua marire e piri ai e oo te verevere,	They subsisted on wild berries and fruits
E verevere aere i Tuanaki.	Found in the depths of the rocks,—
Kua tika paa ia Rongo ia Tumakatea.	Favoured by Rongo and the forest gods.
Kua au te tira ia Veri.	Did they not worship the centipede ? [1]
Mei uta ia te vao !'	(They ran) from the deep valley
Tai puku kakengata, e korua ê !	To the steep hill where both perished !

Unuunu Rua.	Second Offshoot.
" Oro atu koe, ei iaku Teua,—	(At the words) " Run where thou wilt,
Ei iaku Teua ! "	thou shalt not escape—
Kua topa koe i te io,	Thou shalt not escape,"
Kua taka aere, taka io Vivi nei.	Thy heart sank within thee !
Kua tangi te rau o te tuanue ;	Thou didst roll down ! Vivi rolled down,
O te vaevae oki o te tamaki,	down ;
Koputureia e Tamangoru.	The dry fern-leaves cracked beneath
Mei uta i te vao !	The feet of those who cruelly hunted thee ;
Tai puku kakengata, e korua ê !	Tamangoru himself leaped on thy body.
	(They ran) from the deep valley
	To the steep hill where both perished !

---

[1] *The* god of Vivi and Tito was the centipede.

UNUUNU TORU.

Eketia i raro i Teaumoko,—·
    E i Teaumoko.
Tei Takimivera oki te punanga,—
    Punanga i te ao ê!
E kai eki ua, te mikorau ra.
Kua pipi vaitorea, ta te ao manga ia,
Ko te ua i mapura ia no Ukuroi ê,
    E i atoro i te rangatira.
    Mei uta i te vao!
Tai puku kakengata, e korua ê!

THIRD OFFSHOOT.

Once thou wert hidden in a narrow valley,
    In a narrow valley.
Impervious thickets were the fit home
    Of the conquered in war.
Thy food was seeds, and the drupe of the
    pandanus ;
A drink at the stream was oft thy only
    solace ;
The tender shoots of wild taro on the banks
    Were claimed by the victors.
    (They ran) from the deep valley
To the steep hill where both perished!

UNUUNU A.

Tikina i tai ê, tei Motuvera ?
    E tei Motuvera.
Tera roa tei rotopu i te râei.
Tei Tetuokura ; i kake ake na Pei toe
I o pikimato, anau atu i te kainga.
    Mei uta i te vao!
Tai puku kakengata, e korua ê!

FOURTH OFFSHOOT.

Why were ye fetched from the cave near
    the sea,
    Near the sea ?
From the very bosom of the black rocks?
From the mossy couches of the tribe of
    Teipe,
Amidst fantastic crags, weeping for lost
    homes !
    (They ran) from the deep valley
To the steep hill where both perished!

UNUUNU RIMA.

Taura tukua ê i te taeva ê!
    I te taeva !
I te tai paku, tei Ronaki,
Tei putaranunga.   Kua au te are
I Avaavaotno, araviki o te ara,
Na uta, no tai, akaea Teipe manua.
    Mei uta i te vao!
Tai puku kakengata, e korua ê!

FIFTH OFFSHOOT.

A rope[1] was let down yon dreary chasm,—
    That gloomy chasm,—
The wretched abode of the fugitives,
Wandering hither and thither
Through the most inaccessible places.
Teipe[2] is as a defenceless bird, flying
    hither and thither,
    (They ran) from the deep valley
To the steep hill where both perished!

AKAREINGA.

Ai e ruaoo ê!   E rangai ê!

FINALE.

Ai e ruaoo ê!   E rangai ê!

---

[1] This "rope" was the promise of protection given by Mautara. This their last hope failed them.

[2] The tribe is beautifully personified. As the bird seeks the wildest place for its home, so does this doomed race.

This song is part of the "death-talk about Puvai," who was a member of the Teipe tribe, and who died a natural death upwards of a century later.

CHAPTER XVII.

THE INGLORIOUS END OF TAMANGORU.

CIRCA A.D. 1691.

PREVIOUS to his defeat at Mâuene, Tamangoru was chief of Butoa, the district in which the battle took place. By a just retribution, the murderer of Vivi and Tito became himself a homeless fugitive, his lands passing into the hands of his foes. Had he not been fleet of foot, he would have fallen at the hands of the brave brothers of Kakakina.

Rori was a dependant of the chief Tamangoru. *He* sought to hide himself in the inaccessible rocks near the sea, whilst Tamangoru, his former lord, preferred to hover about in the bush of the district once his own. He would sometimes by night enter the narrow valleys of the interior to slake his thirst. He would hide himself for days and weeks together in one of these lonely hollows, stealing food at night, and sleeping by day in the *hibiscus* thickets or in the gigantic fern. He had no friend to seek him out and to supply his wants.

These little valleys—favourite hiding-places of the conquered —were in those times entirely in a state of nature, but are now everywhere well cultivated. The nicest taro, although inferior in size, grows in these sequestered spots.

In the larger valleys, to obtain possession of which so much blood was shed from generation to generation, families would build their huts close together for the sake of mutual protection.

That misfortune had not softened the heart of Tamangoru towards the feeble is clear from an anecdote which belongs to this period of his history.

Kurapeau, mother of Mautara, was inconsolable for the loss of her husband Akunukunu, who had been put to death by *her* relatives (the Tongan clan). She had often assured him that her own tribe would be sure to protect him. In a state of distracted grief she wandered alone over the island; nothing could induce her to stay with her son and his family. One day she fell in with Tamangoru in one of these secluded valleys, and was by

him immediately speared to death.   The attenuated body was
not eaten, but hidden in a neighbouring taro-path.   Eight days
afterwards it was discovered and buried by her relatives.

But Tamangoru was not always so particular; stragglers
were sometimes cut off and eaten by this solitary cannibal.   He
is said to have been a powerful man; so that, though often seen,
nobody cared to attack him.   His career after the battle of
Mâueue was brief, and his end very inglorious.

Under cover of night he crossed the island, taking up his
abode in the rocks and thickets on the western shore, where he
was but little known.   He had no companion but his enormous
club, and experienced great difficulty in satisfying his hunger
from day to day.   Early one morning, soon after his arrival on
the western shore, he saw smoke ascending at no great distance.
Cautiously approaching it, he discovered two boys roasting a
number of rats over a fire,—a joyful sight for a famishing
Mangaian.

In those days—ere the cat had been introduced—rats were
very plentiful.   Rat-hunting was the grave employment of
bearded men, the flesh being regarded as most delicious.   The
rat, though but slightly larger than the English mouse, was the
only quadruped on the island.

Oromanarangi and Oromananuku were brothers, the former
about fifteen years of age, the younger about thirteen.   They
were themselves fugitives and orphans, and subsisted chiefly by
rat-catching, in which they were adepts.   The place selected for
their operations was a wild, out-of-the-way spot.   Jagged rocks
cropped out of the thin soil in every direction, and were covered
with a variety of creepers, the most beautiful of which—*Coix
lachryma*—yields a profusion of vermilion berries, which furnish
necklaces in abundance for the young folks.   A dense growth of
timber shut out the little open space from observation.

On the previous evening the boys dug a deep hole in the
earth and covered the bottom of it with candlenuts, of which
rats are excessively fond.   A narrow pathway was made on either
side for the rats to get down to eat.   The lads lay in wait at a
little distance, until they thought the hole must be pretty full.
Each lad carried a lighted torch in one hand, and a stout ironwood stick in the other.   They quickly killed a large number of
rats.

The boys now made a fire to roast the spoil. They then thrust long green reeds (previously prepared) through the rats, eight on each reed, and grilled them over the fire. There were four skewers or reeds of rats, *i.e.*, thirty-two in all.

Whilst thus pleasantly engaged in preparing their savoury breakfast, to their great discomfiture the formidable Tamangoru made his appearance. Oromanarangi whispered in his brother's ear, " If anything should happen, do *you* look after his *feet; I* will take care of his *head.*"

Tamangoru seated himself quietly on some dry leaves, and, eyeing the boys very attentively, ambiguously remarked, " Cooked *rats* are capital eating." The word " rats " thus used might apply to the lads as well as to the little quadrupeds. A cooked boy would be indifferently called a " fish " or a " rat." Oromanarangi and Oromananuku at once caught at the double sense intended, and so prepared for the worst. When the rats were done, the elder took two reeds of rats (sixteen) to Tamangoru. Cautiously, however, avoiding the front of his adversary, he approached him on the side farthest from the dreaded ironwood sword, sharply eyeing Tamangoru's hands as he carried the cooked rats. The famished man greedily devoured them. Tamangoru now called for the remaining two reeds. Oromanarangi, without uttering a word of complaint, carried them by the same circuitous route to Tamangoru. Approaching him from behind, he put them over his right shoulder. In Tamangoru's left hand was the wooden sword ; the right hand was at this moment engaged in taking the cooked rats from the boy, who felt certain that the cruel enemy would slay both him and his brother as soon as the rats were demolished. The choice lay between killing him or being killed by him.

At this critical moment, when both hands were engaged, the elder lad seized hold of his flowing hair with both hands. It was a death-grip. His feet were firmly planted in the girdle of his powerful adversary. Tamangoru was unprepared for this, not deeming it possible that mere boys should attack one who had been greatly feared by their parents. He was almost helpless, as his head was pulled far back by the strong lad. Recollecting, however, a large Barringtonia-tree growing just by, he walked backwards towards it, of course carrying the adventurous boy with him, purposing to drive his whole force against the

tree, so as to kill Oromanarangi.   But Tamangoru had found his
match; for, as he was just about to crush the lad, his dexterous
foe wriggled on one side, but without relaxing his hold upon the
head or withdrawing his feet from the girdle.   Tamangoru was
much shaken by the heavy blow received against his bare back.
Again and again the trick was played by Tamangoru with a
similar result, until he at length stood still, considerably exhausted.

This was the precise moment that little Oromananuku was
waiting for.   Taking up a large irregular stone, he dashed it
with all his might against the legs of his huge foe.   One leg was
quite broken by the well-directed missile, so that Tamangoru fell
heavily on the ground.   The elder brother cleverly slipped off
the back of the doomed man as he fell.   Tamangoru, feeling
himself to be indeed in an evil case, earnestly begged the boys to
spare his life.   Little pity could *he* deserve who had never in his
life shown pity to others.   The head was now free, but only
because he was no longer capable of defending himself.   The
boys beat out his brains with stones.   The body of Tamangoru
was left to rot where he so ingloriously fell.   But the brave lads
were ever after celebrated amongst their countrymen as the
punishers of this fierce marauder.   The spot where he fell is
known as "the pounding of Tamangoru," being marked by a
rock four feet and a half high.   Boys delight to beat it with
stones, on account of the musical sound it gives forth.

LAMENT FOR KURAPEAU.

By her son Mautara. *Circa* 1691.

Tumu.	Introduction.
Ko Te-moe-au tei Torekaro	(Thy mother) " The-gentle-sleeper " [1] lies
Ei raupoto i Aremangeo,	buried
Akatupu koe i te verevere.	At "Aumoana" [2] amongst her relatives,—
Ka ano ô, kimi tane ô !	She who succoured the perishing.
Tekura tei rangatira reira ô !	Thou the prosperous Kurapeau [3] didst
	choose
	The unfortunate Akunukunu for thy hus-
	band.

[1] "The-gentle-sleeper" was daughter of Ivi, priest of Turanga.   As this tribe,
from Tonga, was the most powerful of its time, *she* is represented as *condescending*
to marry Akunukunu, priest of Motoro.

[2] "Aumoana" (" ocean current ") is the name of their *marae*, where the lizard
was worshipped.

[3] Kurapeau is shortened into " Kura."   The definite article is (as is often done)
prefixed, giving "Tekura" throughout this song.

PAPA.

Mautara kai ngakau ê!
Kimi atu koe i to metua ;
Tei utu ê, i te vao roa,
I te poo i Vaiaua.
Kua pa oki te karanga ê,
Akunukunu e vai ra, e Tekura ê!

FOUNDATION.

Mautara, the wisest of sons,
Sought everywhere for his mother.
He found the corpse in a lonely glen,
In the deep recesses of Vaiaua.
How deep thy grief at the sad news that
Thy Akunukunu had been slain, O Kura-
peau.

UNUUNU TAI.

Te-moe-au ê, tei Torekaro ê,
Tei Torekaro i te ûû o Atakura,
    Tei Nukumau te kino,
    Tei Nukumau te kino ai.
Ko te kiko i oongo mai ana ;
    Kave atu tanumia,
    I oro mai ia Tipou.
    Ka ano ê, kimi tane ê!
Tekura tei rangatira reira ê!

FIRST OFFSHOOT.

(Thy mother) "The-gentle-sleeper" lies
    buried
At "Aumoana," the resting-place of her
    tribe.
    'Twas *her* tribe that was angry—
    That caused us this sore trouble,
Piercing our very hearts with sorrow.
    Bury the dead out of sight,
    And return to thy home.
Thou the prosperous Kurapeau didst
    choose
The unfortunate Akunukunu for thy hus-
    band.

UNUUNU RUA.

Te upoko i mua ê, ia Mautara,
Ko Teuanuku ko te vae tapeka,
    Kai te tai i Pokara.
Ko te upoko tikitiki o Ngati Vara nei,
    Kua kavea i Tangikura.
    Ka ano au ê, kimi tane ê!
Tekura tei rangatira reira ê!

SECOND OFFSHOOT.

Mother of great men! Mautara first of
    all ;
Thy grandson Teuanuku, the brave,
Who avenged the wrongs of his ancestors.
The children of Vara[1] can ne'er forgive
The ancient slaughter at Tangikura.[2]
Thou the prosperous Kurapeau didst
    choose
The unfortunate Akunukunu for thy
    husband.

UNUUNU TORU.

Koai, koai te piritanga ê?
    Piritanga ia Tekura ?
Ko te anau a Tevaki,—
Ko Ngati Vairanga, ko Ngati Vairanga' í.
Aore au e tau, e Akunukunu.
Ko te amo ia Terua i paeke ei.
    Ka ano ê, kimi tane ê!
Tekura tei rangatira reira ê!

THIRD OFFSHOOT.

Who—ah! who—afforded succour ?
Who pitied poor Kurapeau ?
    Save the children of Tevaki,
Descended from Vairanga,—that ancient
    stock !
" My case is hopeless," exclaimed Akunu-
    kunu :
"I cannot escape from my foes."
Thou the prosperous Kurapeau didst
    choose
The unfortunate Akunukunu for thy
    husband.

UNUUNU A.

Mangere ikona ê, tei Ruaiva ê,
Tei Kukupunua, ê Tekura,
    I te akamate aere,
    I te akamate aere ei,

FOURTH OFFSHOOT.

    " Leave me here to die,
I will wander over the hills," said she.
    " I care not for my life,—
    I long to die.

---

[1] " Vara " was the second priest of Motoro in order of succession, and an ancestor
of Mautara.
[2] The slaughter of the " Aitu," or " god-tribe," at Tangikura in the second battle
that occurred on Mangaia.

Taku moe ngauta iaku,
　Ei tiki ia Tetipi,
Tekura te ranga ia Paeke.
　Ka ano ê, kimi tane ê ;
Tekura tei rangatira reira ê !

My dreams are of the dead.
I will join my deceased ancestors.
The death of Kurapeau shall avenge
　Paeke."
Thou the prosperous Kurapeau didst
　choose
The unfortunate Akunukunu for thy
　husband.

Unuunu Rima.

　Ka peke i nunga ê,
Tei Putoa ê, kua ungâ Mautara.
　Ko Tevaki te rave ake ;
　Tei Putuputukiau,
　Tei Tekaeruaie !
　Ka ano ê, kimi tane ê !
Tekura tei rangatira reira ê !

Fifth Offshoot.

　Mautara took flight,
And for awhile was hidden at Putea,
　Tevaki was his only solace ;
　Amidst thickets and bushes
　They both found shelter.
Thou the once prosperous Kurapeau didst
　choose
The unfortunate Akunukunu for thy
　husband !

Akareinga.

Ai e ruaoo ê !　E rangai ê !

Finale.

　Ai e ruaoo ê !　E rangai ê !

CHAPTER XVIII.

THE EXILES.

In two famous instances whole families were driven off the island, to take their chance on the ocean for life or death.

Tauai and Tekaraka, with their respective families and adherents, were exiled by the chief Aeru, of that division of the tribe Ngariki bearing the name Vaeruarangi. The deminant clan wished to kill them on account of an abortive attempt to seize the supreme chieftainship of the island. Packe, priest of Motoro, speaking oracularly, said, "Exile them." Two double canoes of the largest size were prepared, and provisions (cocoa-nuts) laid in for their long and uncertain voyage. These double canoes were connected with each other by means of stout iron-wood poles lashed with strong sennit. A deck was now laid across, a mast set up, and the extempore ship furnished with sails of stout native cloth, mats being unknown on Mangaia in those times.

On the appointed day Aeru ordered these two great double canoes to be launched, and the exiles to embark. Tauai com-manded one canoe, Tekaraka the other. Nearly opposite to the mission premises at Tamarua is an indentation in the reef called "Aeru," commemorating the exact point of departure. At that period the famous Ngauta was but a child; but in manhood he took ample revenge upon the ancient dominant clan for the ex-pulsion of his relatives, Tauai and Tekaraka. The first exiles must have left the island upwards of two hundred and fifty years ago.

In Christian times the fate of these early voyagers has become a matter of great interest. It is believed that they reached the northern island of New Zealand in safety,—that the Tekaraka referred to is the veritable Tekaraka who figures in Maori story. It may be a corroboration of this that the New Zealanders at once fraternize with the Hervey Islanders, and address them as their "ai tuakana," or "elder brethren." Besides, there is a remarkable correspondence between various Maori names and the names of places on the south of Mangaia

10

—Mongonui, Waikato, Waitangi, Waitotara; only in the Hervey Group dialect we print V for the W. The pronunciation of these names is identical. The distance to the nearest part of New Zealand would not be much more than that sorrowfully traversed by Elikana in 1862, in his involuntary voyage from Manihiki to Nukuraerae.

The expulsion of Iro is of a comparatively late date, scarcely more than two hundred years ago. Like the former band of exiles, Iro and his friends belonged to the ever-restless Tongan tribe, whose headquarters were at Tamarua. The valuable "miro" tree (*Thespesia populnea*) grows spontaneously only on the rugged shore, where their ancestors originally landed, bringing the seeds with them.

Ngauta had perished, and with him the overshadowing influence of the Tongan clan. But Iro and Tuavera, wishing to restore the ancient fame of their tribe, plotted the destruction of the leading chiefs of the day. Tuanui was supreme "lord of Mangaia," and Mautara priest of Motoro. The plot was revealed by Tia; consequently the ambuscade of the Tongans failed, and the exile of those concerned in the attack was decreed in the name of the god Motoro. The alleged motive for not permitting these Tongans to be slain was, "that the sacred clothing of the gods might not be defiled with human blood," and so draw down vengeance upon the ruling race. Pati, priest of the exiled tribe, was the sole depositary or maker of the superior paper-mulberry cloth, as thick as cardboard, used exclusively for clothing the gods, great chiefs, and priests. This "lordly clothing" was actually worshipped by the tribe that manufactured it, under the name of "te tikoru mataiapo"!

As soon as the decree of Motoro was made known, Iro and his friends mournfully prepared for their enforced departure. As in the former instance, two large double canoes were built at a spot called "Tuavera," in memory of the event, on the northern part of the island. The timber used was that of the noble *Barringtonia speciosa*, whose large handsome flowers open at sunrise, but fade and fall to the ground at sunset. As the canoes of these exiles were sixty feet long, several of these magnificent trees were required. Like those of Tauai and Tekaraka, these canoes were decked and supplied with masts and sails. A thatched covering or awning was set up in each double canoe, in order to protect the women and children from the sun and rain.

All the valuable movable property of the exiles was taken on board, with a good supply of food and water. Several months were occupied in these preparations, during which time they suffered no molestation.

When no further excuse for delay could be invented, Tuanui gave the command to depart, and led the sorrowful band to the usual place of departure on the west side of the island. A farewell feast made for them by their friends occupied the morning. The sun was low in the horizon when, amid loud lamentations and many tears, they started, with a steady trade wind, on their uncertain voyage. Iro and Tuavera commanded one double canoe, Akaina and Pati the other.

The last words of Iro to his nephew, Arekare, were never to rest until he had avenged their expulsion by splitting up into hostile factions the tribe which ruled the island. They parted to meet no more. Would the exiles perish in the unknown waste of waters towards the setting sun, or would they reach some friendly shore and there revive the fallen fortunes of their race? As the little "ships" pressed towards the edge of the golden sky, and darkness came on, it is said that the distant glimmer of the torches lighted by the voyagers to cheer them on their way was the last ever seen here of Iro and his companions.

Some 155 years rolled on without tidings of these exiles, so that no one doubted that the entire party, upwards of forty, had perished in the deep. Not that the event was forgotten, as may be seen in an interesting song composed in memory of their departure.

LAMENT FOR IRO THE EXILE.

By Koroa; recited at "the Death-talk of Vaiaa."—*Circa* A.D. 1791.

TUMU.	INTRODUCTION.
Taiku io, e Iro e, ia Arekare—	Thy last charge, O Iro, to Arekare was—
Naau ake ia Ngariki.	Split up the clan of Ngariki.
E tae koe i te kao nu momoke	Fell the fair palm soaring above all others
I Araata; te ê o Tetipi ka eva ê!	At Araata;[1] now the tribe of Tetipi mourns.[2]

---

[1] The *marae* of Motoro was named Araata, where only the dominant tribe of Ngariki might worship. This tribe, hostile to the exiles, is compared to a lofty palm growing at Araata, and looking disdainfully down upon all other trees. This was doubtless suggested by the circumstance of a single cocoanut-tree of a rare yellow kind growing in the idol grove. On account of the supposed sanctity of the place it was never climbed, nor was the fruit tasted.

[2] "Tetipi," one of the founders of the Tongan clan.

PAPA.

Tuku atu tei te moana, e Iro ;
Tei ia Pati te vaka i Tuavera.
Ko Akaina, te rû torikiriki tatou ê !

FOUNDATION.

Start now on thy voyage, O Iro ;
Pati has furnished Tuavera with a craft.
Alas, Akaina ! our sun disappears in the
    horizon !

UNUUNU TAI.

Taiku io ê ia Arekare,—
    Ia Arekare,
E momotu koe i te ivi roa,
    Ei oo paa nooku,
Ka rua vaka e Tetipi ;—
E no Tauai tei neê atu,
    Ponakava ia Aeru.
E tae koe i te kao nu momoke
I Araata ; te ê o Tetipi ka eva ê !

FIRST OFFSHOOT.

Thy last charge to Arekare,—
To thy friend Arekare, was—
End their long-continued sway.
This is the solace I crave.
Twice our tribe has been expelled ;
Long since Tauai was driven away
Through the malice of Aeru.
Fell the fair palm soaring above all others
At Araata ; now the tribe of Tetipi mourns.

UNUUNU RUA.

Oioi ake i te motuone,—
    I te motuone,
Tei Vaipia, kua ata paa
I te tikoru i runga ia Pati,
    Kua panaia e Motoro ;
Kua tamutu oki Tamangaro ê,
    Kua naki na e Tia ê !
E tae koe i te kao nu momoke
I Araata ; te ê o Tetipi ka eva ê !

SECOND OFFSHOOT.

The ambush was well laid
    And planned.
The sacred garments of Pati
Scared our hereditary foes.
'Tis Motoro that exiles us.
The attack of Tamangaro failed
Through the treachery of Tia.
Fell the fair palm soaring above all others
At Araata ; now the tribe of Tetipi mourns.

UNUUNU TORU.

Rangakauria ê i te maroro ê,
    I te mâroro ê !
E vaka kura no Tuavera.
    Kua pau Teaaki !
Kua tauna te matakeinga o Tetipi
Poroara io ia Ngariki.
E tae koe i te kao nu momoke
I Araata ; te ê o Tetipi ka eva ê !

THIRD OFFSHOOT.

Our noble canoes are completed ;
    What models are they !
Ornamented with red feathers by Tuavera.
    The tribe Teaaki[1] is gone !
The descendants of Tetipi have disap-
    peared,
Driven away by merciless Ngariki !
Fell the fair palm soaring above all others
At Araata ; now the tribe of Tetipi mourns.

UNUUNU A.

Kua iti te rû ê kumekume tika,—
Kumekume tika kia mâro.
Kia rou te rua i te matangi.
Na kono o te vaka, mei tatakina.
    Kua aae, kua neue—
    I te ara kaa i te torere.
    Kua viri Iro i tai enua !
E tae koe i te kao nu momoke
I Araata ; te ê o Tetipi ka eva ê !

FOURTH OFFSHOOT.

Ah ! the sun shines brightly. Shine on ;
For once hasten not to set.
Let the wind blow favourably,
The ships sail gallantly o'er the ocean.
The sennit strains, the seams open ;
Yet the fragile barks hold on their way.
Perchance Iro will reach some other
    isle.
Fell the fair palm soaring above all others
At Araata ; now the tribe of Tetipi mourns.

UNUUNU RIMA.

Opuopu te uru ê no Mangaia ê !
    No Mangaia !
Kua pueke te ai ki vaenga moana,
    Ki te ata kurakura.
E kaou te kare i te taoa,

FIFTH OFFSHOOT.

The hills of Mangaia are lost to sight.
    Alas for Mangaia !
Torches light our pathway o'er the sea
Where the ruddy sun went down.
The cruel waves attack our ships,

---

[1] "Teaaki," a branch of the once-powerful Tongan tribe.

Oromia io Raunika Nui,
I te papatua e muna ê!
E tae koe i te kao nu momoke
I Araata ; te ê o Tetipi ka eva ê!
 Ai e ruaoo ê ! E rangai ê!

Hoping to sink them in mid-ocean,
 And bury them for ever in its depths.
Fell the fair palm soaring above all others
At Araata ; now the tribe of Tetipi mourns.
 Ai e ruaoo ê ! E rangai ê !

A few years after the introduction of Christianity into the Hervey Group, about 1826, a young Rarotongan accompanied Mr. Williams to Mangaia, and astonished the men of that day by stating that one of those double canoes commanded by Iro and Tuavera reached Ngatangiia in safety. Kainuku, the chief of that part of Rarotonga, gave the exiles a kind reception, allotting to them an entire district at Titikaveka, which occupies relatively the same position at Rarotonga which Tamarua, the original home of Iro, does with respect to Mangaia. Like other heathens of Polynesia, the Rarotongans were always fighting. The valour of these exiles assisted materially in after years in raising the tribe with which they were incorporated to the proud position which it enjoyed in 1823, the date of the discovery of Rarotonga by Mr. Williams. "In proof of this," said Terei, the acknowledged head of this little colony, "we alone are permitted to eat turtle and other royal fish when caught by ourselves."

A block of sandstone in the harbour at Ngatangiia marks the spot where Iro first landed in his new home. At Titikaveka a vast quantity of sandstone (*kea*) is on the beach, and is found on no other part of Rarotonga. It came to be believed that this sandstone foundation of their new home actually accompanied Iro in his flight, and complaisantly settled down in its present position ! The foundation of this wild fancy is the circumstance that pieces of " sacred sandstone " were put on board their canoes as charms to insure the safety of the voyagers.

Terei was a worthy man, and made a consistent profession of Christianity for many years. The old man said that the story of their origin had never been forgotten by the exiles. For himself, he had a strong desire to visit the land of his ancestors (Mangaia), but his duties as chief forbade him to indulge his wish. His name refers to the fading outline of the rocky shore of his ancestral home. This good man has recently passed away to the better world.

A young man named Taora was left behind, detained by his uncle, Manini, who little recked what his fate would be.

Tuanui, "lord of Mangaia," wished to offer a sacrifice to the sanguinary Rongo; none would be so acceptable in *his* eyes as the friendless Taora. It happened that a grand dance was to come off by torchlight; the intended victim would be present as a matter of course. Tuanui resolved to take this opportunity of killing Taora with his own hand, and, for this purpose, under his gay "tiputa," or loose upper garment, concealed a small stone adze.

Just before the torches were lighted and the dance was about to lead off, it was whispered in Taora's ear, "Run for your life; you will be slain to-night." But Taora well knew that if the chiefs were resolved to slay him he could not escape. He therefore refused to run, but dressed himself with unusual care, and even had the audacity to steal the beautiful shells which hung around the neck of the god Motoro. Taora now took his place in the dance, admired of all for his gay trappings and his energetic participation in all the required evolutions. Merrily the dance went on, few suspecting the bloody tragedy to be enacted in the name of great Rongo.

About midnight, when half the songs had been recited, the supreme chief of Mangaia quietly stepped up in front of Taora, who knew that his last moment had arrived, and by one well-aimed blow closed the career of the ill-fated dancer. The blood of the victim besmeared the sacred necklace of Motoro, as the wearer intended. The dance was thus rudely brought to a close, but the required sacrifice was that night laid on the altar of the god of war, and peace was again proclaimed. Happier far if Taora had accompanied the exile Iro to Rarotonga.

The last words of Iro sank deep into the mind of Arekare ="House-on-the-Waves"—a new and sad memorial name. The one object of his life now was to foment quarrels amongst the principal men of the day, with a view to war. Several years of unquiet rule under Tuanui had passed away when Arekare collected a number of his friends and made a successful night attack upon those chiefly concerned in the expulsion of Iro. The murder of Vivi and Tito by Tamangoru a short time previously was thought little of at the time, as they were friendless. But now the case was quite different, and immediate preparations were made for a battle that took place at Maueue, on the east of the island. In that fight, Tuanui, Arekare, the father of Rori, and many others were slain. Iro's wish was gratified, as in this fight for the first time the original ruling tribe was split into adverse factions, brother fighting against brother, thus preparing the way for their final overthrow some years later at the hands of their oracle, Mautara.

The man who wrought all this dire confusion—"House-on-the-Waves"—had a presentiment of defeat and death. The night previous to the battle of Mâuene, Arekare went with his *ten* wives to catch fish on the reef for a final feast. It was an invariable custom to enjoy a feast before going to battle, as one might not survive to eat again. Amongst the many wives of Arekare, Eiau, the beauty of her day, was his favourite. They returned by torchlight to the encampment, each wife carrying her own basket of fish, whilst their joint husband held in his hand a spear. The descent to the interior is still difficult; by night it is dangerous—a single false step might precipitate one to the bottom. All had gone down but Eiau and Arekare. The favourite was about to descend, when *her loving husband pushed her over the precipice!* Eiau was much injured by her fall, particularly her pretty face. Covered with blood, she demanded of Arekare, who seemed quite unconcerned, why he thus treated her. "*It was only an accident,*" remarked her husband. Eiau easily divined the truth; it was the clear presentiment in his mind that he would be slain to-morrow, and then the lovely Eiau would belong to one of his mortal foes. Arekare's grief was that she was not killed outright. She lived many years afterwards, much disfigured by this "accident," a slave in the household of Mautara.

ANOTHER LAMENT FOR THE EXILE IRO; BY KOROA.

Recited on the same occasion.

TUMU.	INTRODUCTION.
Solo.	*Solo.*
Mâtua moana ia Iro,	Hail, Iro, expertest of voyagers,
E eke ua i Karanganui,	Descending (to the beach) at Karanganui,
Ka ana 'tu au kimi kouru matangi,	Awaiting a favouring breeze.
Chorus.	*Chorus.*
Ki te iku anau e araru ê!	List to the south-west wind awaking.
PAPA.	FOUNDATION.
Solo.	*Solo.*
Oki mai Iro i te tumu e reirê!	Return, Iro, to thy natal soil.
Tau akatere i te atianga,	He is pressing through the breakers,
Ua rori aere i Teumi,	After crossing the pointed rocks.
O te akama nui ê!	Alas, the greatness of thy shame!

Chorus.

Ko Iro i tei ungaia ò !

Chorus.

Alas, Iro, thou art exiled

UNUUNU TAI.

Solo.

Mâtua moana ê teia Iro ò !
E eke ua i Annporea,
E ngakinga apinga'i i ano ai ;
E ngakinga apinga'i i ano ai.
Pâii atu na o te kuonga,
Kautaka aere i Araoa,
Te teka nei i te urutonga
Ka ama 'tu au kimi kouru matangi,

FIRST OFFSHOOT.

Solo.

Hail, Iro, expertest of voyagers,
Frequent at the wave-washed cave
Whenever a feast was preparing—
Yes, whenever a feast was preparing.
Thou didst follow the still waters of the
    reef
Plying thine art at Araon.
Ha ! the wind has veered to the south ;
I am awaiting a favourable breeze.

Chorus.

Ki te iku anau e arara ò !

Chorus.

List to the south-west wind awaking !

PAPA.

Solo.

Oki mai Iro i te tumu e reirê !
Tau akatere i te atianga.
Ua rori aere i Teumi,
O te akama nui ê !

FOUNDATION.

Solo.

Return, Iro, to thy natal soil.
He is pressing through the breakers,
After crossing the pointed rocks.
Alas, the greatness of thy shame !

Chorus.

Ko Iro i tei ungaia ò !

Chorus.

Alas, Iro, thou art exiled !

UNUUNU RUA.

Solo.

Taku ara paia ê i te eketinga ê !
I te eketinga ia Poatutokere ê !
I te eketinga ia Poatutokere'i !
O Terei e tu mai, ua iria
Te manava, ua iria te manava'i.
Na reo taiku auta mai te anau.
E eke ua i Karanganui.
Ka ama 'tu au kimi kouru matangi,

SECOND OFFSHOOT.

Solo.

Thy way down to the beach is inter-
    rupted,—
The descent at Poatutokere ;
Yes, the descent at Poatutokere.
Yonder stands Terei oppressed with grief,
With intense sorrow, and the nephew
Treasures up the last charge of his uncle,
As he descends (to the beach) at Kara-
    nganui.
I am awaiting a favourable breeze.

Chorus.

Ki te iku anau e arara ò.

Chorus.

List to the south-west wind awaking !

PAPA.

Solo.

Oki mai Iro i te Tumu e reirê !
Tau akatere i te atianga.
Ua rori aere i Teumi,
O te akama nui ê !

FOUNDATION.

Solo.

Return, Iro, to thy natal soil.
He is pressing through the breakers,
After crossing the pointed rocks.
Alas, the greatness of thy shame !

Chorus.

Ko Iro i tei ungaia ê !

Chorus.

Alas, Iro, thou art exiled !

---

[1] *I.e.*, the sister of Iro, and mother of Arekare by her husband Tuanui, temporal
lord of Mangaia. It was the hate of Tuanui that led to the expulsion of Iro and his
party. The last charge is that referred to in the "Introduction" of the preceding
"Lament," and which subsequently occasioned so much blood-shedding. Nganguru,
the father of Iro and Terei, was offered in sacrifice to the god Rongo.

This song is given exactly as it was chanted, with all the repetitions, by way of
showing how the other dirges in this book were actually performed.

UNUUNU TORU.	THIRD OFFSHOOT.
Solo.	*Solo.*

Tiroia i nunga ê i te rango nei ê!	Gaze once more on the sea-shore!
I te rango nei, te vaa maira i Teanaroa.	Voices sound from the cave Teanaroa.
Tei Pariki tetai kopunga vaine,	It is the hum of women at Pariki,
Tei Pariki tetai kopunga vaine'i,	Yes, the murmur of women at Pariki,
Te tara nei i te râui, na Iro atu na i tamaka.	Discussing thy ejection. Iro is girding on his sandals.
Ka ana 'tu au kimi kouru matangi,	I am awaiting a favourable breeze.

Chorus.	*Chorus.*
Ki te iku anau e arara ê!	List to the south-west wind awaking!

PAPA.	FOUNDATION.
Solo.	*Solo.*

Oki mai Iro i te tumu e reirê!	Return, Iro, to thy natal soil.
Tau akatere i te atianga.	He is pressing through the breakers,
Ua rori aere i Teumi,	After crossing the pointed rocks.
O te akama nui ê!	Alas, the greatness of thy shame!

Chorus.	*Chorus.*
Ko Iro i tei ungaia ê!	Alas, Iro, thou art exiled!

UNUUNU A.	FOURTH OFFSHOOT.
Solo.	*Solo.*

Itiki Mu ê i tona tai ê!	Mu has tabooed the sea,—
I tona tai ia Karanganui.	His sea at Karanganui.
Aore paa e taea ua atu te râui.	It is vain to go, for the *râui* is set up;
Ua tu te râui, e tangata metua	Yes, the *râui* is set up, and that aged man
E mareva aere i te moana.	(*i.e.*, Iro)
Kautaka aere i Araoa.	Is now an exile on the ocean.
Ka ana 'tu au kimi kouru matangi,	Let us go together to Araoa.
	I am awaiting a favourable breeze.

Chorus.	*Chorus.*
Ki te iku anau e arara ê!	List to the south-west wind awaking!

PAPA.	FOUNDATION.
Solo.	*Solo.*

Oki mai Iro i te tumu e reirê!	Return, Iro, to thy natal soil.
Tau akatere i te atianga.	He is pressing through the breakers,
Ua rori aere i Teumi,	After crossing the pointed rocks.
O te akama nui ê!	Alas, the greatness of thy shame!

Chorus.	*Chorus.*
Ko Iro i tei ungaia ê!	Alas, Iro, thou art exiled!

UNUUNU RIMA.	FIFTH OFFSHOOT.
Solo.	*Solo.*

Karanga i uta ê oki maira ê!	A voice from shore is calling, "Come back!
Oki maira, ka ano koe kia?	Come back! Whither art thou fleeing?
Ua tapu oki te tai, ua tapu oki te tai.	The sea is sacred; yes, the sea is sacred."
Ua tioi te tua'i, ua taeke,	Ha! he is getting into his canoe, he starts,
Ua romiromi te oe, i aro ai.	He seizes his paddle and faces the horizon!
Ka ana 'tu au kimi kouru matangi,	I am awaiting a favourable breeze.

Chorus.	*Chorus.*
Ki te iku anau e arara ê !	List to the south-west wind awaking !

AKAREINGA.	FINALE.
Chorus.	*Chorus.*
Ai e ruaoo ! E rangai ê !	Ai e ruaoo ! E rangai e !

In this song the daily avocation of the fisherman and the final sad departure of Iro are dexterously intermingled. Hence the references to places which Iro was accustomed to frequent. When a great feast was in preparation, the custom was (and still is) for fishermen not to return to their dwellings at night, but to sleep in some cave or under some overhanging cliff near the sea.

CHAPTER XIX.

A POISONED BOWL.

On the south of Mangaia, on the margin of a little lake, once-lived the famous priest Tangiia, guardian of the *marae*, and greatly feared on account of his supposed supernatural powers. The worshippers carried to the priest bowls of intoxicating drink —the nectar of Polynesian gods—in the hope of securing a favourable response to their petitions. Cooked taro and fish were given with the " kava" (*Piper mythisticum*), as without the addition of solid food the narcotic effects of this detestable drink would not be evoked.

But *this* priest, affecting to speak in the name of his god Tangiia, required *human flesh* as a relish. From time to time he demanded of his infatuated followers that they should furnish him with a young child "to eat with the *kava*." Such was the terror which this wretch inspired that his cruel demands were invariably complied with. Receiving from the hands of the worshippers the frothy bowl, Tangiia eagerly quaffed its contents, and (it is expressly said) with his own hands slew the little victim and devoured the quivering flesh. In the haggard, bloodshot-eyed priest was recognized, not the man, but their own fierce god, the supposed arbiter of life and death.

One day Tangiia declared to Marere, a member of the royal Akatauira clan, that he required from him the accustomed bowl of " kava" *and his little son!* The father knew that the wily old priest had long cherished an ill feeling towards him. Mad-dened by this demand, which he dared not openly refuse, Marere rose superior to the superstition of his day, and resolved to put an end to the tricks of Tangiia. Luckily for his purpose he had discovered the three sorts of vegetable poisons used to kill fish, and still associated with his name. He resolved to try them upon the hated Tangiia. He accordingly expressed into a small bowl a strong decoction of all three. To test its strength he now threw into it a small salt-water fish and a fresh-water fish, both of which instantly died. The drink was now prepared in the usual disgusting way, by first chewing pieces of the root and then discharging the contents of the mouth into a bowl kept for the purpose. When about three parts full the poison was poured into the stupefying drink instead of water. The whole was now well stirred together and strained off for drinking.

All being ready, Marere led his little boy with one hand and with the other carried the fatal mixture into the presence of the priest, who was delighted to see an unusually large quantity of his favourite drink. Upon taking the bowl, Tangiia looked at its contents and remarked, " Kua tuke te tu "= " It looks strange." Yet, as the little victim was brought with every outward mark of deference, he thought it must be a mere fancy, and drank off the whole. The priest was at once affected by the deadly potion. His face became red; the eyeballs seemed ready to start out of their sockets as he splutteringly said to Marere, " Give me the boy." Reeling about like a drunken man, he advanced a few steps in order to clutch the child, who with his father slowly retreated.

In fact the poison was rapidly taking effect. But Tangiia was not easily to be cheated of his victim. On and on came the drunken priest; his voice became thicker, and his footsteps more uncertain, as with great difficulty he pursued father and son. Soon the old cannibal stumbled and fell heavily on the ground. It was now evident to all that Tangiia was dying and Marere's boy saved !

The body of the old priest remained where it fell eight days; until at length, the stench becoming unendurable, it was dragged away into the bush, where it was left to be devoured by rats. In memory of this, the spot is still called " Paepaeauau "=" disgusting offal."

Hence the common saying, " Beware of the poisoned bowl of Marere."

In a later age the great warrior-chief Ngangati, descended from this Marere, took up his abode in this neighbourhood. A fragment of the once-powerful clan of Tangiia still lived there. Now Ngangati inherited all the hate of his ancestor Marere against the fallen descendants of Tangiia. He accordingly ordered a grand drinking-bout. The intoxicating root had been chewed, and the feast prepared, when Tangikaara, the head man amongst the devoted race, was invited by his companion, Ngangati, to drink. He declined to do so, and by that refusal saved his life, for every other male member of that unhappy tribe found his head seized by his boon companion, and was clubbed to death.

Tangikaara was of almost gigantic proportions. As soon as he felt his hair grasped by his foe Ngangati, he wisely ran to the lake, with his foe on his back, intending to drown him. But just as the desperate Tangikaara was about to leap into the deep black waters, Ngangati wisely gave up his hold, slipped off his back, and, much chagrined at his failure, returned to his more successful companions.

Tangikaara long remained hidden in the rocks. Eventually, however, the drum of peace enabled him to make his appearance in the interior. Unable to wreak his vengeance upon his brave old foe, Ngangati bequeathed to his relative Manini his legacy of hate. To carry this out, Manini sedulously cultivated the friendship of Tangikaara. Early one morning they went together to the *marae* of Rongo to hear the king offer prayers. On their way back Manini walked in front, carrying, according to the wont of aged men, a short spear as a walking-stick. Pretending to have dropped something, he desired his companion to go on. In another moment he came up with Tangikaara, and dealt him a death-blow on the back of the head. The body, still warm, was taken back to Rongo's *marae*, which he had left about half an hour before. Manini had accomplished two good things at once; he had avenged the famous Ngangati, and had provided the god of the invisible world with a bleeding sacrifice. So much for the natural conscience of the heathen.

The children of Tangikaara lived on for future sacrificial use. Said the narrator, " I am a direct lineal descendant of the priest Tangiia and of Tangikaara, and but for Christianity should unquestionably myself have been laid on the altar."

THE DESTRUCTION OF THE TANGIIA CLAN, AND THE ESCAPE OF KEUKEU.

A "crying-song" (*tangi*) pertaining to the " Death-talk " of Arokapiti. Composed by Koroa, *circa* 1817.

TUMU.	INTRODUCTION.
Solo.	*Solo.*
Tiô râ Keukeu tupuna i ora ;	Sing we of Keukeu,[1] our ancestress, who escaped ;
E tangi atu rai ki te pâre.[2]	Weep we for the sad fate of her tribe.

---

[1] Keukeu narrowly escaped the hands of the cannibal Ngako ; her children, half of the present tribe of Tanè, never tire of praising her adroitness.

[2] For " apare "=clan.

Chorus.

Ka tua ra tai kopu o Kanaê!

Chorus.

'Twas resolved that the Kanae should be slain.

PAPA.

Solo.

Aere mai kotou ê!

FOUNDATION.

Solo.

Come on, friends! (said they).

Chorus.

Aere mairâ Tangikaara i te vâinga kava,
Ia te arutoa o; na Rongo i ngau ra.
Ua etu!

Chorus.

The brave Tangikaara came to the assembly
Of drinkers: but murder was in their hearts.
The fatal signal was given!

Solo.

Ei tupa ia Tangiia ia kai ake nga atia-poro ê!

Solo.

'Twas planned for the extinction of Tangiia.

Chorus.

Kapitipitia ê i pau nga pâre e!

Chorus.

Again and again was our tribe slain!

UNUUNU TAI.

Solo.

Keukeu tupuna i ora mai!

FIRST OFFSHOOT.

Solo.

Yet Keukeu, our ancestress, escaped.

Chorus.

Keukeu tupuna i ora mai na.
Tuairiaki tangata motua ia koti
I raua Kanae i te ta ta rikiriki.
I tokiâ Kaara, o Tetupu, o Tepôiarongo,
O Vaikakau, na taomurau i te umu ko-karakara.
Te ranga aina ia Motoro i Tepatiki ê!

Chorus.

Yes, Keukeu, our ancestress, narrowly escaped;
Her father and grandfather all perished.
A stone adze clave the skulls of Kaara,
Of Tetupu, of Tepôiarongo, and of Vai-kakau,
Firstfruits of that harvest (literally *oven*) of death!
In honor of the god Motoro were they slain.

Solo.

Erâ Keukeu tupuna i ora;
E tangi atu rai ki te pâre.

Solo.

Rejoice we at the escape of our ancestress Keukeu;
Weep we for the sad fate of her tribe.

Chorus.

Ka tua ra tai kopu o Kanaê!

Chorus.

'Twas resolved that the Kanae should be slain.

UNUUNU RUA.

Solo.

Tangata reua i Ariki ra ê!

SECOND OFFSHOOT.

Solo.

Alas, that murdered throng at Ariki![1]

Chorus.

Tangata reua i Ariki.
Teia te uri a Marere
E ôra kava ia Tangiia.
Ka rere roa i Paepaeauuu.
O te rangi piri na uu-pae-ngaru,
Na ngarumotuia, ua atea i te ara

Chorus.

That great company at Ariki fell
By the hand of a descendant of Marere,
Who skilfully poisoned the priest Tangiia;
The carcase lies at "Paepaeauau."
Like fish in the billows at the reef,
They fell under the sharp-pointed spear;

---

[1] Ariki is the general name of the district where the famed Ngaugati slew his multitudinous victims.

O te eiva i pakoko i Maraepâpâ ra.
Te ranga aina ia Motoro i Tepatiki ê!

Solo.

Erâ Keukeu tupuna i ora;
E taugi atu rai ki te pâre.

Chorus.

Ka tua ra tai kopu o Kanaê!

Yet he himself barely escaped with life.
In honour of the god Motoro were they slain.

Solo.

Rejoice we at the escape of our ancestress Keukeu ;
Weep we for the sad fate of her tribe.

Chorus.

'Twas resolved that the Kanae should be slain.

CHAPTER XX.

THE STORY OF NAMU.

At Rarotonga it was customary for fishermen and voyagers to take with them in their canoes pieces of wood carved roughly into the human form, as charms. At Rakaanga and Manihiki, islands lying 600 miles due north of Rarotonga, if a king, priest, or distinguished fisherman died, the body after lying three days in the grave was exhumed, and the head cut off. A cocoanut was planted in the grave in lieu of the head, the fruit of which was eaten by strangers. The head was deposited in a finely-woven cocoanut-leaf basket, and placed in the fore-part of the canoe as a sea-god. When overtaken by unfavourable winds on a voyage, or drenched with heavy tropical rains, the head would be taken out of the basket and held aloft by the hair whilst prayers were offered to it for favourable weather. The hands and feet of defunct chiefs, priests, and fishermen were used for the same purpose by people of inferior rank. Upon the introduction of Christianity into those islands in 1850, these ghastly objects of worship were buried.

In heathenism no canoe ever ventured over the reef at Mangaia to fish without first fastening to its bows the fisherman's god. This consisted merely of the extremity of a cocoanut frond secured with fine-plaited sennit tied into a bow.[1] This Mokoiro, as it was called, was supposed to be all-powerful in regard to the winds and waves. The family of Namu were priests of Mokoiro; it was their hereditary office to equip each canoe in the fishing-season (from September to December) with this little protector. No other hand than theirs might perform this sacred office.

The aged king of Mangaia informed me that in those days a fleet of, say, two hundred small canoes—carrying only one man apiece—would assemble in front of the site of the present village of Oneroa at the beginning of the fishing-season. The little leaf-gods would be got ready against the appointed night, which

---

[1] I have deposited one of these charms in the British Museum.

was indicated by the recurrence of the phase of the moon favourable for catching certain kinds of fish. It was for Namu to give the word, and then the entire fleet of canoes would start off. The first night's fishing was in honor of the *elder sons,* who would eat part and give part to their respective gods. The second night's fishing was in honor of the *elder girls,* who likewise ate part and gave part to *their* respective gods. After this the *tapu* was removed; men, women, and children now ate freely, always, however, giving a fish—often the worst—to one of their supposed ocean divinities.

The family of Namu was specially obnoxious to the clan of Tongaiti, or "little Tongans," who are believed to have reached Mangaia at an early period from Tonga, a distance of about one thousand miles. These Tongan settlers were very warlike; they provoked a battle on their first landing on the south of the island. In this engagement they were worsted by the primitive tribe of Ngariki, from whom Namu was descended. The chief ground of hatred was the fact that from the date of their disastrous defeat at Teruanonianga the entire Tongan clan was devoted to the furnishing of the oft-required human sacrifices to Rongo, god of war. At least three other tribes were afterwards set apart for the same vile use; the choice lying with the warrior-chief and the king of the day as to the individual who should be slain and offered on each particular occasion.

One night the boy Namu was sleeping with his father, the priest Motau, in their own reed hut in a sequestered spot named Pakia. Their slumbers were disturbed by the sudden hum of angry voices from a number of armed men who violently pushed aside the sliding door of the hut, and felt all round in the dark for the obnoxious offerer of human sacrifices. The father was discovered and slain; but Namu, taking advantage of the door being for a moment left unguarded, slipped out unperceived, and escaped.

When Namu had grown to man's estate he took part in several engagements fought at that especially turbulent period on the southern part of the island, not far from the cave of the cannibal Tangaka, who, unknown to the combatants, from his lofty hiding-place witnessed these conflicts with grim satisfaction, knowing that, whichever party might win, *he* at least was sure of a feast.

11

In the second of these encounters, at a place called Teaupapa, it is said that eighty persons fell on the side to which Namu belonged, amongst whom were most of his own male relatives. Being, however, fleet of foot, he succeeded in saving his life. At length, gaining the highest ridge of the interior range of hills, he paused to look back at his pursuers, when he saw Pautu and his party exultingly perform the war-dance ere proceeding to occupy the lands and homes of the unfortunate Namu and his slaughtered friends.

The fugitive, under the friendly shelter of night, crossed the island to Ivirua, and hid himself in the thickets and rocks at no great distance from the utterly desolate spot immortalized by the long residence of Rori. Yet Namu and Rori never met until afterwards, in times of peace, when both lived in the interior, under the protection of Mautara and Manaune. Namu spent seven weary months in hiding at Ivirua, occasionally supplied with food by his faithful wife Tetui, whose pretext for going to their appointed meeting-place was the necessity for collecting candlenuts (*Aleurites triloba*) for evening lights. The candlenut-tree grows very plentifully in the neighbourhood of the rocks where Namu secreted himself. The collecting of candlenuts is a grand employment of native women. When obtained, they are slightly baked; the remarkably hard shells then easily crack and fall off, leaving the oily kernel entire. These kernels are skewered together with the midrib of the cocoanut-leaf, not un-like a row of large yellow beads. This curious torch yields a good light, but requires some care, and is attended with a dis-agreeable smell.

At last it became known that Namu was hiding amongst the gloomy rocks, and that the secret of his wife's exemplary diligence in collecting candlenuts was that she might supply him with food. The hereditary foes of his race resolved to make a careful search through the thickets and rocks until they should find him. One morning Namu happened to be cautiously making his way along a narrow fishing-path, when at a sharp bend he caught sight of his foes advancing towards him. Very wisely, Namu, instead of turning back or running on through the bush (either plan would have insured his destruction), merely turned aside and crouched under a low rock, still pointed out, which was at that time entirely overgrown with wild vines and creepers. In extreme terror he held his breath whilst they passed by,—his hiding-place being sufficiently near to the pathway for him to hear his foes breathing out vengeance against him.

Namu now felt that it would never do for him to remain in that part of the island, as his enemies would be sure to resume their search. However, he stirred not from his leafy hiding-place until nightfall, when he made his way into the interior to the dwelling of his faithful wife. He told her of his marvellous escape, and that he must seek a new asylum. Leaving him hidden for a short time in the fern, she ran off to consult her father Keu, priest of the Tongan clan—*i.e.*, of those at deadly enmity with him. Keu seems to have been a humane fellow, for he at once offered to secrete his sorely-hunted son-in-law inside the very recess or portion of his dwelling where his god Teipe was kept and worshipped. In the company of this uncouth ironwood god, Namu spent one month in safety, all that time secretly supplied with food by the priest himself, for the presence of a female in that sacred enclosure would be an unpardonable offence. But a servant of Keu's, wondering at the greatly-increased consumption of food in his master's small family, impiously lifted the sacred curtain and peeped inside. To his disgust he there saw the enemy of his tribe sleeping alongside of the wooden god whom all that section of the Tongan clan adored. It was soon noised abroad that Namu was hidden by their own priest. The enraged tribe assembled to take him out of his father-in-law's hands and put him to death. They did not regard the tears of his wife, although she was one of themselves. Namu had fought against them, and therefore must die. Happily, however, for their intended victim, he caught a glimpse of the killing party in time to force an opening through the reeds of his asylum on the side farthest from his foes. To elude detection the opening was at once carefully closed up by Keu. Namu scampered off to the neighbouring hill, then, as now, covered with tall fern, in which the poor fugitive hid himself. The Tongans had by this time arrived at the house of their priest, who truly averred that the man they were in search of was not there. Disregarding his words, they instituted a strict search, even entering the sacred enclosure itself. This was sacrilege, but they cared not, so that they might kill Namu.

Finding, however, that he was not there, they rushed out again
in search of their victim.   The fern was trampled down in every
direction in the hope of discovering him.   For an instant the
body of the trembling fugitive—who gave himself up for lost—
was actually between the legs of one of his pursuers, without,
however, being perceived by him.   After a long and fruitless
search, it was proposed to set fire to the fern, a perilous trick,
but at the same time a certain means of driving a poor wretch out
of the only covert the bare hills of Mangaia afford.   At this
critical juncture one of their number came upon two nests of
wild ducks.   The fortunate finder shouted, "Here is a lot of
duck-eggs!"   That shout saved Namu's life, as several were
approaching very close to him at the moment.   Several of the
party now made a rush for the eggs.   Hervey Islanders will not
taste a raw egg.   The cooking and eating effectually diverted
their thoughts for the time.

Whilst they were thus engaged, one of the killing party,
gazing down upon the main valley so lately dotted with huts, but
now utterly desolate, said, "There sleeps Ivirua, like a bride forsaken" (*Kua tiraa a Ivirua vaine*).   These words at once passed
into a proverb.   At dusk Namu descended into the neighbouring
valley to slake his burning thirst.   He determined to make his
way to Veitatei, whither his wife had fled to escape the anger of
her tribe for so persistently sheltering Namu.   Had he taken the
ordinary road—a distance of nearly four miles—he would certainly have been captured.   He wisely resolved to cross the nine
deep but narrow valleys which lie between.   This is no slight
undertaking on a dark night; yet he succeeded in making his way
to the house where Tetui was.   Resting awhile on the brow of
the hill, he was greatly pleased to see a light shining through the
reeds of the dwelling.   A pebble thrown lightly on the thatch
drew the attention of Tetui, who, guessing that her husband had
thrown it, went outside.   They wept together as Namu told her
what had befallen him.   He said that he must leave his old
haunts altogether, and would henceforth hide himself in the most
inaccessible rocks of the district where they had happily met
again.   They parted; and ere daylight dawned Namu had reached
his proposed hiding-place.   For another weary period of seven
months did this fugitive conceal himself amongst the thickets
and vine-clad crags of Veitatei.   Still, this was a paradise com-

pared with the inexpressibly desolate home of Rori, who had not
a single friend left to care for him; whereas Namu was regularly, although secretly, fed by his devoted wife.

Namu subsisted partly on wild roots and fruits. It does not
appear that he manufactured anything during his sojourn in the
rocks; for he was not a craftsman, but the mouthpiece of the
gods in regard to fishing and feast-making—quite enough, in the
estimation of that day, for any one man.

Tetui's friends at length got into great straits themselves.
As the only chance for life, she threw herself upon the protection
of Mautara, who had recently worsted her own clan in battle.
Despite this severe reverse of fortune, she contrived, slave though
she had become, occasionally to convey food to Namu. To her
great joy, the all-powerful Mautara one day asked his slave
" whether her husband was yet alive." She answered, " Yes."
" Go, then, and fetch him to aid me in performing the religious
ceremonies preliminary to peace." Raumea, the brother of
Teuanuku, who a few months later fell in battle, was appointed
his protector. Three entire districts (*tapere*) were bestowed upon
Namu as the price of his services, of which however (such are
the rapid changes of savage life) only one remains in the hands
of his descendants. Namu was now at the height of prosperity,
for he lived on good terms with Mautara to the end of that great
priest-chief's days. Tetui was thus abundantly recompensed for
her singular attachment to her husband, who now in his turn
succoured *her* near relatives Kaiara and Tavero, who found a
secure asylum in his home.

The sway of Teuanuku was brief. The murder of that
young chief in his own dwelling at Ivirua led to the battle of
Auâ, where a decisive victory was gained by Mautara over the
murderers of his son. Under the rule of the priest-chief the
island was cultivated, and great abundance prevailed. It is said
that chestnut-trees were covered with nuts even to their very
trunks. Long did the wise old man rule, until " his teeth
dropped out, of sheer old age : " certainly a remarkable event
with a Polynesian, many of whom retain their teeth in soundness
to the age of eighty.

The death of Mautara was the signal for new wars. In one
engagement it was asserted that Namu was riddled through
with a spear, and was left for dead by his enemies. But life

was not quite extinct; and eventually through the care of friends he recovered. This circumstance led his foes to believe that a supernatural power resided in him.

Some years after the visit of Captain Cook, Potai (nephew to Namu) feigned mortal sickness, and sent a special messenger to fetch his uncle and his cousin Manini. Not suspecting mischief, they paid a visit to the crafty fellow, whose couch was spread at a place called Rautauri—a wild spot, under vast overhanging rocks. The couch consisted of dry grass, covered with fine native cloth; his head resting on a pillow of stone (still pointed out), neatly covered over with folds of *tapa*. At his head sat his wife, weeping at the seemingly near dissolution of her husband. Potai had purposely kept himself awake several nights, so that his eyes were red and swollen. It was late in the afternoon when Namu arrived unarmed, so as to spend the night with his dying (?) nephew. According to invariable native custom, he wept long and loudly after he had deposited by the side of the sick man the farewell present. Uncle and nephew slept together that night. Lofty forest trees kindly intercepted the fall of dew. Early on the following morning, as they sat chatting together, Manini made his appearance, also unarmed. When the new-comer was close to Potai, and about to "kiss" him, by a previous secret arrangement the Tongan clan rushed out of their hiding-place, and slew Manini. At the same moment, Potai, hitherto supposed to be dying, seized his uncle Namu's flowing hair, and held him firmly until his ancient foes had put an end to his existence. The limbs of Namu were severed one by one from the trunk, and buried in different parts of the island, lest by some supernatural agency he should live again !

Namu was an old man at the time of his death. Potai would on no account slay him with his own hands, save on the field of battle. But he had no scruple whatever about holding his uncle's head while the body was repeatedly speared through.[1] A son of Manini's happily escaped over the rocks by a narrow pathway left unguarded.

It was not until Namu's peaceful residence in the interior that Tetui bare him a son. " So that," remarked Rouvi, who told me the preceding story, " if Namu had perished in the rocks,

---

[1] A number of similar atrocities has made the name of Potai in Christian times almost synonymous with Satan.

you would never have seen me, his grandson. I had the honor to be one of those who set fire to the idol-groves of Mangaia upwards of forty years ago. The heathen party said that I should speedily die for my sacrilege. I am now aged, but healthy, and have long outlived all those who engaged in idolatrous rites."

LAMENT FOR NAMU.

By Potiki, *circa* A.D. 1790.

TUMU.	INTRODUCTION.
Taia Namu i Tevaenga,	Slain was Namu at Tevaenga.[1]
Kua motu koe ia Potai,	Thy death was planned by Potai.
I te puputu motu no te metua	The garment of the uncle was rent by the
A ngaro ai Namu.	nephew.[2]
O te anau tupu ua te ta ê!	Namu is gone for ever,—
	Smitten by the nearest of kin.

PAPA.	FOUNDATION.
E piri ake Namu i te rau puka ;	Once Namu wandered in the forest ;
Noo mai paa i te makitea.	His home was in the rocks.
Eiea ra tau ai ê?	Who then succoured him ?
Raumea oki te rave	'Twas Raumea that pitied him ;
I te taranguora i noo ei !	His life was secure in *his* hands.

UNUUNU MUA.	FIRST OFFSHOOT.
E pa tikoru i Tekorokoro	In a shrine by the mountain-side
Tetai ora anga ia Namu.	Was Namu once hidden.
O Teipe oki te toko.	Teipe was his guardian.
Auraka e taû are rau i maru ei !	My wife became a tower of safety.

UNUUNU RUA.	SECOND OFFSHOOT.
Mauria Namu tei Pakia ê!	At Pakia was Namu captured.
Tei Pakia, a tai ora anga ia Namu.	Very narrowly did he escape.
Kua motu koe. Tai atani	Thou wast doomed. Yet friendly aid
Na Teipe ia Namu. Kua ora koe.	Was afforded to Namu by Teipe.
O Teipe oki te toko.	Teipe was thy guardian divinity.
Auraka e taû are rau e maru ei !	My wife became a tower of safety.

UNUUNU TORU.	THIRD OFFSHOOT.
Reureu te po e tei paporo e,	In the dark night he was on the hill-top
Tei paporo.	On the hill-top.
Kua ka te ai i Tutapa.	The light was burning in the dwelling.[3]
Ko te roimata o Teaputa,	Plenteous tears were shed by Teaputa
Kua pou te pare i Ariki.	(*i.e.*, Namu),
Kua tangi au i te tava ê!	For his tribe slain in battle.
Auraka e taû are rau e maru ei !	He wept o'er their loss.
	My wife became a tower of safety.

---

[1] "Tevaenga" is the name of the district where Namu fell.

[2] "The garment of the uncle" is a figurative way of saying that the claims of kindred were disregarded by Potai. The garment represents the entire clan, which is now split up by the murder of Namu.

[3] The light in the house occupied by his wife upon his final flight to the rocks of Veitatei.

UNUUNU A.

Punipuni aere i Teauiti é !
   I Teauiti.
Kite ake au i reira ki te ao taka nunga.
Te vai nei te ponga ia Tetuina.
Ee koto na Pautu. Kua piri oki tau
   mata.
Kua kapitiia, e matara koe i te rima é !
Kua kave i te riri ra e ora.
Auraka e taû are rau e maru ei !

FOURTH OFFSHOOT.

He hid himself in the valley,—
   In the valley.[1]
Then did he taste the bitterness of a
   fugitive's lot.
Ah! the undying hate towards our clan;
The shouts of Pautu in chase of me !
Trembling lest I should be o'ertaken
I ran swiftly to save dear life.
My wife became a tower of safety.

---

[1] I have translated "Teauiti" by "valley ;" it is in reality the name of a particular valley. But Namu traversed nine valleys in all on that memorable night, although only one is named. The order of events in the song is not strictly correct; the chronological order is that observed in the narrative.

CHAPTER XXI.

THE BANDAGED FOOT.

CIRCA A.D. 1718.

ALL existing families attribute their preservation to the favour and powerful protection of one man, Mautara, priest of Motoro. For more than a hundred years that family ruled the island. Their two ancestral districts (*tapere*) are the only ones that have never changed hands.

With the rise of this priestly caste the modern history of Mangaia may be said to commence.

Ngauta, "eight times lord of Mangaia," was slain by Ngangati, who assumed the supreme temporal sovereignty. Of Ngangati it is said that, emulating the fame of his predecessor, he became "five times lord of Mangaia." But one evening, when training his yam-vines over some low bushes, he was in turn slain by his nephew, Akatara, who declared himself supreme chief by the will of the gods.

The head-quarters of the new chief were on the eastern side of the island, at Ivirua. The constant wars of that period had hitherto made but little difference to "the mouthpiece of the god Motoro," who was perfectly safe amid all the bloodshed. A change now came over the scene. The bosom friend and confidential adviser of the new temporal sovereign was Aro, who recommended Akatara to root out the priestly family of Mautara, as the surest way of perpetuating his own authority.

A great feast was to come off at Ivirua for the formal installation of Akatara. The principal people of the island would attend it. An armed party were to hide themselves in the long grass to await the arrival of Mautara and his two famous sons. At a preconcerted signal they were to surround and slay all three. Success seemed certain, as no man ever went armed to a feast.

The plot was arranged by Akatara and Aro at midnight, when all were wrapped in slumber. A few yards from the conspirators slept their cousin Kârua, who, roused by a low murmur of voices, drank in every word with intense interest. She inwardly resolved at all risks to save her brother-in-law Raumea, second son of Mautara.

On the following evening the women went on a grand fishing excursion, on account of the approaching feast. Kârua met with considerable success. Arrived within a mile of Raumea's residence, she contrived to lag behind the throng of women; and, quenching her torch, hid basket and scoop-net, having first taken out of it a large fish. Kârua now ran as for her life along a narrow pathway to the interior. The rough road, winding between frowning jagged rocks, is not very agreeable even by broad daylight. Arrived at the house of her brother-in-law, she hastily opened the sliding door, and in so doing aroused Raumea. Kârua gave him the fish, and said, " This is yours ; it may be your last, for your death is resolved upon if you attend the feast. Only let it not be known that I warned you."

She had accomplished her purpose. Away she sped through total darkness by the road she had come. Upon reaching the sea again, she relit her torch, took up her basket and net, and hurried after her companions. To do this she had to walk several miles, fishing all the way, until she found them at a certain spot supping on part of the spoil. Her collected manner, as she referred to her having fished alone through the night with remarkable success, disarmed suspicion. Being expert at torch-fishing, it was easy for her to fill her basket, whilst the others were almost empty.

Night after night torch-fishing for the approaching feast went on whenever wind and surf favoured. As soon as the finny spoil was brought home, it was wrapped in *ti* leaves and cooked, being re-warmed each day until the feast came off. No other plan was possible for people ignorant of the use of salt.

When every precaution had been completed, Aro, in person, made the circuit of the island, delivering a formal invitation to all the chiefs and landowners. Mautara and Teuanuku at once agreed to go ; but Raumea declined on account of the agony he was enduring from a heel scooped by an " ungakoa," or *serpula.* Everywhere on the reef the coral is pierced in a myriad holes by this animal, which often attains the length of several yards. At the top the creature is protected against attacks by a dense shield, whilst the circular edge of the cavity is as keen as the edge of a razor. This animal grows with the bed of coral, the long cavity becoming increasingly large. Young "ungakoa," like young oysters, are easily detached from the coral by means of a hammer. Children eat them raw, not forgetting a supply of cooked taro out of their tiny baskets.

Hence the necessity of using sandals for the protection of the feet. Occasionally the sandals get loose; woe betide the luckless wight who should then tread with his entire weight upon one of these "cobblers' awls!" Round pieces of flesh are in this way scooped out of the foot. The thing most dreaded is when a bit of it breaks off, remaining behind. Months may elapse ere it works out by suppuration.

Aro pressed Raumea to attend the inaugural feast; the assembly would not be complete without so great a man. As a landed proprietor it was incumbent on him to be present. But Raumea, to the evident chagrin of Aro, declared such a thing impossible, for an "ungakoa" had broken off in his foot, and he was in great pain. Aro asked to see the foot, to which Raumea at once assented. The entire foot was covered up with a series of bandages. These were removed one after the other, with much seeming pain, all saturated with blood. And yet the wound itself was not reached! Raumea now assured his visitor that it was impossible for him to proceed further on account of excessive pain. Aro was by this time convinced that Raumea was effectually incapacitated from attending the feast. He at once returned to Ivirua and told Akatara of his ill success. Yet the feast must come off.

How little did they suspect that the bandaged foot was only a ruse, and the abundance of fresh blood which saturated the wrappings had been obtained from *rats.!*

On the day appointed nearly the whole population was present at the feast. There was abundance of such good things as the island could afford. As soon as the sun rose the guests began to arrive; in a short time all had come save Raumea; and perhaps after all *he* would contrive to be present. As a last resource Akatara received the visitors with every outward mark of respect, but proposed to defer the eating of the feast until Raumea should come. Akatara correctly reasoned that it would be of little use to kill Mautara and Teuanuku if the valiant

Raumea survived to avenge their deaths. All three must die together or none.

Hour after hour passed wearily, the guests becoming excessively hungry. Still no Raumea made his appearance. Late in the afternoon this strange feast was disposed of, the invariable custom being to divide out and eat as soon after daylight as practicable.

After the lapse of two or three months a return feast by Mautara and his sons was to come off on the west of the island. A large number of fugitives who had survived the frequent battles of those days agreed to come out of their hiding-places on the appointed day, and, concealed in the neighbouring bushes, engaged to do the bidding of Tenanuku and Raumea. Of these armed fugitives the most brave was Tokoau, ever afterwards associated with his cousin Mautara.

In the centre of the sacred districts of Keia, a spot perfectly level is pointed out as the feasting-place. It is known by the name of "Tapati." It was carefully weeded for the occasion; broad banana-leaves and green cocoanut-fronds were thickly strewed over the ground. On this natural tablecloth was piled abundance of food for the expected guests; but underneath the leaves and food were hidden spears and wooden swords, for a deadly fray!

At length the procession of chiefs connected with Akatara arrived, each carrying a fan of enormous proportions,[1] in token of profound peace. The guests found the feast-makers busy over a preparation of scraped cocoanut and taro called *poke*. In compliance with ancient etiquette, each visitor seated himself opposite to one of his friends, and vigorously began to grate raw taro on madrepore coral.

Raumea wished to save one of these doomed men. To this end he seated himself by his side, and, getting into conversation, obligingly offered to clear his head of vermin—a proposition most acceptable to Polynesians of the olden times, on account of the great length of their hair, and the circumstance that combs were unknown. Ere the task was completed there was a mighty shout, "There comes the lord of Mangaia!" Akatara came alone, some half-hour after his friends, indicating his rank by not deigning to come with the inferior chiefs. On his way to the feast he had

---

[1] About four feet in length.

been stopped by his relative Tuakura, who advised him to retrace his steps. But Akatara scoffed at the idea of danger. Was not the island in a state of peace?

As this great chief came near, Teuanuku rose to his feet, as if to do the honors of the occasion. Wiping his hands, he enigmatically remarked to those about him, "Era te pipi ra e mou," *i.e.*, "Let each seize a mussel-shell." Advancing to meet Akatara he saluted him in the now famous words, "Ah, brother-in-law, how well your new dignity suits you!" They now pressed each other's nose, as in token of affection. Every eye was fixed upon Teuanuku, who instantly seized his adversary by his flowing hair. Almost at the same moment each of the Mautara clan did the same with his astonished neighbour sitting opposite to him. But Raumea, instead of seizing the head he had been cleansing, suddenly grasped another, and forced the unwilling neck under his immense thigh, waiting to see what the other would do. At that moment Raumea saw him stoop to pick up a spear in order to cleave his skull. By a quick movement Raumea caught him, too, by the hair, and dragged him to the ground. And now, with his right hand in the hair of the first victim, his left in the hair of the second, he literally ground his foes to death on the earth by sheer strength! A similar feat of horror was performed that day by King Kanune. Both these warriors are said to have been possessed of wonderful strength, and were the terror of their contemporaries. Those in ambush did their share of that bloody morning's work, in the hope of sharing the lands of the slain. Of the entire party of Akatara, only one escaped to tell the tale. As the solitary fugitive ran past the dwelling of Tuakura, loudly lamenting the unhappy fate of his murdered friends, the only comfort he received was, " May your ears be cooked![1] Did I not forewarn you all?"

The feast was untasted, for it was bespattered with the blood of the guests. Early next morning Mautara and his two famous sons marched a little army over the hills to Ivirua to do battle with the now dispirited tribe of Ngariki, of which Akatara had been the leader. Ruanae now assumed the command. In point of numbers they had a decided advantage, standing "thick as the eaves of thatch." By this I understand that they were eight deep—double the usual number. As the clan of Mautara came

---

[1] A native curse.

in sight, the war-dance of Ngariki "caused the earth (seemingly) to tremble under their feet." The old priest exhorted his clan to do their best, saying, "If we fail, we shall certainly be cooked and eaten."

Williams correctly remarks, in the "Enterprises," "Contrary to the usual practice in the islands, the people of Mangaia do not practise bush-fighting, but meet in an open plain, from which every shelter is removed."

The great clan of Ruanae awaited the onset of their foes drawn up in a line at the base of the hills. Mautara and his clan descended the hills in a single column; but, on account of the disparity of numbers, declined to conform to the usual custom of ranging themselves in a line parallel with their foes. A sudden rush was made at the centre of Ruanae's army, cutting it at once in two. After a well-contested battle Ruanae and his clan were compelled to seek refuge in a gloomy stronghold known as "The Cave of the Tern" (*te Ana o Kākāia*).

Tradition expressly declares that Mautara himself did not fight; that he only carried his enormous fan. To the doomed clan of Ngariki he was the visible embodiment of their god Motoro. To get rid of him the hand of some unscrupulous atheist must be employed.

Mautara remained simply priest of Motoro; the supreme chieftainship was reserved for his eldest son, Teuanuku. On account of the considerable numbers of Ruanae's unreconciled clan the pleasant drum of peace could not sound, and human life was still insecure.

CHAPTER XXII.

THE UNFORGIVING AND THE UNFORTUNATE LOVERS; OR INCIDENTS CONNECTED WITH THE CLAN OF RUANAE.

AN ill-looking but brave warrior of the cannibal tribe of Ruanae, named Vete, fell violently in love with a pretty girl called Tanuau, who repelled his advances and foolishly reviled him for his ugliness. His only thought now was to be revenged for this unpardonable insult. He could not kill her, as she wisely kept close to the encampment of Mautara.

After some months Tanuau sickened and died. The corpse was conveyed across the island to be let down the chasm of Raupa, the usual burying-place of her tribe. There are two openings to this gloomy abode of the dead—a large one for those slain in battle (*te vaa noa*), a small one for those who die a natural death (*te vaa tapu*). The corpse was to be let down the smaller hole by means of immense rope-like vines obtained from forest trees, and sometimes attaining the length of fifty feet. These *kâkâ* ropes are of great strength when green. In general the friends of the deceased were content, after the corpse had descended about halfway, far out of sight, to allow it to fall into the dark waters beneath. Two demons were supposed to inhabit this chasm—a *lizard* of gigantic proportions, and an enormous fresh-water *eel*. This eel-god was believed to be ever on the watch for the descent of a corpse, in order that it might feed on human flesh.

But these *dii inferi* were disappointed of their prey on this occasion. Vete, hearing of Tanuau's death, guessed that her body would be carried to the ancestral burying-place. Now was the time to be revenged. With nine companions he left "The Cave of the Tern" ere dawn of day and hurried to Raupa at Tamarua. On their way they provided themselves with ropes of Nature's own manufacture. Arrived at the mouth of the chasm, Vete and two others were let down about halfway, where a ledge permitted them to take their station in almost total darkness. The rest of the cannibals now drew up the ropes, and secreted themselves in the forest to await the arrival of the burying party.

The sun was high in the heavens when the body of the poor girl was brought and let gently down the gloomy hole, the friends little thinking that three men below were awaiting its arrival. As soon as the body came within reach they drew it on to the ledge and hastily untied the ropes. According to custom, the ropes were thrown after the corpse, and splashed in the unseen waters far below these resurrectionists. At brief intervals came one by one opened cocoanuts and other food offerings to the dead.

As soon as the friends of the deceased girl had disappeared the seven cannibals came out of ambush and let down their ropes again. In a few seconds the body of Tanuau was drawn up, and shortly afterwards Vete and his two companions gladly emerged from their cold and gloomy subterranean prison.

The corpse was quietly carried near the sea to a natural hollow, shrouded from observation by a dense growth of lemon *hibiscus*. It was found to be impossible to eat the decomposed body. It was, however, cut in pieces, and at sunset burnt to ashes. At midnight, finding that a few bones remained, a new fire was made, so that by morning light no trace whatever remained of this poor creature.

A month or two subsequently Vete and his friends met with the due reward of their numerous misdeeds at Pukuotoi, within a short distance of the scene of this barbarous burning.

"The burning-place of Tanuau" is included in the mission premises at Tamarua. During our residence there I had the forest in the neighbourhood of Raupa cleared for the first time, and the rocky soil planted with cocoanut-trees.

It is owing to numerous incidents of this sort that the natives are absurdly sensitive to threats of *burning* anything belonging to themselves. There is no surer way of drawing down their anger than to hint at such a thing as the *burning* of . a canoe, a hut, or even a garment. To *chop the property* of another is regarded as symbolical of an intention to *chop his person*, even as the corpse of Tanuau was cut to pieces.

Among those who escaped at the fatal surprise of Ruanae's clan at Pukuotoi was a young man named Oimara. At the back of the mission premises at Tamarua a curious hollow rock stands out by itself like a round tower. It is eleven feet high, and will comfortably admit one person. The hardened coral surface is so rugged that it is an easy matter for a native to climb in or out.

By day Oimara hid in the savage recesses of the primæval forest, behind vast blocks of stone, or inside one of the thousand natural grottoes. At nightfall he invariably returned to his stone fortress, which is still associated with his name. The starry heavens were the only roof. Ere dawn the fugitive again retired to the forest.

The reason for this strange procedure was that Oimara had a sweetheart, who, though a member of the victorious clan, did not forget her lover. By some means or other, shortly after the battle she became aware that he was still alive. It was agreed upon that he should hide in this curious rock, which was close to the principal path to the beach, so that she might easily supply him with food.

This loved one, whose name is not preserved, at dusk of every evening hastily thrust through a small aperture, most conveniently situated, a small package of food. Sometimes on her return from fishing she would linger behind her dusky companions in order to throw in a fish. Scarcely a word could be exchanged under such circumstances, lest her delay should excite suspicion.

Things went on prosperously with Oimara for some time; but, unhappily for the fugitive, one of her companions resolved to ascertain why this girl was generally a little behind. One evening this curious one hid herself near the narrow turn in his pathway where her friend had so often loitered. Unseen by the lovers, she overheard their brief conversation, and saw the food-packet put through the little hole. This was told to the parents of this over-curious girl.

That very night a party of armed men surrounded the hiding-place of Oimara. Their cruel shouts as they scaled the sides aroused him from sleep. Escape was impossible, as the only means of egress was the very opening by which his enemies were attacking him. He threw himself in his despair on his face on the earthen floor. He was quickly stoned to death, and his body found a grave where he had often peacefully slept under the azure canopy of heaven. Many and loud were the lamentations of his beloved one over his untimely end.

CHAPTER XXIII

CAVE OF THE TERN; OR THE MISDEEDS OF RUANAE.

In the face of a perpendicular cliff at Ivirua, overlooking a picturesque valley cut up into innumerable taro patches, is an opening to which access can only be gained by a long ladder planted on a projecting point of rock. A party of us contrived to extemporize a ladder out of the tapering stems of two papao-apple (*Carica papaya*) trees, and so gained an entrance to the famous cavern which is known as "The Cave of the Tern" (*te Ana o Kâkâia*). Here for many a long day were the head-quarters of Ruanae and his clan. The cavern is extensive, and abounds in beautiful stalactites. A deep natural recess in the side nearest to the sleeping-place of the fierce chieftain was the repository of the weapons of the clan. On each club and long spear was a private mark, so that each warrior might know his own weapon.

Outside, at the entrance to the cave, is the spot where the cannibal feasting was held.. It is in reference to this that it still bears the significant name of "Feasting Hollow" (*Ruekai*).[1] Here we picked up one or two large rounded stones, designed to crack the skulls of any who might be foolhardy enough to attack those who kept watch outside. A fearful chasm runs across the interior of the cave. Great stones hurled down by some of us splashed heavily in the unseen waters far below.

The clan of Ruanae used to cross this abyss on a bridge of long logs. Not having this advantage, we had to descend our ladder and make a considerable circuit. Our worthy guide Rouvi, about seventy-five years old, with the clan of Vaeruarangi, once occupied this cave. He showed us the *secret* entrance to this stronghold through a thick grove of plantains. Near the entrance the roof is very low, but soon becomes loftier. The cave eventually opens up into a noble cathedral-like nave. The arched roof as well as the walls and flooring, being composed of

---

[1] For *Ruakai.*

stalactites, sparkled and glittered magnificently in the light of our torches. Right and left branched off aisles all richly ornamented with a wondrous fretwork of Nature's own moulding. After proceeding a considerable distance, we found ourselves on the brink of the same chasm we had previously approached from the opposite side. The united light of our torches in no degree lessened the gloom of this fearful abyss. Yet Ruanac and his warlike followers were accustomed by torchlight to cross this ill-omened spot daily when bent on a secret descent upon the persons or lands of their foes. The water they drank was drawn up from this deep natural reservoir, which abounds in large eels and shrimps. Until the prevalence of Christianity, and the consequent feeling of security, this impregnable fortress was constantly used by the natives of the eastern part of the island. Rouvi assured us that in those days, lighted by the glare of torches above, he often descended, holding on crag by crag, to fish in these unpromising waters.

Hard by, and connected with this stronghold, is a sort of chapel, small but most exquisite in structure. Column rises upon column of seeming alabaster. No torch is needed to display its beauties, sufficient light coming through the entrance to illumine it. All around and beneath sparkle a myriad gems, walking over which were a desecration. This fairy palace is known as *Te Koatu Kurukuru o Angita*—i.e., "The Cave of Beautifully - Carved Stones." The exit is over moss-grown crumbling stones, *as if* the remains of an ancient flight of steps!

The signal defeat of Ruanac at Arera made the sons of Mantara lords of the island. The entrance to the "Cave of the Tern," the hiding-place of the beaten tribe who were still formidable in point of numbers, is so difficult that to force an entrance would be impossible. Hunger, however, occasionally compelled the men to go on foraging expeditions. On such occasions they generally picked up some stray members of the victorious party of Mantara, whose encampment was on the opposite side of the island. These unfortunates were invariably cooked and eaten. It is asserted that the first person deliberately eaten by Ruanac was Itieve, over whose body was registered the unholy vow to spare neither sex nor age whenever a victim should fall into their hands.

Teange was one morning fishing on the reef about a mile

from the present mission premises at Oneroa, when to his dismay he found his retreat cut off by a sudden descent of Ruanae and his cannibal warriors from the neighbouring rocks and bush. Under cover of a dark night they had crossed the island and hid themselves at a convenient spot where a never-failing spring of fresh water gushes up amidst stones and sand. Delighted to see Teange, a man of no ordinary size and prowess, carrying only a scoop-net and utterly unconscious of danger, they rushed out upon him. The only possible means of escape was to swim out to sea; which Teange did without hesitation, knowing that at a short distance is a block of coral rising up from the ocean depths. At high water it is covered; but even then a man sitting on it would have no fear of drowning. On came the clan of Ruanae like a number of hungry sharks to devour their victim ; but they were astonished that he did not attempt to run in the direction of the camp, but coolly swam out to sea and succeeded in gaining the rock referred to. Teange climbed on it and defied his foes. Many were the stones thrown at him, but at that distance he found it comparatively easy to avoid them. Tired of this, some of the disappointed cannibals swam out to the coral rock on which the brave Teange stood pouring abuse and curses ; but when they got uncomfortably near he wisely swam out to sea. Being an excellent swimmer, he quietly watched his foes until they returned to the reef, when he returned to his old standing-place.

In their joy at the prospect of securing their victim, the cannibal tribe did not notice a little boy sitting in the bush near the pebbly beach, awaiting the return of his father from fishing. At the beginning of the attack the little fellow ran as fast as his legs could carry him through the bush and over the hill towards the encampment,—a full mile. In a few seconds more the entire body of warriors, led by Teuanuku and Raumea, the brave sons of Mautara, were in motion eager for fight, hoping to crush for ever the adverse tribe. On descending the hill which overlooked the scene of conflict they were seen by the scouts of Ruanae. A prolonged shout caused the entire troop of cowardly cannibals to take to their heels. The pursuers strained every nerve to cut off the retreat of Ruanae, and thus terminate the contest which had dragged on slowly for many months. Ruanae, however, succeeded in gaining the sharp-pointed rocks, where it were vain to follow him. The coral rock on which the fearless swimmer rested is still known as " The Standing-place of Teange" (*Te Turanga o Teange*).

A few weeks after this, three women went one evening from the encampment of Mautara to the lake in Veitatei, to catch shrimps and delicate *kokopu* fish, which are obtained at night by the aid of torches. The shrimps are easily caught with coarse cocoanut-leaf baskets.

Now these women had been very successful, and at dawn cooked the fish, for convenience' sake, and to appease the cravings of hunger. The romantic little spot chosen for the oven is in a dense thicket under the shadow of a mass of rock about a hundred feet high, where, if anywhere, they might hope to be unnoticed.

Little did they imagine that Ruanae and his clan were on a foraging expedition in their immediate neighbourhood. They slept in the rocks overlooking 'the lake, without noticing the women. Early in the morning, when about to march back, their attention was attracted by the smoke of the oven. Finding that it was a party of defenceless women, the cowards descended as quietly as possible by a rough pathway, still used, called Raurau. At the first sight of their cannibal foes, Mapi rushed off as fast as she could in the direction of her home. Her path lay underneath those frowning lofty rocks which form an imperishable defence against the advance of the ocean. In a short time she came to a narrow pass, occasioned apparently by the severance and fall of a vast block of rock, overgrown with dwarfed banyan-trees shooting out of the crevices of the stone. The long roots hang like ropes of immense strength from the summit to the ground.

Mapi in her flight recollected that at the distance of ten feet from the earth, and overhanging the narrow path, is a round fissure, opening up into a narrow chamber capable of containing three persons. In a twinkling, with the aid of fingers and toes, sailor-like, she climbed by means of this natural rope into this curious hiding-place, and lay flat to elude notice. Had she been seen, escape would have been impossible, as there is only one way of entrance and exit. Hardly had she lain down on the flooring of her strange retreat when her foes rushed past close underneath, little suspecting that Mapi was hidden there. On, on they pressed at full speed, not thinking it possible that she should escape. At length they stopped and resolved to return, and carefully to examine every bush that could possibly afford shelter to a fugitive, their long spears being thrust repeatedly through the bush without a trace of their intended victim. In passing again under the overhanging rock, in the very heart of which Mapi still lay, they little thought that every threat of vengeance was distinctly heard by her.

In this rocky chamber, on the side nearest to the lake, is a small hole through which she ventured a glance at her retreating foes, and with inexpressible relief saw them disappear in the distance. When all was quiet she cautiously descended from her hiding-place, and descended to the ground. Very warily she made her way through the tall tufts of reeds and clumps of pandanus-trees to the mountain-ridge, whence it was easy for her to gain the distant encampment, *minus*, however, her fish.

The fate of the two other women, who were sisters, was diverse. Koua, the elder, and Anauaukura, the younger, in their affright took different paths. Koua ran into the neighbouring thickets, and thence made her way to the rocks and so escaped, ascribing her safety to the friendly aid of Matarau, the lizard-god, the guardian of all rocks and caves. Her ill-fated sister, after running a short distance in the open country, was caught, her hands tied behind her, and led back to the smoking oven which she and her two more fortunate companions had just left. The savoury contents of shrimps and *kokopu* were speedily demolished by the famished cannibals. But for their haste to enjoy this unexpected feast, it is very probable that the search for the missing woman might have been successful.

As soon as this meal was despatched, Ruanae hurried off his people through fear of a sudden attack from their foes. They started off in single file across the fern-clad hills of the interior to their gloomy stronghold at the " Cave of the Tern," at Ivirua. Anauaukura, with her hands tied behind and well guarded, walked in the centre, *in order to save the labour of carrying her dead body !*

At the top of the first eminence she looked back, and for the last time caught sight of the lake where so lately she had been disporting with her companions. Just beyond was the sad scene of her capture. It is said that she travelled on in silence under a midday sun until they reached the taro patches of Ivirua, where the cannibals felt themselves safe, as in the event of a sudden alarm they could easily betake themselves to their stone fortress. The hands of the victim were now untied, and by a refinement of cruelty she was compelled to collect a quantity of dry firewood and to break off a lot of banana leaves to wrap her own body in. Near the entrance to the cave, and in full view of the women and children, was the large oven used by Ruanae's party in cooking their victims. Anauaukura was directed to heat this oven, which she did. As soon as the stones were sufficiently hot, the poor unoffending woman was clubbed to death and cooked in the very oven her hands had lighted. The body was carefully divided out and devoured by these horrid cave-dwellers.

Upon another occasion a number of women and girls engaged at lobster-fishing at Tuaate were surprised and slain by Ruanae. Eight poor women were cut off by daylight when digging for wild yams. Four females collecting chestnuts were slain early one morning, and, skewered on long spears, were borne with fiendish shouts of joy to the great oven at the foot of the ladder.

Now a man named Matautu was appointed by Ruanae to keep the chiefs supplied with shrimps and eels. He alone lived in the middle of the valley and unceasingly plied his avocation. On the morning of the capture of the chestnut-gatherers he was horrified to see his own aunt cooked and devoured. Burning for revenge, he sent word to Teuanuku, who, with the victorious clan, ventured by night close to the cave where Akapautua was keeping watch, his long spear resting on the earth. The spear was quietly stolen. The clan slept on, all unconscious of danger. A beautiful daughter of Ruanae named Kimiatu, descending at dawn of day to bathe in the neighbouring stream, was at once pounced upon, her hands tied, and led weeping and calling for help to a well-known spot in the centre of the taro patches, in full sight of her distressed relatives in the Cave of the Tern. Dry cocoanut branches were collected and piled up round this unhappy girl, and the whole lighted. It is said that her arms, now released by fire, were stretched out towards her father in the cave, imploring succour. But Ruanae well knew that any effort to rescue his daughter would insure the immediate destruction of himself and his tribe.

Thus it is that the heathen corrupt themselves from generation to generation, "hateful and hating one another." *Only a*
power from above can arrest the downward progress, and trans-
form savages into human beings with kindly affections one
towards another.

We have seen that the elder sister Koua escaped. One of
her direct descendants is Turoua, the present worthy chief of
Tevaenga, one of the six principal governors of Mangaia, a man
of marked character, who has long made a consistent profession
of attachment to Christ.

THE OVERTHROW OF RUANAE.

Composed by Potiki, *circa* 1791, for the "Death-talk of Vaiaa."

TUMU.

Solo.

Kua pau te vaka o Ruanae!
Ana mai nei kua tuā tei Atea,
Te viri nei i te ara ô!

Chorus.

E vaio 'ia ngaere i reira ô!

PAPA.

Solo.

Tipoki te aro o Ruanae,
Pakia io ia mou ei,
Kai riro te papa iaia.
Akapautua i mamao atu,
Oi mai koe ia piri ô!
Kia kapitia i te mate.

Chorus.

Kia vai reka raua katoa ô!

UNUUNU TAI.

Solo.

Kua pau te vaka ê,
No Ruanae ê!

Chorus.

Tei Vaitangi na taukarokaro anga.
Tei Vaitangi na taukarokaro anga' i.

Solo.

Me ô te ô ia taua,
Me kite atu i te rangatira,
Ka ati te ati Tangaroa.
Ana mai nei kua tuā tei Atea,
Te viri nei i te ara ô!

Chorus.

E vaio 'ia ngaere i reira ô!

INTRODUCTION.

Solo.

The tribe of Ruanae has perished!
As the reef covered[1] with dead fish
Is the ground where they fought.

Chorus.

Let the dead rot there!

FOUNDATION.

Solo.

Ruanae lies low in the dust,
Where he rushed on to his fate
In the vain hope of victory.
Akapautua pressed behind (saying),
"Come on, stand shoulder to shoulder,
That we may die together."

Chorus.

Both warriors lie in one place!

FIRST OFFSHOOT.

Solo.

The tribe of Ruanae
Has perished!

Chorus.

By the purling brook the fight took place,
Ay, by yon purling brook the fight took
place.

Solo.

(The chiefs said:) "Should the worst come
to the worst,
Should we be overpowered by our foes,
Our bodies shall lie on the field of battle."
As the reef covered with dead fish
Is the ground where they fought.

Chorus.

Let the dead rot there!

---

[1] At times the reef is almost dry, and the small fish die by hundreds on account
of the excessive heat of the sun.

UNUUNU RUA.
Solo.
Tatari aere
I te vaka nei ê!
I te vaka nei!
Chorus.
Kua kake i te maunga,
Noo atu i reira,
Kua taumate aere,—
Solo.
Kua taumata aere ei.
Te tara nei i tena atua,
E ui paa i te ânû e te kouo.
Ana mai nei kua tuâ tei Atea,
Te viri nei i te ara ê!

Chorus.
E vaio ïa ngaere i reira ê!

UNUUNU TORU.
Solo.
Kimiia te ara ra ê,
Chorus.
———— e marere ai ê,
E marere ai!
E na tai atu i Teone ê,
E na Paeru, na veiveitamaki,—

Solo.
Na veiveitamaki ai?
Na veroinga i te io,
Na ookainga i te korero.
Ana mai nei kua tuâ tei Atea,
Te viri nei i te ara ê!
Chorus.
E vaio ïa ngaere i reira ê!

UNUUNU A.
Solo.
I uiia te ara ra ê,
Chorus.
———— e aere ai ê,
E aere ai!
Tei Arakino Ruanae,
Tei te utu tutai,
Solo.
———— tei te utu tutai ai.
Te pao nei i te ara,
Te kai nei i te ua nono i te râei,
Aore e tumu ia uta.
Ana mai nei kua tuâ tei Atea.
Tei viri nei i te ara ê!
Chorus.
E vaio ïa ngaere i reira ê!

AKAREINGA.
Ai e runoo! E rangai ê![1]

SECOND OFFSHOOT.
Solo.
Waiting for a sign
Of advancing foes,—
Of any advancing foe.
Chorus.
(Ngako) climbed the mountain top,
And long watched there
To get notice of their approach,—
Solo.
Ay, for the faintest token of their approach.
The priest-leader gave the fatal command,
"Climb the trees and bare them of their fruit."
As the reef covered with dead fish
Is the ground where they fought.
Chorus.
Let the dead rot there! .

THIRD OFFSHOOT.
Solo.
The only thought was
Chorus.
———— now of flight,—
Of mere flight!
Shall it be by Teone, the path to the sea?
Or by the hill Paeru, overlooking the battle-field,—
Solo.
Ay, overlooking the battle-field?
Dare thy utmost to live;
'Tis hard to escape.
As the reef covered with dead fish
Is the ground where they fought.
Chorus.
Let the dead rot there!

FOURTH OFFSHOOT.
Solo.
Ask the road
Chorus.
———— by which to fly,—
To fly for one's life!
Ruanae's home had been in the rocks,
Where a solitary Barringtonia grows,—
Solo.
Yes, where a solitary Barringtonia grows.
He subsisted on pandanus berries,
And the sour fruits found in the wilds.
For none befriended him!
As the reef covered with dead fish
Is the ground where they fought.
Chorus.
Let the dead rot there!

FINALE.
Ai e runoo! E rangai ê!
[Meaningless, like our "fal, lal, lah."]

---

[1] This song is printed as actually chanted.

CHAPTER XXIV.

THE STORY OF KAIARA.

AFTER the defeat at Arera, a family of three girls, whose parents had been slain, fled to the rocks at Mataorongo, not far from the hiding-place of Rori. Most of the beaten party took shelter in the Cave of the Tern; but these young girls were sure that they would be singled out for destruction on account of the murder of Paeke, "mouthpiece" of Motoro, by their father Arekava some years before.

One afternoon an armed party, headed by the cruel Ngako, issued from the stronghold of Ruanae in quest of victims. On reaching the crest of a hill on the east, they turned aside to inspect the old battle-field of Mâueue, which marked the rise of the priestly clan of Mautara, and the downfall of their own. In those days the slain were rarely buried, so that some had become mummy-like, dried up in the sun; others were reduced by the rats to skeletons. The fern had everywhere grown about the dead, many of whom were the near relatives of these cannibal visitors.

A thin distant curl of smoke caught the sharp eye of Ngako. It came from the rocks, and must indicate the presence of fugitives. Very willingly they left the unburied bodies of their ancestors on the slope of the hill, and made for the distant fire in the rocks. Upon leaving the open country they became very careful not to give their victims any intimation of their approach. The three girls were cooking nono[1] apples over a fire for their supper, when the quick ear of Kaiara, the eldest of the party, caught the sound of advancing footsteps. She at once ran to hide herself in the deepest recesses of the forest; but her poor sisters were both caught, and led over the distant hill to the lair of Ruanae. That same night they were cooked and eaten by their own tribe! The passion for human flesh had grown so strong, since the destruction of Itieve, that it must be gratified at any cost.

---

[1] *Morinda citrifolia.*

Now the crafty Ngako correctly concluded that Kaiara, whose presence had been thoughtlessly revealed by her sisters, would after a time come back to get some cooked *nono* apples, in order to satisfy the cravings of hunger. Instead, therefore, of following the rest of his party leading the captive girls, he laid himself down by the fire to await the return of his expected victim, of course solacing himself with the roasted apples. At last she came ; but, on espying the huge form of the cannibal, she again ran for her life. Ngako gave chase, calling her to come back and be his wife. He espied the trembling girl crouching down under a ledge of rocks, and put down his long spear to enable her to climb up to him, secretly resolving to club her as soon as she should be fairly in his power.

Kaiara feigned compliance, but, perceiving over her head a narrow opening on the side farthest from her foe, she at once availed herself of it. That she had disappeared was clear, but how Ngako could not make out. The cannibal drove his long spear (twenty-five feet in length) in various directions, but with no good result. He now got round the chasm and gave chase. The poor girl again hid herself in a hollow, hoping that the increasing darkness of evening would effectually conceal her from her relentless foe.

Ngako came up to the spot, and thrust down his spear several times at a venture, once narrowly missing the body of Kaiara, who now gave up all hope of escape. But the cannibal, not dreaming that, after all this riddling with his famous spear, his much-desired morsel lay quietly at the bottom, her head hidden by a mass of magnificent rock fern (*rau kotaa*), went on his way chagrined. He would not return to the cave of Ruanae without his victim, to become the laughing-stock of his friends. He therefore slept in the rocks, hoping to catch this " little fish " in the morning.

But again he was doomed to be outwitted, for Kaiara, after a short but much-needed sleep, rose at midnight, and tremblingly climbed up out of her hollow and pursued her painful way over and over the sharp rocks. She had no sandals to protect her feet, which became much lacerated. Fortunately Ngako was at some little distance sound asleep, so that, when the first streak of dawn admonished her to hide herself from observation, she had gained the " wild rocks " where Rori, all unconscious of her presence, was at that time hidden. The probable reason why they did not meet is that Kaiara kept as near as possible to the interior, whilst Rori lived in the very heart of the *ráei*. Besides, Kaiara was on her way to Ivirua, where most of her time was passed in the solitudes beyond the region frequented by Rori, and close to the site of the present village.

Very slowly did Kaiara traverse this rugged part of the island, grieved at the loss of her young sisters. She subsisted exclusively on what could be obtained in the rocks, without daring to descend to the open country of the interior. Her greatest difficulty was to obtain water : however, she contrived to slake her thirst at the various hollows where rain had collected. In the midst of the rocks she discovered a spacious cave, where she took up her abode and cooked what food she could collect. One night, as she slept, her rest was disturbed by what she regarded as supernatural voices reproaching her with having desecrated a cave sacred to the god Tanè by cooking food. As most of the larger caves have long winding passages leading towards the sea, it is easy to understand how the winds should whistle and howl most ominously in the ears of a terrified solitary woman.

After occupying this cave, named by her "Tevarovaro" (The Whistler), for fifteen days, she again started on her travels. One day she suddenly came upon a wasted woman pounding pandanus seeds to eat. Seeing she was alone, Kaiara spoke to her. The astonished fugitive looked up—it was her near relative, Tavero, who had lately fled for life to the rocks. They cried heartily over each other, and rehearsed the sad story of their escape. Henceforth they would keep together, come what might. They took up their residence at the rocks of Ivirua, having somehow discovered that Ruanae's cannibal clan no longer occupied "the Cave of the Tern." Month after month passed in comparative security, for the cannibal tribe had perished whilst Kaiara was hiding in "the Whistling Cave;" and Ngako, though alive, prowled over the southern part of the island, having now his head-quarters with Vaiaa at Marotangiia.

Meeting with no molestation from day to day, the two half-starved women grew imprudent. One evening at dusk they carried a lot of bitter yams (*oe*) to a stream rushing under the rocks, in order to make them eatable. The children of a man named Mauiki saw them and gave the alarm. In a few minutes

Mauiki himself and his friends overtook the wretched women and drove them to his house in order to slay and eat them, in revenge for injuries received from the now extinct tribe of Ruanae. Thus too late the captive women learned that the drum of peace had not yet been beaten.

Firewood was collected and leaves piled up for a grand feast in the morning. To prevent the escape of Kaiara and Tavero, they were tied up to the two principal posts of the house. The doors were made fast with the strong bark of the paper-mulberry. All hands were to keep awake that night. What so sweet to a savage as revenge? The wretched captives listened with deep interest to their conversation, from which they learned the downfall of their own wicked tribe; that the island was, for a second time, declared subject to Teuanuku, the eldest son of the priest-chief Mautara, and that their cousin Tetui was wife to Namu, the spiritual chief or king of the island.

At midnight the entire household was hushed in deep sleep. Kaiara too slept of sheer grief, not thinking escape possible this time. Tavero was wakeful, and resolved to attempt a rescue. By repeated contractions of the muscles, the cords which bound her to the post slipped down. A dexterous use of her teeth freed her hands. Softly approaching her relative, she whispered in her ear, untied her hands, and set her at liberty. Untying the fastening and withdrawing the door as gently as possible (in Mangaia doors are opened by sliding in a groove), both women got out without any one inside being aware of their escape. At this critical moment Tavero recollected a calabash full of water which would be invaluable in their flight. She coolly re-entered the house, felt about for it, and succeeded in getting out again without being discovered.

Off they ran now at full speed for the rocks and bush. In a few minutes the cool air through the open door roused some of the sleepers, whose first thought was, Are the victims safe? As soon as their exit was discovered, the entire household started off in hot pursuit. The fleeing women could distinguish their cries and threats as they entered the thick bush, and speedily gained the summit of the first ledge of rocks. Every inch of the difficult path was familiar to these starved fugitives, who were soon beyond pursuit. The path they took is well known, but such as only women in extreme peril could dare to follow.

Their feet were bare; but then their forms were extremely light and agile, and they had the great advantage of moonlight to guide them on their way. Daylight found them in an extremely wild place, overgrown with pandanus-trees laden with fruit. They resolved if possible to make their way to their cousin, wife of the spiritual sovereign, in the hope of obtaining shelter and protection.

It was many days before they reached Tamarua, where their cousin lived, a journey which might well be made now by the direct interior road in a couple of hours. Opposite to the king's residence was a small cave called Ruaanau, where they hid themselves till sunset. The children of the chief first discovered them, and ran to tell their mother that two starved ill-looking women were hiding in the cave. Tetui went to see whether the report was true, and was not a little moved to find her long-lost relatives. The children were strictly enjoined to be quiet about this pleasing discovery until the king Namu should come home from the ceremonies connected with the beating of the drum of peace.

Taro was hastily taken up to feast their new-found relatives. What a treat for the starved women! They wished to help their cousin in her labours, but Tetui would not hear of such a thing. Ere the taro was done, Namu came and heard the story from the lips of his wife. He pledged himself to protect them *as slaves.* That night they told the story of their perils and wonderful escapes. At daylight it became known that Kaiara and Tavero had come out of the "wild black rocks," and were under the protection of Namu, who remained at home spear in hand to protect them.

Mauiki heard with infinite mortification of their safety. He had hoped that they would die miserably of hunger in the rocks. Mautara recollected that his grandfather had been slain by the father of Kaiara, and thirsted for the daughter's blood. As "mouthpiece of Motoro," *i.e.*, high priest of the god worshipped by Namu, he declared that the two young maidens should be killed and eaten by Mautara. Three times did armed men come to fetch them "by order of the god Motoro." Three times did Namu nobly refuse to "put his wife in mourning" for her young relatives; for Tetui had threatened to commit suicide if he gave them up to be eaten.

It seems strange that the great priest should have been so

persistent in his endeavours to get possession of these girls; but the ceremonies connected with the drum-beating were not yet completed. Besides, the sacred duty of revenge was never forgotten in heathenism. Only Christianity can originate the true spirit of forgiveness. The devouring of a poor wretch like Kaiara could be a matter of no consequence whatever in those days.

Namu prevailed; and the young women lived. Great must have been the disgust of Tokoau, the unscrupulous factotum of the high priest, who too closely imitated the evil practices of the slain Ruanae, of infamous memory.

Kaiara was resident in the rocks and woods for about two years. This woman and Tavero became slaves to Tetui, and secondary wives to the king. A numerous progeny exists to this day, possessed of a good share of lands. The various places where these poor girls lived in the rocks have given rise to family names. Two individuals are called after "the Whistling Cave;" but all modern inquiries to discover it have failed. Of course the entrance has been blocked up.

A set of songs once existed in reference to Kaiara; but they are forgotten for the most part. The technical name for the set is *"Te Kakai ia Namu,"* or "The Death-Talk about Namu." Here is a fragment:—

SONG OF KAIARA FOR HER SON TENIO.

TUMU.

Tenio pi i te po è!
Kua keukeu takoto.
Kua ara i roto ia metua' i,
Ka eke ai Motoro è!
I to riu i Ivirua' i tara mai,—
O te meringa kai ra i topa è!

INTRODUCTION.

Dear little son Tenio, by night
Painfully tossing from side to side
On the lap of thy sleepless mother,
'Tis the anger of Motoro
Admonishing his erring worshippers,—
"You omitted my accustomed offering!"

PAPA.

Te vâ nei i Vaitepongi,
Te maru nei e tapautu;
O te eketumu ta Kaiara
O Tavero e o metua oki
Mau ki te tama e teia è!

FOUNDATION.

Ah! my home was once in the desolate rocks, ·
Hidden in the densest thickets;
Death stared Kaiara in the face.
Thy aunt Tavero was my companion;
Here (with Namu) we found shelter and plenty!

It is curious that after the lapse of so many (164) years the spot where these poor women were tied up by Mauiki for death is in the possession of one of their descendants.

Kaiara died about the year 1777, from the fall of a green cocoanut. The offending tree was immediately cut down.

CHAPTER XXV.

MANAUNE'S FORTUNATE ADOPTION.

In the olden time, if a man wished to marry he must select a wife from another tribe. To marry into one's own tribe was usually regarded as a heavy offence against the gods. Each clan had its separate gods, customs, traditions, and songs—constituting but one great family, with a single head, and pledged to defend each other to the death. These tribes were almost always at war with each other, so that a man was often compelled to fight against his wife's nearest relatives. In general the boys went with the paternal tribe.

One of the most memorable instances of adoption into a hostile tribe was that of Manaune.

We have seen that the vanquished tribe of Ruanac, after the battle of Arera, took refuge in the "Cave of the Tern," at Ivirua. This cave is very difficult of access; inside is a fearful chasm, down which it were easy to hurl an intruder. Amongst them lived Teora, whose husband and all her sons but one had fallen in successive battles with Mautara's victorious clan. Teora's great anxiety was to save her remaining boy. Night after night she dreamt that she saw her warlike nephew, the priest Mautara, alone on the distant spur of a mountain opposite to their stronghold, slaying some invisible foe. This seemed to the anxious mother a sure intimation that all those in the cavern were doomed to destruction. She resolved therefore to go secretly to her nephew and beg him to adopt the orphan Manaune into the winning tribe. She whispered to her boy her design, and directed him to watch through the ensuing night until the morning star should rise, and then stealthily descend the perilous pathway from the cave and meet her at a certain spot a little way off. The reason for this arrangement was that at midnight Ruanac was in the habit of going round with a lighted torch and counting his sleeping clan, so as to detect any who might attempt to go over to his foes. Now Ruanac and his whole tribe were cannibals, but the victims were usually stray members of Mautara's clan, caught at a disadvantage. Deserters and suspected parties belonging to his own tribe shared the same horrible fate if caught.

As soon as the bright herald of day made its appearance Manaune left the cave and met his mother at the appointed place. The fugitives luckily reached the summit of the interior mountain-ridge without being pursued, and now ran with all possible speed along the narrow path through the fern and iron-wood-trees. By daylight they were beyond the reach of the terrible Ruanae; and whilst it was yet early morning they reached the encampment of Mautara, on the west of the island.

Meanwhile Teko, the wife of Mautara, was quietly cooking her oven for the early morning meal. According to the ancient but now obsolete custom of native women, as soon as the taro was covered up in the oven with leaves she sat upon it to make it retain the heat. If inconveniently hot in one place she would move herself to another part of the oven until the food was properly done. She had fallen asleep over her oven when she was heard by her husband muttering to herself, "My boys are fighting at Tamarua." Mautara roused her by asking what she had been talking about. She replied, "Nothing : it is only a dream." But the sagacious Mautara felt sure it was her god "Tanenga-kiau" addressing him through his wife, and that a great crisis was at hand.

Whilst the priest-chief was pondering over the words, his aunt Teora suddenly entered the back door of his hut, the other and principal entrance being *tapu*—unlawful to her as a woman. Teora kissed the feet of her nephew in token of profound respect. It was usual in this and many other ways to honor the first-born and future head of the family; besides, Mautara was the greatest man on the island at the time.

The priest-chief inquired the object of his aunt's visit. She frankly confessed that she wished to put under his protection her beloved son, Manaune. At that moment the lad came out of his hiding-place, was " kissed " and kindly greeted by Mautara. It was forthwith arranged that Manaune should stay in the victorious encampment and be adopted into Mautara's clan, but Teora should return to the Cave of the Tern for their property.

The oven of taro was now opened, and Teora once more partook of a nutritious meal. In a few minutes more the now

13

happy mother, having succeeded in her purpose, set off towards
Ivirua. Mautara and the lad accompanied her some distance
along the hill-side, and finally, at a spot named from the circumstance, took a farewell with tears. Would Teora's share in the
transaction of that day be discovered and punished with death?
Three times she turned back to get a last look of her son, but
Mautara waved his hand for her to be gone.

The cousins made their way back to the place where the
warriors were encamped. They had heard that some one was to
be formally adopted into the tribe, without knowing whom. For
so important an occasion they put on their war head-dresses and
covered their persons with many folds of twisted native cloth.
With spears poised, as if for an immediate attack, they stood in
file awaiting the new arrival. As the two relatives came in sight
from the hill at the back of the encampment (Mautara shouting
to them with all his might), they were immediately enclosed
between the ranks, and a mimic fight began. As soon as this
was concluded Manaune was led to a sacred stream to wash off
the taint of his old antagonistic associations, and his person
became " sacred " in the eyes of his new companions.

Teora's return to the cave excited no remark from the women
and children left in charge, for the males had that day started
to Tevaenga in quest of food. They obtained plenty, but were
particularly jubilant because they had caught Patea in a lofty
tree collecting Brazilian plums. They ate the plums *and the poor
man who had gathered them.* Fortunately, the wife, Piriau,
escaped through being at a little distance gathering candlenuts.
Thus amid the excitements of the day Manaune's escape did not
attract notice.

That evening Teuanuku, eldest son of Mautara, led his victorious clan to Tamarua, in hope of intercepting the flight of
Ruanae's force, who marched from Tevaenga to Tamarua in
order to collect cocoanuts. Mautara's clan hid in the bushes
until daylight revealed the precise whereabouts of their foes,
who, not suspecting danger, were scattered in all directions,
climbing after nuts. Unhappily for themselves their spears were
all piled up against a large chestnut-tree still standing. To their
dismay Teuanuku and his little army suddenly came in sight,
and stood between them and their weapons. Two or three of
the attacking party got their skulls cracked by green nuts

dexterously thrown by men in the trees. Others, by main force, wrenched off branches of the cocoanut, and belaboured their adversaries. The struggle was brief and disastrous to the cannibals, who all perished, save a few who at the beginning of the conflict ran to the rocks for shelter.

Young Manaune evinced his bravery that day at the expense of his deceased father's nearest kin. Many were laid low by his spear. As a punishment, he was long afflicted with insanity, until he had made atonement to the gods. The reward of his bravery was a "tapere" on the east side of the island. A "tapere" is literally "*a slice*" (as of a cake) from the outer reef to the central hill of Mangaia. He married, and lived with his mother on his lands, where to this day lofty cocoanut-trees bear the name of Manaune. Here he succoured Rori, who lived under his protection in after years.

Many were the battles which he afterwards fought side by side with the sons of Mautara. The lordship of Mangaia twice devolved upon Teuanuku—first, after the battle of Arira; and, secondly, after the surprise at Pukuotoi, just described. Now, for the first time, the drum of peace was beaten, and human life was for a while respected.

Thus originated, in process of time, one of the principal warrior tribes of Mangaia, named after the founder Manaune, and possessing now about half the soil of the island. When the Rev. J. Williams, in 1823, vainly endeavoured to locate teachers, a grandson of Manaune, named Pangemiro, was temporal chief for the second time. Pangemiro did not live to embrace Christianity; but his son, Simeona, became the first deacon, and in connection with Barima laid the foundation of Christian society by sanctioning the destruction of idolatry, the establishment of law, and the protection of the early native evangelists.

CHAPTER XXVI

SCARCELY SAVED; OR THE STORY OF VAIAA.

Amongst the few of the cannibal clan of Ruanae who survived the disastrous surprise at Pukuotoi were Vaiaa and his sister Mangaia, who ran across the island and hid themselves in the rocks and caves of Marotangiia, on the west. The motive for selecting this hiding-place was the abundance of wild food in that neighbourhood. Here they subsisted on crabs, rats, frugivorous bats, and berries, nutritious roots, and cooked herbs. Occasionally they made their way to the reef and caught a few fish, without attracting notice.

One day, to their dismay, Ngako came upon them well armed. His character for ferocity was too well known to them to make his company desirable. They were both young and unarmed, whilst Ngako had been one of the chief warriors of Ruanae, and was particularly addicted to cannibalism. On the fatal day of Pukuotoi he was scout, and, finding that there was no chance for victory in fight, rushed to the rocks, and actually subsisted on the stray fugitives belonging to his own unfortunate clan. Twice Kaiara narrowly escaped his ruthless hands. On one occasion Keukeu with difficulty got away from this noted cannibal—a circumstance which her numerous descendants have not failed to celebrate in song. Month after month passed in this ignoble employment, when Ngako resolved to change the scene of his infamous exploits, and made his way to the western part of the island, where, as we have said, he fell in with the children of Akapautua, the chief next to Ruanae in point of dignity. Ngako proposed that they should all live together; of course, pledging himself to protect the children of his fallen chief. To this the brother and sister assented with as good grace as was possible, seeing they were in his power. The fierce old cannibal went from time to time in quest of human victims, and rarely did he return without one. Especially did he look out for children wandering about the rocks in search of berries

wherewith to satisfy the cravings of hunger. The cooking fell
to the lot of Mangaia and her brother. Nearly two years had
been spent by them in the rocks, when it became evident that
they must in their turn be eaten, for victims had become very
scarce. More than once Ngako had returned without anything,
with an ominous scowl upon his face. The last man living
amongst the rocks was caught, and his body brought home to the
brother and sister to be cooked as usual by night, lest the smoke
should lead to their detection and death. Ngako greedily devoured his own portion; but Vaiaa and Mangaia hid their share
for their dreaded companion. On the following day the old
wretch again ate, and then started off in search of another
victim. At nightfall he returned in no good temper, but was
pacified with the reserved portions of food. Next morning he
again ate, and went off in quest of a victim. At noon Ngako
came back cross and hungry. There was still a bit left; it was
speedily devoured by their grim "protector."

During the absence of Ngako that morning Vaiaa and Mangaia held an important consultation. Should he again come
back without a victim, it was evident that the brother would be
killed and eaten, and afterwards the sister. They must lull
Ngako to sleep, and then run for their lives.

After his meal the old cannibal became cheerful and chatty;
so that Vaiaa ventured to propose that he should lay his head
upon his lap and allow him to hunt for disagreeable insects.
The ruse succeeded, and it was not long before Ngako gave signs
of feeling drowsy under this agreeable operation. A significant
elevation of eyebrows to his sister caused her to rise and cautiously remove to a safe distance, when she took to her heels and
ran by a well-known path towards the interior, never stopping to
get breath until she had reached the summit of the hill Aretoa,
overlooking the beautiful and fertile valley of Keia. This was
about a mile from their old hiding-place at Marotangiia.

At last Ngako went off into a sound sleep, and his head was
gently laid on some leaves collected for the purpose in the morning. Vaiaa felt sorely tempted to take up the cannibal's spear
and drive it through one of his eyes into the brain. But he was
so weak and attenuated, from want of food, that he judged it
best to leave the muscular form of the old warrior alone and
betake himself to flight.

Vaiaa ran a short distance; but, thinking it possible that Ngako might wake up and give chase, he stepped aside from the path and hid himself in the rocks. Ere long his fears were realized, for he heard Ngako running past and grunting, "My little fish have escaped." Vaiaa dared scarcely breathe for fear of detection. After awhile Ngako returned without having caught his victims. With infinite satisfaction Vaiaa saw his huge form and long spear take the narrow path leading to the sea, in the vain expectation of falling in with his old companions.

Vaiaa felt it to be now best to venture out of his hiding-place, and run by the direct path to the hill where his sister lay hid. This he safely accomplished. Brother and sister wept for joy that they were at last safe from the evil designs of the dreaded Ngako, who durst not venture into the open country. But, if safe from their old foe, they knew not what their reception might be upon their discovery by the winning tribe occupying the fertile valleys of the interior.

Having slaked their thirst at a small spring — but without tasting a morsel of food—they slept in the crisp fern. On the day following they could distinctly see the huts studding the valley, but durst not approach. At dusk they made for a picturesque wide valley known as Tongarei; the lights in the various houses became distinctly visible. A second night was spent in the fern. Ere daylight of the third day they reached a very solitary place where a clump of bread-fruit trees grew. Under the rule of Teuanuku the entire island had become fruitful again. Vaiaa got up into the best of the bread-fruit trees and gathered the fruit, throwing it to his sister below.

Not far off happened to be a woman collecting chestnuts which had fallen in the night. Espying a strange-looking fellow in the bread-fruit tree, she left off her work and ran back to the main valley to give the alarm. In a short time the tree was surrounded, and brother and sister were made prisoners. It was resolved to cook and eat both, in revenge for the many who had fallen at the hands of their cannibal clan. Dry firewood and the largest banana-leaves were at once collected for this purpose.

By this time the mother of Teuanuku heard that her relatives, supposed long since to be dead, were caught, and in a few minutes would be in the oven. She said to her son, " Tera ake taù kiko "—" There goes my own flesh." Teuanuku took the hint, and ran towards the place where the prisoners were said to be. Fearing lest he should be too late to save them, he shouted, as only a chief can shout, " Oi, e kiko no Teko ! "—" Spare the relatives of Teko ! "

This timely shout saved their lives. The crowd, disappointed in their hope of getting a taste of human flesh that day, fell back. The captives were led to the feet of Teuanuku ; a coral-tree marks the spot where they met. In a few minutes they reached the home of Teuanuku. Hard by was that occupied by the priest-chief Mautara and his wife Teko. Tears of joy were freely shed, that auspicious day, at their narrow escape. Vaiaa remarked to his sister, " Kua tatara te enga," *i.e.*, " The fear of death has passed away,"—words which have passed into a proverb.

Vaiaa possessed medical[1] knowledge derived from his father : this was one reason for his life being spared. Lands were bestowed upon him at Tamarua, the ancient home of the Tongan tribe. Vaiaa married, and became the father of a number of sons and daughters.

Not long after their happy deliverance, Vaiaa and a number of his protectors made an expedition to the rocks in quest of Ngako, with a view of punishing him for his many cruelties. They found him starved to death in the old domicile occupied by Vaiaa and his sister. They left the corpse to the tender mercies of the rats which infest that wild district.

Mangaia became a dependant of Teuanuku's. Whenever she went on the reef for the purpose of torch-fishing she took *two* baskets, whereas it is customary to carry but one. The best fish she put into the basket reserved for her protector Teuanuku ; all the inferior sort went into the other. On returning to the interior her invariable practice was to present each person she met, whether man, woman, or child, with the best in her *second* basket. If anything remained at the bottom it would be hers ; if not, she would be quite content, for was not her life secure ? When asked why she alone of all women in Mangaia carried a second basket, she would say, " Who can tell but that in some future hour of peril one of those to whom I have given fish may

---

[1] Ta pito.

save my life?" Hence the proverb, "good-natured as Mangaia"
(*e takinga ta Mangaia*).

She was eventually married to Maruata, who was offered in
sacrifice to Rongo when the drum of peace was beaten for Kirikovi, in whose brief reign of five or six years Captain Cook came.
She had the misfortune to see some of her children laid on the
altar.

Rori obtained some of her beautiful hair to adorn the then
newly-carved image of Motoro. At the period of the surrender
of the idols to Mr. Williams the hair of this woman was still
on it.

Mangaia lived to a very advanced age. Some now living
(1872) well remember her.

The identical bread-fruit tree in which Vaiaa was caught was
blown down in the dreadful cyclone of March, 1846. A sucker
from one of its decayed roots has grown into a noble tree.
Standing on the interesting spot, I heard the story in all its
particulars. I once heard a native pastor run through the outline of the story in illustration of a greater salvation.

At the commencement of Potiki's reign a set of songs were
prepared in honor of Vaiaa, who had just died, and whose son,
Nguare, had rendered important service to the ruling tribe in a
recent battle. These are known as *Te Kakai ia Vaiaa*, or, "The
Death-talk about Vaiaa." *The sister is not referred to in these
songs*, marking the low estimation in which the sex was held.

THE CAPTURE OF VAIAA: "A DEATH-TALK."

Composed by Temaru, *circa* A.D. 1791.

TUMU.	INTRODUCTION.
Tongarei te kuru i kuke ei Vaiaa. 　Kitea i Maruia, 　Kua ngara i te mate ra aia!	In Tongarei is the bread-fruit Vaiaa 　climbed. 　　Found in a shady vale, 　　He thought his last hour had come!

PAPA.	FOUNDATION.
Kitea mai Vaiaa mei uta i Tongarei, 　Kua rongo koe i te pati e, 　Tetai mama ia Vaiaa. 　Kua rave a Teuanuku. 　Te kou raunika tapa ê!	Found was Vaiaa in the valley of Tonga- 　rei. 　　He heard each one asking 　　For a bit of Vaiaa. 　　It was Teuanuku that saved him. 　So the leaves for cooking thee were useless!

UNUUNU TAI.

Tongarei te kuru i kake ei,—
Tei kakea, kapi oki a raro!
Kua kapi oki a raro ê!
    Te kete kuru manin,
    Te matapa, no uta i Tongarei.
    Kitea i Maruia,
Kua ngara i te mate ra aia!

FIRST OFFSHOOT.

In Tongarei is the bread-fruit he climbed.
The ground was covered with foes,—
Covered, alas! with foes.
Oh, the baskets of choice bread-fruits,—
The fine fruits that grow in the vale of
    Tongarei.
    Found in a shady vale,
He thought his last hour had come!

UNUUNU RUA.

Nooia ra te Kâtara,—
Te Kâtara, tei Tutama te ai!
Tei Tutama te ai, tei motu ii karoa ê!
I ui mai te vaine, Vaiaa oki teia.
    Kitea i Maruia,
Kua ngara i te mate ra aia!

SECOND OFFSHOOT.

Thou didst tarry on the hill-top,
On the hill-top where thou didst see the
    grove of tall chestnut-trees.
A woman asked and found it was Vaiaa.
    Found in a shady vale,
He thought his last hour had come!

UNUUNU TORU.

Ka akapiri i te ara ê!
    Na Katongi ïa.
Na Katongi tei Kâpune,
Tei Kâpune te ara nui,
Te vao roa koe i Tongarei.
    Kitea i Maruia,
Kua ngara i te mate ra aia!

THIRD OFFSHOOT.

The crowd led thee by the narrow path
    Through the valley,—
Through the dell and past the waterfall,
Until they gained the main road
From the long valley of Tongarei.
    Found in a shady vale,
He thought his last hour had come!

UNUUNU A.

Tapiri i roto, ei te pu meika,
I te pu meika, kua nânâ te mata ê!
    Kua ta tatou ika ê!
    Aore au e pa atu;
    E kiko oki no Teko.
    Kitea i Maruia,
Kua ngara i te mate ra aia!

FOURTH OFFSHOOT.

Hidden in a banana grove,
On peering through the leaves (they ex-
    claimed),
    "Here is our sweet morsel."
(A shout was heard:) "Slay him not!
    He is the kinsman of Teko!"
    Found in a shady vale,
He thought his last hour had come!

Ai e ruaoo! E rangai ê!

Ai e ruaoo! E rangai ê!

THE WANDERINGS OF VAIAA: "A DEATH-TALK."

Composed by Temaru, A.D. 1791.

TUMU.

Akapautua tei poro io ia Vaiaa,
Ei Ivirua te ora ake ia tatou,
    Reviri ake i reira.
Kua maru te rakau o te ao ê!

INTRODUCTION.

Akapautua's last words to Vaiaa were,
"Let the survivors fly to Ivirua,
And take refuge in the rocks."
The shade of the forest is the home of the
    conquered.

PAPA.

Noo mai Vaiaa i te makitea,
E tai paa, tei ora ake ia tatou;
Taumata io i te uru mato.
E roimata te manga ê!
E marere mai nga rau aoa ê!

FOUNDATION.

Vaiaa's shelter is the rocky heights
Near the sea. From a distance we
Wistfully gaze at our old homes,
Tears being now our constant food,
Sere banyan leaves falling all around!

UNUUNU TAI.

Akapautua ê, tei poro io ê,
    Tei poro ia Vaiaa,
    E tatari ra, e roa e,

FIRST OFFSHOOT.

Akapautua's last charge,
His parting words to Vaiaa, were,
    "Watch the event of the fight:

Kua pau akarere, kua pau akarere ai,
   Te vai ra i Pukuotoi,'
E tauna kapitia io e te puruki.
Ei Ivirua tei ora ake ia tatou,
   Reviri ake i reira ē!
Kua maru te rakau o te ao ē!

Should we be utterly worsted,
And our bodies cover Pukuotoi,'
Slain and mangled by our foes,
Let the survivors fly to Ivirua,
And take refuge in the rocks."
The shade of the forest is the home of the
   conquered.

UNUUNU RUA.

E ū te ara aerenga ē,
I te aerenga i te raei i Toua ē!
Kua tairo aere ē, tairo atu Vaiaa ē,
   Te pou toa i Rangimotia,
   Te pa puku i tu maunga,
I te karara i Kotikoti tei Paugorua.
Ei Ivirua tei ora ake ia tatou,
   Reviri ake i reira ē!
Kua maru te rakau o te ao ē!

SECOND OFFSHOOT.

'Tis difficult to discover the path,—
The track o'er rocks and sharp stones.
Carefully note, Vaiaa, each turn of the
   road.
Yonder are the ironwood-trees of the in-
   terior,
And the gently-sloping hills
We have so often gazed upon.
Let the survivors fly to Ivirua,
And take refuge in the rocks."
The shade of the forest is the home of the
   conquered.

UNUUNU TORU.

Ka ka ano au ka kimi e,
   Kimi ra i Tomoariki ;
   Te reira te uinga ao,
   Mai te uinga ao.
E kimi i to ara e, e umi to inangaro,
E naea ra Vaiaa, o na tai aina ?
E eke i raro atu, mei eke atu ki raro,
   I raro i te tapa utu,
Kua akarongo aere i te varara rakau.
Kua ariu ki miri, e tamaki aina ?
Kua eanga, moanga aere atu.
   Te mua paa to mate,
   Te tangi nei te atua.
Akatapa Vaiaa ko Temakavetai ē !
Mei Temakavetai ra, o naea taua ō ?
E naea taua ē ? Ei tai ngai atu.
Kua meamea i te nooinga,
Kia kite te mata i te enua ;
   Mai kite atu Vaiaa!
E te tangi nei ia Akapautua.
Ei Ivirua tei ora ake ia tatou,
   Reviri ake i reira ē!
Kua maru te rakau o te ao ē!

THIRD OFFSHOOT.

They will hunt about for thee
E'en as far as Tomoariki,[2]
The usual haunts of the conquered,
Where they meet together.
Seek out thy path ; take heed to each
   step.
How, where shall Vaiaa now go ?
Descend to the beach, hide there awhile
Amongst groves of Barringtonia-trees.
Start not at the rustling of the leaves.
Lookest thou behind thee for a lurking
   foe ?
Ah ! how timidly thou turnest round !
Perhaps a deadly foe is at hand.
Hark to the cry of a guardian bird !
Call, Vaiaa, upon the god Temakavetai,[3]
"Oh, guardian spirit, go with me ;
How shall I proceed ? How can I escape ?
I weary of this desolate place."
Oh, to set foot again in the interior !
How would the heart of Vaiaa then re-
   joice,
Who now grieves for his father, Akapau-
   tua !
"Let the survivors fly to Ivirua,
And take refuge in the rocks."
The shade of the forest is the home of the
   conquered.

---

[1] " Pukuotoi " is the spot where the surprise took place. This " death-talk " was gone through within a stone's-throw of the fatal battle-field.

[2] " Tomoariki " is the designation of a very desolate tract of rocks where Vaiaa once took refuge.

[3] Temakavetai "—" Single Ringlet "—was the supposed guardian of all " black-wild-rocks." Temaru, the composer of these songs, in his youth, *ate his female slave*, Rongo-ika-eke !

Unŭunu A.

E kitea koe ra ô, i te nooinga e,
   I te nooinga i te vao ô,
   Mei raro i Tongarei,
   Mei raro i Tongarei,
Te ui nei i te kotu ma te katitaa ;
Karangaia ia eke, teia te mate iaau.
Ei Ivirua tei ora ake ia tatou,
   Reviri ake i reira.
Kua maru te rakau o te ao ô!
   Ai e ruaoo! E rangai ô!

Fourth Offshoot.

Thou wast captured in a tree,
   When at ease in a shady valley,
   In the vale of Tongarei,—
   Ay, it was in the vale of Tongarei,
Thou wast plucking young bread-fruits,
When they shouted, " Descend to die ! "
   Let the survivors fly to Ivirua,
   And take refuge in the rocks."
The shade of the forest is the home of the
   conquered.

CHAPTER XXVII

SIN AND ITS PUNISHMENT.

CIRCA 1727 (POSSIBLY 1730).

ONE day, as Râei, a chief of secondary rank, was playing at quoits, he noticed the stately figure of Tcuanuku gliding towards his hut in the sequestered hollow of Rupetau. Coincident with this, the monotonous music of his wife's cloth-beating hammer ceased. Ere the day closed she confessed her guilt, and Râei had laid his plans for revenge. The seducer being, like himself, a worshipper of Motoro, he dared not take satisfaction with his own hand; but this did not in heathen morality render it improper in Râei to arrange with Kikau and his Tongan tribe for the murder of "the lord of Mangaia" as soon as the affair should apparently blow off, and the intended victim be put off his guard.

Day after day Râei, like one demented, defiled the sacred district of Keia—the home of the gods—by wearing a *scarlet* hibiscus flower in each ear, a sin which in a previous generation had sealed the fate of Tiaio. The sagacious old priest inquired of Tcuanuku the possible reason for this extraordinary conduct, and, discovering the truth, passed over the insult to his god.

The just anger of the husband at length seemingly cooled down, and nothing further was dreaded. Tcuanuku therefore cheerfully went back to his home at Ivirua. But that night he was slain by Kikau and the Tongans.

The younger brother, Raumea—a man of giant strength—had fallen in the battle of Pukuotoi, about two years previously, when the cannibal clan of Ruanae was exterminated. The exulting force led by Kikau collected most of the men of the northern half of the island, and encamped in great force at Keia, with the declared intention of crushing the remaining adherents of Mautara, and of conferring the supreme chieftainship upon Râei. Luckily for the hitherto unconscious followers of Mautara, a swift messenger warned them of the near approach of their foes. In a short time the sorrowful old priest, with as many of his family and retainers as lived in the neighbourhood, crossed the hills to Ivirua to secure the corpse of the murdered chief. At the entrance to his hut lay the disfigured body, guarded by his weeping widow. Restraining his feelings until he had taken revenge, Mautara hastily wrapped up the corpse, and hid it in the tall fern on the hill-side. He now beat up for recruits; but it was not until he had reached the ancestral seat of his tribe in Veitatei that he met with much success.

Night came on, but sleep was out of the question. Would he be able to cope with his foes and avenge the murder of his first-born? One-half of his extemporized army consisted of raw youths and *women*, most of the acknowledged warriors being ranged on the opposite side.

In a corner of Râei's camp that same night a secret con-ference was held by Namu, the royal husband of the famous Kaiara; Manini, husband to the only two daughters of Mautara; and Pârae, priest of the Tongan tribe which had slaughtered Teuanuku. Said Manini to Namu, " Whom should we pity?" Namu unhesitatingly replied, " Our god [represented by his priest Mautara] alone deserves our pity "—words which after-wards became famous. The three resolved to save Mautara at at all risks, and deputed Pârae under cover of darkness to go off to his camp and divulge to him their plans. Mautara's force was to take a hasty meal, and make a sudden attack upon Râei's hungry army, when the three conspirators with their friends should attack them in the rear.

Pârae's visit did not transpire. Upon his return to Keia he ordered a grand feast requiring several hours to prepare,—a feast that he well knew would never be tasted. In the midst of their cookery, to their dismay, the brave little army of Mautara appeared on a hill overlooking the camp. Each warrior rushed inside the enclosure for a spear or a club, and hastily put on his war gear.

Meantime Mautara was preparing to descend by a short narrow path, where half a dozen brave men could easily keep an army at bay. Pârae saw at a glance that Mautara's cause was lost if he trod that narrow causeway. Taking advantage of the desperate confusion which momentarily prevailed in the camp, and under pretence of washing his hands in the running stream (his face towards Râei's camp), he most energetically beckoned Mautara to a circuitous side-path. Mautara at once understood the signal, and, making a slight *détour*, crossed the taro-patches in the rear of the hostile encampment. The fight now took place in right earnest and on more equal terms, as the nature of the ground prevented a considerable portion of Râei's army from engaging at all.

Namu, Manini, and Pârae had stationed their friends in the rear. In the heat of the battle they mercilessly attacked their former comrades, so that, hemmed in between the two, there was no chance whatever of escape. The slaughter was great. Amongst the slain was Râci, but Kikau was taken alive.

When the fight was over, this wretched man, bound hand and foot, was conducted to Mautara. His fingers and toes, hands and arms, feet and legs, were cut off joint by joint with flint knives. As each limb was severed the writhing victim was asked, "Why did you not spare our brother?" The unvarying reply of the unhappy Kikau was, "*Kua é ia Ra*" (Râci)—"I was misled by Râci,"—now a proverb. The sufferings of the victim were terminated by his stomach being ripped up, and his intestines entwined on the trees shading the dwelling of Mautara.

That same day Teâ was laid upon the altar of Rongo; but Mautara deferred the ceremonies connected with beating the drum of peace until he had buried Tenanuku in the ancestral *marae*. In the re-division of lands which followed, the three arch-conspirators received ample shares. Mautara was declared temporal sovereign,—the first since the days of Tiaio, but not the last instance in which a priest was invested with a dignity strictly pertaining only to warriors.

Mautara's reign of twenty-five years is the longest on record. Unbroken peace prevailed. Few vanquished warriors survived; but their little orphan children grew up to maturity " under the shadow of Mautara," and the island again became populous. Ikoke, the third son of the priest-chief, had six wives; his slave Terimu boasted as many—widows of those they had slain.

The sway of Mautara is looked upon as the model one of historical antiquity; for no blood was shed, and no one of note died, during the entire period. At his death he must have been over fourscore.

In that wondrously long interval of peace the enormous fan and ornamented staff took the place of the spear and the club. The old priest-chief was ever chanting to himself the well-known words,—

Ua purukia e au tamariki,	My boys have won many a victory;
E maraerae io Mangaia ô!	Have crushed every foe in Mangaia,
Ka aere ua ra to raua metua.	That their old father might rest in peace.

As soon as death closed his eyes, the new generation thought the time had come to avenge the slaughter of their sires. A battle was fought at Tuopapa, where Ikoke fell. His slave Terimu, having abandoned him, was afterwards, despite his grey hairs, selected for sacrifice, when the drum of peace declared Uarau sovereign. A short reign of two years was terminated by the last surviving son of Mautara seizing upon the reins of power.

Ngarâ, like his father priest and chief, slew and laid upon the altar the woman Ike. After a peaceful reign of fifteen years the priest-chief died. Under the shadow of that romantic pile of rocks called "the Cave of Terau" a battle was fought, which conferred the supreme power upon a grandson of Mautara, known as Kirikovi, Maruata being the victim for the altar. In this reign (1777) arrived the famous Captain Cook. It was not until the year 1814 that the supreme temporal power passed into other families, and the Mautara clan could henceforth boast only their ancient prowess in arms, and the richest collection of traditionary songs in the Hervey Group.

Koroa sung thus, *circa* 1815 :—

Karake te au o Mautara ra teaore ê!	Long and peaceful was the rule of Mau-
E rima tau aitu.	tara,
Na nu rou o te Amama ê!	Enduring five sacred lustrums.
	Like a tall palm was the priestly sway.
No Karainga[1]	His descendants, Potiki
No Ngarâ nga tau ra e toru ê!	And Ngarâ, reigned three lustrums apiece;
Ie tiria i raro,	Then Rongo willed
Unuia e Rongo te aratoko e tu i rae-	That those who had been chiefs should
ngapu.	be slaves.

[1] "Karainga" is better known as "Potiki." In point of time, Ngarâ's title should precede Potiki's by many a long year.

CHAPTER XXVIII.

RORI, THE HERMIT.

ETIQUETTE in the South Seas, as at home, requires an express invitation to a great feast. One morning a nephew of the chief at Tamarua entered the mission premises, walked up to the door of my study, and inserted the extremity of a cocoanut frond in the thatch. Without uttering a word he departed to act similarly at the houses of all the parties expected to attend—*i.e.*, the king and six principal chiefs, beside the three native pastors. There was a peculiarity in this silent invitation—the separate leaves amounted to fifteen, the meaning being that the entire household should go. Two or three leaves would be but a poor compliment.

Not wishing to be deficient in courtesy, on the following morning at break of day I rode over to the village of Tamarua, and rested awhile at the native minister's house. At length a messenger announced that all was ready. Accompanied by the valued native pastor I proceeded to the feasting-ground, which is a level spot in the centre of the settlement, covered with long grass and neatly enclosed. Huge heaps of food were arranged in two long rows opposite to each other, one for the guests, the other for the entertainers themselves. At eight o'clock silence was called for, hats of all descriptions were taken off, and a blessing was asked. The chief of Tamarua then called out the names of the guests over the respective piles of food, beginning with the missionary and the three native pastors, to evince their respect for the word of God. Then came the king and six great chiefs, whose names were announced in a certain order handed down from time immemorial. Curiously enough, these chiefs at once said to the subordinate landowners, " Divide our food ;" and, when that was done, the chiefs got no more than their people. But they *alone* had the *honor of their names being called out* before the assembly ; so that in reality the food became *their* gift to those who according to ancient feudal usage followed them.

My heap consisted of sixty baskets of taro, large bunches of ripe bananas, cooked fish, which no European would care to eat, and a large quantity of the cocoanut *poi* for which Mangaia is famous. This concoction, which is sour and disagreeable to foreign palates, is made of scraped cocoanut, allowed to ferment, and afterwards mixed with cooked taro. It is regarded as a great treat by the natives ; no great feast is complete without some. Each basket of raw taro had a lot of this *poi*, well packed in broad fern-leaves, on the top.

Surmounting the whole heap were several joints of pork, an entire pig half-cooked, and—rare treat !—a joint of raw beef. The pile was also garnished with young cocoanuts intended for immediate use.

The problem now was, how one solitary mortal could dispose of a heap of food nearly as high as himself. This was quickly decided by dividing the whole amongst our servants, students, gratuitous doorkeepers of our church at Oneroa, and some Rarotongans on a visit to their friends. In this way the whole pile of taro, *poi*, fish, and pork disappeared in the course of a few minutes. I reserved for ourselves merely the piece of beef.

The guests quickly disappeared ; their friends and retainers bearing away huge baskets of food, cooked and uncooked. To leave anything behind were an insult.

Three valuable fish-nets had just been made at Tamarua, their united value being nearly £20. The entire pecuniary value of the food disposed of would be about eight or ten times the worth of the nets. But then it is ever considered a mean and disgraceful thing for a chief to make and use such nets without inviting all the magnates of the island to a feast. The waste of food is only in appearance ; for at certain seasons it is necessary to replant the taro-patches by planting the tops of the old taro.

A VISIT TO THE " RAEI."

Desirous of a little change, I now expressed my wish to the native pastor to visit the *rāei kere*—" wild black rocks," so famous in Mangaian story. Notwithstanding a long residence in the island, I had never been there. It was agreed that we should start at once. Three young men from Oneroa got an inkling of my intention, and followed us. After a walk under the shadow of the continuous belt of rocks which, like a second

14

reef upraised by some mighty subterraneous agency, surrounds the island, we reached the nearest pathway to the *rdei*.

At first the ascent over the stones was tolerably easy; but the atmosphere was stifling on account of the extreme luxuriance of tropical vegetation, often literally growing out of the very rocks without an inch of soil. At length it became needful to wear native sandals, made of the twisted bark of the lemon hibiscus, and secured by thongs of the same material wound round the toes and ankles. As I had on a stout pair of boots reserved for the occasion, there was some difficulty in fastening them on. This happily accomplished, there was little danger of slipping, — a misfortune inevitable to a visitor with only European shoes on.

We soon emerged upon a perfect wilderness, where no leaf of any description was to be seen. This was the *rdei kere*— "black rocks," of which I had heard so much from old warriors! In every direction, save that we had just left, spread out before us an unvarying succession of black pointed rocks, over which it was difficult to believe that a human being could pass. Our party preferred keeping strictly to what the natives satirically call a pathway, which in truth was only a faint track over the rocks. Off that track only a native could venture: at each step the pointed stones cracked ominously. Yet native boys, well sandalled, run races over the more tolerable parts. Our guide walked on in front. Each step had to be taken with the utmost caution. In one hand I held a long pole; a native lad held my other hand.

There are in all eight ridges, each bearing a distinct name. Midway we found a rock recently levelled by a sledge-hammer to form a comfortable standing-place, although not larger than a table. An excellent view of this Land of Desolation was obtained from this spot. The *rdei kere* extended on every side, being about three miles in length and two in width. The low mountains of the interior were here lost to view. Before us rolled the vast, blue Pacific. About a mile from our resting-place was the spot where of old Rori hid himself from his relentless foes. Looked upon from a distance, the *rdei* closely resembled a map of the moon; the hollows appearing as mysterious black spots enclosed by strangely-contorted ridges. We resolved to press on to the sea. But as the sun was nearly vertical, and there was no tree or even a low bush to afford shade—we could not even see one—we suffered greatly from thirst. I inquired for the waterholes where Rori used to slake his thirst; but the search of our guide was unavailing. The walk across occupied two hours. On reaching the beach we rested awhile, despite the burning thirst, on the sandy floor of a cave.

Anxious not to return by this rough path, we now endeavoured to skirt the shore, as the water was high on the reef. For some time we persevered, but eventually found it impossible to go on. A small yellow creeper had so completely covered the many fissures and holes in our course that more than once our party nearly disappeared from sight in these natural pitfalls. With great difficulty we made our way back to the old resting-place in the cave by the sea, and prepared to wade along the reef as best we could. Sometimes the water was up to our chins; at times as low as our waists. The force of the current made it difficult at times to maintain one's footing. Occasionally we were compelled to swim, clothes and all.

On first wading on the reef, the feeling was one of delicious coolness, allaying our thirst in no small degree. But before long the weight of water in our clothes became intolerably fatiguing. Midway we espied a little cavern, hollowed out of the overhanging rocks by the ceaseless beating of the waves, and known as "the Cave of Uanukutea." Here we rested for a few seconds, and listened to the

STORY OF UANUKUTEA.

In the days of Tiki a woman from the island of Mauke, named Uanukutea, took up her solitary abode here. The reason of her being exiled was that on more than one occasion she was caught by her father, Uanukutaketea, eating human flesh and drinking human blood. Without hesitation he drove her away from her pretty island-home. Sent to sea alone in a small canoe with a mat sail, and a scanty supply of cocoanuts to serve for food and drink, she reached Mangaia, a distance of one hundred miles. Landing unobserved on this wild part of the coast, she sent the canoe adrift and took shelter in the cave that bears her name. Uncertain what her fate might be, she did not wish her arrival to be known.

She had lived some months on the island, when Matariki,

priest of Tanè, third in order of succession, met her in the dusk of evening prowling about the adjacent rocks. Learning the name of the stranger woman, he inquired, " What are you *crunching*, Uanukutea ? " Her reply was, " Only *the legs of a god* "— words which have since passed into a proverb. Matariki's impression was that she referred to the legs of land-crabs, which abound in that neighbourhood. In reality Uanukutea was picking a human bone. To this incorrigible female cannibal nothing was so delicious as human flesh : she never wearied of it. It is asserted that her habit was to waylay any solitary young person who might lag behind the bevies of women and girls engaged in torch-fishing on the reef whenever the tide was favourable. In the utter darkness of moonless nights the stranger woman might easily escape notice, or, if seen by the distant glare of the torches, be mistaken for one of their number. Uanukutea used an iron-wood dagger, two feet long, called a *tui* or " needle." A stab in the naked back whilst her victim was intent on picking up a drowsy fish or chasing a lobster would be sufficient for her purpose. The body was of course borne to the little cave which bears her name, to be devoured at leisure.

An inquiry was set on foot respecting the fate of several young persons who had mysteriously disappeared. Matariki advised that a visit be paid to the lair of a stranger woman from Mauke whom he had accidentally met and conversed with. A new sense was given to her famous words. The suggestion was at once complied with, and abundant evidence of her guilt was discovered. Uanukutea was forthwith speared to death. The name of this monster in human form is indelibly associated with this little cave, which now forms a pleasant resting-place for the wearied traveller, despite the cold drops of purest water which occasionally fall from the stone roof upon his head.

So runs the ancient story. That a stranger woman so named once met her fate there is doubtless true. The story of her crimes may have been a mere excuse for the murder committed by these islanders, who looked with an evil eye upon all visitors. Vaipo in his *fête* song (*circa* 1819) refers to this woman :—

[*Call for dance to begin.*]	[*Call for dance to begin.*]
Uanukutea te vaine ê !	Ah, Uanukutea !
Ka aere i to piaki roa : Mataorongo ê !	That wanderedst by the shore of Mata-orongo,
Kua taia koe.	Thou hast met thy deserts.

Solo.	Solo.
Taipo ê!	Go on!
Chorus.	*Chorus.*

Noo maira i te rua roa tei tai ê!	There once dwelt in a cave by the sea,
Tei tai te rua roa o Uanukutea.	Far away from the dwellings of men,
Te ara e kai tangata ua ê!	A she-cannibal, a stranger, named Uanu-
Te raro aturâ Uanukutea ê!	kutea.
Te raro atu Uanukutea i te papa	Her home, scarcely noticeable, was
I te moana. O Tane-aiai, e vari Tautiti ê!	Where the white breakers ever foam.
Kua kitea, e kitea mai ana,	Tanè,[1] the evening-star god, revealed her;
Te kai maira te kai a te Atua :	He who presides over the merry dance.
Turinga, turinga mou ai rai.	She was devouring the food[2] of the gods :
	Utterly addicted to eating human flesh.

Again we pressed on our way; perpendicular rocks at our back threatening us with certain destruction should the sea suddenly rise, this being the weather-side of the island, where the trades unceasingly blow in all their mighty strength. After an hour's wading we happily reached the well-known "Big Cave," which has a tragic history of its own. Here was the path by which we thankfully made our way back to the interior, dripping as we were with sea-water, through a thick growth of candlenut and other trees. At last we emerged upon a cultivated spot, where grows a clump of low cocoanut-trees. Here we soon enjoyed most refreshing draughts of cocoanut water. Overheated as we were, we knew that we might drink without fear of evil consequences : a striking instance of the Divine Wisdom which adapts food and drink to the climate.

We now returned to the village of Tamarua, weary and footsore. Forthwith, mounting my horse, I rode home much gratified with my brief adventure. But to my surprise I found that I had suddenly become famous; for it had got wind that "the missionary had gone to see the *rdei*," which very few on the west side have ever visited. Many were the kind congratulations, as I rode along in my tattered garments, that I had returned from so famous and so rugged a spot without accident.

There were several points of interest connected with this trip, of which the principal is

RORI'S HOME ON THE "RAEI."

Rori's grandfather, Una, arrived on the eastern coast of

---

[1] "Tanè" is put for Matariki, priest of Tanè. The evening-star was "the eye of Tanè."

[2] The dead were regarded as food for the gods, which she was impiously devouring.

Mangaia in a drift canoe from Iti, the only name by which Tahiti was formerly known there. By a Mangaian wife he became the father of Rongoariki. Now, father and son were famed for their skill in all manner of carpentry and fine sennit work. Una died; but these well-guarded secrets were faithfully transmitted in the third generation to Rori, the only son of Rongoariki.

When Rori was a lad of say eighteen years, the decisive battle of Mâucue was fought on a pleasant hill-side within a stone's-throw from the home of these artisans. The immediate occasion of that fight was anger at the expulsion of a section of the Tongan clan, who were imagined to have been swallowed up in the ocean, but in reality had found a comfortable home on the southern part of Rarotonga.

Sixty fell on the losing side, to which Rori and his father belonged. The old man fought as a warrior in the ranks; behind him stood his son, spear in hand, ready to occupy his father's place should he fall.

Their party being utterly routed, they both ran for shelter to their hut. But, seeing the victors in hot pursuit, the old man urged his children to leave him to die, and take refuge in the *rdei kere*—"wild black rocks" on the east of Mangaia. Rori and his two sisters willingly obeyed, and ran in the direction indicated.

During the few minutes wasted by the attacking party in killing the father and disposing of the valuable articles which his skill enabled him to produce, Rori succeeded in gaining the summit of the cliffs not far from his future home; but from that inaccessible height witnessed the unhappy fate of his sister Amio, and a younger one, whose name is forgotten. To kill women was contrary to the ordinary usage of war here. So swift were the brother's movements that his pursuers gave up the chase as fruitless.

Finding himself no longer an object of pursuit, Rori looked carefully about for a place of refuge in the very bosom of the "wild black rocks." He deliberately made his home in the very worst spot in all Mangaia, because it was impossible that any one approaching his hiding-place, however cautiously, should escape his observation.

The spot selected by the young exile as his head-quarters was a hollow about thirty feet square, towards the interior effectually sheltered from observation by a rock. Here he resolved to settle down as in an utterly unknown or forsaken land. He worked hard night by night to level the sharp-pointed rock, until at last he succeeded in making it tolerably smooth. The only hammers used by him in breaking off the tops of these rocks were large pieces of basalt, stolen by him in his nocturnal visits to the interior. Thus in the midst of this fearful scene of desolation he had gained an unsuspected hiding-place, just midway between the ocean and the fertile interior, where dwelt his foes.

Tradition asserts that, after he had thus levelled the surface of this hollow, the place was still rough and uncomfortable. Rori found amusement in chipping sharp stones into the appearance of sea-worn pebbles, such as are invariably used to adorn the dwellings of Polynesians. In the course of time the irregular surface of "Rori's hollow" was neatly covered with artificial pebbles.

The heavy dews and rains of the tropics admonished the solitary fugitive to build a house. Abundance of suitable wood could be procured for this purpose at night from the dense forest skirting his barren domain. But he had no adze wherewith to cut down a single branch. Nothing daunted, Rori set to work to make a set of stone adzes out of pieces of basalt stolen from the interior under cover of darkness. These adzes are made by ceaselessly chipping with sharp fragments of red flint. A mountain of red quartz exists on the north-east of the island, which, tradition says, *travelled all night of its own accord from Rarotonga,* and at daylight settled down where it now is! Natives go from all parts of the island to this spot, appropriately called *Maana*, the Rarotongan word for "hot," for supplies of quartz, which they use as flint, and which are obtained by roasting the rock.

Handles must be sought for these adzes. Sennit must be plaited to fasten them on the top of the wooden handles. In all this Rori was an adept: it was to perpetuate this invaluable knowledge that the father begged his boy to leave him to his fate. But the fugitive dared not venture so near to human habitations as would be needful to obtain the materials for making sennit. In those times cocoanut-trees were only planted in the immediate neighbourhood of the dwellings of the proprietors, who kept constant watch, spear in hand. A substitute was hit upon in the bark of the banyan-tree, which here grows best on the rocks skirting the barren kingdom of Rori.

The set of adzes was finished. A few dark nights enabled Rori to obtain from the forest the wood required. Two small houses were now built—one for a workshop and for sleeping; a second for storing and cooking food. The ordinary pandanus thatch was unattainable to a man in his circumstances. Rori therefore had recourse to a beautiful broad-leaved fern (*rau kotaa*) which abounds in the moist recesses of the rocks outside this desolate domain, and which is well adapted for temporary dwellings, being perfectly impervious to rain. But there was one serious drawback to this sort of thatch—it must be renewed every fifteen or twenty days. At the present time, if a party of natives felling timber in the forest are overtaken by darkness or by rain, they extemporize a house of this kind for the night. A couple of men with sharp Sheffield axes can run up a house of this sort in half an hour—a labour of many weeks to Rori, with his clumsy tools.

The fear that his solitary home would eventually be discovered, and that he would be surprised and slain, led to his seeking an additional hiding-place. At no great distance was a cave admirably suited for this end. Here was carefully hidden his treasure of red feathers and stone axes not in use. When a strong sense of danger crept upon him, here, too, he would sleep in safety during the day—the period when most liable to be discovered. After the death of Rori the entrance to this cave was carefully built up with stones by his sons, so that it might prove to them a refuge, as it had been to their father, if needed. This famous little cave has of late years been sought for in vain —so completely have the stones closing its mouth assumed the blackened, mossy appearance of the rocks around them.

Water exists in the crannies of the rocks sufficient to sustain life, although a superficial seeker like our guide could find none. "The well of Rori," in the midst of this waste, is a natural hollow, to which the ingenious fugitive adapted a stone cover. In a second visit to this romantic spot we found it, and tasted its water. The purport of the cover was to hide the water from sight, and to keep it free from insects.

. Rori subsisted on a sour wild fruit, known as the *nono* (*Morinda citrifolia*), a species of wild yam, candlenuts, and pandanus

drupes, which have a pleasant flavour. To obtain these neces-
saries of life he made frequent expeditions to the neighbouring
woods. His main support during the early months of the new
year was the fruit of the chestnut-tree (*Tuscarpus edulis*). A
single nut, divested of its thick husk, is usually four inches long,
three wide, and one thick. Not far from the *rắei* in the interior
of the island there grew at that time a noble grove of seven of
these valuable trees. Three of the seven still stand, and bear
the name of "Rori's chestnuts."[1] Though they have weathered
the storms of centuries, they are still magnificent trees.

At dusk Rori approached as near as was safe : as soon as it
was pitch-dark he boldly left the rocks and made for the well-
known trees. If there was nothing to excite suspicion, he ventured farther into the interior to a second clump of trees, to
collect worm-eaten chestnuts, which he easily distinguished from
the good by their lightness. Rori's basket being full of these
worthless nuts, he would return to the grove which bears his
name, and feel about the ground for good chestnuts. For every
good nut he picked up he substituted a worm-eaten one, in order
to avoid suspicion. Nobody would imagine that a fugitive would
venture to the distant clump of chestnuts ; but the frequent disappearance of the fruit of the trees so near the rocks could not
but eventually lead to his destruction. So cleverly did Rori
manage matters that his existence was for a long time unsuspected.

The sandals of Rori—so necessary to his safety—were made
of prepared banyan-tree bark, the best possible for this purpose.
It was needful to beat the bark out on a log of wood, after being
steeped in water. The same sort of bark yielded him a coarse
coverlet (*tiputa*) and the never-forgotten girdle. The paper-mulberry tree (*aute*) is invariably used for these purposes ; but Rori
was an outcast and a fugitive. The all-important point with
him was to have a good supply of sandals to enable him fearlessly to run over these spear-pointed rocks ; a single pair lasting
him only two or three days. Throughout the Polynesian islands
cloth-beating is a female employment. To dull the sound of his
cloth-beating he half-buried his log (*tutunga*) in the ground,
taking care to beat out the bark very gently. The cloth made

---

[1] Often designated " Rori's delight."

under such disadvantageous circumstances was of the coarsest
description.

Rori usually slept soundly during the early part of the day,
after the toil of the night in providing and cooking. His
favourite employment in the after part of the day was the manufacture of stone adzes, articles of the greatest value in these
islands before the introduction of iron. His unwearying in-
dustry is attested by the abundant chips of basalt and red quartz
which may yet be seen in his solitary home in the very bosom of
the *ráei*, which is simply hardened coral. These stones are never
found there unless taken by some clever fugitive from the interior
in order to beguile the weariness of his exile. These stone adzes
require continual sharpening on hones, obtained from softer portions of the mountain of red quartz. A hone of this sort was
hidden in the garden where he had once lived in peace. He
tremblingly ventured there one night, and, finding the place
entirely deserted, succeeded in carrying away his treasure. That
hone, much worn by use and broken, was long in my possession.[1]

Close to the hiding-place of this industrious fellow is a small
quarry of the finest stalagmite, used in making valuable pestles
(*reru*) for preparing food. It is said that he made numbers of
these useful articles during his long exile in the *ráei*. A beautiful specimen was presented to me lately by the native pastor,
saying, " It is the best stone ; it came from the quarry of
Rori."

A favourite employment of Rori was to tame wild birds,
which at that time were numerous. The gun and the wild cat
of the white man have effectually thinned them out. Some
species are entirely extinct. Having with some difficulty succeeded in taming one or two young tropic birds (*tavaki*), he fed
them on a rock near his home, taking care to secure one foot
by a string. By means of snares he caught numbers of the
birds, in order to get the beautiful red feathers (two only) found
in the tail. These feathers are still prized by the natives, but
were then of much higher value for head-dresses. Other birds
yielded to him black and blue and golden feathers, without,
however, preventing his winged companions from seeking their

---

[1] Now deposited in the British Museum.

own livelihood. The dark feathers were in those days used to decorate their dances in time of peace, and their long spears on the battle-field.

However short of food he might be, he never killed these birds, as they were in his estimation his special guardians in time of peril. Two species were sacred to the god Tanè; the rest to Tamakavetai, the spirit of the "wild black rocks." If, when on his nocturnal marauding expedition, one of these birds would cross his path and cry over his head, Rori devoutly believed this to be a hint from these divinities that he had better hide himself from impending danger, or fly for his life.

To facilitate his movements, he built a rough pathway, half a mile in length. The stones were so fixed that whilst capable of bearing the weight of Rori they would rattle; so that, if discovered and pursued in his strange asylum, he would thereby get timely notice of danger. In running away at his wondrous speed from danger, he was careful to take a direction contrary to his home, lest his retreat should be discovered. The stone pathway referred to approaches the sea route which our party so painfully traversed. A practised eye is required to see that it was made by human hands at all, as time and weather have made all the stones equally black.

Seasons came and went; years rolled on in this monotonous way with Rori, whose existence was unknown, and whose name was all but forgotten. It was known that he had taken refuge in the rocks after the fatal battle of Mâucue, but it was believed that he had long since starved to death. One or two individuals professed to have seen an ill-looking, cadaverous fellow flying like the wind over the most inaccessible rocks; surely this must be Rori. But this was regarded as a wild imagination. Such was Rori's wonderful fleetness of foot, when once sandalled, that it was hopeless to chase him. Upon one occasion he ventured on the reef to fish for sea-eels. He had caught several, and, for once, unwisely cooked and ate on the sandy beach. Meanwhile a number of armed men, themselves exiles from a later battle-field, but who eventually all perished of hunger, caught sight of Rori. These fugitives were in quest of human flesh, and stealthily approached so near to their intended victim that escape seemed impossible. Rori, perceiving their shadow on the white sand, raised his head, and, to his dismay, saw his foes preparing to spear him from an overhanging crag. With the wonderful instinct of a native, he instantly caught up a cooked fish in one hand and his sandals in the other, and, making a desperate leap, happily succeeded in gaining a projecting point of rock on the side farthest from his pursuers. Running a short distance with his naked feet, he deliberately stopped to fasten on a single sandal; then, holding the other in his hand, he advised his foes to go back, as they would only cut up their feet (they were without sandals) in pursuit of Rori, without catching him. They gave chase, but to no purpose. Rori purposely led them over the worst places, and disappeared from his foes like an apparition.

Seven pitched battles had been fought during the long years of Rori's first exile in the *rdei*. Five times had the brave Ngangati been declared " temporal lord of Mangaia," and at length fell by the hand of the rival chief Akatara, who thus succeeded to the chieftainship. The priestly tribe of Mautara had avenged the death of Ngangati by the well-arranged daylight murder of Akatara. In the battle of Arira that followed, the great tribe of Teipe, of which Akatara had been head, was worsted; the remnant, still powerful in numbers, taking refuge in the " Cave of the Tern, " at Ivirua.

The present chief of this unfortunate class was Ruanae, who had introduced cannibalism, in order to strike terror into the hearts of his victorious enemies. Numerous instances of cannibalism are remembered of solitary hungry fugitives, but Ruanae was the first chief to practise it openly in the presence of his entire tribe.

The chief adviser of Ruanae was old Butai, a near relative of Rori, the only one living who remembered and cared for him. Now, Butai had incurred the hatred of Ruanae by foolishly boasting that, " let worst come to worst, *he* should be safe at the hands of their foes." From that day his fate was sealed, although well known to be " the wise man " of the tribe.

Now, Rori, in his nightly peregrinations, had become increasingly daring; he ventured once as far as the neighbourhood of the " Cave of the Tern," and overheard the gossip of some stragglers. Learning from these unwitting informants that Butai still lived, he made himself known to his relative, and consented to share the waning fortunes of the clan. Although living with Butai in the cave, he wisely forbore to give information of his old hiding-place, as he might have occasion yet to return. It does not appear that Rori had any definite purpose of leaving his old haunts; but upon hearing that Butai, his near relation, was living close by where he had chanced to wander, an irresistible yearning for human society and sympathy induced him at once to join the cannibal clan, although himself not a cannibal.

It so happened that on the day afterwards the entire body of well-armed men left the cave in search of food, leaving the women and children in the care of Butai. About a mile distant, in a sequestered hollow, was a grove of wide-spreading Brazilian plum-trees (*Spondias dulcis*) covered with fruit, so that it must have been the month of February. On account of his lithe and wiry form, Rori was chosen one of the fruit-gatherers. A very large quantity of fruit was obtained and packed in baskets, to be cooked inside the stronghold. Said Ruanae to his cousin Akapautua, "As soon as we get back we will eat that prating old fool Butai, and the new-comer, his relative Rori; for one victim would not be a taste all round." Little did these intended victims imagine that their bodies were to be the relish for these half-ripe plums.

But Akapautua in his heart pitied the unoffending Rori. Without being seen by Ruanae, he contrived, whilst washing his hands at a brook, to give a hint to Rori. As soon as the tribe had arrived at the foot of the long ladder leading to the cave, Rori deposited his basket of fruit on the ground, and, saying to those about him he must collect some dry sticks for the great oven of the clan, disappeared in the bush. Thought Ruanae, "Those sticks will serve nicely for the cooking of Rori himself." But so it was not to be; for Rori darted through the bush as fast as his legs could carry him. The wind bore to the ears of the fugitive the death-wail of old Butai, "Aue tou e! Ka mate au e?" (Alas! alas! Must I, too, die?)

Congratulating himself on his narrow escape, Rori did not stop his flight until he knew that he was beyond pursuit. Embittered at heart at this brief sojourn amongst mankind, he once more made his home in his old quarters in the desolate *rdei*, where he could live comparatively without fear, for it was difficult to take him by surprise.

One good resulted from his short residence with Ruanae's clan in the stronghold—he became acquainted with Manaune, at that time a mere youth.

It was after this narrow escape of Rori that Manaune was adopted into the winning tribe of the priest Mautara, and so rose to power and fame.

To Rori's apprehension every human face was that of a foe bent on his destruction, and doubtless intending to cook and eat him. He resolved to end his days where he had so long lived, in the "wild black rocks." Years passed on during this second flight to the *rdei;* two more pitched battles were fought, of which our hero was happily ignorant. The cannibal tribe of Ruanae had been swept utterly out of existence. Again had the chieftainship of the island changed hands, while Rori lived on in his wild home. Only once before during these long years had the drum of peace been beaten, making it safe for a poor fugitive like him to enter the interior of the island by daylight, and yet live. *Altogether Rori could not have spent less than thirty years in his solitary residence among the rocks;* and when eventually he returned to the interior he had not a single relative living !

Tenanuku and Raumea were dead. Their clever father, the priest Mautara, now held undisputed sway over the island. Peace reigned; consequently food became plentiful again. But Rori was still in the old place in the rocks, ignorant of this, and dreading every human being.

He had, however, grown less careful of himself. One evening, as he approached the outskirts of his barren domain, he saw a number of women going to fish by torchlight on the reef. He hid himself near the beach until they returned, and had, according to custom, cooked and eaten part of their fish, and then returned to the interior. As soon as the women had disappeared, he went to pick up the morsels of fish and ends of taro,—food untasted by him for many a long year. Whilst thus engaged, two men—one of whom was the Manaune he had become acquainted with in the "Cave of the Tern"—passed along the reef with scoop-nets in their hands. They caught sight of a wild-looking elderly fellow entirely absorbed in consuming his dainty meal of odds and ends. They advanced in perfect silence towards him, and when tolerably near ran to catch Rori, who started to his feet, and with his ancient agility leaped on the rocks. He could now easily escape, as he had no equal in the art of running. Manaune now saw that this bird of the desert was his old acquaintance Rori, who was supposed to have perished with the scattered remnants of Ruanae's cannibal clan. Knowing that he possessed the invaluable secret of working in wood and stone and sennit, he earnestly called out to him, "Rori, come back and carve my god for me." The fugitive, astounded at the mention of his name and craft, stood a second to inquire who was lord of Mangaia, and whether the drum of peace had been beaten. Finding that Mautara was chief, and that perfect peace prevailed, he altered his purpose of flight, and, descending from the cliff, gave himself up to Manaune.

Fishing was out of the question now. All three made their way to the beautiful valley of Ivirua, where the lands of the chief Manaune were situated. The pathway from the sea was that by which the writer gained the interior, after his expedition to the home of Rori in the "wild black rocks." The welkin rang with merry shouts of "*Kua tau mai Rori!*" (Rori is found!) The news spread all over the island the same day, so that crowds came to see this poor fellow. And a miserable skeleton he was, his skin almost black through continual exposure. A feast was made for him by the people of Ivirua, but he scarcely tasted the unaccustomed food. He was then led in procession round the island by his protector and others; the crowning point was for him to bathe in "Rongo's sacred fountain," in token of his being cleansed from a state of bondage and fear, and being allowed to participate freely in all the good things of the dominant tribe.

A day or two afterwards he went back to his old haunts in the rocks, to say farewell to the guardian deities of the *rāei*, to look after his old feathery friends, and to bring away as much as he could of the treasures he had accumulated during his long residence there. Many subsequent visits did he pay, until all his stone adzes, pestles, and feathers were removed,—a fortune in those days.

When he first took up his abode in the rocky wilderness he could not well have been more than eighteen years old. He came back with a large sprinkling of grey hairs.

A granddaughter of Mautara, named Motia, was given to Rori as his wife. By her he had several children. The spot

where his house stood is still pointed out; and a number of
ancient cocoanut-trees, planted by Manaune a little before his
discovery and adoption, are still growing. These palms, about
106 feet in height, are the oldest on the island.

His employment now was to instruct the young men of the
time in the art of carving, plaiting sennit, the manufacture of
adzes, and the building of houses. He not only carved Tiaio,
the god of his friend Manaune, but all (excepting Teipe) the
other gods of Mangaia, once kept in the idol-house of the king,
but about fifty years since removed by the Rev. J. Williams to
the museum of the London Missionary Society. During Rori's
residence in the rocks the former idols had all been destroyed
by fire—a significant hint that, being thus unable unitedly to
take care of themselves, they could still less succour those who
trusted in them.

Beautiful red parrakeet feathers, brought to this island by
his grandfather, and concealed with Rori's other treasures in the
rŵei, were used by him to adorn Motoro, to the great admiration
of the men of that day. His last great work was to build a
temple to Tanè, supported by a single post. This temple had
just been completed at the time of Captain Cook's visit in 1777.
Rori lived happily with his family in the district generously
assigned to him by Manaune, and died at a very advanced age.

Some years afterwards his sons resolved to celebrate the
sufferings and happy escape of their father in "*e tara kakai,*"
or "death-talk." The food was planted for the feast, and most
of the songs got ready, when war again broke out. In the battle
of Akaoro, which followed, three grown-up sons were slain.
Contrary to promise to their mother, they took up arms against
her clan. Hence it is said that when Motia heard of their
death she refused to weep, and cursed their memory!

The intended "death-talk" *in memoriam* never came off, and
most of the songs were forgotten; but the story of Rori will
never be forgotten, so long as there exists a native of Mangaia.

Two younger sons of Rori did not go to battle, and consequently were allowed to live as slaves to the victors. There is
now living a venerable man, Vainekavoro, about ninety-five years
of age, who was born just after the said battle. It is certain,
therefore, that the three sons of Rori fell about 1780. The
heirlooms of the family were hidden in a cave, to which the only

means of access was by holding on to the roots of a banyan-tree which, like a strong cable, ran over the precipice to the soil below in a deep fertile gorge. A lad, hunting for bats to eat, saw a number hanging from a tree, paralyzed with the cold of early morning, and in climbing discovered grand head-dresses, wooden drums, adzes, and sennit. These were the property of the slain sons of the hermit of the *rdei*.

The most popular of the songs about Rori is the following:—

RORI HIDING IN THE ROCKS.

TUMU.	INTRODUCTION.
Mâueue te taua ê,	Mâueue was the battle-field,
E taua puruki na Arekare,	The fighting-ground of Arekare,
I ao ei Rori i te makatea,	When the fugitive Rori fled to the rocks,
Kua oki au ki miri:	Everything was lost ;
Kua piri atu ki te rau puka ê!	My home was where the laurel-trees grow.

PAPA.	FOUNDATION.
Akatu koe i toou are, e Rori ê,	Thou buildedst thy house, O Rori,
Te are rau kotaa e!	Thatched with broad fern-leaves ;
Noo mai koe i te râei i Mataorongo.	Thy home was in the rocks of Matao-
Kua tupu te mato ia Maurangi ê!	rongo until
Aere, akatu are i nunga i te râei ê!	The *very stones grew* in the presence of
	the Rockite,[1]
	So long was thy home in the *rdei !*

UNUUNU TAI.	FIRST OFFSHOOT.
Mâueue ra te taua nei ê,	Mâueue was the battle-field,—
Te taua e puruki mataati,	That unfortunate battle-field,
E paeke to vaevae, paeke to vaevae, e	When Rori became a fugitive, a poor
Rori ;	fugitive.
Kave atu te riri i Akatangiateriro,	Thou didst thy best on the hill-slope,
Kia kite atu i tau metua.	Once more to see thy father.
Kua oki au ki miri,	Everything was lost ;
Kua piri atu ki te rau puka ê!	My home was where the laurel-trees grow.

UNUUNU RUA.	SECOND OFFSHOOT.
Kukupa te manu ra e tangi nei ê,	The cooing of doves was thy only music,
E tangi nei i nunga i tau tukiavake,—	Sounding warnings over thy head,—
Tau tukiavake!	Over thy devoted head!
Ko te râi pare koe e karanga nei.	In pity they called to thee ;—
Tai ataai na Temakavetai ia Maurangi ;	Sent by Temakavetai to save the Rockite.
Kua oki au ki miri,	Everything was lost ;
Kua piri atu ki te rau puka ê!	My home was where the laurel-trees grow.

[1] Rori was originally named Barapu—"West." Whilst yet living peacefully in his father's house, a little sister died through eating a poisonous *rori* (*bêche de mer*). To evince his grief at her loss, he thenceforth assumed the name of the poisonous fish *Rori* (all *roris* are not poisonous ; the poison arises from the sort of food they have been devouring). After his return to the interior he was nicknamed "The Rockite" (Maurangi), in allusion to his long residence in the rocks. In his death-lament only the latter names occur.

Unuunu Toru.

U, kua tu ei to are,
Are raukapakapa kotaa ô !
   Kua kapitia e te ua,
Kapitia Rori e te ua nui i te rôei ô !
E noa te tamaka e nere ei i te rangi piri ô !
   Kua oki au ki miri,
Kua piri atu ki te rau puka ô !

Third Offshoot.

Ah ! such a miserable hut—
A single side covered with fern !
   Oft wast thou drenched ;
Often was Rori drenched with heavy
   showers.
Rori's sandals were of banyan bark for
   the hour of peril.
   Everything was lost ;
My home was where the laurel-trees grow.

Unuunu A.

Kapara te ii e, i te piaki ô,
I te piaki koi aere atu i te kapara o te ii,
   Koi aere atu a Maurangi e,
E i te ngai tapureu atu i reira,
   Kua kapitia e te ao.
   Kua oki au ki miri,
Kua piri atu ki te rau puka ô !

Fourth Offshoot.

Ripe chestnuts covered the vale ;
In that vale thou didst gather the ripe
   nuts ;
Laboriously were they gathered by the
   Rockite ;
And ofttimes ere they were cooked
   Grey dawn surprised thee.
   Everything was lost ;
My home was where the laurel-trees grow.

Unuunu Rima.

Kakea i nunga i te rôei ô !
I te rôei i Mataorongo,
I nunga i te tau are o Ue na,
Te reira nga vairanga i te kura ô !
   Kua oki au ki miri,
Kua piri atu ki te rau puka ô !

Fifth Offshoot.

Thou didst roam o'er the sharp-pointed
   rocks,
The sharp-pointed rocks of Mataorongo,[1]
Near the ancient home of Ue.
'Twas there thou didst hide thy treasures.
   Everything was lost ;
My home was where the laurel-trees grow.

Akareinga.

Ai e ruaoo ê !   E rangai ô !

Finale.

Ai e ruaoo ô !   E rangai ê !

The companion song of the foregoing is not destitute of interest :—

RORI PROSPEROUS IN THE INTERIOR.

Tumu.

Akatauria i te tura,
I te kainga ia Manaune,
Kua anau te tama.
Tai piritanga i maru ai au ô !

Introduction.

Kindly succoured by a friend,
On the lands of Manaune,
Rori reared up a family.
Oh for a rock [2] under whose shadow I
   might rest !

---

[1] " Mata-o-Rongo " is a general name for the east of Mangaia ; it means literally " the-face-of-the-god-Rongo," because originally his *marae* and sandstone image were there, face towards the sunrising ; but were subsequently removed to the west. The reason alleged for the change was that the afternoon's sun burnt his back.

The present generation have taken such an interest in the adventures of Rori that scores have lately visited the lonely *rôei*, hunting after memorials of the fugitive. Not content with surveying the interesting spot, they have pulled up the neatly-built flooring, in the vain hope of finding some of his famous stone axes ; *as if* he would have left such precious property behind him, having now a secure home in the interior in the midst of plenty ! Bits of flint and basalt left by him are plentiful enough.

[2] The " rock " so long wished for was Manaune, under whose " shadow " Rori lived happily in later years.

PAPA.

Tai tuamata i kite ia Ruanae,
O te rangi piri tei ia Aro.
Kau mai Rori i te uru enua
Ia Mangaia : kua ngara ua i te mate.
Ka piri i te rau puka i tangi e !

FOUNDATION.

A curse upon thee, Ruanae !
And on all thy warrior friends ;
Rori has again set foot in the interior
Of Mangaia : he who once seemed doomed
    to die,
A fugitive hiding in the rustling forest.

UNUUNU TAI.

Akatauria i te tura, i te tura e !
    I te kainga ia Manaune,
Kua anau te tama, kua anau te tama.
Ko Amio i te atu e Rori
    Naai e rave ake ?
Tai piritanga i maru ai au e !

FIRST OFFSHOOT.

Kindly succoured by a friend,—such a
    friend,
    On the lands of Manaune,
Rori reared up a numerous family ;
Yet still laments for his sister Amio,
    On whom none took pity.
Oh for a rock under whose shadow I might
    rest !

UNUUNU RUA.

Kauanga kore, tavare onge,
Kua noo Rori i te toko pe
In Maruata : naai e rave ake ?
Tai piritanga i maru ai au e !

SECOND OFFSHOOT.

Utterly friendless and starving,—
Thy god, Rori, proved but a rotten stick,[1]
E'en as Maruata's, who left *him* to die.
Oh for a rock under whose shadow I might
    rest !

UNUUNU TORU.

Moemoe rango e, i te ana roa e !
    I te ana roa i Turu-atua.
Kua tae to eka, kua puapua to ina,
    I te ruaine metua,—
I te ruaine metua noou, e Barapu
Tai piritanga i maru ai au e !

THIRD OFFSHOOT.

Thy bed was at the entrance of a deep cave,
A cave hard to discover in the rocks ;
Thou wast wearied out with thy long re-
    sidence,
Grey hairs had made their appearance ;
Old age was fast creeping upon thee,
    Barapu.
Oh for a rock under whose shadow I might
    rest !

AKAREINGA.

Ai e ruaoo e ! E rangai e !

FINALE.

Ai e ruaroo e ! E rangai e !

---

[1] A *god* was usually designated a "stick," or support, on which the worshippers were accustomed to lean. The unknown poet considers that Rori's own god Teipe had left him in the lurch, *almost* as badly as Maruata, and in his descendants, who generation after generation 'were offered in sacrifice to Rongo. As the god's name, Teipe, means "the rotten one," it almost reads like a pun : I think this was the design of the poet.

CHAPTER XXIX.

SELF-SACRIFICE.

A YEAR or two previously to Captain Cook's visit to this island, a canoe, with half a dozen men on board, sailed from Aitutaki to Manuae (Hervey's Island), a distance of fifty-five miles, in order to collect red parrakeet feathers. Having succeeded in their object, after a brief stay on Manuae they started upon their return voyage, but were driven out of their course by strong contrary winds. After a few days, food and water began to fail, and a miserable death stared them in the face.

Routu, the commander of the canoe, now addressed his companions,—"I see why we are thus driven about over the ocean by unfavourable winds. We have sinned in taking away the sacred red parrakeet feathers. A costly sacrifice is demanded by the angry gods. Throw me into the sea, and you will yet safely reach home."

Very sadly the voyagers, as their last chance for life, complied with this request, and Routu speedily disappeared in the unknown depth of the ocean.

The question now arose, Who should be captain? Tamacu, son of the drowned Routu, said, "I will be captain. My father taught me the course by the stars." The others looked upon this as a piece of presumption on the part of so young a man; but Tamacu persisted, and they yielded out of respect to the memory of Routu.

That same night the anxious captain roused his sleeping companions with the remarkable words, "Wake up, friends; we have reached 'Mangaia-Nui-Neneva!'" The canoe had happily drifted to the southern side of Mangaia. A number of women engaged in torch-fishing on the reef at once fled to the interior at the sight of strangers, fearing they might be slain.

Tamacu and his companions, having hauled up the canoe, followed the retreating lights, but missed the true path. To aid their painful progress over the extremely rugged rocks on that part of the island, the visitors built up part of the road. Through the livelong night, notwithstanding the moon had risen, they succeeded in travelling but half a mile.

On the following morning the islanders came down in search of the intruders, intending to exterminate them. They were found fast asleep on the rocks, with their priceless parrakeet feathers concealed in calabashes between their legs. For the first time in the modern history of these islanders they pitied their defenceless visitors, hoping to share their treasures. This was doubtless owing to their inconsiderable numbers.

These Aitutakians remained some months on the island, and built a *marae*, on which human sacrifices were subsequently offered. It is said that Tamacu first called this island by its present name, " Mangaia-Nui-Neneva"—"Mangaia Monstrously Great," which suited the fancy of the men of that day, and almost supplanted its original designation " Auau."

The path which the Aitutakians traversed that night bears the appropriate name " Bad Road " (Arakino) ; the part built up by them is known as "the work of the visitors" (*koro o te manuiri*). Eventually, Tamacu and his companions safely got back to their own pretty island-home, thus realizing the prediction of Routu.

The beautiful red feathers presented to those who had so kindly entertained them were collected and put on their god Motoro. When that idol was given up to Mr. Williams these identical red feathers adorned it.

It is to this Tamacu that reference is made in the song of Captain Cook.

CHAPTER XXX.

CAPTAIN COOK'S VISIT TO MANGAIA.

WHILE conversing with one of my native teachers (a very intelligent man) and another native of this island respecting Captain Cook's visit to Mangaia in 1777, I showed them a picture (from "Cook's Voyages") of Mouroa,[1] the only Mangaian who ventured on board his ship. Mouroa is a fierce-looking fellow, with a knife stuck in his right ear, and wearing a beard. They said, what I had often heard before, that they had never heard of *Mouroa's* going on board Tute's (Cook's) ship; but that everybody on the island knows that *Kavoro* was the bold fellow who ventured on board the first ship that ever touched at Mangaia. They stated that this Kavoro received from Captain Cook an axe, a knife, some large beads and nails, and a few yards of print. At the date of our first landing, in 1852, the axe and knife were in existence. The blue beads were especially valued; they were buried, as a mark of great distinction, with a woman named Rimarima.

I have remarked above that, beside the teacher, another native of this island was present. That other native is a grandson of Kavoro, who went on board the "Resolution" March 29th, 1777. I asked him to relate the native tradition of Cook's visit to this island. The tradition coincided with the printed account in the "Voyages," with but few variations. For example, only one ship is mentioned in the tradition; whereas the "Resolution" and the "Discovery" visited Mangaia. I find, too, that the native of Raiātea (Ulietea in the "Voyages"), called "Omai" in Captain Cook's account, who was the medium of communication with these islanders, is in the tradition called Mâ-i. Mâ-i, in the Hervey Group dialect, is written without a break—Maki—and signifies "sick," a very common name indeed throughout these islands; I dare say we have a dozen or two of that name

---

[1] The natives of Mangaia were much surprised that I possessed a minute printed account of the transactions of March 29 and 30, 1777, and still more to find that there exists a portrait of their savage countryman Mourua.

on this island alone. The "O" is simply a prefix to a proper name, not by any means a part of it. Thus "Otaheite" is now more correctly written "Tahiti." The only remaining difference between the native tradition and the printed account is that the man who went on board the "Resolution" is named by Cook "Mourooa;" whereas the natives of Mangaia insist that his name was Kavoro. Feeling sure that, like most of his living countrymen, he had two or more names, I inquired whether Kavoro might not have been also named Mourooa or Mourua. Kavoro's grandson now recollected an old lament about this man, beginning thus :—

> Mourua, burning star of heaven, how pleasant in life!
> Grief fills thy widow as she turns (on her pillow).

The natives now found that Mourooa and Kavoro were identical, and that their missionary had a veritable likeness of this celebrated native. The news brought great numbers from all parts of the island eager to get a sight of Mourua (or Mourooa) and his distinguished friend Captain Cook. Some old men remarked that the peculiar short twist of his hair was an invention of Mourua's to prevent his being caught by the head when fighting, and so put to death.

Captain Cook mentions a scar on the forehead of this native (which does not, however, appear in the portrait lying before me). Mourua got it by fighting — not with invaders from another island, but with a tribe of his own countrymen living at Tamarua. These hostile natives had been cutting down wood for a canoe in one of the valleys. Mourua, and his companion Kirikovi, were walking along the ridge of hill above, unconscious of danger. So good an opportunity of destroying a foe was not to be lost. Overpowered by numbers, they were left for dead ; but their loud cries ere they fell brought help. On coming up with Mourua and Kirikovi, their people found them insensible, with terrible gashes on the forehead. The father of one of them pulled out by the roots the hair on the great toes. A slight vibration of the foot assured him that life was not extinct. Both ultimately recovered ; and the spot, which I have visited, is known as the "fighting-ground of Kirikovi." This Kirikovi afterwards became "lord (or great chief) of Mangaia."

Mourua took his new name—the name by which everybody on Mangaia knows him—Kavoro—*i.e.*, "skin and bones"—on account of the death of his mother, who wasted away to a skeleton. To the great English navigator he appeared to be a very docile, agreeable fellow. His real character will appear by the following anecdote : Mourua had a sister named Teão, who married Moenga, a member of the very tribe who handled him so roughly on the mountain ridge. The head-quarters of that tribe were at the "Cave of Tautua." Mourua went to the mouth of the cave professedly to pay his brother-in-law a friendly visit. They met. Mourua told his relative that if he would meet him the following evening at dusk at a certain place he would give him a valuable stone axe. The bait took. At the appointed hour Mourua met his sister and her husband. Moenga was delighted with his beautiful stone adze ; but, whilst bending over it, found his flowing raven hair seized by his powerful and pitiless brother-in-law. The poor fellow struggled hard for dear life, but in vain. Teão, horrified at this tragedy, rushed in obedience to her husband's dying word to the cave, to seek protection from her husband's relatives from the cruelty of her own brother Mourua, who afterwards confessed that he intended to murder both that fearful night. That his sister Teão had married one of the hated tribe who attacked him many years before on the mountains was with him sufficient reason why she should die : she happily escaped.

Mourua had a very pretty daughter, named Kurakaau. Tradition says that the crafty parent was very anxious to get Captain Cook to come on shore and become his son-in-law. Through this projected splendid alliance he hoped to become all-powerful among his countrymen. However, the great navigator declined the proposal. He sent a few yards of print to furnish Kurakaau with a decent dress.

Mourua was, after his fashion, very devout. Captain Cook correctly guessed that he had invoked the protection of his idol god ere he ventured to take hold of the line thrown to him from the stern of the "Resolution." That idol, named Motoro, is a rude representation of the human form, carved in ironwood.

My own impression is, that the captain would never have got off alive again had he taken Mourua's advice in coming ashore. There being no boat harbour, he must have trusted himself entirely to the tender mercies of the heathen, and they are cruel.

After a life of bloodshed, Mourua was murdered on a sandy

beach, about one hundred yards from our island residence. He was one of a party of five who had been fishing. They had returned, and were asleep when their foes surrounded the house. Only one escaped, by creeping through the legs of the attacking party. Three were speedily despatched, but still Mourua struggled hard with his cruel foes. Whilst some were vainly endeavouring to twist a cord round his neck to strangle him, another chopped his legs with a large stone adze. This sealed his fate, for he fell. A single blow on the head closed this sad episode of a warrior's life. Mourua perished about two or three years after Captain Cook's visit.

It is not unworthy of remark that the full name of this island (but little known now) is given by Captain Cook with but a slight deviation from the true spelling. This full name, as a native would write it, is *Mangaia Nui Neneva*, which may be translated "*Mangaia, Monstrously Great.*" This is pretty well for a little island about twenty miles in circuit. We had lived amongst these people more than fourteen years before I learnt the full name from the lips of an old man, who was reciting to me a scrap of an ancient song in which the name occurs. This is a striking proof of the general correctness of the observations made by the illustrious Cook.

On sailing from Atiu, the natives asked where he had come from. He told them " From Mangaia." The Atiuans called it by the queer-looking designation of " Owhavarouah," which, being so dissimilar from Mangaia, Cook conjectured (very naturally) to be the name of another island contiguous to Mangaia. Such, however, is not the case—it is only an ancient name of this island. It should be written "Auau," the "O" being merely the prefix to *all* proper names preceding the verb. I may remark in passing that "Auau" means "terraced." Mangaia signifies "*peace.*"

Some of our teachers have lately come back from the Loyalty Islands. I asked one of them, who has laboured long and usefully in that group, where the natives of those islands got their pigs from. The reply was, " From Tute (Cook), the first white man they ever saw." Tute's name is preserved, amid a vast variety of dialects, in these Southern Seas, as the material benefactor of the natives. A dog was the only animal that he left in the Hervey Group.

A LAMENT FOR MOURUA.

Pertaining to "the Death-talk of Vaepae," in the reign of Kirikovi, *circa* A.D. 1774.

TUMU.

Mourua! te etu ka i te rangi ê!
Kua reka te taa ora.
Ua tangi rai to vaine e uri mai ei!

INTRODUCTION.

Mourua, burning star of heaven,
How pleasant in life!
Grief fills thy widow as she turns (on her pillow).

PAPA.

Ko te atiu mua na Vaepae ê!
Ua riro te au inia ;
Ua mou paa i te mouranga,
I Auau no Motoro.
Ua ta ê! Te rû i mou ki tau rûma ê!

FOUNDATION.

Beloved son of Vaepae,
Victorious in battle,
Hold firmly thy own,
Won in Auau through Motoro.
Thou hast slain, in the day of thy strength.

INUINU MUA.

I tangi, i tangi atu ki te tama ê!
Tama û Vaepae. Ua punipuni aere ê!
*Kia punipuni aere kia ugaro paa raua.
Tei Aramoi te rua i te piritanga ê!
Ko te piritanga akera ê!
Ua tangi rai to vaine e uri mai ei!

FIRST OFFSHOOT.

Weep, weep for the eldest son!
Son of Vaepae, hiding himself—
*Hiding himself, perchance with his father,
In Aramui, the unknown cave.
Yonder is that cave.
Grief fills thy widow as she turns (on her pillow).

INUINU RUA.

Ii rare i te karanga ê!
Karanga'i i Bukamaru—
Ua taiku. E autaa ê!
*E ano rai i reira.
E ano rai i reira. Aea'i?
Apopo taua e ana atu, ana mai.
Ana mai. E rua ê!
Ua tangi rai to vaine e uri mai ei!

SECOND OFFSHOOT.

How they startle at the call,
The call from Bukamaru—
The shout. Yonder ones!
*Thither let us go (*i.e.*, to take food),
Thither let us go. Ah, when indeed?
To-morrow we will go and return.—
Come back, my husband, come back.
Grief fills thy widow as she turns (on her pillow).

INUINU TORU.

Eke e, eke atura ki tai ê!
Te tai i te kavakava ê!
Ua mana ia Rongo
Ua mana koe i te koatu Ovaiomaao.
Ei ara paa no taua—
E aere ei ki te rau puka.
Ua ao eera ê!
Ua tangi rai to vaine e uri mai ei!

THIRD OFFSHOOT.

Go, go to the shore,
The shore by the valley.
Mighty art thou by the power of Rongo,
Mighty by the stone (idol) Ovaiomaao—
The protector of us both,
As we walk where the laurel-trees grow.
Daylight dawns.
Grief fills thy widow as she turns (on her pillow).

INUINU A.

Aengara te ata ê!
Ata ka mârama
E tu ra e tama ê!
Ua ao ê! Ua iterere i te moe.
Iterere ake Kavoro nei i tana moe.
Ua mou te tamaka e!
Te mua oki te mate,
Ua tangi rai ki tona tama, e uri mai ei!

FOURTH OFFSHOOT.

The shadows of night are breaking!
Light is increasing.
Rise, eldest son,
It is day. He has risen from sleep.
Kavoro has risen from sleep.
His feet are sandalled.
But death is at hand.
Grieves for her eldest son as she turns (on her pillow).

AKARPINGA.

Ai e ruaoo ê! E rangai ê!

FINALE.

Ai e ruaoo ê! E rangai ê!

This lament refers to a disastrous period of his life, when Mourua was a fugitive hiding in a cavern. It may seem strange for a wife to address her deceased husband as "the eldest son" ("c tama c"); but it is common, and is a mark of respect. In the lament two parties would be engaged. The song would be recited slowly, in a plaintive voice. At two points (marked by me with asterisks) both companies—*i.e.*, the men and the women—would wail loudly in unison. Although a lament for the dead, there is no reference to the future; for the obvious reason, it was altogether too gloomy and uncertain a topic for a heathen to dwell upon. "Without hope in the world!"

After the lapse of some ninety-eight years this song is for the first time written. In quoting from it, a native would give not only the words, but the stanza in which the words occur. In some such way as this all the remains of extreme antiquity (as the Homeric poems) must have been handed down from generation to generation.

CHAPTER XXXI.

THE DRAMA OF COOK.

THE following song is a pantomimic description of Captain Cook's visit to Mangaia. For several years after that event constant wars prevented the more agreeable employment of song-making. But when peace had at length been secured and plenty reigned in consequence, a chief named Poito resolved to give a grand feast, with the indispensable accompaniment of dancing and music. A level spot was selected for the festival and carefully weeded. From one end to the other, a spacious canopy of plaited green cocoanut-leaves protected the many hundreds present from the heavy dews of night,—as such entertainments never took place by day. Men only, or women only, not men *and* women, might take part in the dance and song. Sometimes men danced, and women held the flambeaux. At other times women danced, and men held the torches. Poito's dance was for men, numbering, it is said, nearly two hundred; the entire remaining population being present as spectators and as flambeaux-holders. Twenty songs were required for one *fête:* these songs were usually encored. At sunset the performance began, and continued till midnight, when refreshment was taken, and once more the entertainment proceeded. As soon as the day-star appeared, the last song (reserved for the purpose) and the last dance were gone through, and the whole concluded. Six artists were usually employed to compose the songs, and to arrange the whole proceedings.

The words were slowly chanted in a pleasing though monotonous tone; sometimes by the master of the ceremonies only, who stood on an elevated platform, and sometimes by all the performers. In what is termed " the introduction," no musical instruments were employed, and consequently the dancing, which was to keep time with the music, had not commenced. The musical accompaniment consisted of a " kaara," or large wooden drum hollowed out of " miro " (*Thespesia populnea*)—a beautiful dark-red wood. It was prettily carved all over, and was suspended from the neck with strong cords, being beaten, not as with us, on the *end*, but in the *centre*, the long slit emitting a considerable volume of sound.

Another sort of drum, called the " paû," was used on such occasions. A round piece of *Thespesia* was dug out at one end, and the aperture covered over with a tight-fitting piece of shark's-skin. It was designed to stand upright. The drum-sticks were the tips of the musician's fingers.

A subsidiary musical instrument was the " riro," a sort of harmonicon, consisting of two pieces of dry hibiscus wood, supported at each end by banana-stalks, and lightly tapped with ironwood sticks.

The great wooden drum used for Poito's dance is still preserved, and is used by the police in drumming their prisoners to court. The " paû " has entirely disappeared. The " riro " now gives amusement only to idle boys. But the dance itself was invariably connected with very serious evils ;[1] so that upon the establishment of Christianity it was entirely abolished. ·

This dramatic song was composed by a warrior named Tioi, who was afterwards slain in battle. It is complete, and is now written for the first time—an interesting proof of the power of memory in thus retaining a song during a period of three generations. It begins with a reference to Tamacu, who drifted here in his canoe from Hervey's Island a year or two before Captain Cook's visit in 1777.

A year was required for getting up one such entertainment, so that the number of such festive occasions served to chronicle the duration of peace. This long interval was required, first, for the making of the songs and the rehearsal of the performers ; secondly, for the growth of taro, &c., &c., requisite for the grand feasting, which is a necessary sequel to any assembly in the mind of a Polynesian ; and, thirdly, for the very important purpose of *blanching the complexions and fattening the persons* of those who were to take part on the occasion. The point of honor was to be the fairest and fattest of any present.

Each such entertainment was in honor of the gods. Thus,

---

[1] The chiefs, whether married or not, often wore phallic ear-ornaments in order to allure the opposite sex. Two of them may be seen in the British Museum.

if the originator were a worshipper of Motoro, all those devoted to the service of that idol would feel bound to take part. In the present instance, the dance was in honor of Tiaio (the shark-god) and Tanè conjointly; consequently the entire body of worshippers of those gods were performers. This inherent idolatrous tendency was one reason for. the suppression of these dramatic efforts.

The fate of Poito, who got up this exhibition, is an instructive picture of heathen life. In his old age a battle took place, in which some of his sons fought with the father, and some on the other side. In the hour of conflict, it was Poito's unhappy fate to find himself opposite to his second son Pakuunga. As there was no retreat, the old man made a faint thrust at his boy; whereat Pakuunga gave his father a lunge, which at once terminated the old man's career! This occurred a few years previous to the landing of the first teachers.

The reader will bear in mind that Captain Cook never set foot on the soil of Mangaia, although very desirous to do so, so forbidding was the aspect of the armed natives.

PE'E MANUIRI.

TUMU.

Chorus.

Koaniia e Tu ma Tangaroa
Ei tia i te aru oa a Tamaeu.
E kutu i te rangi.

Solo.

Nga utu ake utu.

Chorus.

Ngu! Ngu!

Solo.

Nga puru ake puru.

Chorus.

Ngu! Ngu!

THE VISITOR'S SONG.

INTRODUCTION.

Chorus.

Great Tangaroa[1] and Tu assist
In caulking the canoe of Tamaeu.
Oh! the deafening noise (of the workmen)!

Solo.

Caulk[2] the seams.

Chorus.

Aye! Aye!

Solo.

Here is plenty of fibre.

Chorus.

Aye! Aye!

[1] Tangaroa was not worshipped on Mangaia; but, as the god of some other islands, it was supposed that he had led the voyagers to the island.

[2] The individual who uttered the words " Caulk," &c., held in one hand a wooden mallet, and in the other a stone chisel, which he struck vigorously, as if instructing his workmen in the art of caulking canoes with cocoanut fibre. Upon this signal the entire body of performers, uttering simultaneously the cry " Aye, aye," drove stone chisels brought for the purpose into logs of soft wood for the occasion, and extending from one end of the dancing-ground to the other. Canoes were " caulked " from time immemorial. This scene was twice enacted.

Chorus.

Unuia, e Tumatangirua,
I te varo kia rauorooro,
Tauaua i Avarua,
Kia peka te iku i te mataugi.

Chorus in falsetto.

" Nako! Nako ! "
" Iko! Iko ! "

Solo.

Tokonga kumi o Avarua ê.
Tukua maira tai ori i te vaka.

Chorus in falsetto.

" E Bere !³ E Bere !"

" Maîo! Maîo ! "

Chorus.

Ikâ! Kua rau; kua rau
Te toa, te toa. Kua ta, kua ta,
Kua ta Mangaia, kua ta te pai !

Te Karanga Mua.

Solo.

No Tangaroa te vaka :
Kua tere i te aka i te rangi ê !

Chorus.

Grant, O thou ruler of the winds,
That the weather may be propitious,
Surfless be the reef of Avarua,[1]
Compel thy slave to obey.

Chorus in falsetto.

" This way !² This way ! "
" No ; that way, that way ! "

Solo.

O that vast ship off Avarua !
Launch speedily a canoe.

Chorus in falsetto.

(They say :) " We are Britons. We
are Britons."
" Maî, Maî."

Chorus.

We come ; hundreds on hundreds
Of warriors to fight ;⁴—yes, to fight !
The Mangaians will attack and destroy
the ship.

The First Call[5] (for the dance to
lead off).

Solo.

Tangaroa has sent a ship,
Which has burst through the solid blue
vault.

---

[1] " Avarua " is the name of the spot where Cook wished to land.

[2] " This way," &c., grotesquely describes the contradictory directions given to
Captain Cook by the natives as to where he should land. The " falsetto " throughout is an absurd mimicry of the language of the visitors.

[3] " Bere " is a shortened form of " *Beretane*," for the sake of rhythm ; just as
Captain Cook's usual designation, " Tute," is for a similar reason abbreviated to
" *Tu*." " Maî " is of course the " *Omai* " of the " Voyages," to whom the captain
naturally appealed from time to time.

[4] Their aspect was very warlike ; but they wisely abstained from hostilities. The
heathen of Mangaia looked upon all strangers as mortal foes, to be opposed and
slain, if possible. The only exceptions recorded by tradition are those referred to in
this song. Tamaeu and his friends escaped because they carried a priceless treasure
—red parrakeet feathers for adorning the gods. When Mourua found that the
foreigners were after all men like himself, he slapped his thighs, and shouted with
all his might,—

> A mate! A mate !! A mate !!!
> Kia mou! Kia mou !! Kia mou !!!

> Let them die! Let them die !! Let them die !!!
> Seize them! Seize them !! Seize them !!!

It appears, however, that his courage afterwards evaporated.

At the stanza, " We come, hundreds on hundreds," &c., a mimic attack was
made with real spears upon imaginary invaders.

[5] Hitherto *no* drum had been beaten, nor any dancing performed. Hence " the
call " now is for dancing and music, beginning with the words " which has burst
through," &c., and pausing awhile at the word " Britons." After a moment's rest
the master of the ceremonies gives the " *second* call " in a very soft and plaintive
voice : on again pronouncing the words, " which has burst," the whole two hundred
performers were on their feet once more, chanting and performing those remarkable
evolutions which they term a " kapa," or dance. On again uttering the word
" Britons," a slight pause occurred ere " the finale " was gone through.

Solo.

No Maîo tai manuiri ê!

Chorus.

No Tu te tere i tau ê!

Solo.

Koai ma ô?

Chorus.

Tei tai te vaka manuiri a tae,
Ouarauranae!

Solo.

Nai ua rau te vaka ô!
E manuiri. Maîo no toi enua ê!

Solo.

Veroîa!

Chorus.

Veroîa, e Tu, te rua i te matangi,
Tirangoa te moana ia tiai.

Solo.

Terô!

Chorus.

Tero. Tero.

Solo.

Terô!

Chorus.

Aere mai! Aere mai, e Beretane!

TE KARANGA RUA.

Solo.

No Tangaroa te vaka ;
Kua tere i te aka i te rangi ê!

Solo.

No Maîo tai manuiri ê!

Chorus.

No Tu te tere i tau ê!

Solo.

Koai ma ô?.

Chorus.

Tei tai te vaka manuiri a tae.
Ouarauranae!

Solo.

Nai ua rau te vaka ô!
E manuiri. Maîo no tai enua ê!

Solo.

Here is a stranger, Maî.

Chorus.

'Tis Cook, who has paid us a visit.

Solo.

Who has come?

Chorus.

A boat full of guests is here.
What gibberish they talk!

Solo.

Numberless are the boats.
They are foreigners. Maî from some
other land.

Solo.

Blow softly!

Chorus.

Blow softly, ye winds, from your holes,[1]
That the ocean may be smooth.

Solo.

Where are they?

Chorus.

Yonder, yonder.

Solo.

Aye, there they are.

Chorus.

Come on, come on, ye Britons.

THE SECOND CALL (for the dance to
lead off).

Solo.

Tangaroa has sent a ship,
Which has burst through the solid blue
vault.

Solo.

Here is a stranger, Maî.

Chorus.

'Tis Cook, who has paid us a visit.

Solo.

Who has come?

Chorus.

A boat full of guests is here.
What gibberish they talk!

Solo.

Numberless are the boats.
They are foreigners. Maî from some
land.

---

[1] At the edge of the horizon are supposed to be a set of holes, through which the god of the winds amuses himself by blowing away with all his might, often much to the discomfort of mariners. It is hoped that he will be propitious on this occasion.

Solo.

Kiritia!

Chorus.

Kirikiritia atu tai ua manu,
E Tu, kia pârai i te tua o te manuiri.

Solo.

Kua ta te râ e!

Chorus.

Kua ta! Kua ta!

Solo.

Kua ta te râ e!

Chorus in falsetto.

O murenga oa. O murenga oa, e
Beretane!

MAUTU.

Chorus.

E pai parere i tau mai
No tai tuamotu e!

Solo.

E pai kua aa teia?

Chorus.

A! e atua mataku oki.

Solo.

E pai kua aa teia?

Chorus.

Taau ariki o Avarua.
No Tu oki e Maî te râ e!

Solo.

E pai kua aa teia?

Chorus.

E pai omurenga!
Auere toa.

Solo.

Lord of the winds!

Chorus.

Lead forth some bird to settle down
Upon the shoulders of these guests (*i.e.*,
to detain them).

Solo.

Splash[1] go the oars!

Chorus.

Aye, splash, splash.

Solo.

Splash go the oars!

Chorus in falsetto.

They are white-faced—they are white-
faced men and Britons.[2]

CONCLUSION.

Chorus.

A people of a strange tongue have arrived
From some distant land.

Solo.

Of what sort are they?

Chorus.

Oh! they are a godlike race.

Solo.

Of what sort are they?

Chorus.

A great chief is off Avarua.
The ship belongs to Cook and Maî.

Solo.

Of what sort are they?

Chorus.

A people with white faces.
Unheard-of event!

---

[1] "Splash go the oars." At this stage of the entertainment, a mimic rowing takes place with the arms. The way in which Europeans handled oars was a very wonderful thing in the eyes of the men of that day.

[2] It is interesting to find that the name "Beretane," or "Britain," was enshrined in the native dialect long before the first preachers of the Gospel had set foot on any of these islands.

16

CHAPTER XXXII.

The island of Atiu, called "Wateeoo" by Cook, lies a hundred and twenty miles north of Mangaia. These are the twin islands of the Hervey Group, being nearly alike in height, shape, extent, geological formation, and products. It is remarkable that the great navigator, in sailing from New Zealand, should discover in succession Mangaia, Atiu, Takutea (spelt "Otakootaia" in the "Voyages"), Manuae, or Hervey's Island, and, lastly, Palmerston's Island, and yet miss the only two rich and fertile islands of the group (Rarotonga and Aitutaki), possessed of harbours and capable of furnishing all the supplies urgently needed by the "Resolution" and "Discovery." During a recent visit to Atiu I inquired of some aged men what their fathers, who had seen Captain Cook, had told them of the first visit of white men to their rugged coral shores. Their verbal account agreed well with the printed narrative, with a few additional particulars.

Atiu was sighted March 31st, 1777. On the following day Lieutenant Gore, of the "Discovery," landed on the southern shore at an indenture in the reef called "Orovaru," which the natives pointed out to me. Thence the visitors were conducted to the interior by a passable road, and all honor shown to them. That the people would have forcibly detained their wondrously fair-skinned friends but for the extravagant statements given by Maî (Omai, the interpreter) of the prowess of Europeans, and the effect of firearms, is certain.

The natives of Atiu pretended to be greatly surprised at the question whether they ever ate human flesh. Many now living have confessed to me that they had often gorged themselves therewith. A native of the neighbouring island of Mauke told me that in 1819 most of his countrymen were slain and devoured by the victorious Atiuans. The people of Mitiaro were similarly treated by the "meek-faced Atiuans," as they amusingly nickname themselves.

Originally there was but one chief on Atiu. At the period of Cook's visit there were two possessed of equal authority—viz., Tiaputa and Tangapatolo.

Captain Cook did not go ashore himself. On Lieutenant Gore's landing, the chiefs asked him, amongst other things, "Are you one of the glorious sons of Tetumu? Are you a son of the Great Root or Cause, whose children are half divine, half human?" According to their mythology, Tetumu was the father of gods and men, and the maker of all things. The white complexion of the visitors, their wonderful clothing and weapons, all indicated, in their opinion, a divine origin. To these inquiries no reply was given; in all probability they were unintelligible to Maî as well as to Lieutenant Gore.

On that memorable day the strangers were the guests of Tiaputa, who ordered the dances and other amusements in honor of the occasion. The *kava* - drinking, the nectar of the Polynesian gods, and the feasting were extravagant. Forty pigs, mostly small, were cooked and presented to their visitors, who were led to the *marae*, where a sort of worship was paid to them as the favoured children of Tetumu.

The Atiuans maintain that the ships were four days off their island, whereas the "Voyages" seemingly give an account of the transactions of a single day. But if we recollect that the uninhabited islet of Takutea (where Cook took in a supply of cocoanuts, &c.) is regarded by the Atiuans as an integral portion of their own territory, only separated from the main island by a narrow channel of fourteen miles, the discrepancy vanishes. Atiu was sighted March 31st, and sail was finally made from Takutea April 3rd, proving the correctness of the native tradition.

A curious heathen prophecy[1] was known to these islanders previous to the discovery of Atiu by Captain Cook. A god named "Tanè-mei-tai" — "Tanè-out-of-the-ocean" — would some day visit their shores. This new divinity would speak a strange language, would introduce strange articles and customs, and would ill-treat the natives. This oracle was at once applied to their illustrious visitors, so that no little distrust and fear

---

[1] The old men of Rarotonga invariably apply to Christianity the following ancient oracle : "Yonder are the children of God, floating over the ocean like birds on drift cocoanut fronds—some are in advance, and others are following!"

mingled with the pleasure of seeing "Tute." "Tanè" was regarded as one of the "glorious sons of Tetumu." Hence the appropriateness of the question proposed to Lieutenant Gore upon his arrival.

For the first time they now became acquainted with the exist-ence of a race entirely different from their own. Many were the gifts bestowed upon these islanders in return for their hos-pitality, such as beads, iron nails, knives, strips of cloth, and several iron axes, exactly corresponding with that given to Kiri-kovi, the warrior chief of Mangaia, a few days before. The crowning present of all was Maî's dog, the first ever seen in the Hervey Group.

Captain Cook expresses his astonishment at their "incredible ignorance" in making the "strange mistake" of calling the sheep and goats on board the "Resolution" "birds." The word actually used by them was "manu," which means any living thing moving on the earth or through the air. The term is frequently applied to human beings, so that the Atiuans were strictly correct.

It is much to be regretted that the great navigator and his officers never gave them a hint as to the existence of the One living and true God. It was not until forty-six years after that the Gospel was introduced to Atiu by the martyr of Eromanga. The idols so long cherished and worshipped, as visible repre-sentations of the invisible and glorious sons of the unworshipped Tetumu, were speedily given up. Some were burnt; others are now, and long have been, in the museum of the London Mis-sionary Society. Amongst the latter is the famous Terongo, to whose *marae* the guests were taken.

Atiu is said to be the name of the first man on the island. A singular myth is related in reference to this Adam of Atiu. A pigeon, the pet bird of Tangaroa, sped hither from spirit-land, and rested awhile in a grotto still known as "the Pigeon's Fountain." Big drops of water kept falling from the stony roof, producing little eddies in the transparent water beneath. As the pigeon was refreshing itself by sipping the cool liquid, it noticed a female shadow of great beauty in the fountain. Now the pigeon of Tangaroa was in reality one of the gods, and there-fore readily embraced the lovely shadow, and then returned to its home in nether-land. The child thus originated was named

" Atiu "—" First-fruit," or " Eldest-born "—and from him the island derives its name. It was on this account that "they dignified their island with the appellation of ' A Land of Gods,' esteeming themselves a sort of divinities, and possessed with the spirit of the gods."

The double canoes of Atiu are usually fifty feet in length, provided with a mast and mat sails. The cordage is made of the bark of the lemon hibiscus. As many as a hundred and fifty men, women, and children are often accommodated on board one of these primitive vessels. In launching them, one may still hear the following song referring to Captain Cook's visit to Atiu. It was composed somewhere about the year 1780 :—

ATIUAN CANOE SONG.

SOLO.

Tuku ake au o Tahiti Nui,
O arina, O Tu-papa, O Tangaroa,
Mea ò, kua oti.

CHORUS.

Reti ê!

SOLO.

E te tupu ò, kua oti.

CHOUUS.

Roti ê!

SOLO.

Tangi mai te pupui, te pupui,
Te pupui iea?
Te pupui i teimaa ê!
I teimaa iea?
I te teimaa i nga tamariki.
Tuoro mai i te pai o Tute ra ê!
Ritana.

CHORUS.

Ae, ritana, ritana!

SOLO.

Tuoro, tuoro atu iea?
Tuoro atura i te kiato mua ia Otu,
Tangi mai i te tangotango,
Taku rakau mei apitia ;
Mei ia tauae te vaka ê!
Tavai te ruê!

CHORUS.

Tavai te ruê!

SOLO.

I sail to Great[1] Tahiti ;
O ye divine Tu and Tangaroa,
Be propitious, and I am off.

CHORUS.

Tug away.

SOLO.

Friends, 'tis done.

CHORUS.

Tug away.

SOLO.

Hark ! the guns, the guns are firing.
What are these " puffers " ?
Terrible weapons.
Whom do they terrify ?
The whole of the people, calling
That Cook's vessels have arrived.
Tug away.

CHORUS.

Aye ; tug, tug away.

SOLO.

To whom do these guns speak ?
To the offspring of divine Tu,
Startling even the spirit-world.
Ah ! the sleepers are slipping ;
The canoe is upsetting !
Right her.

CHORUS.

Right her !

[1] To the native mind there are two Tahitis, the Greater and the Lesser, united by a narrow isthmus. The latter is now commonly known as Taiarabu.

SOLO.

Tavai te ruê i te rakau, ko mea ra
Ko vaka, o taurekareka, o pai taia.

CHORUS.

Aea, e pai ô!

SOLO.

Steady her—all of you,
Our noble ship is afloat.

CHORUS.

Bravo, ship!

In examining the best charts of the Pacific, it is puzzling to the novice to find that in very many instances two, three, or even four positions are given for a single island or reef, owing to the unskilfulness of observers. But it is no slight praise to our great navigator, Cook, that the positions of islands laid down by him remain unaltered to this day.

CHAPTER XXXIII.

THE STORY OF AN AXE.

One day an old man came to me bringing in his hand a bit of old iron. I was surprised that he should set store by such rubbish, and desired him to take it away. The old man then said, " You have been inquiring about Tute's (Cook's) visit here. This axe[1] came from Tute; it is the first foreign axe ever seen here. I give it to you as a countryman of his." Feeling interested, I made careful inquiries, and learnt that whilst Captain Cook was in his boat, on March 29th, 1777, looking about for a landing-place, several natives swam off to him. To the most influential man amongst them, named Kirikovi (commonly known by his nickname, Tiâci, or " Beardy "), the near relative of Mourua, and the then " lord of Mangaia," this axe was given. It is of a very peculiar shape, and of course is much worn with constant use. It is, in fact, merely a bit of iron : doubtless it was beaten out on the ship's anvil to please the natives. It has one excellence—it is easily fastened on a wooden handle with sennit.

I was not previously aware that anything was left on this island by Captain Cook on the occasion of its discovery in 1777 but what was given to Mourua, who alone of his countrymen had courage to venture on board the " big canoe." Yet, in the " Voyages," after referring to the " beads and nails " given to Mourua, Captain Cook speaks of taking with him in the boat " *such articles* to give the natives as might serve to gain their goodwill." Tradition says that strips of cloth were freely distributed by him among his visitors, who seem to have been very unceremonious, according to the great navigator's account. These bits of cloth, instead of being applied to their legitimate purpose, were wrapped round the head as ornaments and as marks of distinction from the vulgar crowd.

---

[1] Now in the British Museum.

The strips of cloth would quickly perish; but this bit of iron, unquestionably the first ever seen on this island, must have been a wonderful object in the eyes of the men of that generation. The native adze was with great labour chipped with pieces of flint out of bits of basalt. Some of these adzes are beautifully finished off, and constituted the gold and silver of former days. A present of two or three was usually sufficient to insure protection to one of the vanquished.

Kirikovi at once understood the value and use of the present he received from Captain Cook. A suitable handle was prepared for it, and the axe secured by strong sennit of the finest quality. When not in use, it was kept wrapped round and round with many folds of "tapa." The old man who gave it to me had had possession of it for nearly fifty years. It was almost forgotten, as it had become useless on account of the numerous American and Sheffield steel axes on the island at the present time.

The axe was in constant requisition amongst the chief people of the island for preparing smooth blocks of wood, on which their wives and daughters beat out the bark of the paper-mulberry for cloth; also for the finishing off of the wooden troughs which, in native life, answer to our tubs, buckets, and basins. The beautiful finish of some of the existing "tamanu," or native mahogany troughs, is said to be owing to Tute's famous iron adze. It is to be regretted that the first Tahitian teachers caused these mahogany-trees[1]—the growth of centuries—to be burnt, on account of their supposed connection with idolatry.

Another use to which it was applied was the making of long spears and wooden swords for battle. To a Mangaian heathen the one object of life was to fight, and, as he thought, gain an imperishable name in the traditions of his countrymen. From the date of Captain Cook's visit here (1777) to the year of grace 1823, when the gospel of peace was first brought, no less than *six* general pitched battles were fought, involving in every case a total or partial redistribution of lands. More than one powerful tribe at the date of the Captain's visit has long since disappeared. For each battle this iron axe, with numerous stone auxiliaries, was put into requisition in preparing weapons. The old man who gave me this unattractive-looking curiosity was himself in

---

[1] *Callophyllum inophyllum.*

four of these battles. But times have happily changed, and he has changed with them.

A painful point of interest in regard to this relic of Captain Cook is, that it was used in slaying human sacrifices for Rongo, who was supposed to feed exclusively on human flesh. His chief representative was a conch shell (Rongo means "The Resounder"). A large block of stone, rudely shaped like a man, was also regarded as an inferior representation of this Poly-nesian Mars. Many years ago, when these people embraced Christianity, this huge stone idol was utterly defaced, and the fragments form part of the stonework of the church at the prin-cipal village.

About the year 1810, Ngakauvarea, a leading warrior of the now almost extinct tribe of Tongaiti, was appointed to guard the entrance to the cave of Tautua, where they took refuge after having been defeated in battle. Unluckily for themselves, they had resolved on a midnight attack upon their victorious adver-saries. This plot was revealed by a woman, and consequently failed. The dominant party, greatly incensed at this discovery, doomed the entire tribe of Tongaiti to destruction. · But it was no easy thing to carry out this cruel design. The cave in which they had taken refuge is large and very difficult of access. Underneath the vast pile of hardened coral rock there passes on towards the ocean a stream of water from the valleys in that part of the island. There were two entrances, a "sacred entrance" for warriors, guarded by Ngakauvarea; the other entrance was for women and children employed in collecting food, where, Robinson Crusoe fashion, a ladder was placed, to be drawn up when not required. At the top another armed man kept guard. The interior of the cave is spacious, with a level earthen floor, at that time covered with dry grass, on which the poor refugees huddled together as best they could, and where in the earlier days of the siege they amused themselves with dancing. Beyond is a dreadful chasm, over which a single plank was laid, to enable the entire party to gain the other side should the entrance be forced. The grand difficulty was how to get food. It was only possible to get supplies at night under cover of darkness.

On a given night it was resolved to attack these cave-dwellers. The leaders of the attack were anxious to ascertain the will of the gods in reference to their intended expedition.[1] A number of centipedes, green lizards, and dragon-flies were collected, and, at the same instant, thrown into a folded leaf of the gigantic taro plant, filled with water—a single leaf will easily hold half a bucket of water. Only one insect perished out of the entire number; therefore it was sagely concluded that the gods had decreed that only one person should that night die at their hands.

That very evening, as Ngakauvarea (or " Deceived Heart ") was sleeping at his post, with his spear by his side, a foe named Terake (or " There-he-is ") climbed up the almost perpendicular rock with his hands and feet, and succeeded in gaining the sacred entrance unobserved. Had Ngakauvarea been awake and given the alarm, nothing would have been easier than to have hurled down the daring climber on the sharp-pointed rocks below, a depth of thirty feet. In the moonlight, Terake plainly discerned the form of his unconscious victim, and, with a single blow of Captain Cook's axe, clove the skull of the sleeping warrior. The body was hastily thrown to those below. The noisy formula for killing sacrifices—" Taumaa, Rongo, toou ika," *i.e.*, " Rongo, slay thy fish " — roused those within, so that the attacking party were glad to retire with a bruise or two from a shower of stones, bearing away, however, their bleeding victim in triumph. The supposed command of the god Rongo had been obeyed—at any rate, their malice was gratified.

The slaughter of the devoted tribe had thus favourably commenced. A most vigilant watch was kept on the starving wretches who tremblingly crept out at nightfall in search of food. Relatives from the attacking tribe still visited their starving friends inside the cave, but were carefully searched lest a bit of taro or cocoanut should perchance be hidden in their long hair or within the girdle. Scarcely a day passed without some of them being caught and killed. All the dead bodies were collected and

---

[1] Sometimes the will of the gods was supposed to be made known by the success of a fish hunt. Three or four large fish of a certain species would be seen enjoying themselves in the shallow waters of the reef. It was known beforehand that these fish, if chased, will *not* return to the ocean, else the chase were vain. They invariably make for the shore, or for some hiding-place in the reef. A most exciting chase now takes place : the fish are literally hunted to death. Sometimes one will escape the utmost efforts of the hunters by rushing past them and taking refuge in some large hole in the coral too deep to permit a human hand to reach the coveted prize within. The number of fish caught was believed to prefigure the number of the doomed.

laid in rows on a rising ground, where in after years a church for the worship of the living and true God was erected. About fifty in all, when sufficiently dried in the sun, were borne across the island to the *marae* or idol-grove of Rongo, "to feed him and his mother Papa," according to their mythology. At length it was resolved that the drum of peace should be beaten, and that Marokore should, in the name of the gods, be declared "lord of Mangaia." To accomplish this, another bleeding victim must be expressly slain and offered to this insatiable Rongo.

Few men were by this time left in the cave, and they were reduced almost to skeletons. Nevertheless, they kept watch as well as they could. Ngutukû was the guardian of the common entrance, where the ladder was occasionally let down. One morning, by broad daylight, the grandfather of one of my deacons, being on the watch, observed from a distance that Ngutukû had laid himself down to sleep. Axe in hand, the murderer crept round stealthily to the foot of the ladder, and, finding that his approach had not been observed, he boldly mounted it and slew Ngutukû. No attempt at rescuing the body was made by the poor dispirited creatures within. The body was at once carried off to the *marae* in the sacred district of Keia as an offering to the gods. To show the thorough change which has passed over these people, I may mention that this very spot was many years afterwards presented by the chief of that district to the missionary, my esteemed predecessor, as a *pen for his cows!* After being exposed there for some days, the body was taken to Orongo=O (definite article) Rongo—where the great stone idol Rongo once stood—and was eventually thrown into the bush, *not* buried. The gods thus appeased, the drum of peace was beaten, and the few half-starved wretches yet living in the cave were permitted to crawl out and show their faces once more in the light of day without fear of being clubbed.

So much for the history of this old axe. About the same time the aged king gave me two beads, the size of large marbles, which had recently come to light when digging a foundation for a new house. A string of these beads was tied with some nails to a piece of wood and thrown by Captain Cook to Mourua and Makatu, in the hope of establishing a friendly intercourse with these islanders. The beads, the first ever seen here, were greatly admired. As their blue colour corresponded to that of the supposed "solid stone vault above," they were named "sky pebbles," as if veritable chips of the azure arch which encloses earth and sea. To this day all beads are designated "sky pebbles," although their *earthly* origin is well known. A solitary nail is yet preserved as a relic—not of the giver, Captain Cook, but of his dusky friend, who alone of his countrymen ventured on board the moving monster. A neat ironwood handle was made for this nail. It was long used as a bradawl for boring holes, so as to secure the different portions of canoes with strong sennit.

TUMEA'S LAMENT FOR HER FATHER NGAKAUVAREA.

1.

Na metua-noo-rua e ketu i te metua.
Teiia râ Ngakauvarea?
Tei te ana o Tautua, vai ake i reira.

1.

A daughter is seeking for her cave-dwelling father.
Where, oh, where, is Ngakauvarea?
He who guarded the cave of Tautua.

2.

Vai ake i reira, tiki na te rima,
Retia mai, mauia e,
Paria ra i te toki pai e!

2.

Asleep there, his hands were stealthily grasped:
Cruelly seized and dragged was he,
And slain with the white man's axe!

3.

Toki pai ê, noou ua rava
Te tokotoko i raku atu.
O te toa ua te tua iaau!

3.

It was the white man's axe that slew thee,—
So utterly unlike all others!
Why did not the wooden spear lay thee low?

4.

Toki pai ê, aue koe i o teina,
Aue Uruata e, aue te tamaki e,
Aue ka mate, ka mate ei au!

4.

Oh, that white man's axe! Alas for thy brother,
Alas for Uruata! Oh, that cruel stratagem!
That fearful blow! Oh, that I too had died!

5.

Kounuunu ia Kaarau.
Kâku oki te metua, e tama,
E Ngakauvarea; kavea ra i raro.

5.

Kaarau saved his own skin.
Was not Kâku his father? But thou,
Ngakauvarea, wast pitilessly hurled to those below.

6.

Kavea ra i raro, koai te tarava i to vaka e rava'i?
E rave ua ake i o matou tokotoru ua e,
Kua rai oki te tara, akairia ake koe ra!

6.

Pitilessly hurled down! Who now will fill up the ranks?
Would that these three (warriors) had been saved!
Why did the babblers oppose thy wish (to fight)?

7.

Akairia koe ra ; kopunga i raro,
Naoe ra te karanga e, aere mai a puruki.
Ariana ia karo ake ia te ao e!
Kua mataku oki Avaiki.

7.

They opposed thy wish. The foes beneath
Kept shouting, "Come out and fight."
"Wait, that we may for awhile gaze at the light of day,"
Said his death-fearing friends.

8.

Avaiki e! a reru ra te tāki, akavo ra te
kura,
Ei tiki ki te rua e, te aa maira te tara i
te rua.
Aore, te noo ua, ka mate rava i reira.

8.

Death! Dance the war-dance: send a
message of defiance.
Fight the cave-dwellers.   Will they
venture out?
No, they will not.   *There* they are doomed
to perish.

9.

A mate rava i reira.   Kua ruma te aiai,
Tuatu, ka aere tatou.
Kua tangi i te metua i te vairanga ua.

9.

Aye, doomed to perish!   The sun is
setting.
Come, let us go and greet our father
In his miserable abode.

10.

I te vairanga ua e,
Oro i Butoa, tao mai
I te paka raurangi.

10.

Alas, that wretched abode!
Let us go to Butoa to collect and cook
His repast of wild leaves.

11.

Te paka raurangi, e tatari i te metua.
Aore e taia e vero,
E tiaki na te ara.

11.

Yes, a repast of cooked leaves was ready
for our father.
He was not killed by hunger.
Our approach (to the cave) was prevented.

12.

E tiaki na te ara, kua pa te rongo
Kua pou te puruki, kua ingū Ngakauvarea
Te vai rai i Tamarua.

12.

Our approach was prevented. We heard
a report,
"The fight is over; Ngakauvarea is
slain."
His corpse lies exposed at Tamarua.

13.

Te vai ra i Tamarua : vairanga kino e!
Vairanga taurere e!   E taeake e!
E Tuturi i rave ake ai.

13.

Lies exposed at Tamarua : sad resting-
place!
Exposed on a rock!   Ah, my brother,
O Tuturi, why didst thou not save him?

14.

E rave ake ai ra, tiki na, retia e!
Te arouga ē tangi i te tuaine e!
Kurakaau i vai ake ai.

14.

Why was he not saved?   He was
dragged and slain.
Such was your pity for your sister!
Kurakaau is left utterly desolate.

This is a specimen of the ballad poetry of olden times.   In
general, each stanza catches up the last words of that preceding,
and carries forward the train of thought.   This mournful ballad
was composed by a daughter of Ngakauvarea.   The "Kurakaau"
referred to in the last verse was the pretty daughter of Mourua,
whom the father wished to marry to Captain Cook.   As the
great English navigator declined this kind offer, she afterwards
became the wife of the ill-fated "Deceived-Heart," but did not,
however, share her husband's fate.

All their weapons of warfare were made of ironwood.   Ngakauvarea (third stanza) fell by a weapon previously unknown.
Their own adzes were of stone.

Kaarau (verse 5) was a near relative of the three warriors (verse 6) slain in the cave—namely, Ngakauvarea, Uruata, and Ngutukû.   It seems that through his wife, who was nearly related to the attacking party, Kaarau received more than once a hint about an intended attack, and retired into the interior of the cave, thus "saving his own skin."   In verse 7 the idea is that, seeing death was inevitable, Ngakauvarea proposed that the unhappy tribe should give battle, and so perish honorably ; and not be cut off one by one.   The starving cave-dwellers would not fight against such fearful odds—one to four or five.

Butoa (verse 10) is a wild but pleasing spot not far from the cave where the daughter is represented on the evening of his death as going to collect leaves—the only food obtainable—for her parent's supper.   She had married into the attacking party in happier days ; but persisted in going by stealth to take a little food to her father.

In this ballad style of composition the verses are invariably designated " *knots,*" in reference to an ancient method of counting by making knots in a piece of cord.

A son of Ngakauvarea who was spared was ever afterwards known by the name of " Wild-Leaves," in memory of the wretched food on which the old man subsisted in the cave. " Wild-Leaves " died a year or two ago.

Thank God that the grandchildren of the murderers and the murdered meet in Christian friendship now at the table of the Lord Jesus ; " for *He* is our peace."

CHAPTER XXXIV.

A STONE THROWN IN THE DARK.

CIRCA A.D. 1781–89.

THREE or four years after the discovery of the island by Captain Cook, an elderly chief named Paî—brother to Kirikovi, supreme warrior-chief of Mangaia — was sitting one evening warming himself at the oven his wife was preparing. The reverie of Paî was rudely interrupted by a smart blow on his bare breast from a stone thrown out of the darkness. The incensed chief rushed into the bush in the vain hope of catching the unknown offender. Finding it impossible to overtake him, he solemnly charged his grown-up son Paoa never to rest until the stone-thrower should be discovered and slain.

Some months after, Toê, belonging to the unhappy tribe of Teipe, confessed to his friend Paoa that *he* had, from sheer wantonness, thrown the stone on the night referred to. On learning the name of the offender, Paî greatly wished to club him, but out of respect to his brother, the paramount chief at the time, restrained his feelings. He commanded his son Paoa never to consent to any intermarriage between the two families, lest such an alliance should prove a hindrance to revenge at a future day.

About this time Paoa married and set up a separate establishment in a neighbouring district, a sister living with them. One day Paî was astonished by hearing that Paoa had been stupid enough to give that sister to Toê to wife, notwithstanding the pledge solemnly given to his father. Toê and his wife started off to the opposite side of the island to avoid the anger of the old chief.

Upon hearing of the marriage, Paî hurried off to see his son. High words ensued. Paoa excused himself as well as he could; but the proud father, growing wild with anger, ordered his disobedient son to quit the island for ever! Paî returned home. That same night Paoa went fishing, and secured a great cavally.

In the morning he called together a few friends to announce his resolve to take his chance on the ocean. The remonstrances of his friends were without effect; so they moodily feasted together for the last time. Paoa afterwards went to the *marae* to take a farewell of the gods, by playing on his famous wooden drum, with the tips of his fingers, his best tunes in their honor—for he was an excellent musician.

Next day Paoa went to the edge of the reef and launched his little canoe all alone, for he desired no companion on his ill-starred voyage. The entreaties and tears of his wife, who with their two infants accompanied him to the top of the hill over-looking the point of departure, were unavailing, and Paoa started on his unhappy expedition.

By this time it had got wind that Paoa had gone. Several near relatives, not in the secret, ran as fast as they could to the beach, but did not arrive in time to detain him. Determined to save him, they launched a number of small canoes, paddling with might and main after the runaway, who madly hurried on far out of the lee of the island to escape their importunities to return.

Meantime the sky became overcast, and the wind, which had been blowing steadily from the east, veered round to the north and blew with considerable violence. The friends assembled on the reef, watching the chase after the fugitive, could only discern tiny specks on the boisterous inky waves. Darkness came on, but no canoe returned. Numerous torches were now lighted ; but the chiefs, fearing that they could not be seen at so great a distance, ordered *the hills to be set on fire !* The dry fern and reeds quickly spread the fire over the interior, consuming all the ironwood and pandanus trees on the hills, and numerous cocoa-nut-trees in the valleys.

Guided by this magnificent beacon-light several canoes got back about midnight, with the sad news that the foremost canoes, containing the King Teivirau and his brothers, when within hail of the runaway, whom they entreated to return, were suddenly engulfed by a mighty wave, which at the same time drowned the infatuated Paoa. The remaining canoes escaped by being nearer shore, out of the track of the pitiless billows.

Thus the folly of this wilful youth cost him his own life and the lives of four relatives, one of them the grandfather of Numangatini, the present King of Mangaia. An essential emblem of Teivirau's dignity was a conch-shell, used to summon chiefs and leading men to council whenever he thought fit. This shell, bearing the name of "Ororakiau," or "The Royal Messenger," is in my possession.

But where was Paî? After his memorable quarrel with his son he remained in his own dwelling, nursing his anger, not dreaming of the fate of Paoa. But when the news came that his unhappy boy and four others—all men of mark in their day— were lost, he became as frantic with grief as he had a short time before been with anger. He sought out his cousin Mourua, the friend of Captain Cook, who was always ready to shed blood, and arranged a plan of revenge. Toê, his hated son-in-law, must perish, as the prime author of all these troubles.

On a starless night these worthies set out for the other side of the island to murder Toê and his aged father Aretere. As father and son occupied different houses, it was arranged that Paî should club Aretere, whilst Mourua should despatch Toê— the old chief not liking to kill his son-in-law in the very presence of his wife. Mourua, however, was never troubled with scruples of any sort when his services were required. He sat in the dark before the open door of the unsuspecting inmates. The wife was busy weaving a cocoanut-leaf basket, by the light of a candlenut torch, whilst the doomed husband lay asleep at her side on the dry grass strewed over the hut. For some seconds Mourua watched his cousin's work without being himself observed; but at length growing impatient he rushed through the open doorway past the astonished wife, and transfixed the sleeping Toê! The spear with which the victim was thus pinned to the earth was left standing upright, whilst Mourua, without uttering a word to his cousin, so lately wedded but now a widow, strode out of the dwelling to rejoin Paî, who had about the same time despatched the father of Toê.

But this was only the beginning of years of bloodshed and anarchy. The charm of peace was broken; Paî and Mourua and their retainers went about killing people day by day. The entire population had resort to arms; a pitched battle was fought at a place known as "Taukuera," in which Kirikovi was worsted by his brother Paî and Mourua, and the proud Paî was declared "lord of Mangaia" instead of his brother.

17

But ere the ceremonies preparatory to the beating of the drum of peace could be completed, war again broke out. Kirikovi, aided by his friends, one dark night surrounded the house on the rocky beach where Mourua and several others were resting after a fishing expedition. Of the sleepers but one escaped. The struggle with Mourua was protracted, by his immense strength, long after his companions lay dead at his side. His brave wife stripped off her clothing to enable her the better to ward off the blows intended for her husband; her left arm, however, was broken in the contest. Forced to retire from his side, Mourua received the fatal blow which he had long since richly deserved.

All this resulted from a stone wantonly thrown in the dark by one heathen at another.

It is pleasant to be able to add that a grandson of this irritable old chief Paî, and nephew to the foolish Paoa, named Taata, was for many years a valuable deacon of the Church.

Throughout the preceding narrative I have called the proud chief by his later name of Paî—"Canoe." In point of fact, however, his proper name was "Kaiau." When his son perished miserably at sea, according to their national custom he adopted the new name of "Canoe," to evince his grief at the loss of his foolish boy. It is by this later designation that he is invariably called by his countrymen.

A LAMENT FOR THE KING TEIVIRAU.

By Potiki, *circa* 1790, for the "Death-talk" of the drowned King.

TUMU.

Taugi te maunga, e Teivirau.
Koai a uta ia tatou, ko Temokomoko!
Ko te karava i reira,
Ko te kaivi maunga i roa ê!

INTRODUCTION.

Weep for the mountains, O Teivirau!
For friends left behind in the land.
Oh, those pleasant hills,—
The long range of mountains at home.

PAPA.

Ka pura te ni i te uru kare, e Teivi e!
Ei ukatere ia,tatou.
Oe atu koe i te tai roa.
Kua maru te maru i tuitui nunga
Kua reu te reu po.
Kua meaki te kare nga tama ê!

FOUNDATION.

Lights are seen by Teivi[1] o'er the white-crested waves,
Intended for thy guidance.
Why venture so far out to sea?
The island is lessening in the distance.
Darkness o'erspreads the ocean.
The king is lost to sight in the waves!

UNUUNU TAI.

Ka tangi te puku ê tei te maunga ê!
Tei te maunga, kua kapu i raro,

FIRST OFFSHOOT.

Weep for the well-known mountain tops,
Now hidden by the swelling waves ;—

· [1] For Teivirau. In the last line of this verse he is termed " eldest son :" all kings were so called out of respect. I have simply rendered it "king."

Kua kapua ei i raro ki te tapa rakau,
Ki te tapa rakau Pouekakeariki,
  I te taata roa i Angara,
  Ko te oroki i te nu tauu.
    Ko te karava i reira,
Ko te kaivi maunga i roa ê!

Though hidden they are covered with
    verdure,
Pouekakeariki[1] is lost to view ;
Stretching towards the *east*,
  With a smooth summit and cocoanut-
    tree.
    Oh, those pleasant hills,
The long range of mountains at home!

UNUNNU RUA.

Maunga i uta ê kua teitei ê!
Kua teitei, kua aaura i runga,
  Kua aaura i runga 'i.
Tau tangi e i te poo i Tongarei,
  Ko te taparere i raro ê!
    Ko te karava i Teroto
Ko te kaivi maunga ra i roa ê!

SECOND OFFSHOOT.

How lofty[2] those distant hills,
Lying piled one above another!
  How vast are they !
Weep for the sight of Tongarei,[3]
  And its precipitous sides.
Oh, those pleasant hills on the *west*,
The long range of mountains at home!

UNUNU TORU.

Ka vero te ai tei te maunga :
Tei te maunga ; kua tui ki te moana
  Kaa tui ki te moana.
Kua ka te vera i Poue.
  Kua tungia Mangaia ê!
    Ko te karava Uira,
Ko te kaivi maunga ra i roa ê!

THIRD OFFSHOOT.

Smoke is rising from the hills ;
The mountain ranges are on fire !
The fierce heat is felt on the ocean ;
  The blaze is extending all around :
All Mangaia is on flames !
Oh, those pleasant hills on the *south*,
The long range of mountains at home !

UNUUNU A.

Kau mai Taa ê i te poiri ê!
Ite poiri tatango ; kua noo tona io—
Kua noo tona io 'i, ko Tiaio rangi ê!
O Keretoki : kua mataku te ika i noo
  reva ê!
Uru mai koe i te tauirangiapa.
Ko te kaivi akau ra i roa ê!

FOURTH OFFSHOOT.

Taa[4] has gained the shore in the dark.
In the starless night he was preserved.
The "shark-god" was his protector,
And Keretoki too, to save him from
All monsters of the deep, and to bring
  him to shore.
Oh, the far-extending *reef* at our home !

AKAREINGA.

Ai e ruaoo ê! E rangai ê!

FINALE.

Ai e ruaoo ê! E rangai ê!

LAMENT FOR PAOA.

A song pertaining to the "Death-talk of Teivirau." By his repentant father, *circa* 1790.

TUMU.

Tumatuma te pau i Itikau na Paoa.
Oro mai ana, e tau ariki, kia ongi ake
  tana ê!
    To pou kino i oro ei!

INTRODUCTION.

At Itikau[5] Paoa beat softly his drum.
Come, beloved son,[6] let us once more kiss
  each other.
    Why this ill-omened flight ?

---

[1] A prominent hill, serving as a landmark to those on the ocean.
[2] This is amusing, considering the highest hill of Mangaia is about 500 feet above the level of the sea !
[3] Another prominent hill.
[4] Taa was one of those who got back alive. Of course it was Taa and his more fortunate companions who saw the lights ashore on the edge of the reef, the prominent hills, and that awful spectacle, an island on fire. Hence the pleasing change in the chorus, intimating the course taken by the returning canoes, until they joyfully set their feet on "the far-extending reef at home."
[5] "Itikau" is the name of a place close to Paoa's dwelling.
[6] "Beloved son." In the native it is "my king," a common appellation for a beloved *elder* son.

PAPA.

Tamaki na te medua i ara 'i Paoa ê!
Auraka kia akamoû, kua crueru i te
  one.
  E tangi ai Moeau i te takanga.
  Ei kona korua e, ka aero ê!

FOUNDATION.

The angry words of the father exiled
  Paoa.
Yet bear not malice. The mother, in
  grief
For her lost son, scratches the dried grass.[1]
Alas (those words)! "Farewell! I leave
  you for ever!"

UNUUNU TAI.

Tumatuma te pau ô, tei Itikau ê,
  Tei Itikau na Paoa ;—
  Ko te uinga ïa o te karioi.
Kua akarongo mai nei au taeake
  I te pau tangi reka :
  Tangi reka te pau a Paoa!
Oro mai ana, e tau ariki, kia ongi ake
  taua ê!
  To poû kino i oro ei!

FIRST OFFSHOOT.

Softly sounds the drum at Itikau,
  The famed drum of Paoa.
It is the gathering of young men.
Entranced by the music of their friend.
  Oh, that sweetly-sounding drum!
  The incomparable touch of Paoa.
Come, beloved son, let us once more kiss
  each other.
  Why this ill-omened flight?

UNUUNU RUA.

O Mumuu te are ra e moe ai ê!
  E moe ai i te avatea.
Kua akapiripiri Paoa ê
  Na nunga i Aparai,
Ka kitea mai au e Moenoa!
Oro mai ana, e tau ariki, kia ongi ake
  taua ê!
  To poû kino i oro ei!

SECOND OFFSHOOT.

Sequestered was the dwelling
  Where he slept when the sun was high.
Paoa loved to saunter about
  The shady hill-side Aparai
In company with the lovely Moenoa.
Come, beloved son, let us once more kiss
  each other.
  Why this ill-omened flight?

UNUUNU TORU.

Te umea te maro ô, ka uapen ê,
Ka napea to maro i Vairotokava,
Kua pou ai to angai urua.
  Aere tu tei tai ê!
Tu mai koe i Aratau!
Oro mai ana, e tau ariki, kia ongi ake
  taua ê!
  To poû kino i oro ei!

THIRD OFFSHOOT.

Thy girdle is adjusted and well secured
  (for flight),
'Twas done in desperation at Vairotokava,
  After feasting on a great cavally.
Ere starting on that fatal voyage
  Thou didst take a last lingering look.
Come, beloved son, let us once more kiss
  each other.
  Why this ill-omened flight?

AKABEINGA.

Ai e ruaoo ê! E rangai ê!

FINALE.

Ai e ruaoo ô! E rangi ê!

---

[1] The custom still obtains of scratching the grass or earth where the deceased last sat, in token of excessive grief.

CHAPTER XXXV

A STORMY NIGHT IMPROVED.

Somewhere about A.D. 1785 nearly a hundred persons took refuge in the cave Touri, and double that number in the great cave Eruc, about three miles distant. Both companies owned the authority of the clever but unscrupulous Potai. Unfortunately for the smaller party, a hostile chief named Poito, with a number of warriors, took up his quarters under Touri, and laid siege to this natural fortress. The long ladder, which hitherto had enabled the fugitives to collect supplies from their old plantations, was at once destroyed. The secret subterranean passage conducting to the forest on the hill-side was so difficult to traverse as to be of little use. It became evident that, unless Potai came to the rescue, the whole party inside the cave must die of starvation.

By the secret path a message was sent to Potai acquainting him with their critical state. They were promised assistance on the first stormy night.

Potai was afraid to attack Poito, as he had already had painful experience of his bravery. The women and children could not hope to escape by means of the perilous secret subterranean path. The only feasible mode of rescuing these despairing fugitives was to draw them out of the cave with ropes. The main force of Potai at Eruc was unwatched, and enjoyed plenty. Four-stranded ropes, of great length and strength, were twisted, sticks being inserted at one end to enable the poor creatures to *sit* whilst being drawn up.

Potai now watched with great anxiety the appearance of the heavens. It so happened that on the first moonless night a tremendous storm burst forth. Those who have not seen a tropical storm can form no adequate conception of its terrific grandeur. Poito and his warriors took refuge inside a neighbouring cave, which still bears his name. In fine weather he delighted to seat himself at the entrance and play the harmonicon—a rough sort of music, set to the war-songs of his tribe.

Potai and his well-laden followers arrived on the crest of the overhanging rocks by the forest path in the early evening, before the tempest had reached its height.   The starving and expectant creatures inside the cave soon perceived, by the flashes of light-- ning, a number of ropes dangling in the air, but far out of reach, opposite the entrance to their rocky asylum.   In a few seconds the ropes were brought near by means of long fishing-rods with hooks fastened to the extremities.   Those above—a distance of some eighty-eight feet — feeling, by the weight, that some of their friends were perched on the cross-trees below, joyfully hauled them up.   A father would clasp his child in his arms whilst being pulled up.   Women with their infants in this way escaped a miserable death; of the entire number not one lost his life that night; but, when Taaki, the last to ascend, arrived at the top, it was discovered that two of the four strands of the rope, by which he had been pulled up, had been cut through by the sharp projecting rock !

All this time Poito and his besieging force were fast asleep. So near were they that any of those drawn up could easily have thrown a stone amongst the slumberers.   The time chosen for hoisting up the fugitives was when the thunder was the most terrific, and the rain the heaviest.   The strife of elements went on through the livelong night; by dawn the poor creatures had all reached the magnificent stalactite home of Potai at Erue, to the utter chagrin of their foes beneath.

This famous relief of Touri long remained an enigma.   But many years after, when Poito was dead, it was whispered that *one* of the sleeping guards beneath was aware that the fugitives would that night be rescued.   That individual was the clever harmonicon-player, himself chief watcher !   As a last resource the crafty Potai selected the prettiest girl in his tribe and sent her stealthily to Poito, who, heathen-like, readily fell into the snare.   This woman acquired such influence over Poito that he yielded to her entreaties and tears to permit the escape of her perishing tribe.   On the night of the storm he told the guards that they might as well sleep, as *he* himself would keep watch. He felt sure that on such a dreadful night no foe would venture out.   When the exit of the fugitives was discovered on the following day, Poito apologetically said that he supposed he must have fallen asleep !   Poito would gladly have made this girl his wife, but by so doing would have betrayed his secret and dis-- graced himself in the eyes of his own people.

CHAPTER XXXVI.

MAIKAI'S CHESTNUT-TREE.

CIRCA A.D. 1787.

ONE of the noblest trees in the Pacific is the chestnut (*Tuscarpus edulis*), which almost rivals the cocoanut in height, and for shade has no equal. The timber, however, is worthless. At the beginning of the year it puts forth innumerable tiny white blossoms, filling the air with fragrance. The fruit is a staple article of diet, not of luxury; it lasts from the middle of February to the end of June. This tree attains to a great age, far exceeding that of the cocoanut. The oldest cocoanut-trees now standing on Mangaia were planted at the commencement of Mautara's chieftainship, *i.e.*, about one hundred and fifty years ago;[1] whilst certain chestnut-trees at Tamarua are believed to have been planted by Amau, about four hundred years ago. The age of the chestnut is, however, exceeded by the banyan, which is almost imperishable.

A striking peculiarity of the chestnut is the circumstance that the trunk of the full-grown tree throws out five or six lateral supports, each about an inch thick, and running out some distance into the soil. A fall from one of the lofty branches of this tree on one of these plank-like buttresses would be certain death. The skull would be cleft in two. I have known several fatal accidents to occur in this way. The larger trees, if beaten with a stick, give forth a very pleasant sound, which can be heard at the distance of a mile. In former times it was usual to select the most musical for beating, in order to assemble the population of an entire district for dancing, reed-throwing matches, &c.

Not long since I went to see a particular chestnut-tree which has become historical. With some difficulty we climbed up its

---

[1] Mr. Ellis, in his "Polynesian Researches," thinks the cocoanut-tree may attain the age of fifty or sixty years, or even more. I have no hesitation whatever in doubling this estimate.

ancient trunk, and there I listened (not for the first time) to the following incident :—

About ninety-one years ago, Maikai, wife of Tetonga, went with a number of other women to a distant plantation to obtain food for her family. They did not know that their foes, under Moerangi's guidance, had that morning left their stronghold in the rocks for the same spot in quest of plunder. A year or two previously, in a time of peace, one of Moerangi's clan had been abused in no measured terms by Maikai for lurking about their premises after nightfall. Upon relating to his tribe the indignity he had undergone, it was resolved to murder Maikai if ever she should be in their power. It is a point of honor with a heathen *never* to forgive.

On the day referred to they were delighted to see amongst the women the very one they wished to wreak their vengeance upon. They therefore gave chase to Maikai, allowing the rest to escape. Maikai ran for her life, well knowing their cruel intentions. She wisely left her friends, who ran by the accustomed path through the open country, where she must have been overtaken and slain. She chose for her hiding-place a narrow valley where a number of fine chestnut-trees grew. She recollected that in the largest of these trees was a hollow occasioned by the limbs of the chestnut shooting out of the stem at the same distance from the ground. Maikai made for this clump of chestnuts. Running to the side of the tree farthest from her foes, in a second she climbed the tree and completely secreted herself in the natural hollow, which was just big enough to admit her.

Now it fortunately happened that one of the pursuing party, named Raimanga, was greatly in advance of the rest. He caught a glimpse of Maikai making for this large tree, and at once divined her purpose. But, being secretly anxious to save her, he ran at full speed a good distance up the valley, and threw some large stones into the sluggish stream to make it muddy, and pretended to be looking everywhere for the fugitive. When the rest of the pursuers came up with him and saw how turbid the water was, they concluded that Maikai had taken to the bed of the stream. On and on they rushed up the valley, in the vain hope of overtaking their victim. After a long and fruitless search for Maikai, they returned by the same path to the very tree in the top of which she lay hid. Tired with their chase, they piled up their spears against the trunk of this chestnut, and sat down under its grateful shade to refresh themselves. They slaked their thirst from the stream at their feet, and chatted about Maikai's marvellous disappearance. The majority thought she must have been specially helped by the gods; but Raimanga was sure that it was due to her wonderful fleetness of foot. After awhile Raimanga remarked, " Let us be off, or our enemies will catch us." At this the entire party took up their spears and returned to their old haunts.

All this time Maikai lay crouching down in the hollow of the great chestnut, scarcely daring to breathe, and expecting every moment to be discovered and speared to death. At first she distinctly heard the rush of feet and the voices of eager pursuers on their way up the valley, for the pathway then, as now, ran under the branches of the tree, and then all became quiet for awhile. But again the sound of human feet and human voices was heard. She was conscious that the entire party, hot and angered by their bootless chase, were resting under the chestnut. It is said that not a word of their .conversation escaped her. But when they finally departed she could scarcely credit the truth that her life was safe.

At last she ventured to rise from her cramped position, and cautiously peered beneath to see if there were any traces of her foes. Finding there were none, she descended to the ground, and ran as fast as her legs could carry her along the narrow mountain-path to her husband and children, who, on hearing the report of the women who had seen her chased, gave her up for lost. Hence the commemorative name still kept up in their family, " Ate-ru " (Trembling Heart), as descriptive of Maikai's feelings while she lay trembling in the curious recess of this famous chestnut-tree.

Her preserver was called " E koinga ta Raimanga " (Raimanga the pitiful), an epithet that would be appropriate to but few of his heathen countrymen.

The narrator of this story, a deacon of the Church, is grandson of Maikai.

CHAPTER XXXVII

PADDLING FOR LIFE.

An old and respected native of the village of Oneroa gave me the following account of the escape of his maternal uncle Matenga from a miserable death about the year 1810.

During the long and peaceful rule of Potiki, Matenga grew up to manhood, and married the sister of the chief Raoa. The rival factions which eventually overthrew the government of " the supreme temporal lord " brought sorrow and tears to Matenga and all the Tongan tribe. The crimes of former days were remembered against them, so that they resolved to take refuge in the impregnable natural fortress known as " the Cave of Tautua."

Underneath flows on to the ocean a never-failing stream of water; but the difficulty of obtaining food was considerable. At first their wives and children were permitted to collect food to supply the wants of the warriors inside the cave. But at last the then all-powerful tribe of Mautara resolved upon their extermination. For a distance of one hundred yards lofty palisades were firmly planted in the soft soil in front of the cave, in order to prevent all egress. Armed men were appointed to keep constant watch that nothing eatable should be taken into the cave. Any member of the doomed tribe venturing outside was at once clubbed. Persons connected with the winning tribes wishing to visit their starving relatives inside were first rigorously searched, so as to prevent the possible concealment of food in the narrow girdle or flowing hair.

As Matenga's young wife belonged to the dominant party, she went inside to see her husband as often as she pleased. Months of misery passed away, and yet Matenga lived on, though but the shadow of his former self. The fact was that his faithful wife was in the habit of stealthily conveying food by a long and circuitous path to a certain hollow nearly a mile from the carefully-guarded entrance. This secret entrance is now shaded by lofty cedars,[1] covered during the summer months with delicate lilac-tinted blossoms. The subterraneous passage is exceedingly tortuous and difficult. A yawning chasm, bridged by a single plank, ran across the cavern. A lighted flambeau was absolutely needful. But the instinct of self-preservation enabled Matenga to find his way to the secret entrance, where his wife awaited his arrival with a small basket of cooked taro.

This could not go on for ever. The leading men of the unhappy tribe had been slain. It was evident that the clan was doomed. In a nook of the cave a sad meeting was held, when the father and brother of Matenga urged him to escape and leave them to die. To make sure of Raoa's favour, a valuable fish-net,[2] called a *nariki*, an heirloom of the family, was given to Matenga. This treasure was conveyed to the secret entrance, and intrusted to his wife to be carried across the island to Raoa the chief. On her way to her brother she fell in with a party of armed men, who at once took possession of the fish-net, as being the property of the cave-dwellers. Raoa was not disposed to relinquish so valuable a net; he therefore made a formal demand for it, and succeeded in recovering it. Thus the price of protection had been paid; but the difficulty now was how to get Matenga across the island in safety to the district where Raoa exercised authority. Intercession with the cave-watchers would be futile. Happily, however, a plan concocted by Raoa and his sister proved successful.

On a given day Matenga met his faithful wife at the unsuspected opening amongst the rocks near the sea. A morsel was eaten; few words were exchanged, for the fugitive had just taken a last farewell of his nearest relatives. Carefully threading their way through the bush and over jagged rocks to the beach, they fortunately found a small canoe with a paddle in it, belonging to one of the watchers and murderers of the unfortunate tribe. In a few minutes the frail bark was on the ocean, and the wife hastening back through the bush to give tidings to her brother Raoa.

The fugitive paddled leisurely towards the west, taking care that the canoe should not be sufficiently near the reef to permit his features to be recognized. Every now and then he made a

---

[1] Introduced by myself. [2] Such a net will now fetch £6 in cash.

pretence of dropping his line for fish, and after a time, as if
unsuccessful, would take up the tackle and press forward.   Had
Matenga met any other canoe that day he would undoubtedly
have perished; but, fortunately, he succeeded that afternoon in
getting opposite to the boundary-line of the district where his
brother-in-law resided.   The poor fellow now breathed freely.
Being well provided with fish-hooks, he began to angle in right
earnest.   The fish-hooks of those times were laboriously manufactured with bits of round coral out of the hardest cocoanut-
shells.   Twenty fine "*nanui*" rewarded his exertions.   These
were intended as a gift to his future protector.   Thus the life-
work of the serf had commenced.

The sun had set when the fugitive, with his stolen canoe,
arrived at the usual landing-place on the west.   Though un-
assisted, he succeeded in shooting his canoe through the breakers
at the right moment on to the rugged coral reef, and dragged it
through the shallow water to the beach.

Matenga had paddled a distance of five miles.   With his face
well hidden with native cloth, and lugging his fish, he started for
the interior, about a mile away.   Once he gave himself up for
lost, for one of his foes passed him; but happily the muffled figure
moving in the dark was not recognized.

My friend Kerimaniania, referred to at the commencement
of this story, was that day engaged with his father Raoa in digging a new taro-patch.   Though a tall youth at the time, he was
not intrusted with the secret of Matenga's escape, lest it should
be betrayed to some of his bloodthirsty foes.   As the evening
shadows from the neighbouring hills fell upon their romantic
home, the lad observed that Raoa frequently paused in his work
and glanced uneasily at "the Rat's Pathway," the only road
thereabouts to the sea.   At last a figure hurried over the brow
of the hill to the spot where they stood.   It was Matenga with
his load of fish.

To avoid a surprise he was at once concealed in a tiny hut
built on long poles as a sort of watch-tower.   His companions
were his nephew and his wife, who had also been on the watch,
whilst Raoa went to his principal neighbours to induce them to
promise their assistance in saving the poor fugitive.

. Only one refused — Tavare, who had already imbrued his
hands in the blood of the Tongans.   Apprehensive that Tavare

would some day slay his brother-in-law, a small cave near at hand was selected as the temporary home of Matenga. It was well strewed with dried grass. His constant companion was his nephew, whose duty it would be to give the alarm at the first appearance of danger. Tavare again and again asked permission to dispose of "*the bird in the hole;*" but was invariably refused.

For many months this little "bird" durst not leave its nest in the rocks. Matenga was well supplied with food by his wife. But when at length Ngutukû had been offered in sacrifice to Rongo, arbiter of peace and war, and the drum of peace had been beaten all round the island, the fugitive left his hiding-place and ventured to walk about in open daylight, taking care, however, to keep to Raoa's district.

Matenga lived to see the first native evangelists land on Mangaia, and witnessed the earlier triumphs of Christianity. But he would have nothing to do with the new religion, because his kind protectors were at that time averse to the new order of things. Raoa fell in battle two years prior to the landing of Papehia and Haavi. A son of Matenga was a truly pious man, and, after leaving a most cheering testimony to the truth of the Gospel, a few weeks since passed away to the better land.

The real cause of the extinction of the Tongan tribe was their excessively warlike propensities. The clan was familiarly called "Tumu o Miro," *i.e.*, "*The Root of all Bloodshedding.*" The common saying in reference to this tribe was, "E kuru i tai vaa koatu ei ako ia Tonga-iti," *i.e.*, "Carve out a *stone mouth* that will never weary of admonishing the Tongans."

CHAPTER XXXVIII

A BRAVE WIFE.

WE have seen that the priestly tribe of Mautara retained absolute sway over the island of Mangaia for about a century. They claimed descent from Papaaunuku, who came as a vassal in the train of Rangi from Avaiki. In successive battles the descendants of Rangi and his brothers were almost exterminated. The vassals became lords, the ancient masters being fearfully massacred and often literally devoured.

In 1814 this once all-powerful clan lost their power and most of their lands, as the inevitable result of several years of bitter dissension and constant fighting amongst themselves.

About A.D. 1811 one of the factions into which the tribe was split, led by Kaunio, made a raid upon Ata-toa, chief of Keia, and his aged father Tukua, because they were firmly attached to the opposite party. This was but a prelude to the battle of Rangiura, the last fatal victory of the shattered clan.

Taking a sorrowful farewell of their families, Ata-toa, Tukua, and several others awaited the onset under the shadow of the romantic overhanging rocks of Okio. I have stood with Ata-iti, the present chief of the district, whilst he pointed out to me the stone on which Tukua's brains were pounded by his foes, and, a little higher up, the place where Ata-toa fell with a ghastly spear-thrust in the neck. Several others fell in that unequal fight.

The heroic wife of Ata-toa fought bravely by the side of her husband. To save him from the fate of Tukua, as soon as he fell she picked up the still breathing body and succeeded in carrying it off to some distance, where she laid him on the grass. Finding their enemies on their track, she again took up her living burden, and carried Ata-toa to a large cave, hoping to be able to staunch the wound. Again they were pursued: again the noble-hearted Kie refused to leave her husband to his fate. Eventually she secreted him in a cavern, named Teakautu, near the sea. Here she tended him for seven days and nights, till the unfortunate man died. Their *little* children brought food by stealth every evening.

Now Ata-toa had a grown son, Muraai, who afterwards became chief of Keia. By a singular arrangement he and his brothers were adopted into the *maternal*[1] tribe, at the tearful solicitation of Kie. Hence it was that during the fight *they* were sitting secure in their house listening to the distant clashing of spears.

The present (1870) chief, Ata-iti, whose name frequently occurs in the songs, well remembers the sad events of that day, —the farewell, the fight, the stealthy visit by the sea, and finally the well-wrapped-up body gently let down the gloomy chasm with long cords, without a ray of light regarding a future life.

Kie, then a grandmother, lived several years after the introduction of the Gospel to Mangaia. When old and decrepit, it was a great pleasure to her to attend all the services of the sanctuary. It must have been a significant fact to her mind that the spot on which the church is built is where she once hid her husband from the cruel vengeance of his foes. The singular love and tender care of this poor heathen woman was commemorated in the songs of the clan.

KOROA'S LAMENT FOR HIS FRIEND ATA.

Pertaining to the "Death-talk" of Arokapiti.—*Circa* A.D. 1817.

TUMU.	INTRODUCTION.
Kua maru te rā i Okio ê !	The shades of evening rest on the rocks
Kua tangi atu Muraai ki te roronga,	of Okio.
No Ata koia te mate, te metua tatari	Muraai is disconsolate and wretched,
roa ê !	For Ata-the-Elder, who perished so
	miserably.

PAPA.	FOUNDATION.
Kaitanga, e Kie,	Distressed indeed was Kie
Ia Makitaka no ta iaku.	With the priests who slew Ata : said he,
Na tika ra ka maru au ia korua,	" Had ye befriended me,
Kua noo au i te vao ;	I had still dwelt in prosperity,
E Tamarua karotonga e Mariki.	And my children would not be in tears."

UNUUNU MUA.	FIRST OFFSHOOT.
Kua maru te rā ô tei Okio ô !	The shades of evening rest on the rocks at
Tei Okio ! Ariu te mata i Auroa, e Metua-	Okio.
iviivi !	From Okio I glance fondly towards our
	dwelling.

---

[1] Exactly like Manaune in a preceding generation.

Te noo ua maira tau mokopuna,
O Ata-iti, kua anau e Taoro nei.
Ei ara vou i Rautetiki ka arara.
No Ata koia te mate, te metua tatari
   roa ê!

Yonder lives my beloved grandson,
" Ata-the-Little," he whom Taora bare.
Her children
Are like the many-rooted pandanus on
   the mountain-side.
Alas for Ata-the-Elder, who perished so
   miserably!

UNUUNU RUA.
SECOND OFFSHOOT.

Mata mai oki ê i mamao ra ê!
I mamao ra. Te noo maira
I te utu ruru na ngati Mautara ;—
Ka ano paa ka koke e, ia Keia.
Mei vai te aka o Muraai ka arara.
No Ata koia te mate, te metua tatari
   roa ê!

Yet glance again towards me,—now far
   away,
Aye, far indeed! Bitter as fish poison
Is the tribe of Mautara against me.
Perchance they will utterly root up my
   family,
Lest one of its branches avenge my
   death!
Alas for Ata-the-Elder, who perished so
   miserably!

AKAREINGA.
FINALE.

Ai e ruaroo ê! E rangai ê!

Ai e ruaoo ê! E rangai ê!

TUKA'S LAMENT FOR HIS FRIEND ATA.
Recited on the same occasion.

TUMU.
INTRODUCTION.

Kua mou te piro ia Kie.
Runaio i te putiki.
Ka ano paa, ka rave i te tane.
Aurâ koe e râvao e, kia uuna atu i te
   mata ra i te metua ê!

Kie has girded on her war-petticoat ;
A gay yellow band well secures it.
She fights to-day to save her husband.
Forget not the day when thy father's
   face was hidden (*i.e.*, in death).

PAPA.
FOUNDATION.

Pikaio, e Kie, i to tane ;
E apai atu i te ana-roa, i te ana-iti,
Akarongo ake, e Mariki e,
I te koumu e, " Apai atu i te ao:
I Auraka tanukere ai rai ê! "

Tenderly wrap up thy husband, Kie,
And carry him from cave to cave ;
For did not thy daughter overhear
The cruel words, "Take away the
   wretch !
Throw him down the gloomy depths of
   Auraka " ?

UNUUNU TAI.
FIRST OFFSHOOT.

Kua mou te piri ê, i te popongi ê,
I te popongi no Kie ê, no tera vaine,
No tera vaine! Nani ra e ranga ?
Na Tamarua, na Meduaiviivi,
Na tama vaine ia Tane ê! E Muraai,
Aurâ koe e râvao, e, kia uuna atu i te
   mata ra i te metua ê!

At dawn she girded on her war-petticoat.
Thus did that brave woman Kie—
That heroic woman—equip herself.
Will not Tamarua and Muraai avenge
   thee ?
Are they not adopted into the tribe of
   Tanè ?
Forget not the day when thy father's
   face was hidden.

UNUUNU RUA.
SECOND OFFSHOOT.

Pikaio e i te putiki ê, i te putiki o
   Mariki,
Tau kata Takinga e to tama akarongo,
To tama akarongo ei, to anau, e Kie.
E titiri atu ia maua kia mate ua atu,
I taua matenga i Okio, e Ata,
Aurâ koe e râvao kia uuna atu i te mata
   ra i te metua ê!

Tenderly wrap him up in thy gay yellow
   cloth.
Ah, beloved Takinga, and thou first-born,
Ever-obedient children of Kie—farewell!
Grieve not, little Ata, at our fate,
Slain on the jagged rocks of Okio!
Forget not the day when thy father's
   face was hidden.

UNUUNU TORU.

Tikitikie, e Kie e, i to upoko e, i to upoko,
  ka mate ê!
Kua pou to manava, kua pou to manava,
  e Kie e!
Na tika ra ka maru e kia tamaru ia
  Itirere,
Ei kokou i to upoko, e Ata-iti ê!
Aurâ koe e vâvao kia uuna atu i te mata
  ra i te metua ê!

AKAREINGA.

Ai e ruaoo ê! E rangai ê!

THIRD OFFSHOOT.

Shave off thy locks, thy raven hair;
For thy heart is breaking for sore grief,
  O Kie!
Oh that those had helped who *could*
  have helped
To shield thy head, little Ata!
Forget not the day when thy father's
  face was hidden.

FINALE.

Ai e ruaoo ê! E rangai ê!

How strikingly does the repeated call for vengeance (" Forget not the day," &c.) contrast with our Saviour's dying words,
" Father, forgive them ! " Here lies the essential moral antipodes
between the religions of the world and the religion of Christ.

ANOTHER LAMENT FOR ATA; BY KOROA.
For the same " Death-talk."

TUMU.

Purunga ra o Mariki ê!
Akanooia e Kie ra,—
Te tauinu para o Marua,
Kua pipiri tane âna ê!

PAPA.

Papaio i te parai o rircio o Ata ê!
Ki te akaunoanga rai, na Maikai oki rai.
Kua kake e ariki tiare rautonga ra na
  Kie.

UNUUNU TAI.

Purunga oki ra ko Mariki nei ê!
O Mariki nei : kua pipi te vai o Marua,
Ei enua taurere, ei enua taurere,
Tei Poiria te are i Motuariri ra.
Kua karanga ia Kie e,
  I te tauinu para o Marua,
  Kua pipiri tane âna ê!

UNUUNU RUA.

Tiarctiare rautonga ê, rautonga ê,
No tai matavaka no Motuaaereroa.
No Motuaaereroa 'i ; tena, e kua ‘kakau
I te tititai : kua rere nui mai e,
Te moe atura i Teakautu.
  I te tauinu para o Marua,
  Kua pipiri tane âna ê!

INTRODUCTION.

Thy aged mother-in-law, Mariki,
Cherish fondly, my Kie ;—
Thou fair-leaved " tauinu '" of Marua,
So tenderly faithful to thy husband!

FOUNDATION.

Piles of cloth were heaped around thee, O
  Ata,
On that joyful day when Maikai's wish
  was realized.
Kie had gained a princely husband.[2]

FIRST OFFSHOOT.

Yonder sits thy aged mother-in-law.
Poor Mariki ! sprinkle on her the sacred
  water
Against her day of departure, of sad
  death.
Her hut is at Poiria, near to Motuariri ;
She delights to address thee, Kie, as
  " The fair-leaved ' tauinu ' of Marua,
  So tenderly faithful to thy husband."

SECOND OFFSHOOT.

Thy loved husband, thy chosen com-
  panion,
Travels slowly and painfully along
The rocky shore ; clothed with seaweeds
And wild creepers, he eventually gains
His last hiding-place, the cave Teakautu.
Thou fair-leaved " tauinu " of Marua,
So tenderly faithful to thy husband !

---

[1] The beautiful leaf of the " tauinu " tree is almost white, and is poetically supposed to grow at the sacred fount Marua, where Kie (who is said to have been
exceedingly fair) lived.

[2] Literally " a flower to wear in her ear," alluding to the ancient custom of wearing a single flower of the beautiful and fragrant Gardenia in the pierced ear. Hence
a husband is designated " a precious ear-ornament " by the wife. A similarly
endearing phrase is used by the husband towards a beloved wife.

18

UNUUNU TORU.

E laua tamaine, e tamaine,
E Tamarua, e Mariki ra,
Kua reuiui reui atu nga taokcto ;
Muraai oki tci mavae ia maua,
Kua akarongo i te tara tu,
I te tauinu para o Marua,
Kua pipiri tane âua ê !

THIRD OFFSHOOT.

My beloved daughters,
Tamarua and Mariki,[1]
How pleasantly we once all lived together !
Muraai now is separated from me,
Protected by his mother's clan.
Thou fair-leaved " tauinu " of Marua,
So tenderly faithful to thy husband !

AKAREINGA.

Ai e ruaoo ê ! E rangai ô !

FINALE.

Ai e ruaoo ô ! E rangai ô !

TAUAPEPE'S LAMENT FOR ATA.

For the same occasion.

TUMU.

Ka tuku ra nga tama e kei te te metua.
Ei rave ake, e Tetonga e ; akamoeria te
    ivi
To tama kai kino ra, e Ata ô !

INTRODUCTION.

Go, my sons, to your new parent.
Adopt them, Tetonga. Take to thy
    bosom
This poor orphan grandson, "little Ata."

PAPA.

Me ka maara rua ô, ei metua tangiia !
Mei e tangi atu, e Ata e, ceuria i te ruru,
Kia karo atu i te metua ka aere ;
    Vai ake te tama urunga ô !

FOUNDATION.

Cease to grieve for your father, so well
    beloved.
Yet once more, " little Ata," untie the
    bandages,
And take a last look of love at thy grand-
    father,
    Ere thou turn homeward in peace.

UNUUNU TAI.

Kua tuku i te tama ei te metua, i to
    metua,
Akaurunga reka i te tama ka aere,
E nga tama tangi ei, nga tama tangi ei.
E takipu te manava ô ! Kua tae mai te
    ta rai.
Tena Rongo tatâ ô ! Ia taua tipoki atu
    to matu.
Akamoeria te ivi to tama kai kino ra, e
    Ata ô !

FIRST OFFSHOOT.

Go, my sons, to your new parent.
I leave you in safety, beloved children.
Beloved ones, my heart yearns for you all.
Terror seizes me ; the slayer is at hand.
Pitiless Rongo approaches to close for
    ever my eyes.
Take to thy bosom this poor orphan
    child, " little Ata."

UNUUNU RUA.

Ka urunga te tara vaeakauta ia taua.
    Ei kona ra, e tau ariki !
Ka aere koe kimi metua ke atu,
Ei kona ra, e Aro, e Muraai !
Auâ e anau ki te metua, e karo atu te
    mata.
E riu ke atu taua, to tama kai kino ra, e
    Ata ô !

SECOND OFFSHOOT.

Rest in the pledge so solemnly given.
    Farewell, dearest child !
Go seek another parent.
Farewell, Arokapiti and Muraai !
Leave me to my fate. Gaze not on my
    face.
Turn away, my poor orphan grandson,
    " little Ata."

UNUUNU TORU.

Ka unui te o ô i te aerenga,
I te acrenga i te puruki Takinga ô !

THIRD OFFSHOOT.

Hold on firmly to thy god on thy journey—
The journey to the battle, oh, thou father
    of Takinga !

---

[1] The " Mariki " in the " Introduction " was the grandmother of this one ; the former being the mother of Ata-toa, the latter his daughter.

O Ata tangi i te anau ;
Mei tangi i te anau tokoitu rai i te ao,
Nga tama ra e aere ki te titirimoe,
I te akaarnara e ara. Na Rongo-toi-maui,
Na Rongo i toi tamaki tamauria i Ma-
racara.
Te tama aia e ko te vaarangiuui.
Na Takinga akera ko Ata ra i mamao
Ia uti tane au, e Kie, te aroa tangi atu.
   Mei tangi akera, e Mura,
Kua autaa te reo i te tara taiku,
E to ai tuaine Takinkaumu-i-te-vai-ta-
maki.
E kua tokatua aere te metua.
Ka ngongoro te anau tangata.
Ku ngongoro ana, e Kie, te anau,
Kua pingoi koe ra, e Ata,
E riu ke atu tauа, to tama kai kino, e
Ata ô!

Ata weeps for his children—
His seven children living yonder—
As he goes sadly to his last sleep,
He marches forth to meet Rongo,
The war-god Rongo worshipped in yon
   grove,
Ever imperious, the arbiter of destiny.
Takinga and "little Ata" are far away,
Whilst Kie lovingly bears along her hus-
   band.
Grieve not for me, Muraai :
Remember my last solemn charge,—
To protect thy sister who watched the
   fight,
And ministered to her outcast father.
Ah! the children must weep.
Yes, Kie, even thy loved ones will weep,
And "little Ata," too, will bitterly grieve.
Turn away, my poor orphan grandson,
"little Ata."

UNUUNU A.

Ka tuku te tama e vaekauta ia taua.
Naau ake, e Aro, e Muraai, te tama,
   Mei maru ake te tama e aroa,
E tutakiria ia Takinga o Metuaere to
teina akáui.
Na Rongo-aroa-kai, ko Ata te tuku i
runga,
Ko Ata te tuku i raro, taumaa atu ia
Naupata,
Papaaere, Enguengu to tuaine, O Mariki
ru.
Kua kokou, kua reva te tama korikori,
Tuku ua mai, e Ata,
E mei roto i te itiki i te akeke,
E aitu tutakina, o Rongo-tutakina-te-toa ;
Tatakina te uru tupu ariki.
Te rangi tuku ki raro. Tei Tukua mai
Ata ô.
Ei maringi te vai ki Avaiki ; maringi mai
te vai i Avaiki.
Te tangi nei Takinga ô i tongi paâ Toko-
toko,
Kua rikavika nga tama i te tainga—
   I te metua titiri, e Ata ô!

FOURTH OFFSHOOT.

Go, my son, and rest in the pledge so
   solemnly given.
O Arokapiti, be a parent to Muraai, my
   first-born :
Lovingly shelter my children.
Remember Takinga, and Matuaere, his
   brother.
Yonder is Rongo-giver-of-food. Ata will
   be hunted
From crag to crag. The father of Nau-
   pata must die.
Alas for Papaaere, and their sisters Engu-
   engu and Mariki!
Who lie huddled up and cling together
   in terror,
Whilst their father Ata is driven out
Of his strong enclosure,
To become a disfigured corpse, to please
   pitiless Rongo,
   Amid deafening shouts (of triumph).
Tukua and Ata, once so great, have fallen.
Their blood like water is poured out on
   the ground.
Takinga is weeping, and Tokotoko too.
They shudder, my "little Ata," to see
The slaughter of their forsaken father !

UNUUNU RIMA.

Vairanga kino ô, tei Okio ô, tei Okio.
Kia pange to metua te vairanga otai ;
E uui paa to toa i te komata toto,
Ei ta paa ia Tukua i te riu koatu,
Kia kapiti i te tama. Ka aere taua i te
puokia—
Te puku : kake atura i runga i te mau-
nga tauri.
Kua taparere Tukua ; kua motu te ivi i
Avaiki.

FIFTH OFFSHOOT.

Sad scene of blood at Okio ; yes, at Okio!
Fell father and son in one place,
And thirsty spears drank in their life-
   blood.
In a romantic pile of rocks fell Tukua ;
By the side of his brave son was he slain.
Death o'ertook both on that mountain of
   safety.
The death of Tukua will ever divide the
   tribe.

Motuia ra kia motu. Tatari atu taua.
Taua tei rongo—ko te puipui matangi
Te kave kura i tai—Auenei, apopo, ooku
  rā,
E taū ariki, e kare ei i te ao,
Karo ake paa, e Mariki e, i te tangi paa
  a te toko'oko,
  Kua rikarika paa nga tama e,
    I te tainga ki te metua titiri, e
    Ata ē!

Now rend it to fragments. Await events.
I hear something—a faint breath of wind,
A whisper—To-day or to-morrow.
Pet grandson, I cease to gaze on the light
  of day.
Gaze, Mariki, on the clashing of spears.
Well may the poor children shudder, my
  "little Ata,"
At the slaughter of their forsaken father!

AKAREINGA.
Ai e ruaoo ē   E rangai ē!

FINALE.
Ai e ruaoo ē! E rangai ē!

"Little Ata" lived to see better days. When the Gospel was first introduced in 1823 he was a young man. In 1840 Muraai died, and "little Ata"—then about forty years of age, and father of a family—became chief of Keia. In rank he came next to the king, and for many years acted as chief judge. Ata was of a remarkably humble and gentle disposition, and yet he could be firm as a rock when duty dictated. I never knew him to be guilty of a mean or a wrong action; indeed, he was always scrupulously careful not to bring the faintest slur upon his Christian profession.

CHAPTER XXXIX.

A DIRGE FOR TUKUA AND ATA-TOA.

(Accompanied by the harmonicon and drums.)

By Tangataroa, son of Ata-toa, *circa* A.D. 1817.

Tera!—	Now!—
Tutangoria ïa kopu ka aere ê!	Go root up this family—
Kuriki ê! kuriki ê!	Utterly, ayc, utterly!
Te pakupaku a miri!	(List to) the trampling of feet—
Te pakupaku a miri, a miri!	To the trampling of feet yonder.
O Ata e, apopo a titiri.	To-morrow, Ata, thou must die!
Mokopuna te amo i te aitu.	Mokopuna bears the corpse.
Ka ia ruru apopo?	How many more to-morrow?
Tai kura tu no korua.	'Twas no fair open fight.
Kua ta Kaunio, kua ta tai vaka.	Kaunio smote and crushed his foes.
Oi Avaiki teia Rongo ê!	Rongo has come up out of Avaiki.
Kua tu i miri.	(Ata) makes a brave stand;
Tu e tu ka aere ê!	Though brave, he must die.
Te ui mai na Rongo ê,	Rongo demands of each
Tai okiri, tai korare,	A spear and a club,
Tai okiri, tai korare;	A spear and a club;
Tai naau peiaa ê,	An army longing to fight,
Tai naau peiaa ê!	An army longing to fight.
Tai okiri oki ê,	Each now wields a spear.
Ka tu ê ka puruki.	Lead on to the attack.
E tu, e Rongo, e tukatakata;	O Rongo, arise, laugh heartily!
E tu, e Rongo, e tukatakata.	O Rongo, arise, laugh heartily!
Taúna aea tai o tukatakata na.	This work of slaughter is thy delight.
Tingiri—ringiri.	
Rangara—rangara râ takiri.	Harmonicons and drums only.
Rangirira tatangaa.	
E popo ta i miri;	A wooden sword for the battle;
E popo ta i te tangata.	A wooden sword to slay warriors;
Popo taia atu na;	A sword that has often been proved;
Kauariki i te toê.	To transfix the foe.
Anangirira tatangaa.	Harmonicons and drums only.
Kutu mai te ta i miri ê!	War weapons are clashing.
Kutu mai te ta i miri ê!	War weapons are clashing.
Kutu mai te ta.	'Tis the crash of battle.
I karuru te ruru i tiria,	Bind up the slain for burial,—
Pururu atu na i ruro ê!	To be hurled down some deep chasm,
Ei papa one i au ei.	To rot and mingle with the soil.

Tikirikiri, &c.

Harmonicons and drums only.

Titiara kokopu e, maua e,
Kikaoa a tua te utu i Rangiue,
Kua riri koe nei, e Rongo,
Vâvaiia te upoko ô!
Je kutu ana Tane ô!
Je kutu ana, e reru ana,
Je tu ana i te aiti puruki aere.
Kua pau maira i te mate,
Viri ake te kiore,
Ina kokopu e, Ina ô!²
Te ngurenguro kiore;
Te ngurenguro kiore.

We are like the fish on the hook ;
Cut down like a stately "utu"¹ at
    Rangiue.
Art thou very wroth, O Rongo?
Split open your skulls.
Fight bravely, O tribe of Tanè!
Fight on ; beat them down.
In that narrow space fight it out,
Until the last be destroyed,
Like rats in a snare,
As Ina's fish in a net.
The rats are squeaking,
The rats are dying.

Tingiri—ringiri.
Rangara—rangara râ takiri,
Anangirira tatangaa.

Harmonicons and drums only.

Ana taia ora Tukua.
Taia ora Tukua,
Aitoa koe ia mate,
In tiria i te rua nui no Akaotu,³
I te rua nui no Akaotu,
Oa tangi to upoko,
Kutu i te rangi a ta ô!
Viri ake te ina i raro ;—
Viri ake te ina i raro.

Scatter the brains of Tukua,
Spare not the aged Tukua.
Ha! thou must die,—
Must be thrown down the terrible
    chasm,—
That dark chasm, the grave of the slain.
The club resounds against thy skull,
Like thunder. He falls!
Thy white locks are scattered about ;
Aye, thy white locks are scattered about.

O na tui atu i Tuakiva.
To ngaoro, te ngaoro.
Tu ka aere e miri ô!
Mau takitai ua i te arua,
Ei tautipitipi na Aropee
I te tâci a titi ô!
Kua ora paa Nguare ;
Kua ora paa Nguare.

(Ata-toa) was borne over the cliffs
To a level grassy spot ;—
But still hunted by his foes,
Each armed with a war-club,
To smite him like Aropee (of old);
Or like a defenceless bird (= titi⁴).
Yet one escaped the fight ;—
'Twas Nguare⁵ who escaped.

Tikirangiti—ngitingiti.

Harmonicons and drums only.

This species of song is called an "eke"="descent;" because it refers to the descent of friends to the spirit-world, and of their bodies to the grave. Despite this, they believed that the spirits of the slain eventually attained to the warriors' paradise above.

---

¹ The "utu" is the *Barringtonia speciosa*. This is a covert reference to the extinction of the Tekama clan at Rangine some centuries ago.

² An allusion to the pretty myth of Ina. See "Myths and Songs," Chapter VI.

³ "Akaotu"="Terrible," a name applied to "Auraka," one of the grand repositories of the dead.

⁴ The particular bird in the native is the "titi," which is easily deceived by an imitation of its cry, and is then caught by the hand.

⁵ Nguare was a relative of Ata's who escaped at the battle of Akaoro. This was intended as a compliment to that branch of the family who were present at the performance of this dirge.

The alliterative sounds produced at intervals by the harmonicons and drums are, though very remarkable, destitute of meaning. The object evidently is to make the instruments "speak." Thus "takiri" must not be taken for the word meaning "entirely;" although the coincidence of sound is singular. The fascination for the native ear is great. Our own " Fal, lal, lah " is meaningless.

CHAPTER XL

A COMPLETE LIST OF BATTLES FOUGHT ON MANGAIA.

Place where fought.	Victor and consequent real "Lord of Mangaia."	Tribe defeated.	Priests of Motoro in Order of Succession.	Remarks.	Recognized "Lord of Mangaia."
1. Teruanonianga, in Keia	Rangi	Tongan colony	Papaaunuku	...	Rangi.
2. Tangikura, in Veitatei	Rangi and Tamatapu	Tribe of Tanè	"	Teuriitepitokura fled to the rocks. 140 slain	Teakatauira.
3. Raumatangi, at Tamarua	Moke	Rarotongans under Kateateoru	"	...	Vaeruarangi.
4. Iotepui, at Tevaenga	Amû	Aitutakians under Toapini and Toarere	Vara		Teinaorātea.
5. Ikuruākā, in Keia	Tiaio	Atiuans under Matatia	"		Tiaio.
6. Parainui, at Karanga	Tirango	Tekama tribe	Terau		A member of the tribe of Ngariki, name unknown.
7. *First* oven of men at Tutaeuil Putoa	Ungakute	Teaitu, *i.e.*, Tanè	"	...	Ungakute.
8. Rangiue, at Ivirua	Tirango	Tekama tribe	"	*Circa* A.D. 1570	A member of the tribe of Ngariki, name unknown.
9. Areutu, at Ivirua	"		"		...
10. *Second* oven of men at Angaitu, in Tevaenga	Kaveutu	Teaitu, *i.e.*, Tanè	"	Autea offends his lord *Circa* A.D. 1600	Kaveutu.
11. Vaikakau, *i.e.*, Maungarua, in Veitatei	Ruaika	Tirango and the Tongan tribe	"	Tirango slain	Tenau.
12. Taaonga, in Veitatei, at the Tuitui	One	Ruaika	"		One.
13 Kunekume, in Veitatei	One and Panako	Vete and his tribe of Vairuarangi	"	...	Panako I.
14. Kouramuii, in Veitatei	One	Mokora and Tekama	"		" II.

15. Tepapa, in Veitati ...	One	Kotaa and Tekanna ...	Pueke ...	Tauai and Tekaraka exiled ...	Panako III.
16. Teruakeretonga, in Karanga	Ngauta	Runika ...	,, ...	The original Mautara turned cannibal, and fled to the rocks at Ivirua	Ngauta I.
17. Arakoa, in Keia ...	,,	Tata and Panako ...	,, ...	Panako slain ...	,, II. Thia nominally enjoyed the dignity.
18. Auruia, in Tevaenga ...	,,	Maruataiti and tribe of Teipe ...	,, ...		Ngauta III.
19. Iotepui, at Tevaenga ...	,,	Motuoro and Akatauira tribe ...	Akunukunu		,, IV.
20. Punanga, at Tamarua...	,,	Tiauru and Tuma tribe ...	,,	Kauate and Reketia fly to the rocks. They fall in with and eat the original Mautara. 100 warriors slain	,, V.
21. Teruanouiangu, at Keia	,,	Ngariki ...	,,		,, VI.
22. Ikuari, in Keia ...	,,	Arepee and tribe of Teipe	,,	Circa A.D. 1666 ...	Terea, by consent of Ngauta.
23. Each-slave-slew-his-own-master throughout the island, the same night	Ngangati	Ngauta and the flower of the Tongan tribe	Mautara	Circa A.D. 1670. Iro and his clan expelled	Tuanui, by consent of Ngangati.
24. Mâueue, at Tamarua ...	Tauii	Arekare and his clan ...	,,	Rori fled. 60 warriors slain	Tauii.
25. Ariki, in Veitatei (1st)	Ngangati	Namu and his Vaeruarangi	,,	Tangka feasts on the slain after this battle and the four succeeding engagements	Ngangati I.
26. ,, (2nd)...	,,	Tribe of Tangin ...	,,	This battle was fought on the third day after the preceding one	,, II.
27. ,, (3rd)...	,,	Tribe of Kanae ...	,,		,, III.
28. Teaupapa (1st)	,,	Koluku (father of Nga-uta) and Tongan tribe	,,		,, IV.
29. ,, (2nd)	,,	Kaoa and his Vaeruarangi	,,	Namu fled to the rocks. 80 warriors slain	,, V.
30. Auâ, in Keia (midnight surprise)	Akatara	Ngangati and his tribe	,,		Akatara.
31. Tiipâtiu (daylight surprise)	Sons of Mautara	Akatara ...	,,		No chief declared.

Place where fought.	Victor and consequent real "Lord of Mangaia."	Tribe defeated.	Priests of Motoro in Order of Succession.	Remarks.	Recognized "Lord of Mangaia."
32. Arerá, at Ivirua ...	Teuanuku ...	Tuókura and Teipe ...	Mautara	Ruanae, &c., fly to the rocks and turn cannibals. Kaiara flies to the rocks	Teuanuku I. No drum of peace beaten.
33. Pukuotoi, at Tamarua...	,, ...	Ruanae and his cannibal clan	,,	Vaiua saved. Kaiara and Tavero saved, after spending two years in the rocks	Teuanuku II. Drum of peace beaten.
34. Auá, in Keia ...	Mautara ...	Ráei and his clan ...	,,	Rori saved by Manaune. Namu saved by Mautara	Mautara (25 years).
35. Tuopapa, in Tevaenga...	Uarau ...	Amai clan ...	Ngará ...		Uarau first, thenNgará.
36. Teopu, in Karanga ...	Kirikovi ...	Tongia and Tongan clan ...	Teká ...	Captain Cook touched at Mangaia in 1777. The woman Ike offered to Rongo in sacrifice	
37. Taukuara, in Keia ...	Paí ...	Kirikovi and his divided clan	,, ...	...	Paí.
38. Akaoro, in Keia ...	Potiki ...	Potai slain; clan Ngariki clan	,, ... Makitaka	*Circa* A.D. 1787	Potiki. Marokore.
N.B.—Marokore seized the government, after presenting the needful human sacrifice.					
39. Teatuapai, at Ivirua ...	Koroa ...	Marokore slain; one section of the priestly clan	,, ...	...	Koroa.
40. Rangiura, in Veitatei ...	Makitaka ...	Koroa slain; other section of the priestly clan	,, ...	Reigned three years	Makitaka.
N.B.—Temporal lordship peaceably transferred to Pangemiro after offering Teata to Rongo as sacrifice.					
41. Araeva, in Keia ...	Pangemiro ...	Tukua and Makitaka, *i.e.*, the whole priestly clan of Mautara	,, ...	Reigned seven years / Second reign of three years	Pangemiro I. A.D. 1814. Pangemiro II.
42. Putoa, at Tamarua ...	Teriovai and the heathen	Numangatini	,, ...	Fought on February, 1828	Numangatini.

CHAPTER XLI.

THE PRIESTHOOD.

SUCCESSION OF THE PRIESTS[1] OF MOTORO (=TE ARA PIA O NGARIKI).

1. Papaaunuku, from Avaiki.
2. Vara.
3. Terau.
4. Packe; slain by Ngauta at Keia.
5. Akunukunu; slain by Ngautu at Veitatei.
6. Mautara.
7. Ngarâ, youngest son[2] of Mautara.
8. Tekâ.
9. Makitaka. Died in 1830: professed Christianity.

SUCCESSION OF THE PRIESTS[3] OF TANE (=TE ARA PIA O TANE).

1. Turuia, from Iti (=Tahiti); slain by Tamatapu.
2. Mouna.
3. Matariki; offered in sacrifice to Rongo, at Ariki.
4. Tiroa; offered in sacrifice to Rongo, at Ariki.
5. Tepunga; offered in sacrifice by Tuanui, at Tamarua.
6. Tevaki; saved by Mautara, priest of Motoro.
7. Taeimua (i.e., Kakari).
8. Vaekura.
9. Pangeivi (=Erekaa). Died in 1830, a Christian.

---

[1] All these, except the two indicated, died natural deaths at extreme old age. Sometimes a tenth priest, Tereavai, is named. But the truth is, Tereavai was never invested with the priesthood of Motoro, as at the time of Makitaka's death Christianity was altogether in the ascendant. Tereavai was the last priest of the shark-god Tiaio. He died in 1865.

[2] The succession was from father to son.

[3] The first five priests were worshippers of that unpopular but feared deity Tanè-ngaki-au. The last four were priests of Tanè-i-te-ata, i.e., Tanè-kio, regularly descended from Terangai, who came from Iti (= Tahiti).

SUCCESSION OF THE PRIESTS[1] OF TURANGA (=TE ARA PIA O
TONGAITI).

1. Teaô, from Tonga : time of Rangi.
2. Tâmakeu : time of Teakatauera.
3. Ivi : time of Mokoiro, *i.e.*, Vaeruarangi.
4. Tirango ; slain at Angamoa.
5. Tamangaro ; driven, with his friends, off the island.
6. Moa.
7. Ngangaru ; slain by Ngangati at Tamarua.
8. Pârae (whom Potai vainly sought to kill).
9. Teâ, *i.e.*, Poa.
10. Ivi.
11. Mâueue.   Died in 1828, a heathen.

The above is a correct list of the three principal orders of
priests on Mangaia, from the date of the first settlement on it
until the subversion of idolatry.   There cannot be any material
error in the list, as I derived it from the proper depositaries of
such knowledge.   The three orders fairly tally, the priests of
Motoro ever taking the proud pre-eminence due to their superior
rank in heathen society.   When Captain Cook visited the island
in 1777 Ngarâ had been dead some three years.

LINEAL SUCCESSION OF THE "RULERS OF FOOD," FROM AVAIKI DOWN
TO 1829 OR 1830 (=TE PA ARIKI NO TE TAPORA KAI).

1. Mokoiro, from Avaiki ; buried at Rangikapua.
2. Mokoiro ; died a natural death, and buried at Karorâ.
3. Amû.
4. Maru.
5. Kaoa ; drowned at Teruavaaroa.
6. Namu ; slain by Ngauta, at Te-uma-tuna.
7. Kaoa ; slain by Ngangati, at Teaupapa.
8. Motau.
9. Namu ; the friend of Mautara, slain by Potai.
10. Kaoa ; held office during the sway of Potiki.
11. Metuarangiia.

.[1] All descended from Teaô (*i.e.*, The Man of the Long String. See "Myths and
Songs," p. 287, note), who came from Tonga.   The two last priests, however, were in
the *female* line from Teâ, eighth priest of Turanga.

12. Mauri;[1] visited by the Rev. J. Williams in 1829, but died soon after without accepting Christianity.

It seems to me that a comparison of this list with the three preceding ones irresistibly leads to the conclusion that the island has been populated only some five or six centuries. (See pp. 23–25 of "Life in the Southern Isles.") The list of kings proper is disputed ; but the most accurate list obtainable contains only twelve names, from the days of Rangi down to the reign of the present worthy king Numangatini.

THEIR PANTHEON.

Opposite to the *marae* of Motoro and the altar for human sacrifice was the idol-house, known as "The Prop-of-the-Kingdom" (Te Kaiara). Inside were the principal gods of Mangaia, which, with the exception of Rongo, all consisted of rude representations of the human form, carved by Rori about one hundred and sixty-five years ago. They were as follow :—

1. *Rongo* = "The resounder." Tutelar god of Mangaia, dwelling in the shades, and feeding exclusively on mankind. His chief representative was a triton-shell, used only by the king, and deposited at the entrance. A block of stone, shaped like a man and covered with cloth and coarse sacrifice-nets, was set up at his *marae*, "O-Rongo," for the convenience of worship and sacrifice ; where also stood a smaller image named "Little Rongo," or Rongo-of-the-red-tongue.

2. *Motoro ;* proudly called "te io ora" = "living-god," as his worshippers were *not* eligible for sacrifice. His *marae* was named Àraata. Supposed to be enshrined in sennit-work, in the "Oronga"-plant, and in the blackbird (Mo'o).

3. *Tanè, i.e., Tanè-papa-kai* = Tanè-giver-of-food.

4. *Tanè-ngaki-au* = Tanè-striving-for-power ; worshipped at Mapûtû. Supposed to be enshrined in *birds*—the Kanâ and Kereearako.

5. *Tanè-i-te-utu* = Tanè-of-the-Barringtonia-tree ; worshipped at Maraetêva. Supposed to be enshrined in *fish*—sprats.

---

[1] The connection in each case was that of father and son. This remarkable list is undisputed, and was given me by Kouri, the brother of Mauri. Many old men that I knew at Mangaia in 1852 were well acquainted with Kaon, who lived to a very advanced age.

6. *Tanè-kio*=Tanè - the - chirper; worshipped at Maungaroa. Supposed to be enshrined in *planets*—Venus and Jupiter —and in sennit-work.

7. *Tiaio;* worshipped at Mârâ. Supposed to be incarnate in the eel and the shark.

8 and 9. *Tekuraaki* and *Utakea;* worshipped at Nuvêe. Supposed to be incarnate in the woodpecker (Tatangaêo).

10. *Turanga;* worshipped at Aumoana. Supposed to be incarnate in the white and the black-spotted lizards.

11. *Teipe;* worshipped at Vaiaua. Supposed to be incarnate in the centipede.

12. *Kereteki;* worshipped at Araata and Tauangaitu. Believed to have no incarnation.

13. *Tangiia;* worshipped at Rangitaua. Believed to have no incarnation.

INDEX.

GEORGE DIDSBURY, Government Printer, Wellington.